Gwyneth

Angela Sanner

EerieLit House of Publishing— Bridgeville, PA
ISBN: 979-8-218-33705-6
Library of Congress Control Number: 2023923145
Title: *Gwyneth*
Author: Angela Sanner
Digital distribution | 2023
Paperback | 2023

Dedication

Thank you to the people who pushed me and encouraged me to never give up. Times have been tough but I'm making it through. I've made it through the darkness and I've entered the light at the end of the tunnel. Without any of you, this book would have never been written. Thank you for all your help and support!

Chapter One
Present Day

Winter has finally arrived.

Winter. In December.

It's the season she loves the most and the coldest season of the year. Icicles sparkle like dazzling diamonds as they hang from dead tree branches. Leaves have frozen; making a crunching noise as they're being stepped on by heavy-booted feet. Bugs and critters have scattered; hiding deep into the ground. Are they hiding from the weather or are they hiding from her? That is a question that will never be answered. It's a possible speculation of both.

A light dusting of snow has covered the ground. The sun is setting; causing a dark and gloomy atmosphere. It's just the way she likes it. That's the mind of a gloomy human being. It's someone who fills their brain with hatred and unthinkable decisions. A gloomy atmosphere controls that temptation of unthinkable acts. Acts that are so violent but they slip through her cranium just like blood drips from a knife. Her cranium is filled with jumbled electrons that have no path. They don't know where to go; just like her.

She likes the darkness; deep grays and black. If she could crawl through the black hole, she would. It's the hole that could end life for eternity. That very hole that she is destined to be part of… feels like it is right within reach.

Sometimes, she reaches out her hand but the black hole resists. It resists her temptation.

That's just how her mind works. She doesn't know any better. To be quite honest, she should be locked up in an insane asylum. That is long overdue and something she's never even thought of. She doesn't even know what an insane asylum is. She doesn't know a lot of things outside of "her world." Her world involves this winter blast of cold and watching trees sway in the breeze. Her world revolves around her and how she must survive.

She likes it here though. It's peaceful most of the time. She loathes other human beings. They better not even think about stepping one foot onto her territory. This is her way of living. This is her environment. This is HER space to create what makes her feel comfortable. She hates feeling uncomfortable and she hates it when she's being disturbed.

Whatever comes her way; these human beings have to pay the consequences.

There always has to be a consequence to their negligent appearance. Yes, these disrespectful human beings are negligent for their own safety. They don't even know it, but she ALWAYS waits. Again, she ALWAYS waits.

She waits to hear them. She waits to see them.

It makes life worth living. Seeing their frightened expressions and listening to their dreadful screams. Their actions are pitiful; begging and crying for their lives. They cry like small children hiding in the corner of a room. They cry like children being beaten with belts. Only, they're being ripped apart like the mouth of a bear when he eats during feeding time.

Their blood is an enjoyment of warmth just like gulping a flavorful cup of coffee. The warmth flows through her veins and gives her the chills. It reminds her of tasting a piece of hot apple pie topped with a scoop of vanilla ice cream. The moisture is a delightful taste to her lips.

Hot apple pie used to be her favorite dessert. It's the only "good" memory she has of her mother. That was the only dessert her mother knew how to make. Her cakes were always dry and her brownies were always hard as a hockey puck. The woman didn't know from her ass to her elbow let alone how to bake. She was such a piss poor mother, but strangely, she didn't understand why her daughter hated her so much.

But Gwyneth never asked for this. She's never asked for this kind of life. She's accustomed to it now though. She knows how to survive. She knows how to take care of herself. She doesn't need anyone. She definitely doesn't need anyone in this type of environment.

Especially…her mother.

A mother who never had a heart. A mother who should've taken a stroll through that black hole. That would've been extremely satisfying and well-worth the watch.

Gwyneth is twenty-four-years-old now. She's a grown woman.

A woman who has been through HELL and back. This is a woman who has suffered pain and sorrow, abandonment and abuse; things that no one should have to suffer through. It used to make her scared out of her mind. She was deathly afraid of the trees, of the wild animals and the creepy noises at night time. She used to be afraid of other human beings.

But now, she has accepted it.

She's accepted it throughout all of these years.

But she feels like a child lost into the abyss. She looks like a child with her baby-face features and filthy, long black hair. Her high cheek bones give her blue eyes an icy glaze; an everyday angry look upon her face. She's owned that angry face since she was a child.

But, she acts like a grown woman who was thrown to the wolves. When you read about it, she was literally thrown to the wolves, or bears, or squirrels, or coyotes.

Take your pick because she's seen them all. She's eaten them all. And she's killed them all.

Gwyneth is dragging a dead woman's body through the wet lands of the woods. It's surprisingly quiet. It's like the wild animals saw her from afar and bolted like a scared kitten. The snowflakes are landing softly like a fitted sheet landing on top of a mattress.

It's terribly convenient that the dead body is her forty-five-year-old mother, Ruby Glacier.

Gwyneth is wearing a dirty gray Eskimo coat with the fur on the hood. She wears a grimy, shredded, white T-Shirt that's displayed over her nose and mouth like a mask. She's also wearing black fingerless gloves to cover her cold, filthy hands.

She never asked for this, but it happened. And it happened at the right time. Either way, she doesn't feel any remorse. She doesn't feel some sort of saddened pain. She has no feelings for this woman whatsoever. She's like a stranger to her. She never really had the chance to know her mother like a daughter should. It's like she woke up from a nightmare just to live inside of another nightmare. It's completely mind boggling that someone her age could be spit out like the burning embers of a blazing fire.

Gwyneth has no empathy and absolutely no sorrow for this woman in her grip.

There's nothing there that awakens the black hole in her heart. She has a black hole inside of her body that spins like a tornado; spitting out hatred toward anything and anyone. It has, especially, spit hatred out toward her mother. The worst mother anyone could ever ask for.

The Bitch asked for it.

Ruby is wrapped in a soiled and unwashed blanket. Her head, her left arm and hand are exposed to the frigid cold. Her knuckles are causing drag marks through the snowy ground.

It's impossible to imagine what was going through Ruby's mind. Or Gwyneth's for that matter. We as humans don't truly know what goes through someone's mind while they're being tortured or murdered. Sure, they might scream or cry but we can't read their minds; unless someone has that super natural capability.

Gwyneth wishes that she could read minds. She would've loved to hear her mother's thoughts about her. She's always wanted to hear Ruby's true thoughts and not the lies that spat out of her mouth. She was like a dragon blowing hot fire throughout the air.

Gwyneth could use some hot air right about now. The tips of her fingers are frozen and her eyeballs have formed little crystals on her eyelashes. She's losing breath with this T-shirt mask covering her dry mouth. She's thirsty and hungry again. She's been getting a lot of exercise lately and it's taking quite a toll on her body. She just needs to rest a bit.

But rest will come once she's finished with her mother.

As Gwyneth drags her lifeless body, she approaches her run-down shack in the woods. It's made out of simple wood, logs and good-old fashioned nails and screws. The front door is cracked open because it's hard to close it all the way. It's been like that since the beginning; the beginning of her nightmare. It was the beginning of the black hole spinning inside of her body. It was the beginning of the hatred toward other people.

The whole entire shack is crooked in shape. The front door is covered with scribbles of colored crayons. Different shades of reds, blues, greens and purples are fading as each winter approaches. It looks like someone purposely dug their sharp nails into the wood; forming a bear claw shape. It wasn't just SOMEONE; it was

Gwyneth when she became angry about life. She's been angry for years and she has every reason to be.

But this shack is HER home.

A home she has been accustomed to for twelve years.

Yeah, she didn't ask for this.

There's a fire pit ten feet away from the shack that contains fresh, half eaten chicken bones. The bones are causing smoke to filter throughout the air. There's a dirty, open dog cage that's placed next to the water well. Another grimy blanket unfolded and rolled into a ball looks like it was tossed into one of the corners of the cage. A picnic table is placed just five feet away from the fire pit. The splinters of the table stand upward like it's ready to stab someone in the back.

Just like her, stabbed in the back. If only she was stabbed with a knife, that would've felt better. She would've rather have felt the twists of the tip of a knife digging into her skin. She would've loved to have felt her blood quickly dripping down the spine of her back.

But this has been HER life now.

Because of HER mother.

Tit for tat Bitch.

Gwyneth lifts Ruby's dead body on top of the picnic table, slightly struggling. Ruby is not big at all. As a matter of fact, she feels like a handful of skin and bones. Gwyneth giggles inside. Her mother's body is blue from death and her lips are purple and cracked from the cold.

Gwyneth is only struggling because she's incredibly tired.

She's tired of not getting enough sleep because she's still afraid that someone will stumble upon her. She's tired of having to go on scavenger hunts for more food.

She's tired of looking for THEM.

She's tired of this bullshit.

Ruby has a faint smell of cigarette smoke on her clothing. That's something that Gwyneth loathes entirely. It brings back too many memories; memories that she absolutely hates remembering. It's that awful smell and the sound of her mothers' hacking through her raspy throat. She doesn't miss Ruby blowing her cigarette smoke straight into her face either. That's what made her hate cigarettes for as long as she can remember.

She really hates a lot of things.

Gwyneth swiftly and angrily removes the blanket from her mother.

Ruby is wearing a dirty, white tank top with metal buttons and filthy, gray sweatpants covered in mud and snow. She's not wearing any socks; Gwyneth took them off. Mud is caked underneath all of her toe nails. Her feet are disgusting with gashes, cuts and dried blood.

She's just a disgusting person in general. Well, she WAS. She was disgusting toward her daughter and treated her like she was from another planet. Ruby was a horrible human being who didn't care about anyone but herself. She never cared about her children either.

Gwyneth trudges toward the shack. Reaching the cracked front door, she suddenly whirls around to take another peek at her dead mother on the picnic table. She looks around the woods; watching the snowflakes land softly onto the trees and the muddy ground. She wishes for a split second that she could hear the beautiful sound of birds chirping and deer chewing on grass.

She has to wait until spring for that. She wonders why she suddenly wants to see rainbows and butterflies. That's not her style. She likes snakes and bugs and killing people.

But this is HER home.

Because of HER mother.

She wishes she could just throw her mother's body into the black hole and watch it spin in circles as it sucks deep inside. That would give her so much enjoyment. That very thought gives her goose bumps. For once, it's not the freezing cold wind.

But, she very rarely gets what she wishes for. Wishes are like dreams that don't come true.

Well, maybe someday one of her wishes will come true. It has to. She's been wishing in one hand and shitting in the other. Not literally, but she does shit in the woods and sometimes the feces smears on the side of her hand.

She hates that too but it's become nature to her. She has to use leaves and grass to wipe her private areas. That causes scratches and itching that can last for days.

Gwyneth makes sure that the coast is clear and steps inside.

Inside the shack, there are old, filthy, raggedy dolls with missing eyes sitting upright against a wall. Some of those dolls have buttons sewn into the eye sockets. They stare back at her as if they're asking for help. Help is something that she will never give them.

Gwyneth doesn't understand a lot of things. Her brain has the capacity of a younger elementary school child. But she is smart in her own way. She knows what actions are right and wrong. She knows that what she's doing is not acceptable to society.

But, she doesn't care.

And what does society know? Society truly doesn't know her life or what she's been through. And would they care?

Probably not. That's why she's still here. That's why she's stuck in this disgusting life. Well, she's not really "stuck" but she chooses it because it's something she's been used to. That's what human beings do. They make choices that are not always the best. It's a repeated behavior that transforms the brain into something more psychotic.

A line of dingy coats are hanging from fishing wire nailed to the wall. The coats are missing buttons from their proper spots. They are also raggedy and old. Some are covered with old feces stains and blood from wild animals.

The whole entire shack is completely filthy. There are no carpets or any rugs to cover the wooden floor. A wood burner containing tree logs is crackling; heating the small area. An empty dog bowl is flipped over onto its side. A small white desk sits in the corner with a broken lamp with no lamp shade. The desk is covered with crayon drawings of a fire pit, trees, squirrels and bears. A container with a lid colored with blue and black crayons sits on top of the desk.

A tattered cot sits in another corner with a dark brown blanket with holes in the middle of it. Her pillow is covered in dried mud and saliva stains.

Gwyneth is actually quite calm right now. She doesn't ever have happy thoughts or feelings. But she feels content and slightly excited for the dead body that awaits her.

She's an independent twenty-four-year-old woman.

A killer.

Gwyneth opens the container on the desk. She searches through sewing needles and thread.

She picks a ten inch, silver sewing needle and black thread. Gently, she closes the container. She's a stickler for not breaking her valuables. Everything she owns is precious to her.

She picks up the scissors next to the container and walks over to a coat dangling over the fishing wire. She cuts the last button off of the coat.

She then picks up an old doll and cuts off the button from the doll's eye socket.

Staring at the doll for a moment, her eyes are suddenly frightened as if she just saw a ghost. Just as quickly, she blinks and snaps out of her thoughts.

Gwyneth leaves the shack; not realizing that the snow has stopped.

She approaches the picnic table and places her items on the bench.

There's no emotion anywhere upon her face. With her evil and hatred eyes, she stares down at her mother's lifeless body; a body that she has waited for twelve years to kill.

Shoving her fingers into her mother's eye socket, she pulls the eye out; popping it out of the skull. She tosses it next to her six-year-old black Labrador, Buttons. Buttons is lying on the snowy ground. He growls in enjoyment as he devours the eyeball.

Buttons likes to mind his own business; until his owner needs him.

For some reason, she needs him a lot. Maybe it's the loneliness or the depression. Maybe it's the anxiety she feels every single day from being all by herself in the wilderness.

Or maybe it's because she can't talk.

Either way, Buttons is always there for her, ready and willing to do as she commands. He's been doing that since the beginning; since she was there for him when he needed her the most.

Gwyneth places the black thread through the loop of her needle. Her fingernails are caked with dirt and blood. That doesn't faze her though. That's also something she's accustomed to.

Dirt. Blood. Filth. Just plain old nastiness.

She's used to playing in dirt.

She's used to tasting blood on her skin and fingers.

Carefully, she ties the thread into a knot. Picking up a button, she sews it into her mother's right eye socket. The gooey sound is rather disturbing but it's like music to her ears.

The wind has picked up. Snowflakes sporadically flutter through the wind once again.

The snow can't make up its mind either. It doesn't know if it's coming or going.

Buttons smells the cold air.

Of course, he's minding his own business. He's a good dog. No, let's take that back, he's a GREAT dog. He always protects his owner. He loves her more than anything. He wouldn't harm a hair on her head. She's like his knight in shining armor.

Gwyneth ties a second knot of thread into her needle.

And just when she thinks that all is quiet, Gwyneth's empty tin cans that are tied to the surrounding trees and connected to a trip wire...begin to jingle.

Buttons' ears perk forward. His growl is low and deep.

It's time to protect his owner once again.

He briskly stands up and exposes his sharp teeth.

Gwyneth clicks her tongue at Buttons.

Chapter Two
Six years prior

The dingy water inside of the pond smells of dead fish and rotten eggs. The brown color is dark like coffee beans and the stench gives off a gas-like haze throughout the grime and filth. Beautiful dragonflies perfectly illustrated in shades of blues and purples, carefully fly toward the murky water. They abruptly turn away from it; flying through the air then landing on the wet grass. They can't even stand the smell of this pond either.

Dragonflies are like mystical creatures. They're delicate, charming and beautiful in nature. They are something that many of us humans may wish to be. Some of us want to be delicate flowers while others want to be repulsive, dirty and downright hateful. Those people are gloomy as they take death by its horns. They pass the torch as they come across the finish line. And that torch may get into the hands of the wrong people.

A pretty red and orange dragonfly flutters through the air; enjoying the soft breeze. A fist, big enough to clobber the Stonehenge into a pile of rocks, swats at the dragonfly as it peacefully soars through the sky. The dragonfly isn't hit, thank you to the lucky stars, but it flies away in distress. The man's loud belching stirs the other dragonflies as they leave in fear.

Why can't humans just leave nature well alone? HE is in THEIR territory; sitting his beer-belly ass on his scuzzy, red, beer cooler. It might break if he applies any more pressure onto it. That would send his ass straight onto the wet grass and into dirty mud. It's not like he's clean anyways. His white tank top is covered in jelly donut stains and he smells like a stale ashtray. The bottoms of his ripped blue jeans are completely covered in dried mud.

He looks like he hasn't slept in days. His mouse-brown hair is disheveled and his beard is covered in spaghetti sauce. He's like a pig at a farm. He smells like cottage cheese and bad odor. It wouldn't be a problem if he fell into the nastiness of the pond water because he would blend right in. He's a scoundrel and a no-good man. He's the true definition of the word, "Shit."

That torch was unfortunately passed along to him. His brain is filled with malice and hatred. His eyes should be red because he is like the devil himself. His evil presence make the bugs dig deeper into the ground. Birds hide in trees and worms hide in mud.

The man is a Fisherman if you will. He has nothing better to do with his time. He's newly retired and he can do whatever he wants, whenever he pleases. It's a different kind of lifestyle; something he hasn't gotten used to just yet. It pleases him to sit here and watch for fish in his filthy pond. He likes to watch the overgrown weeds in the distance as they blow in the wind. He likes to watch the leaves on the trees as they fall delicately onto the ground.

He likes to make people nervous. He wants people to be scared of him. He likes it when people ignore him when he drives into town. The entire grocery store is quiet when he steps inside wearing his tall, brown, muddy fishing boots as he inhales the last of his cigarette. He'll flick it out into the parking lot and laugh hysterically as it lands on top of some poor shmucks windshield. He has no care in the world for other people he doesn't love.

And he only loves one person.

As he chugs a can of beer, he clutches his fishing pole in his other hand. He closes his eyes in ecstasy as the bitter taste slides down into his throat and into his jelly donut-filled belly. He continuously gulps as beer dribbles down the sides of his mouth and onto his tank top.

He opens those evil brown eyes and sees the sky darkening. He finishes the last gulp of his beer, and then he crushes the can into his fist. He throws it into the pond and then swats at a gnat buzzing alongside his ear. It's surprising that he doesn't have bugs crawling outside from the inside of his ears. It's surprising that he doesn't have any maggots crawling from the inside of his wet boots. He washes his clothes inside of a metal tub outside in his backyard. He refuses to buy a washer and dryer. He says, "I don't have time for that other bullshit," every time someone asks him why he washes his clothes in filthy water.

Well, no one asks him that anymore. He's just so angry and demented that people just ignore him. He has no social skills and his ability to make friends has diminished completely. He absolutely loves being the most hated man in town though. It's like his specialty; a hot plate of shrimp, a piece of rare steak, a baked potato and rice. That's his ultimate favorite.

Thunder rolls through the sky. Lightning flashes quickly like a whip.

The Fisherman isn't scared, but he's nervous to get stuck in the rain on the way back home. He whips his head behind his muffin top body and notices that his harpoon and tackle box are still sitting where he left them. That's that good ole harpoon he's used to kill many wild animals. He loves to eat squirrels and raccoons. He even killed a bear once. He cut that thing right open and cooked the meat inside of a hot, camp fire.

Well, that's the story he likes to tell people. No one has ever witnessed his bullshit. He's not sure if anyone ever will. He never invites people over to his home. He just doesn't like people in general. His friends don't even like him either. That's okay though, he found this new fur ball that he's going to keep as a companion.

He hasn't given his new puppy a name yet. He wants it to be something different or unique. He wants him to stand out. He wants to train him to be mean. He wants his friend to be vicious and learn the skills needed to hunt animals. He's going to have so much fun with him.

The Fisherman glances down at the puppy. His black Labrador coat is dirty. Something is sticking to his fur and making hard clumps that need to be cleaned out. The Lab is lying on the dirt gravel path that leads to the Fisherman's home. The puppy peeks up at the dark sky as thunder booms once again. He quietly whimpers as he then glances at the Fisherman staring at him with crazy eyes. The Fisherman smiles at his new friend with broken, crooked, yellow teeth.

The puppy watches as the man's fishing pole line moves erratically. Hurriedly turning, the Fisherman quickly pulls the fishing pole toward his body and cranks the reel.

"Wooooo Hooooooo!" the Fisherman yells toward the sky, "Gimme that home cooked meal!" The Labrador quickly stands up; panting as drool drips from his tongue.

He awkwardly turns his head to the side as he watches his owner struggle with the reel. The Fisherman pulls but he's nervous that the line will snap. The reel won't budge anymore and he pulls so hard that he falls onto his buttocks. He pulls the line one last time and watches as a crappie fish flops back and forth on the grass.

"Woohoo puppy! Look at this bad boy!" he yells.

A thunderous boom scares the daylights out of the dog. He lies back down on the ground and whimpers. This might just be too much for him right now. He's scared out of his little mind and it seems like he just wants to go home. He's shivering and he stares at his owner with those sad puppy-dog eyes.

The Fisherman looks up at the sky like he's never heard of thunder before. He has this strange, confused look upon his face. He watches the lightning crack once again like a whip.

"I'm so glad we were able to catch some supper before the rain starts. We have to hurry home!" he tells the dog.

Some might say that the Fisherman is off his rocker. Some might say that he's just an asshole. Some might say that he lived a horrible life with horrible parents and that's why he acts the way he does. Some might even say that his ex-wife cheated on him with a woman and left him to fend for himself. Some might even say that he killed his ex-wife.

Wait a minute; no one would say that because no one knows.

But there's always that possibility that someone could find out. He didn't hide her body very well and if the police would have actually LOOKED around this area, they would've found her instantly. They would've seen her poor mangled face and her body parts chopped off.

The smell of that pond is overwhelming sometimes. The Fisherman smiles as he watches gnats and other bugs fly above the dingy water; struggling as he tries to un-hook the crappie fish off of the fishing hook. He always seems to be distracted nowadays when he's trying to focus on just one project. His mind wanders into the abyss. That's why he struggles and becomes angry.

It is his own fault for being so dramatic about everything.

He's angry now. The poor puppy doesn't like it when the big man is angry. He's scared; knowing that the huge man in front of him will start screaming. He's going to be physically violent anytime soon. The puppy watches him as he shivers in fear. He watches him as he shoves the sharp hook deeper inside of the fish's guts, killing it.

The puppy licks his chops. He's starving. He's drooling as he watches the fat man place the dead fish onto the wet ground. The

Fisherman then licks the blood and guts from his dirty fingers, eyeing the dragonflies that dare to circulate above the nastiness of the pond.

If only dragonflies could talk to humans. If only bugs could tell crazy and wild stories of the violent acts of human beings toward each other. That would be a miracle in its self. Could you imagine if bugs could talk? Oh! The things they could tell us! They could even help crack cases of murder and missing people.

But, they don't.

And in an instant, that Labrador puppy quickly snatches the dead fish with his sharp little teeth. It happened so fast that even those dragonflies and bugs didn't realize what was going on. But then that Fisherman notices, screaming at the top of his crusty old lungs. He coughs then spits what looks like a yellow and red substance.

"AHHHHHH!!! No... you little shit! Give that back!" the Fisherman yells.

The puppy is terrified; unsure of which way to run with the dead fish dangling from his drooling mouth. He's never been so scared in his short life. This man is incredibly dangerous and should never have any pets. He can't even take care of himself. It's a wonder why he thought he could take care of and handle a puppy. That poor thing didn't know what he was getting himself into. Not everyone is a good person and not everyone should have pets; especially violent, murderous men who love to be hated.

The puppy has put himself into an awkward and frightful position. He's extremely hungry though. It's been two days since he was fed meat of a raccoon.

If only dogs could talk as well. He would've told his owner that the meat tasted like shit. He doesn't know how to cook a simple meal over the fire. The giant man is truly useless. If only the puppy could've taken over the preparation of their four-course meal. He would've seasoned that raccoon meat to perfection, smashed the chunks of potatoes into a smoother base, lathered that corn with some creamy butter, and he would've taken those burnt, disgusting biscuits out of the oven at its proper time.

But dogs don't talk to humans. They bark to get your attention and they whimper; just like this poor puppy does as the Fisherman grabs him by the top of his furry head; squeezing. His hands are so big that he could squeeze a human's neck and make their eyeballs pop out of their sockets. He actually fights with this poor dog; trying to pull the fish from his teeth.

It makes you wonder what his parents did to him and why he's so crazy in his mind.

He pulls on the puppy's teeth. The puppy growls back, snapping at his filthy fingers. The fish falls to the ground. The dog has nipped at the Fisherman's thumb, making it bleed.

"Ouch!" the big man yells, sucking the blood from the wound.

The poor puppy doesn't know what to do. He's frozen in place. It's like his paws all of the sudden lost feeling. He's scared out of his mind. His heart pounds so quickly that it feels like it's about to burst. Who knew that he would be stuck in this type of life? He would've been better off scampering through the woods alone. Anything would be better than living with this beast.

The woods actually have a natural beauty about its surroundings. If you think about it, the glow from sunshine can brighten its colors. The strong backbones of animals gleam with pride.

It's a beautiful sight to see if you can imagine the green, red, orange and yellow leaves falling from the trees. It's a pretty remarkable scene to watch flowers blooming in the spring. The bright color of the horizon when the sun slowly rises from the east is something that sends shivers down Gwyneth's spine.

It might not be dark and gloomy but the sight is something to surely watch. She likes to watch it every morning. She also likes to watch the sun set at night time. That is what gives her an adrenaline rush. The stars shine bright up into the dark sky. She likes to watch them form the Little Dipper or the Big Dipper. Of course, she doesn't know that's what they're called. She likes to think of them as, "spoons."

Gwyneth tries to live a simple life. Well, what she thinks as "simple." Left alone in this wilderness is something that she cherishes the most. But she has come to realize that human bodies are essential for her daily growth. They are a great source of vitamins and minerals. It tastes just like eating chicken. It's best for it to be cooked over the camp fire.

Speaking of eating, she's famished. She hasn't caught a squirrel or any animal for that matter, in days. She's afraid to venture off farther. She doesn't know the whole entire area yet, and she should after living here for six years. She's eighteen now but she acts like that twelve-year-old lost, little girl. She is so scared to leave her comfort zone. She doesn't know what's out there, waiting for her. She doesn't know if she will be abducted or murdered by the hands of a stranger. She doesn't know where she will go because she doesn't know where her mother is.

It's been so long that she doesn't know anything outside of these woods. She hasn't developed the courage to go beyond and find what's out there. It's been depressing.

It's been stuck in her mind that something bad will happen to her if she leaves this spot, even for a moment. She's only gone as far as thirty-five feet from the trees at the edge of the camp fire. Her heart starts to pound when she ventures too far and she can't see the shack. All of this pent up anxiety starts to burst through the seams and she suddenly turns back, running to the picnic table to catch her breath. She doesn't want to be caught either.

She knows she's being silly. What could be out here besides wild animals and trees? She's tried to hear the sound of flowing water, but there is none. She's tried to hear the sound of cars passing by, but she doesn't hear them. She doesn't understand how deep she could actually be in these woods. It's like she's buried into some sort of cave and can only see ten feet of wall space.

This isn't nothing new for her though, remember, this is how she likes it.

As Gwyneth sits cross-legged on the bench of the picnic table, she examines a map. The map has roads highlighted in red, huge trees highlighted in green and woods highlighted in brown. The map is cartoon-like. It's like a painted canvas with bright colors jumping out of the paper. The top of the map has a hand-drawn illustration of a crooked sun colored in orange.

The words, "SISTER" and "BROTHER" are written in black marker underneath the sun. At first, the words were actually misspelled. But then, she remembered how to spell them correctly. There's no one here to help her spell or write correctly. The words look like they're climbing a crooked mountain. She could never spell correctly anyways before she was left alone. Her mother used to get so frustrated with her because of the lack of reading and writing skills in her brain. Ruby would be so embarrassed when someone would ask her to spell her name or write a simple word. She couldn't do it. It would upset Gwyneth so much that she would start to cry like a little baby. Then, Ruby would apologize to that person and say that Gwyneth was "stupid."

She sure isn't "stupid," she just needs the proper teachings of reading and writing. Her school teachers would get frustrated as well and refuse to have her in their classes. She was bounced around from class to class and couldn't learn how to properly spell words or learn any math. She knows how to count, but it takes her a while.

With a red marker in her fingers, she writes the word, "MOTHER" on the map with a question mark. An area of roads is already circled, another area is squared and a third area has a triangle drawn around it. Of course, these things are hard to see as the map has fold increases and dried mud smeared all over it. She has no idea what this is a map of or what area it is referring to.

Her knuckles bump the dead body that lies across the top of the picnic table. She stares at the body's leg; gently touching it with the tip of her pointer finger. Tears well up in her blue eyes and she suddenly tosses the red marker onto the picnic table. It lands next to the black marker and onto the crinkled map. Thinking that she's acting like a baby, she picks up the red marker.

She wipes her tears away with her dirty hands. She stares up into the sky like she's staring into the abyss; trying to remember her life long ago. She sees the darkened sky and the crack of the lightning when she suddenly hears the howling and crying of a dog and a man screaming at the top of his lungs. Her concentration has been disturbed, but she doesn't realize at first that the sounds are real. She quickly looks around, searching the area. Hearing the howling once again, she's fast on her feet, snatching the map and the markers. She makes her way toward the shack as thunder booms once again.

Chapter Three

Learning how to sew from the shaky hands of Ruby Glacier was just like crawling inside of the black hole and spinning in circles. Her directions didn't make sense and Gwyneth was too focused on Ruby's tobacco breath to even care about sewing. Ruby's nails are tinted yellow from pinching her cigarettes between her fingers. Gwyneth would always stare at those long, sharp pointed nails with disgust while wishing that Ruby would just stab her in the eyes and ears so she wouldn't have to deal with this drab of a woman.

Gwyneth hated sewing. She hated learning how to sew and she hated hearing her mother cough a hundred times as she spoke about sewing. It was awful. It sounded like she was throwing up or coughing up a lung. Her mother disgusted her every which way possible. She would accidently close her eyes and drift off to sleep; only to have Ruby nudge her with her bony elbow and disturb her nap.

Learning how to sew was like listening to the Devil talk about once being an Angel. You can only hear the story so many times before you get sick and tired of it. And Gwyneth was sick and tired of pricking her poor fingers with the needle and getting frustrated over the thread breaking because she would pull too hard. It was such a daunting task that Gwyneth often thought many times of stabbing herself in the face with the needle so Ruby would leave her alone. She would hold that sucker right up against her skin, but she would back out and cry instead. Ruby would then make fun of her for crying over such a simple task of placing the thread through the loop of the needle.

I mean, who seriously does that to their child? Ruby should raise her hands into the air and yell, "I do! I do!" That would make her look like an asshole.

Again, she was a fool and a piss poor mother.

Gwyneth enters her shack and marches directly toward the container on the desk. *That man will not hurt that dog anymore*, she thinks to herself. *Whoever it is, he better leave that poor animal alone or I'm going to have to do something about him.*

In a heart-beat. In a snap of a finger. In the blink of an eye.

She hurriedly opens the container and picks up her ten inch sewing needle, inspecting it like it's the first time she's laid eyes on it. She has this twinkle in her eye as her breathing becomes rapid. The dirty T-Shirt mask sucks in and out of her mouth like a vacuum, sucking dirt off of the floor. Her heart is pounding like a performer beating on a bongo.

Nonchalantly, Gwyneth places the ten inch sewing needle inside of her right fingerless glove. If anyone is going to be prepared for a battle, it is going to be her. She feels fearless right now. She feels like she can take on anyone of any size and shape. She doesn't quite understand why she feels this sense of empathy toward an animal she has never seen. She quite suddenly feels this overwhelming love toward this dog and she doesn't even know anything about it. She doesn't know what it looks like and she doesn't even know how it will approach HER.

Oh no, she thinks. *What if it ends up hating me the way I hate Ruby?*

Approaching the wood burner, she quickly grabs the fireplace poker. She touches the sharp tip with her finger and rubs the excess soot between her pointer finger and thumb. It reminds her of the black hole. It's a twirling tornado ready to suck her blood just like a Vampire. It chomps its teeth down onto the side of her neck, making her squeal with delight.

Sometimes she questions the state of her own mind. Why did she have to be born with this type of brain? Why did she have to be born by a heartless mother? What did Ruby do to Gwyneth and to her own body while she was pregnant?

Again, all unanswered questions that will never be answered. That's all Gwyneth seems to ask herself lately. She knows she won't have the answer she's looking for. She finds it to be dull and boring to repeatedly ask the same questions over and over in her mind. But she also finds them fascinating as she gravitates toward finding the correct words to put together, like a puzzle.

Gripping the poker in her hand, she stares at the shack door with mischievous eyes.

If dragonflies could talk to humans, they could tell Gwyneth the story of the Labrador puppy from start to finish. They can tell her that all he wants to do is eat. The poor thing hasn't had a decent meal in days. The fat man is currently being greedy and doesn't want the puppy to eat the whole entire fish. They can tell Gwyneth that he beats the puppy with his fat fists and he's been doing that since the day he found him.

But dragonflies can't tell her anything and they don't have to. She's watching with her own eyes as she peeks through the trees at the Fisherman as he grips the poor puppy with his bear-like claws. The puppy cries out, scared half to death.

The dog's eyes are wide as the fat man clenches his disgusting yellow teeth, spitting as he yells, "You stupid mutt! I should've gotten rid of you!"

He grips the poor puppy's neck high up into the air.

Gwyneth might not be so smart in her brain, but she does understand that hurting an innocent animal is against the rules. It's against the law. She knows this from reading a ripped piece of paper she found long ago in a bush resting against a tree one night. It must have blown through the wind while someone was picking up their garbage somewhere farther away.

Or maybe someone intentionally put it there to give HER a hint. But who would do that? No one knows… no one knows that she kills innocent deer and squirrels for food. No one knows that she lives in a condemned shack deep into the woods. She's making herself paranoid and it's affecting her vision and concentration.

Gwyneth rapidly blinks her eyes. She can't believe what she's watching. She can't believe that someone could be so cruel toward this innocent puppy. This kind of cruelty reminds her too much of her awful mother. Those memories start pouring inside of her mind like bats leaving their cave. She dares to close her eyes; envisioning her mother is just as bad as watching someone walk off of a cliff.

Ruby's house was medium-sized but the inside of the dreadful place was always covered with clouds of smoke. The light-blue wall paper was tinted yellow, just like her grimy teeth. All she drank was coffee; always spilling the grounds onto the counter and floor. She refused to clean it up and would make Gwyneth do it.

She was such a lazy asshole but she thought she was tough. She abused Gwyneth every chance she could get. She beat her with belts, brooms and even one time with a bag of yarn.

Gwyneth's bedroom wasn't anything to boast about. She had a twin bed made of metal with the springs poking into the bottom of the mattress. Ruby could never keep the sheets clean on the mattress because Gwyneth had a bed-wetting problem. That used to infuriate Ruby so much that she would tie the sheets into a lasso and whip Gwyneth's butt with it.

This time, Gwyneth is in for it. She thought about it as soon as the mess happened. She can't help being a clumsy little twelve-year-old girl; always testing out the patience of her psychotic mother. Gwyneth always wondered at that point, how far her mother would actually go with all of her verbal threats. "I'll kill you," was something that the little girl always heard.

Ruby stands over Gwyneth with a cigarette pinched between her fingers. She is definitely in for it because Ruby looks around the floor with a hateful but, "I'm not surprised," look upon her face. She seems shocked as well. She looks high from smoking her dope but she is very much alert. She's angry, but above all, she looks exhausted.

Gwyneth suddenly raises her arms in surrender as Ruby's fist comes crashing down onto the top of the poor girl's head. She slams her fist down once again as Gwyneth tries to block the blow. There's ringing in her ears but she can still hear the other children in her bedroom screaming and crying.

"You stupid mute! Why do you have to be so slow? Why can't you just be normal?!" Ruby pauses, waits for an answer that she won't get. "Speak girl! Damn you!"

Ruby suddenly pushes Gwyneth's head backwards. She feels a snap, like her muscles were pulled. It isn't broken but the pain shoots up into her brain, causing flashes of light to appear inside of her eyeballs. It's something she has never felt before and something she never wants to experience again. Her neck hurts, her brain hurts and her ears hurt from all of the commotion.

Gwyneth's teary eyes slowly move, resting on the twins; her five-year-old brother and sister who are hiding in the corner of the room. They're holding each other, crying. They're embracing for the impact they anticipate from this hell of a beast.

"Look! You've upset your brother and sister! You are such a stupid little girl!" Ruby yells as spit dribbles down her chin.

She inhales a long puff of her cigarette, blowing the smoke up into the chipped-painted ceiling. Speaking of the ceiling, it needs replaced in this awfully small bedroom because it's leaking. A big water bubble waits in silence above Gwyneth's bed; ready to be popped like an over-filled water balloon. Some nights when Gwyneth is lying in bed, she stares at the bubble and imagines herself busting it open with one of her mother's sewing needles.

She gets a kick out of that. She pictures Ruby bursting inside of the room like she's an officer of the law; yelling and screaming obscenities while puffing her cigarette. Then, maybe she would accidently swallow that cigarette and choke on it.

She gets a kick out of imagining that too. If only Ruby would choke and die. She could finally be free and her siblings wouldn't have to cry anymore. They wouldn't have to be scared of the big bad wolf. She could bury her in the backyard without anyone knowing.

But that isn't going to happen.

Gwyneth grips the sewing needle in her hand as she watches the twins close their eyes. There's black yarn strewn all over the floor. Yes, that's her mess and she knew she was in for it.

She knew the consequences but she made the mess anyways. If she could talk, she would tell people that she did it on purpose to get a rouse out of her mother. She can't explain why though. Sometimes, this adrenaline rush would consume her whole entire body and it would make her think of doing evil acts. Yes, it would MAKE her think of these things.

"You can't even properly sew. Such an incompetent waste!" Ruby drones on and on.

Gwyneth isn't even listening to what's coming out of her mouth. She's too busy watching the tall ash burning from the tip of Ruby's cigarette. One swift move and that sucker is going to fall right onto the dirty, hard-wood, floor.

Ruby instantly snatches the sewing needle out of Gwyneth's grip. And there goes the ash! Gwyneth's eyeballs follow it as it lands onto the floor. Ruby's cowboy boot smashes onto the crumble of ash just as she steps back from leaning forward.

"You need to clean up this mess," Ruby continues, "I don't

understand you!"

Gwyneth stares at her mother with an evil glare. She doesn't move. It's like she's frozen in time. Her butt feels frozen to the floor. She's actually afraid of what she might do to her mother. However, she deserves whatever bad thing comes to her. Gwyneth is just scared of what's going to happen AFTER she hurts her mother.

What can I do? She asks herself. *I can choke her with my hands but that won't work. She's stronger than me. Let's see… I can hit her over the head with something.*

Ruby grabs Gwyneth by her shoulders. The nasty cigarette stench wafts into the poor girl's nose and mouth. Gwyneth holds in her breath as to not smell her mother's bad odor.

"Did you hear me? Hello?" Ruby yells, violently shaking her daughter's shoulders.

Ruby pounds her knuckles on Gwyneth's forehead like she's pounding on a door. If only Gwyneth could just punch her right in the face. If only she could knock her down and climb on top of her to choke her to death. If only she was strong enough to break every muscle and bone and vein in Ruby's neck. She would squeeze so hard that her eyeballs would pop out of their sockets. Gwyneth imagines this happening as she stares straight ahead at Ruby's slimy, coffee stained lips. Whatever the Bitch was eating earlier is now stuck in between her two front teeth.

"Anyone in there?" Ruby asks as her knuckles leave imprints on Gwyneth's forehead.

As Ruby tries to knock on her forehead a third time, Gwyneth slaps her hand. Instantly, Ruby grabs Gwyneth by her hair. It happened so fast that Gwyneth didn't even have time to react. Her long-black hair is being pulled as if she's a string to a lawnmower.

Ruby shoves Gwyneth's face into her mattress. The twins cry harder, hugging each other as if this is the last time they'll see their sister.

Gwyneth refuses to cry. She doesn't want to give this beast the satisfaction. She doesn't like to cry in front of her anymore because Ruby makes fun of her for that. She just says her prayers every night in hopes that someone will come and rescue them. Then, she could cry in the arms of her rescuer and never let go.

Ruby shoves the tip of the sewing needle an inch away from Gwyneth's eyeball. She doesn't give her the satisfaction of flinching either. She stares at her urine-stained mattress as the needle slowly proceeds toward her eye. She can see it in her peripheral vision.

"If you ever pull a stunt like that again, I will kill you. You hear me? Huh?!" Ruby yells into her ear. The tone of her voice can break a mirror.

Gwyneth's ear drums are vibrating and her head feels like it's about to explode. The migraine is creeping up the back of her neck and into her skull.

Ruby violently spins Gwyneth onto her back and then grips her throat with her ashtray-smelling hands. The look on her face is pure hatred. She's angry and evil… but Gwyneth can be eviler when given the chance. And Gwyneth wants her chance. No, she NEEDS her chance.

As Ruby squeezes, Gwyneth's eyes fill with tears. She doesn't want to cry in front of this beast but she isn't sure if she can keep holding them in. This day has been a disaster and she just wants to run away and hide. She wants to run into the arms of a savior.

Ruby slowly lowers the tip of the needle even closer to Gwyneth's eyeball. She's afraid to blink. She's afraid to release the tears. She's even afraid to admit that she does love her mother and this abuse hurts her not only physically, but mentally as well. Sometimes, she often wonders if she was like her siblings, would her mother love her even more.

Gwyneth is frightened. The needle is a little too close for comfort. She suddenly nods her head in acknowledgment. She blinks her tears and they spill down the sides of her temples.

Ruby smiles but continues to squeeze Gwyneth's throat with her other hand.

Leaning forward, Ruby whispers, "Good, then we have an understanding. Now, go pick up that yarn you threw all over the floor. If you don't, I'll beat you to a bloody pulp."

Ruby lets go of her throat. Gwyneth tries to catch her breath as she falls to her knees on the floor. Picking up the tangled yarn, her tears are making her eyes blurry. She honestly can't see what she is doing. The yarn looks like jumbled shadows. She just wants to disappear and never look back. That's like a dream to her. It's a wish that will never be fulfilled.

Deep down however, she would miss this house and her mother. She would miss her siblings and the way they run to her and give her gigantic hugs.

She would actually miss it all and she's not sure why. Surely it's because she's accustomed to this lifestyle. It's the only thing she's ever known.

Ruby tosses the sewing needle onto the floor next to Gwyneth.

"You know something girl," Ruby continues, "you're about as brave as your father was. He was always trying to save himself or other people. You try to save your brother and sister all the time too."

Gwyneth ignores her but tries to secretly listen to this compliment her mother is trying to give her. She never compliments her and Gwyneth actually feels a little awkward.

She continues to spin the yarn into a ball. She seems disinterested in what Ruby is saying but her mind is peeked and intrigued.

"The only difference is," Ruby drags on, "you're dumber than him. Well, sometimes I think that. But sometimes, I think he's dumb for letting another woman mess around with a married man! *Ha ha!* Not once, but twice!"

Ruby laughs hysterically. It sounds just like a witch hackling. It makes Gwyneth want to stab her ears so she can't hear it any longer. It makes her want to scream bloody murder. It's like nails on a chalkboard. She can't stand her mother's awful laugh.

Gwyneth glares straight ahead at the wall, careful not to look at her mother. She slowly spins the yarn with tears in her eyes.

Chapter Four

When Gwyneth is ready to pounce on her prey, she becomes quiet like a Ninja. Her filthy black boots tip-toe across the mud, slithering its way across the grass like a snake toward the fat man. She's been creeping upon animals and human beings for so long that she knows the drill. She knows how to silently watch as she takes her time in waiting for the right moment. She knows that the "right moment" means everything. She can lose this opportunity to save this puppy if she isn't careful.

And she's always careful. She has to be. It's just like looking both ways before you cross the street. However, she doesn't have to worry about that. But she understands the necessity of having to be extremely quiet when her prey is within reach.

She stares at the Fisherman's back as he continues to hold the puppy high up into the air. He's choking the poor puppy's neck with his big Hulk-like fist.

Quietly approaching from the woods, Gwyneth violently swings the fireplace poker at the man's lower legs. Dropping the dog, he screams in agony as he falls to his knees.

Again, Gwyneth might not understand a lot of things, but she is most certainly smart when it comes to survival skills. She's had to teach herself to not be vulnerable. She's had to teach herself on how to be strong. The wilderness has helped to make her strong and this is how HER life is. And quite frankly, she's tired of being alone. She's tired of facing this world alone every single day of her worthless life. This opportunity has presented itself right in front of her face and she must act upon it. She must save this poor thing and help make it strong, just like her.

This puppy is in dire need of help and she must continue her duty of protecting the innocent. This puppy is alone, just like her, and she knows she can keep him safe; unlike this unlucky Bastard who has no one here to protect him.

Gwyneth feels hot suddenly. She's perspiring as she swings the poker once again. The man quickly grabs it with his fat fist; pulling it out of Gwyneth's grip. Lazily, he swings it at her but it misses her by an inch. The poker lands onto the ground with a thud. The poor dog is lying on the ground, whimpering as he stares at Gwyneth with those puppy-dog eyes.

The look on his poor face makes Gwyneth's heart melt. She hasn't felt like this since she used to stare into the sad eyes of her siblings. All she's ever felt in the past six years is hate and disgust toward anything and anyone. Now, she looks at this vulnerable creature as tears well-up into her eyes. She isn't really sure why she's crying but she knows she must kill this fat man.

Pulling out her ten inch needle from the inside of her glove, she grips it with all of her strength and runs toward the man as he looks up at her in pain. In one swift move, she stabs him in his right eye. The tip of the needle is suddenly stuck inside of it like an icicle stuck to a roof. He screams in pain once again, toppling to the wet ground.

Thunder booms again and the puppy cries out. Gwyneth glances at him with sadness in her eyes. She hurriedly looks up into the sky and watches the dark clouds float by.

She quickly snatches the needle, extracting it out of the Fisherman's eye. As he continues to scream in agony, Gwyneth gently picks up the puppy in her fingerless-gloved hands. Petting him like he's a newborn baby, she slightly yanks down her T-Shirt mask. Nudging her nose on the puppy's wet nose, he licks her. Gwyneth makes a grunting sound while giggling.

"You stupid Bitch! I'm gonna kill you! I swear it's gonna be you and not me that dies tonight!" the Fisherman yells.

Smiling at the puppy, Gwyneth lifts her mask back over her nose and mouth.

She just doesn't like to be seen, especially by strangers. She has these big, beautiful, blue eyes that she doesn't mind people to notice, but the rest of her face makes her embarrassed. She doesn't like the shape of her jaw line. She doesn't like her teeth to be shown and she doesn't like to smell anything rotten. She can't help to live the way she lives and sometimes the smell of rotting food and human flesh of her dead corpses makes her belly flip-flop like a fish.

She enjoys killing. She just doesn't enjoy the repercussions afterwards. It's like getting into trouble with your parents after you did something bad. Gwyneth wants to laugh as she thinks about that. She doesn't have to worry about parents beating her ass. Her mother ended that right years ago. It's surely been a learning experience for her and it makes her tingly inside.

She gently places the puppy inside the hood of her coat. She then gathers up her fireplace poker. Noticing the man's items on the ground, she snatches up his harpoon, placing it over her back like a backpack. The Fisherman cries out as he watches her with one eye open. Blood oozes from his right eye as he tries to cover the wound with his dirty hand.

Shoving both of her fists underneath the Fisherman's armpits, she begins dragging him into the woods. It's a struggle for her though. She knows she's strong but this guy is just so fat that she feels like her back is about to break in half. She fights through the pain as she takes each step with a pull of his heavy body. She grunts each time, making the puppy whimper and the fat man cackle with laughter. His laugh reminds her of her mother, which makes her angrier.

The Fisherman struggles to get out of her death grip. He kicks his boots in fear, yelling intelligible words that Gwyneth has never heard before. He's whimpering like a toddler as he tries to stop her from dragging his body by placing his hands on the ground. It's not working though. His hands are being cut and stabbed by branches and rocks. They're all muddy now too and his dumb ass keeps touching his wounded eye; rubbing the mud inside with the blood.

"What are you gonna do with me huh?" the Fisherman asks, "Hang me by a tree? You stupid girl! You're not stronger than me! I'll get you Bitch!"

He wiggles his fat body like a worm, thrusting himself as he tries to get out of her grip. She watches his blob of fat jiggle as his shirt rides up his back and exposes his belly.

Gwyneth suddenly lifts her boot and smashes the bottom of it onto his giant belly. The man cries out, coughing as he folds himself into a fetal position.

She lets' go of his arms and quickly raises the fireplace poker high into the air.

Beating him with the poker, the Fisherman yells, "Stop it! Goddamn it! I just wanna go home." He's crying as drool slips out of the corner of his mouth. "I won't tell anyone about you! I promise! Just let me go!"

She slams the poker onto his stomach once more, ignoring his cries. At this very moment, she could care less what this man has to say. He could die right here in the middle of the woods and she wouldn't think twice about taking him back to her shack. He has a lot of meat to eat. She would never pass up this opportunity to get this much food for them. She has this puppy to take care of now, she needs the extra nutrients.

The puppy whimpers, grabbing her attention. Gwyneth stops and glances back at her hood.

If only she could talk to the poor thing. She would tell him that everything is going to be alright, there's no need for him to cry. Sure he's scared, but now he has someone to properly take care of him. She isn't sure how exactly, but she will make sure that he's well taken care of. *That's what people with animals are supposed to do.*

Her inability to speak has plagued her throughout her whole entire life. That is one thing that no one understood. Her mother didn't understand it. She originally thought that Gwyneth just refused to do it. Doctors thought that she was deaf but she hears perfectly fine.

When she was seven years old, a doctor did tell her mother that she had some damage to her vocal chords but not enough to keep her from talking. Ruby refused to believe that Gwyneth had any issues with her throat. She continuously told every doctor that Gwyneth was, "Doing this bullshit on purpose to make people feel bad for her."

Gwyneth daydreams and stares into the abyss once again. Her eyes are looking past her hood but the puppy's loud bark disturbs her trance.

She blinks as she sees the puppy shaking in fear. She turns toward the man on the ground once again, grabbing his armpits as she continues to drag his body through the woods.

Gwyneth's belly is empty and she feels like she hasn't eaten in days. Well, she really hasn't. That dirty old raccoon she ate two days ago was caught sniffing around her camp fire. His poor little beady eyes stared at her as she shoved the poker through its plump body. At least he was able to eat good for a while.

As she drops the Fisherman by the picnic table, she feels like she's about to throw up.

She isn't sure what has come over her. Maybe it's the hunger feeling or the fact that she keeps thinking about that poor raccoon's saddened eyes as she devoured him.

Snap out of it, she thinks to herself. *YOU HAVE TO EAT!*

The Fisherman grips his stomach in pain as he coughs up blood. Gwyneth stares at him in disgust. She kicks his legs with the heel of her boot. He cries out but doesn't say anything. He's literally choking on his own blood and Gwyneth watches, shaking her head.

If only she could talk to him. She would tell him right now how pathetic and pitiful he truly is. This is his fault. If he would've left this poor dog alone, he wouldn't be in this predicament. This is what a person gets when they abuse animals. Well, in HER mind, these are the repercussions of abuse and violence toward another person or thing.

Still shaking her head, Gwyneth takes the weapons to the shack.

Once inside, she drops to her knees in front of the wood burner. She has this sudden excitement for finding her new companion. He's beautiful and her heart is racing with love. She never thought that she would ever find something so valuable and lovable. Most of the animals that she comes across either try to kill her, steal her food, or become such a nuisance to her that she can't concentrate. Not that she has a lot to concentrate on, but she does like to relax sometimes. When there's a squirrel that scurries across the ground or up the tree, she tends to kill it because it's on her nerves. Maybe she should be nicer to animals.

Gwyneth laughs as she takes the puppy out of her hood. The only animal she plans on being nice to is this sweet, adorable little Lab right here. She massages his bones and then his neck. He licks at her gloved hand and then her fingers. He then licks the dirt and blood off her fingernails.

He's shivering. Gwyneth pokes at the logs inside of the dying fire. It's gotten chilly inside of the small shack because of the temperature dropping outside due to the storm.

Spotting a dirty towel lying on the floor, Gwyneth snatches it up and then wraps it around the puppy for warmth. Thunder rolls, making the dog jump. Gwyneth places her pointer finger up to where her lips are behind the mask and makes a "SSHHHH," sound.

The poor thing looks hungry and thirsty. At this point, now she HAS to make sure that there's food here. Sometimes she goes for days without eating because she either doesn't feel like hunting that day or she can't catch anything. Some days she'll kill multiple animals at one time and then store them in her mini refrigerator. Now that she knows about that pond, she can go back there to catch some fish.

Worried about the puppy's health, she goes to the cupboard and takes out a food-stained plastic bowl. It wasn't washed very well but it will have to do.

She fills the bowl with cold water from a bucket placed inside of the refrigerator. She likes to use the water well outside and fill buckets of water to keep it nice and cold.

Replacing the bucket back inside of the refrigerator, Gwyneth then sets the bowl onto the floor next to the puppy. She feels this glowing happiness inside of her body as she watches him slurp up the water. He seems to be dying of thirst.

She saved him.

Approaching her desk, she opens her crayon-colored container and pulls out her scissors and some fishing wire. She always feels extremely satisfied when she's able to finish a project. This one seems more captivating than others so far. If only she could find her mother…

Gwyneth grunts. One day she will find that Bitch and give her what she deserves. Maybe she should leave these woods right now and go search for her again. Well, maybe not RIGHT now. Knowing Gwyneth's luck, she would find Ruby and the Bitch would take her puppy away. That's just how she is. And Gwyneth would NOT let that happen.

Back outside, Gwyneth approaches the picnic table and proceeds to cut the tied wire off of the dead body. She has no idea who this girl is but at this rate, she doesn't even care. All she knows is that she shouldn't have stepped onto her territory. Those are the rules. That's HER law. Stepping into these woods is just like stepping into the black hole.

Gwyneth drags the dead girl further into the woods. The Fisherman whines as he watches her. He was pretty quiet up until now. Maybe she should just go and hide inside of the shack while he bleeds to death out here. His silence actually made her forget that he was still lying on the ground in his own blood. She thought that he died already.

He tries to lean forward on his hands and knees. Falling back down, he says, "Hey, hey girl. I.. I'm a... sorry. Hey look, we can make a deal. I won't tell anyone. I just want my life. Please... you can have that mutt. I don't want him anyways."

Gwyneth returns from dumping the body. See, that's what she's talking about. This dip-shit of a man is willing to give up that defenseless, poor animal off to someone he doesn't even know. Which is okay by her, but he doesn't care about that puppy at all. He never did. She could be a killer or something and he's willing to just give him up as fast as the snap of a finger.

The fat man tries to get up again. Gwyneth kicks him in the head. He immediately topples to the ground. She can't even stand looking at this beast of a man anymore, nor listen to his mouth.

Struggling, she tries to lift the Fisherman onto the picnic table. This is why she gets the extra exercise that she needs. Just in case she meets people of his size, she will be ready for the strength that's needed. She likes to stay fit in case she has to run for long distances. Sometimes a bear will show up and she either runs like hell or stands her ground like a fool.

"Hhhmmm... please... I need to see a doctor. Help me to the hospital," he begs.

Gwyneth snatches her scissors in frustration. *If only he would just SHUT UP!*

"Who are you?" he continues, "Why don't you talk?"

She smacks his mouth with the sharp end of the scissors. She's done with his bullshit. She's done listening to him cry like a little Bitch. *Toughen up fat man! You're going to let a young, eighteen-year-old girl kick your ass?*

"You stupid girl!" he yells at the top of his lungs as blood and spit fly into the air.

As calm as she can be, she cuts three long pieces of her wire. The fat man is crying intelligible words again. Her brain is ready to burst but she doesn't want him to see how his annoyance is getting to her. He just needs to die already. It's been going on too long.

Faster than a flash of lightning, she thrusts a piece of wire over the front of his neck then ties it underneath the picnic table. She then ties his wrists and ankles to the sides of the table as he struggles to set himself free. He's too weak. He's too dumb to even fight.

He desperately wiggles his body, struggling to break the wire. All he's doing is hurting himself. This wire is thick and sharp. He's not too smart in his brain either.

Gwyneth cuts a piece of the man's shirt with her scissors. She stares at him for moment, contemplating on just stabbing him in the throat with the scissors.

She can't though. That type of death is not satisfying to her right now. She needs something MORE. Something that will give her the goose bumps. Something that will give her butterflies in her stomach. She needs to feel relieved as well as some sort of happiness about the death that will consume this man.

She quickly stuffs the shirt into his mouth. His muffled cries penetrate the air. It's like music to her ears. She loves to hear the panic in her victim's voice. She loves to hear the fear that jingles their vocal chords. It gives her this insane pleasure of excitement when someone is about to die. There's something about their begging and pleading for their lives that gives her this sensational feeling DOWN THERE.

Of course, that's not appropriate but it's something that helps her to get other things off of her mind. Things like her awful mother and her beloved siblings. She has this strong feeling that her mother killed her siblings. She was crazy like that. She always threatened to kill them and hide their bodies inside of her freezer down in the basement. She always used to tell them, "Your little bodies are small enough. I'll get away with it."

With the shirt stuffed inside the man's mouth, Gwyneth heads toward the shack once more. He's full blown crying right now. Tears fall from the corners of his eyes. He watches her walk away as she enters the shack.

Gwyneth checks on the puppy. He's still drinking water but the bowl is almost empty. The towel that was wrapped around him has fallen half-way off of him.

Stepping to the refrigerator, Gwyneth chooses a large piece of a chicken drumstick. The refrigerator is filthy. A sticky, red liquid is stuck to the bottom alongside crumbs of food.

Picking small pieces of chicken, she feeds the puppy. As she pets him on his head, he licks the chicken juice off of her fingers.

The Fisherman is outside struggling. His cries are muffled. He wants and he needs to get out of here. He needs to figure out how he's going to escape. He's tied to this stupid picnic table and he has no idea how he's going to cut the wire by himself. He has to think of something nice to say to her. Maybe she will let him go if he offers her food or water from his home.

He tries to lift his head, forgetting for a split second that a piece of wire is strangling his neck. The wire cuts through and draws blood. He panics even more.

His cries are still muffled as he begs, "I'm sorry! I'm sorry! Please!"

He searches around for Gwyneth as he has an anxiety attack. He can't breathe and he's sweating profusely. The smell of his body odor enters his nose and he gags. He feels like he's about to vomit. His eyes frantically look around as they stop at the shack door.

What Gwyneth hates the most about her victims is their begging. It's not only exhausting to hear, but she gets frustrated because she can't tell them to shut up. She can't yell back and tell them that there's no point in begging because she won't let them live. Their begging of her to let them go is just like stabbing her ears with a sharp knife. Their crying is just like twisting that knife and stabbing her brain.

The sound of the fat man's muffled cries interrupts Gwyneth's concentration. She covers her ears with her hands. The puppy watches her with wide eyes.

She frantically shakes her head no. She's sweating and whimpering as she closes her eyes.

Chapter Five

Gwyneth feels as though closing her eyes is a sign of weakness. Somehow it gives the abuser more power because the victim can't even look into their eyes. Sometimes though, she has a hard time looking into the eyes of her awful mother.

It's not because she thinks that Ruby has all the power, it's because she can't look at the woman's dreadful face. She's lost more weight from not eating properly. Her eyes have sunken into her skin. Her cheek bones have sharp points like their ready to stab someone. Her teeth are extremely grimy from smoking like a chimney. It doesn't help that she will not brush them either. She complains of the pain that it causes on her gums.

No one is perfect, but Gwyneth doesn't understand why her mother doesn't take care of herself in a better way. She may be just a twelve-year-old with mental issues, but she knows that something doesn't seem quite right with Ruby and she isn't sure what it is. She isn't competent enough to know that her mother has mental issues herself and she shouldn't be taking care of children. Ruby should be locked up in a mental institution.

Unfortunately, Gwyneth and her siblings aren't lucky enough for that. Gwyneth just sits in the corner of her room while covering her ears and violently shaking her head no. The beast of a mother stands over the poor girl, gripping her ten inch sewing needle in her skeleton-looking hand. Her veins are thick but her hands seem fragile. She's losing strength but she doesn't want Gwyneth to have any suspicions of this fact.

Ruby stares at her daughter as if she's a trash bag on the side of the road.

That dumb look on her face is embedded in Gwyneth's brain. She knows that she's nowhere near like her siblings, but that look on Ruby's face is never a look that's given to the twins. It's a look of disgust and pure hatred.

She never asked for this. Gwyneth never asked for this kind of life. She never asked to be mute. She never asked to have mental issues. As a matter of fact, she NEVER asked to be born.

No one asks to be born. It's the way life is.

Ruby leans forward and yells, "You stupid mute, can't even learn how to sew! You need to learn these things to take care of yourself when you get older. You are worthless girl! I should never try to teach you anything! You are so incompetent!"

Gwyneth starts to cry. She didn't want to let the tears flow, but those words that constantly come out of her mother's mouth, hurts her to her core. It's like a burning candle inside of her stomach. It makes her heart pound like a drum inside of her chest. It gives her so much anxiety that her whole body shakes with fear and resentment.

Ruby throws the needle at Gwyneth.

"Pick it up! You need to learn how to properly hold it!" Ruby continues to yell.

If only Gwyneth could stab her mother in the heart. She would twist the needle into circles and chip at it as if it was broken ice. Her heart is black ice. It's there but no one can see it, hear it or feel it. Someone should make it stop beating for good.

Gwyneth is suddenly angry. She refuses to pick up the needle and violently shakes her head no. Ruby is now extremely angry and suddenly throws her knees to the floor. They make a cracking noise as if she's broken them. She grabs the needle and shoves it into Gwyneth's face.

Snatching the poor girl's arm as if she's running across the street, Ruby struggles to open Gwyneth's hand. She has her fist tightly closed as Ruby digs her sharp, pointed nails into the girl's skin. Gwyneth cries out in pain.

"Open your hand now! Hold the damn needle!" Ruby yells.

While struggling, Ruby suddenly smacks Gwyneth across the face.

It feels like a thousand knives stabbing her cheek. There's a tingling feeling and sudden soreness. Ruby does it again, only harder this time.

Gwyneth is in full blown tears; screaming and crying up into the air. She holds her face in her hands, rubbing the numbness.

"You stupid… little girl!" Ruby continues to call her names.

This is why Gwyneth hates the fact that she was born. Well, at least born from a beast with absolutely no parenting skills whatsoever. This woman shouldn't have ever spread her legs. She should've used protection at least. Whoever decided this was a good idea clearly had no suspicion that she would be an unfit mother.

Ruby grabs Gwyneth by her shoulders and aggressively shakes her as if she has marbles in her brain. Maybe she does but at least she knows what's right from wrong, SOMETIMES.

Ruby shoves the needle into Gwyneth's hand. Then, raising the needle up into the air, Gwyneth screams a blood curdling scream in Ruby's face.

For a split second, Gwyneth sees fear in her mother's eyes. It's fear that she has never seen before. It actually gives Gwyneth an adrenaline rush. Her heart skips a beat. She feels fearless and powerful. This beast has finally shown that she's scared.

Well, she should be.

Gwyneth slams the needle's tip into the floor. It feels as if the room is spinning inside of the black hole; the black hole that Ruby should be thrown inside of like a pile of waste.

The black Labrador puppy whimpers as he watches Gwyneth wildly shake her head no. She needs to get a grip and wash all of these bad memories out of her mind. Thinking about that awful woman will get her nowhere in life.

Still, she wishes to find her one day. Even if it's for the sole purpose to just listen to her yell one last time. That's all it would take; one time. Ruby Glacier doesn't deserve to breathe. She doesn't deserve anything good happening in her life.

Well, for all Gwyneth knows, she could be living out on the streets. She could be married to a wealthy man, popping out babies left and right. She was a whore like that. She could be living in that old, tiny house with the roof caving in. She could be living in someone's basement as she watches them from the peephole of the basement door. She's a creeper like that.

Gwyneth suddenly stops crying. She's angry and she isn't sure why. She slowly takes her hands off of her ears as she watches the puppy curl into a ball on the filthy floor.

She gently pets him as she kisses his head.

She feels so much happiness toward this small bundle of joy. It's so nice to find something worth living for. She was ready to give up on everything. She had lost all hope into finding her mother and siblings. If she can find this precious animal, then she has faith that she can find her family. But, someone has to pay the price and that person right now is outside crying like a baby.

Gwyneth angrily storms out of the shack and stomps her muddy boots toward the Fisherman. She approaches him with that same look that her mother used to give her.

It must be in the genes and it's something that Gwyneth has never been proud of. She didn't ask to be this way. She didn't ask to hate the human race and she certainly didn't ask this fat man to come into her life unexpectedly.

She wants people to know that she holds no fear. She wants them to be scared of her and to fear her like she's that spinning black hole. She loves the look on people's faces when they are about to die. She honestly feels no remorse. She feels no empathy. Sometimes she doesn't even have feelings. It's like darkness lives inside of her whole entire body.

Quickly pulling the sewing needle out of her coat pocket, Gwyneth stabs the Fisherman in his left eye. The man screams in agony, begging for his life with more intelligible words. Mumbo jumbo and things she can't quite understand. She isn't even sure if he is speaking words. It reminds her of her mother when she used to yell. Gwyneth couldn't comprehend what she was saying half the time and she didn't know how to express that toward the beast. She didn't want to get beaten for the simple fact that she knew that the woman was calling her bad names but she didn't really know what those things meant. Her siblings tried to explain things more easily but it was hard for them to express their knowledge because they were so young themselves.

Re-living most of those memories all of a sudden is making Gwyneth even angrier. Growing up with a mother who completely hates their own child is like being buried alive. It's like being suffocated and tortured every single day. Not having any adult to run to is even worse.

Gwyneth shakes her head and closes her eyes.

She's sitting on her bed as the beast towers over her. Gwyneth looks up as her brain scrambles for a reason why the woman is in her room. She's unsure of what her mother is going to make her do now. She's gripping a pair of scissors in her filthy hand while her crusty mouth curls into a crooked smile. Her lips are chapped and bloody. It looks like she was biting the skin off her lips and made them bleed.

Gwyneth cringes. If she could never ever look at her mother's disgusting face again, she would be the happiness twelve-year-old in the universe.

She smells her cigarette stench and coffee breath.

This Bitch needs a shower.

"You need to pay attention girl! It's time to properly learn how to sew! Let's try this again," Ruby demands as the coffee stench wafts into Gwyneth's poor nose.

Ruby looks down as Gwyneth's doll is gripped tight in her hand.

Gwyneth absolutely loves dolls. She loves how pretty they are because she hopes that one day she can be as pretty as them. She loves their smooth skin and the soft material of their clothes. She knows she can love them and they can love her back. They smile at her with kind eyes. Sometimes she even imagines them winking at her.

Her very first doll was a present from the twins. Of course the beast bought it, but they picked it out for her as a birthday present. They just knew that she would love it and take extra good care of it. They knew she could be gentle and loving.

As that doll is gripped in her fist, Ruby suddenly snatches it right out of Gwyneth's hand. She cuts the eyeballs out with the scissors. Stuffing falls out and onto Gwyneth's lap.

Smashing the stuffing into her fists, Gwyneth cries out as she violently shakes her head.

Ruby opens a bag of buttons and takes one out. She sits onto the bed next to Gwyneth with a smirk upon her face. Under the word "ugly" in the dictionary, a person would find the picture of Ruby Glacier.

The beast places the buttons, thread, her scissors and a needle next to Gwyneth. For an instant, the poor girl imagines taking that needle and stabbing her mother in the side of the head, puncturing her brain. Her hand twitches with the notion that she can pull it off. It would be so simple to just end her life right at this exact moment.

She stares into the abyss again as she visualizes the blood oozing from the side of her mother's head.

Ruby snaps her fingers, "Pay attention!" she yells. Gwyneth blinks.

Ruby gently cuts a piece of thread and places it through the hole of the needle. She then ties a knot. She shows her work in front of Gwyneth's eyes like it is part of a fashion show on the runway. Gwyneth could care less.

Ruby begins sewing a button into the eye socket of Gwyneth's doll. Gwyneth watches intently with tears in her eyes.

Holding the needle toward Gwyneth, Ruby says, "Now you try."

She doesn't want to fight with her mother right now but she can't help but refuse. This is her precious doll. It is sacred to her. It is the only gift that she has ever gotten from her siblings.

She refuses as she shakes her head no.

"Take the needle…NOW!" Ruby yells.

If only Gwyneth would listen. She knows what her mother wants. She knows if she just obliges to her commands then she won't get yelled at or beaten. She feels like she brings this upon herself. She thinks of giving up sometimes and just doing what her mother tells her to do. It would make her life a lot easier.

But, Gwyneth refuses once again.

Ruby grabs Gwyneth's hand. She angrily opens it and shoves the needle inside of it, careful not to stab her. For once, she purposely made sure that her daughter wouldn't get hurt.

Gwyneth won't grip it but Ruby places it between Gwyneth's pointer finger, her middle finger and her thumb; making her hold it like a pencil.

"You will do this now Gwyneth. Do it or I will beat your ass with my belt again! We're not doing this fighting anymore!"

Gwyneth sighs then takes a deep breath.

Ruby tosses the rest of the thread onto Gwyneth's lap where the stuffing to her poor doll is still clenched in her fist. If only she could stuff it straight into her mother's mouth and down her throat; make her choke to death. That would be just as satisfying as drinking Ruby's blood from an expensive wine glass. The imagination of the warmth and taste of this red liquid as it slides down Gwyneth's throat, gives her the chills.

She immediately smells the nastiness of Ruby's cigarette breath and the thought immediately disappears from her mind. The taste of her blood would be toxic anyways. A poison dipped in acid. It probably tastes like fungus and vomit.

This very thought gives Gwyneth the giggles. She hasn't yet

realized that her eyes are closed and she misses the nasty look that was given to her by the Bitch of a beast. Quite swiftly, and honestly taking Gwyneth off guard, the beast grips onto her daughter's jaw and applies pressure with her sharp nails. With her other hand, she shoves the scissors into Gwyneth's clenched fist.

Now, Gwyneth is no genius, BUT, why in GOD'S name would you shove a pair of scissors into the fist of an angry twelve-year-old who's ready to rip your throat into tiny little pieces?

Ruby isn't a genius and she sure as hell doesn't know how to be a wonderful parent.

"What are you gonna do… huh? Stab me with the scissors?" Ruby chuckles that annoying witch cackle from deep inside her throat. "Oh, I can see it in your eyes girl. The thoughts are endless."

Gwyneth desperately wants to tell her, *you're pretty smart for a dumb ass.*

Ruby lets go of the poor girl's jaw as she watches tears form into her eyeballs. It's not even the pain of her crusty, yellow nails that's making her want to cry. It's the frustration and holding herself back from not making the move she needs to make in order to survive.

Kill her mother right now. This instant. This moment. It would be perfect.

All she needs to do is lift those scissors that are gripped nice and firm in her fist and swing the tip into the side of her temple. Or maybe slash her throat. Or MAYBE, JUST MAYBE, stab the broad in both of her eyeballs. That's right, make her blind.

Instead, Gwyneth does what is commanded of her and shakily cuts pieces of thread. She knows she is defeated, although she doesn't know what that word means, but she does feel like her mother has won this battle too. She wins all of them.

Gwyneth struggles to place the thread through the loop of the needle.

"You can do this girl. Take your time," Ruby says encouragingly.

Gwyneth feels a cough tickling the back of her throat and she's half tempted to spit her saliva into the beast's face. That would give her so much joy.

Instead, she shakes her head no, defeated.

Ruby continues, "Stop being so damn negative!" as she pauses, a quizzical look upon her dumb face, "Do you even know what that means? You know, that attitude makes you look even more stupid!"

…. Says the person with grammar issues. What a joke.

Gwyneth slowly places the thread through the loop. The dirt and filth underneath her fingernails are getting in the way.

She looks up at Ruby for approval…. for some sort of positive response.

Ruby is ecstatic and claps her hands like a red-nosed clown. She's so high that she feels like she's about to float through the air like a red balloon.

"That's it! Now tie the knot!" Ruby demands excitedly.

Gwyneth is shaking. Her adrenaline is through the roof. She's not happy that she's witnessing her mother dancing in this over-exaggerated glory, she's just happy that she FINALLY put this damn thread through the loop. It's been eating at her for weeks.

She smirks as she successfully ties the knot. Her mother cheers wildly like an ecstatic fan in their seat at a hockey game after a big score. What a dumb ass. Gwyneth laughs. It's not because of her mother's electrified behavior, it's because she sincerely hates this woman with a passion.

Chapter Six

Gwyneth doesn't feel relieved or even slightly impressed with the nasty blood that's now oozing from the filthy, vile, Fisherman's eyeballs. He's crying like a newborn baby on her picnic table. *What a waste of space.* It would be nice to throw him into that black hole and watch him spin in circles until he choked on his vomit.

Boo... Hoo. *Bitch.*

Tissues from the inside of his right eye socket now dangle alongside of his face. Gwyneth glances at it for a moment, thinking, *it kind of looks like a large intestine.* She only remembers this from a picture in a health magazine that her mother once showed her. It was a disgusting image of blood; captivating the depiction of the insides of a human body.

Gwyneth shrugs her shoulders. Maybe that's why she loves blood and gore so much.

She's angry though; storming toward the shack with hatred in her eyes. Being angry is her way of life. She's angry at the world. She's angry at her mother. Hell, she's even angry at her siblings for never trying to make any attempt to find her.

Well, she doesn't know if that's even true, BUT, she's just going to assume they haven't made any attempt. This saddens her heart very deeply.

She's angry at this stupid baboon for torturing that poor, defenseless, beautiful puppy. Who would do such a thing? Well, fat ass (aka crying little Bitch), over there, would do such a thing to someone. He doesn't have positive brain cells in order to treat others with respect and love.

There's a slight giggle in the back of Gwyneth's throat.

Neither does she.

And that's RUBY'S fault.

The fat man's whimpers are weaker. Instead of just being dumb, he'll be deaf and blind.

Upon slamming the front door of the shack, even though it re-opened immediately because it doesn't shut all the way, Gwyneth spots Buttons drinking his water. Wagging his tail, he happily jumps up to her. She immediately brightens up, smiling from ear to ear. Of course, her T-shirt mask is covering this gigantic smile, but it's there.

She pets the top of his head and then clicks her tongue. She will have lots of time later to play, but for now, she has to finish ending that poor schmuck's life.

What an asshole. His life must have been terrible as well in order to act this way and treat people like crap. It's not an excuse but too bad he didn't have someone to help guide him in the right direction. It's awful that he didn't have someone who could've helped him see life in a different and positive way.

Opening her container, Gwyneth pulls out more thread; noticing a small black button stuck to the bottom of the container inside a sticky, red substance. Digging the button with her dirty fingernails, it lifts out of the substance as it makes a "ripping noise." Gwyneth's eyes light up.

While bending down onto her knee, Gwyneth points to the button and then points to the puppy. She rubs the back of his ears and then does it again. She jumps up excitedly; pointing to the button and then to the puppy once again.

Piercing her lips together, she tries to say the word, "Buttons." A slight "ba" sound comes from her lips but she can't say the whole word.

This type of activity usually frustrates her when she tries to talk. At one point when she turned twelve, her five-year-old siblings tried teaching her how to talk. She wanted them to teach her how to say, "Bitch," to their mother. It came out as "bi" like the word, "bit." It was useless and Gwyneth would cry for days because she felt so incompetent.

Tossing the black button back into the container and closing the lid, Gwyneth then kisses the top of the puppy's head. He's panting; slightly barks and wags his tail.

The Fisherman is absolutely appalled by Gwyneth's actions. His mind is a jumbled mess and he can't seem to understand what is happening or where he's at. He listens for any type of movement coming from the direction of the shack.

He's sweating; the T-shirt is still stuffed inside of his mouth. His lips are dry and cracked. He's losing momentum, he's losing his breath and he's losing his life.

He's slowly dying. This is what torture feels like. Now he knows how the puppy has felt.

"Please," he muffles, "Let… me… gg..." He barely gets the words out of his mouth.

He's too tired, wounded and he knows he's going to die. His body relaxes as his mind gives up. There's no use into fighting this crazy, mad, lunatic girl. His mind is a black hole. His eyes are gone from their sockets. The pain is unbearable. His face feels like it's on fire.

Gwyneth can see the bones protruding from the beast's backside as she continues to dance like a moron. The poor girl glances down at her favorite doll as she continues to sew a button into the right eye socket. She's trying to get over the fact that her mother has now made her doll looking like a psychotic demon.

Maybe it's a good thing.

Gwyneth chuckles as her nose sniffles. Tears are welled inside of her eyeballs and she's desperately trying to not let them fall. Her mother will make fun of her for crying.

"See, I knew you could do it," Ruby says calmly.

Is this beast serious right now? She never thought that Gwyneth could ever do ANYTHING let alone sew a button into a doll. Not only is this Bitch psychotic like this demon baby doll, but now she's delusional and seriously stupid.

Not enough brain cells.

Gwyneth ignores her mother and gently touches the doll's cheek. Then, as the tears escape her eyes, she pets the doll's hair like a dog. Ruby continues her idiotic speech.

"Just like I know you can talk too but you choose to be a mute. There's something wrong with your brain girl," she points to her own brain as she taps her pointer finger onto her head.

Gwyneth looks up at the beast with hatred in her eyes.

"One day you will thank me for trying so hard with this sewing stuff. I need to teach you. You need to learn how to make things on your own. You never know what could happen to you."

Well, you never know what could happen to you either, Bitch.

The possibilities are endless. She could choke on a cigarette as she's being punched in the back of the head. Oh, who would do such a thing to this beautiful woman?

Her throat could be slit from her own ten inch sewing needle. *Now, that's an idea!*

The poor girl doesn't want to listen to this old bitty bat. Okay, she's not old but she is annoying and obnoxious. She always just talks on and on as if she's standing in front of a crowd.

Gwyneth quietly stares; her eyes transfixed on her doll. She plays with a button on the doll's face with her dirty fingernails. She can't remember the last time she took a bath. Ruby the Twig Beast won't let her; told her she needs to save her water for, "more important children in the house." Of course Gwyneth isn't important. Otherwise, she wouldn't be in this predicament.

"I know that's your favorite doll," Ruby continues, "It had to be done. We had to use something. And that's the best thing in a tight spot to practice with. Always do the right eye first. Then you could make the left eye as even as possible."

That doesn't even make any sense. *Why does it have to be the right eye first? To make the left one jealous?* Gwyneth doesn't understand this explanation at all.

Ruby is still an idiot. She's still a dumb ass.

Ruby strokes Gwyneth's long, black, hair. Her breath smells as if she ate the inside of a butthole. Her yellow teeth gleam in the sunlight. It should be getting dark soon and hopefully this shit of a mother goes back to her room and chokes on her drugs.

"My mother taught me how to sew," Ruby's crusty lips continue to move even though Gwyneth is half-listening. "She used a doll of mine. I was so upset with her. I know how you feel. But my mother was crazy. That's why you kids will never meet her." Ruby giggles. "I guess that's why I'm crazy too!"

Ruby cackles like a witch again. That sound burns a hole through Gwyneth's brain. For her, it's the worst sound in the world. She would rather hear screaming coming out of her mother's throat as the girl tortures her. If only she had the guts to torture her.

Gwyneth pictures it in her mind. She ties her mother to her bed and then –

Ruby rudely interrupts the girl's thoughts by clicking her filthy fingers in front of the child's face. Her nails are still sharp, yellow and brown. It looks like she has feces stuck underneath her nails. This realization makes Gwyneth want to gag.

"That's why your father didn't want nothin' to do with me too!" Ruby laughs hysterically.

Gwyneth is surely not amused. She leans back onto her pillow and hugs her doll tightly in her arms as she imagines stabbing her mother in the temple.

Gwyneth just wants to get this over with. This situation has been going on for far too long. The fat man should've been dead by now. The dog has become a distraction to her. Deep down, she hopes that doesn't continue to interfere with her future killings. She would like to be optimistic and say that it won't, but right now she doesn't know and time will soon tell.

With the scissors, Gwyneth cuts three pieces of the thread. Realizing she has no buttons, she looks down at the coat she is wearing. See, the dog distracted her from retrieving all of the items needed. This is not satisfactory and Gwyneth will put herself down for it later. She usually smacks herself in the head or she will wrap her T-shirt mask around her throat and try to choke herself when she makes herself angry.

Swiftly, she cuts the last two buttons off of her coat. Her heart is pounding but she manages to calmly place the thread through the needle. This is the adrenaline rush that she feels every time she's about to finish murdering someone. It feels like her heart is about to jump out of her chest. She's shaking as she quietly approaches the Fisherman.

She's not scared of him. It's just the pure enjoyment of her heart pounding with excitement.

The man is pitiful and weak. His dry lips make a small attempt to move but no words come out. He's breathless and tired.

He's dying and this makes Gwyneth smile behind her makeshift mask.

Without further ado, she shoves her fingers into his right eye; pulling it out of the socket. Calmly, she places it onto the table.

Back inside the shack, Buttons jumps onto the small card table. Whimpering, he watches Gwyneth through the window. If she only knew what he thought about her? His heart races every time he sees her now. He loves her unconditionally. She is a savior.

If only dogs could talk to humans. If only dogs could talk to those dragonflies. They would have similar stories in order to compare notes. The dragonflies could tell Buttons what they have witnessed from the fat man. They could tell him to never step foot near that pond water ever again. It is disease infected and they should never drink it.

Buttons licks his chops.

Gwyneth can hear Buttons as he whimpers. She feels this sudden sadness but she will allow him to come outside once she's finished. He probably thinks she's keeping him inside forever.

She pulls out the Fisherman's left eye and places it on the table next to the other one. The "slurp" sound that both eyes make as they're being ripped from their sockets is like music to her ears. These choking, gurgling, slicing sounds is what she loves to hear; not her mother talking or this fat man crying like a suffocating baby with its pillow over its mouth.

She sews a button into the man's right eye socket. He makes gurgling noises. She's quite shocked to be honest. She can't believe that he's still alive.

If anyone else was there, they could clearly see Buttons continuously peeking through the window. He watches Gwyneth with wide eyes. He's still whimpering and continues to pace on the card table. Saliva drips from his tongue as he pants; staring at the eyeballs on the picnic table.

He barks; but he immediately puts his head down because he becomes scared. He isn't sure if Gwyneth will punish him. The fat man did. The poor dog wasn't allowed to bark at all.

Jumping down from the table, he sniffs the refrigerator and claws at the door. He then growls; pacing the shack floor.

Barking a second time, he sniffs the garbage can and knocks it over. He scares himself; jumping at the noise and immediately looking toward the shack's front door.

Gwyneth listens to Buttons as he barks and whimpers… *just a little while longer*.

She sews the second button into the fat man's left eye socket. Finishing, she takes a deep breath. That takes a lot out of her because she holds in her breath for some reason. She's afraid to breathe. She thinks the wind of her breath will mess up the thread.

Glancing up at the sky, she closes her eyes. She feels the cold breeze on her face. The storm clouds have passed and the rain has stopped but it left behind a soft breeze that blows the hood of her coat. She feels at peace. She feels her heart pounding with joy. This is so incredibly relaxing.

The Fisherman makes a slight whimpering noise and the sound of Buttons whining from the shack makes Gwyneth slowly open her eyes. The poor puppy will be let out shortly.

Looking down at the fat man, she places both of her hands on top of his mouth; it is still stuffed with his clothing. He can't struggle, let alone move. This makes her completely ecstatic.

She presses harder, taking a deep breath while slowly letting it out until she finally kills him.

She would give up everything to kill this Bitch. Anyone with common sense would see the hatred in the poor girl's eyes every single time she even looks at her mother. That's why she tries to keep her head down. Eye contact with this beast is like looking at Medusa. Gwyneth might turn to stone. She might even die from holding her breath in from the nasty stench that overpowers Ruby's dirty mouth. Her teeth are crying, "Brush me! Brush me!"

Gwyneth has this surge of laughter bubbling at the back of her throat but she stops herself from laughing. Sometimes her thoughts get away from her and she forgets that she's sitting right in front of her mother. The woman could just easily backhand her face and that's not something that Gwyneth is prepared for. Sometimes Gwyneth lets her guard down and Ruby will hit her out of nowhere; stealing her soul from her body.

Gwyneth continues to hug her doll; her guard is downright at this moment. She can't help it. The softness of her doll's plastic skin makes her feel like she's floating in a dream. This helps her to block out her mother's bullshit. The words that are coming out of her mouth sound like a group of bees buzzing in their hive.

Ruby continues to cackle; oblivious to Gwyneth's attention toward her doll.

"Your father was a no good cheater! He used to call me a hussy! His poor wife! They're all stupid!" Ruby continues. She laughs hysterically once again.

Gwyneth suddenly removes herself from her bed. She can't take any more of this woman's drastic and pitiful behavior. She's psychotic and doesn't deserve to be in this room. Shit, she doesn't deserve this house or the kids!

Ignoring her mother even more, Gwyneth strolls over to a corner of her room.

Ruby just boasts on and on; laughing like the witch that she is.

Gwyneth points to her dolls who are sitting nicely in the corner by the window. As she points, she tries to count how many she has left. Ruby suddenly stops babbling and watches her.

"Pretty soon they're all gonna lose their eyeballs!" Once again, she laughs hysterically while pulling out a cigarette and a lighter from her jeans pocket.

Gwyneth snatches three dolls off of the floor and gently touches their hair and cheeks. She rubs their eyeballs with her fist as if she's telling them that they will be next. They probably will. If Ruby gets her way, they will have buttons for eyeballs too.

She returns to her bed with the dolls.

Ruby lights up her cigarette. Gwyneth tries everything in her power to ignore this beast. Sometimes she hates her life so much that she wishes her mother would just come through with her threats and kill her. Other times she wishes she had the balls to kill her mother herself. Well, not balls. She doesn't know what those are. Maybe she wishes that she had the NERVE to kill her mother. She would do it quickly and maybe even quietly so the neighbors down the street wouldn't hear the commotion.

Speaking of the neighbors, they once called the cops on Ruby. It was a nightmare. The beast left all three children alone and caged them inside of a small dog cage. Gwyneth managed to break the cage's lock and released her siblings from being prisoners in their own home. All three children ran outside with no pants on and no socks and shoes. They were filthy from not taking baths and they were starving from not being properly fed.

The cops found Ruby at a nearby bar and arrested her.

The kids were taken into custody but after just one day of an investigation, they were released back to Ruby. Unfortunately, she was so pissed off that she beat the kids with a belt and threw them back into the cage. They were locked in there for three days until finally Gwyneth's brother took a dump inside the cage and smeared the poop all over his twin's face with his own hands. The smell overpowered the whole entire house and Ruby couldn't take it anymore.

As the beast sits down next to Gwyneth on the bed, she blows the smoke into the girl's face. Gwyneth coughs and waves the smoke away with her hand. This action was apparently entertaining because Ruby cackles like a witch once again.

"I'm sure one day you'll do this too. Might as well get used to it now," Ruby laughs as she inhales another hit of the cigarette.

Gwyneth shakes her head no and then lines up her dolls on her bed.

Ruby continues, "No huh? You think so." Ruby thinks for a second. "You know, talking to you is like talking to a brick wall. Just a blank stare. Says nothing back."

Gwyneth hums to herself while playing with her dolls.

Ruby continues her babble talk, "I know you tryin' to ignore me like you always do. It won't work. Normally, I walk away and leave you alone. I'm not today. No siree Bob!"

Who the Hell is she kidding? Ruby does NOT leave that poor girl alone, EVER. She nags her and tortures her mentally, emotionally and physically. It's almost every single day of her life. The only time she isn't torturing her children is when she's drunk and passed out on the couch or drugged up half-dead on her raggedy, bed-bug infested bed.

She truly is a vile human being.

Gwyneth's sister strolls into the bedroom holding onto a can of corn and a spoon. Not knowing that Ruby is in the room as well, she stops dead in her tracks when she suddenly sees her sitting on the bed. Ruby doesn't say a word as she watches Gwyneth reach out to her sister. The five-year-old hands her the food and quickly runs out of the room.

As Ruby chuckles, she says with a snotty attitude, "I got you kids so afraid of me. I love it." She pauses for a moment to think. "Are you afraid of me Gwyneth?"

Without answering, Gwyneth takes a huge bite of her corn; stuffing her mouth like a squirrel collecting nuts for the winter. She's too afraid to look up so she stares at her dolls as if they will answer for her. If only dolls could talk. They could tell this beast of a woman to go to HELL.

They might even kill her if they were alive.

"Hello? Did you hear me? Are you afraid of me girl?" Ruby continues on.

As Gwyneth takes another bite, Ruby slaps the spoon out of her hand. The corn flings onto her dolls; the corn juice splashing on their plastic skin.

"I'm talkin' to you girl. Look at me," Ruby demands.

Gwyneth ever-so-slowly and angrily looks up at her mother. She quickly snatches her favorite doll with the buttons for eyeballs; scared that the beast will torture it some more.

"See, was that so hard to listen? Now answer my question. Are you afraid of me?"

Gwyneth thinks for a minute. Her mind is like flashes of lightning in a storm. It cracks on the left side of her brain and then her right. She looks left and then looks right as if she's watching the lightning flash before her eyes. She's not really looking at anything. She stares into the abyss again as her eyes refuse to blink.

Ruby watches her and waits for an answer. She's becoming inpatient and starts to click her tongue. She then takes a long drag of her cigarette.

Gwyneth shakes her head no. She immediately regrets her response as Ruby snatches the doll out of her arms. Gwyneth suddenly lunges forward and tries to grab it out of Ruby's tight grasp. Ruby lifts it up into the air; swinging it side to side as Gwyneth reaches for it.

"Still not afraid of me huh? What if I rip this doll to shreds?"

What if I rip you to shreds? The Bitch is asking for it. She just needs to collect some courage in order to gain momentum. She needs to fight her and stand up for herself.

She needs to kill her.

Ruby throws the doll at Gwyneth's face. She laughs hysterically as she takes a puff of the last of her cigarette. She smashes the burning embers out onto Gwyneth's sheet and mattress.

Gwyneth feels like she can't breathe. Her anxiety has just now slammed into the roof. Her heart is racing and it feels like it will beat right out of her chest. She's angry, she's annoyed and she's seeing red through her eyes as she stares at the cigarette lying on her bed.

Ruby suddenly stands up and takes off her belt. *A belt for what?* She's ninety pounds soaking wet. She's not even technically a beast. She's a pile of bones with a witch's face.

Gwyneth grips her doll in her arms.

"You afraid of me now? You're so fun to mess with. You're so stupid," Ruby says.

She suddenly swings her belt and slashes the bedpost; missing Gwyneth by an inch. She swings again and hits the mattress.

"I think it's time for an ass whoopin'!" Ruby yells.

Gwyneth clutches her doll and squeezes her eyes shut. She waits for the snap of the belt to sting whatever body part the beast reaches for.

Ruby cackles again and then tosses the belt onto the bed.

"See, I knew you were afraid of me. I'm not stupid like you," Ruby taunts.

Of course not, you're even more stupid than what anyone has ever thought. Gwyneth seems confused but has realized that the belt is lying next to her. She stares at it as if it will grow eyes and a mouth and tell her what to do. She wishes it would come alive and strangle the Bitch.

Ruby plops back onto the bed and then suddenly snatches the doll out of Gwyneth's arms once again. Gwyneth begins to stand up.

Ruby points her shit-smelling finger at Gwyneth and yells, "Sit down girl! Don't you dare move!"

Grabbing the sewing needle that Gwyneth used earlier, she shoves it into the right eye of the doll; stabbing the button. The poor girl cries out, then quickly clutches her other dolls in her arms. The beast continues to stab the doll and pulls out the white stuffing. She tries to shove it into Gwyneth's face but the girl backs away.

"Does this make you mad? Huh?" Ruby taunts.

Gwyneth immediately nods. She suddenly feels brave and clever. She wants this Bitch to be afraid of HER. She wants her to cry over something that she loves.

Gwyneth suddenly snatches the needle out of Ruby's hand. In a fit of rage, she stabs the eyeball buttons of the doll repeatedly as if she's stabbing her mother's heart. The button comes loose out of the thread.

"You're going to fix that you little brat!"

You're fixing it Bitch! You did it!

Gwyneth suddenly grips the can of corn and throws it at Ruby's forehead. Ruby lashes out like a cat in heat. The stench of her breath catches Gwyneth off-guard. The beast then grabs the poor girl's hair and pulls; struggling in a punching match.

Gwyneth repeatedly punches Ruby's arm. She can feel the bones protruding through her mother's thin skin. It feels like she's just punching a skeleton.

Ruby's left hand swings out of nowhere and slaps Gwyneth right across the face. She feels slightly dizzy but she shakes the pain away. The heat from the slap burns her cheek. All of her pent-up anger tries to rush out of her body all at once.

Ruby yells, "Who do you think you are?! Huh Gwyneth?! Who the hell do you think you are you little Bitch?!" *If only you knew Bitch!*

With all of that anger deep inside Gwyneth's soul, she swings her fist as hard as she can and punches Ruby dead center in her face. The beast falls off of the bed and lands onto the filthy floor. She's crying like a newborn baby while holding her broken, bloody nose with her poop fingers. She's such a disgusting waste of space.

Gripping the ten inch sewing needle in her angered fist, Gwyneth jumps on top of Ruby's chest. Making some kind of a screaming sound, she raises the needle high up into the air. Ruby's eyes are wide and scared. *Now who's scared? Huh???*

Gwyneth swings the tip of the needle downward; stopping just an inch away from Ruby's eye. She makes that screaming sound in Ruby's face; her saliva dripping onto Ruby's mouth.

Chapter Seven
Present day

They should be on their way home, he knows this, but he can't stop trudging through the woods like he's looking for something specific. He's not quite sure if this specific *thing* is even "waiting in the wings." One thing is for sure, he shouldn't have brought his mouth-flapping son with him. The kid can't shut up for two seconds and enjoy the fresh air.

It seems like they've been walking for miles. William St. Rose is only forty-seven-years-old but right now he feels like he's eighty. His knees crack with every single step; cringing to the sound as he listens to his seventeen-year-old son, Roman, babble on and on about girls, his schoolwork and what he wants to eat for dinner for the next week and a half. It's truly daunting. He wishes he would've brought his ear plugs. But then he wouldn't be able to hear anything else.

Maybe that's a good thing. He wouldn't hear his poor knees crying in agony.

William looks up at the dark clouds. The weather has been shitty lately but it didn't stop them today from doing what William loves to do the most: hunting for rabbits and deer. They're dressed in their camouflage vests and pants. They're both wearing thick, black boots in order to make their way through this soggy mud.

Roman is wearing a bright orange mask covering his mouth and nose. He's a wimp when it comes to hunting. It's not really "his thing" to do. He only comes along to shut his father up. He would rather be messing around with his brand new camera and filming a short movie. That's what he loves to do and his father gives him slack over it. William wants him to follow in his footsteps but Roman is just not interested in that type of lifestyle.

While Roman's rifle slowly points upward toward the sky, his attention falls onto his fanny pack. As he rummages through his pocket knives and Snickers candy bars, William slows his pace.

Roman bumps into his father just when he finds the life-size Snickers bar he was searching for. William quickly turns to look at his hot-headed son.

Roman looks scared for a moment. The look on William's face reminds him of the "Chucky" doll. "Child's Play" is one of Roman's favorite horror films. Right now though, he wishes he could fly through a time machine to be on that film set instead of staring at the glare from his father's pissed off face.

Roman slowly and silently offers William the candy bar. William shakes his head in disgust then turns back toward the open woods. Roman shrugs his shoulders, opens the candy bar, lowers his mask and shoves the bar into his mouth. As he chews like a cow, he moans, "MMMMMM. Yeah… this is good."

William peeks through his binoculars and scans the area.

"I thought we weren't allowed to hunt in these woods, dad!" Roman says sarcastically as he chomps on the candy bar like a shark chomping on someone's leg in the water. Or someone's head. Or someone's torso. Maybe even their whole entire body.

"We're not," William answers while he continues to look through the binoculars.

"Then why are we? It's your rule. It's always been your rule. Your way, right? I mean, these woods are private property, not the state's business." Roman continues as he licks the chocolate off of his lips.

"Why do you have to be such a Debbie Downer?"

Roman looks confused. This isn't surprising to William.

His son makes it seem like he doesn't have enough brain cells to function properly most days. Don't get him wrong, Roman is smart when it comes to book smart, but the kid doesn't think before he speaks. He lacks communication skills and sometimes he nags people to the point to where they yell at him and tell him to "shut up." Or, "Shut the fuck up" and "Shut the hell up." All three statements work because he immediately closes his mouth and then sulks like a child. He will cross his arms and huff like he has a breathing problem.

"What the hell does that mean?" Roman asks with a mouth full of chocolate. The candy bar is nearly gone and he tosses the wrapper onto a tree stump.

"Watch your language kid," William demands. He stops looking through the binoculars and glares at Roman. "It means that you're bringing negativity to this situation. You're bringing down my mood." He scans the area once again.

"Well, we shouldn't be here. Sounds like I'm more responsible than you are."

William is angry. He whips his head and yells, "Shut up!"

So, sometimes Roman will sulk like a child. Other times, he will antagonize his victim like a knife does when it digs through a chalkboard. It's the sound of his voice. It's like a whiny, "I told you so," bad attitude. He thinks he's slick.

"Daaannnggg! What's up your ass?" Roman asks as he lifts his orange mask and places it back over his mouth.

"I should've come alone. You're not even into this kind of stuff. Too busy into your film dreams. Wanting to make movies." William answers, placing his binoculars into his backpack.

This is a sensitive issue for Roman. He and his father do not see eye to eye with this career move. Roman is frustrated with William's ignorance and ill opinion about making his dreams come true. The poor kid doesn't think it is fair at all and he just wants his father to not only understand, but to welcome his positive vibes about movie making.

"So what?" Roman whines. "You got a problem with that? Oh what? ... I'm not into hunting and sports like you? Well, I'm not you. I'm into other interesting things. Speaking of...my film class requires me to create a documentary film. I'm not sure what to do. Any ideas?"

Is this kid for real? William asks to himself inside of his brain. Roman will not accept the fact that William does not care about his son's film interests. Honestly, William doesn't even understand why himself. He doesn't understand why he hates the fact that his own son wants to become a filmmaker and not the future Sheriff.

Maybe it's jealousy. Maybe it's the fact that Roman could seriously make something of his life. He could potentially make a lot of money in his lifetime and William resents this notion.

"Yeah," William answers sarcastically. "A young boy got on his father's nerves and the father snapped out on him in the woods. Thought he was a deer and..."

Roman interrupts his father, "Whoa! Where are you going with this? That's not a good film idea. You're evil I tell ya! Evil!"

"Never mind son. Let's go this way...to the west."

Roman pulls out his compass from his coat pocket. William rolls his eyes.

"I think we should go north," Roman replies.

William is nervous. "No! West! Will you just listen to me for once?!"

Gwyneth loves how quiet her surroundings can be within her small area of these woods. Sometimes she sniffs the air as a soft breeze blows the hood of her Eskimo coat. She likes to close her eyes and dream of playing outside in a backyard of a huge house alongside her brother and sister. She watches them climb onto swings while laughing hysterically at each other's jokes. They turn to her and yell, "Push us Sissy! Push us please?"

Gwyneth usually smiles back and nods her head. She pushes them so high it's like they float through the sky. They look like small angels with wings just having a good time flying through the air. Her sister's hair slaps onto her forehead as if it's holding on for dear life.

Then, just like the wind, they blow away and Gwyneth is left standing alone in the backyard. That's when Gwyneth opens her eyes and realizes where she truly is. She realizes that her siblings are not with her and this angers the inside of her shaking body.

She's shaking because her heart beats like a drum. Her adrenaline rips out of her body and shoots up into the bright sun. The lightning inside of her brain strikes like the mouth of a snake. It strikes the right side of her brain and then back to the left side. The light continuously blocks her vision until she sees red. When she sees red, her killer instincts take over her entire body. It's like she has no control over her hands, her legs or even her mind.

And that's what scares her the most. It's the only thing that does scare her.

At twenty-four-years-old, she should be used to this by now. But sadly, this behavior isn't something that she wants to be accustomed to. This behavior is something she *has* to do because her mind isn't normal. It never has been.

And that's something that she usually accepts, whether she wants to or not.

She also accepts the fact that the only thing she has in her life is her loyal and lovable black Lab, Buttons. Buttons has been there for her through thick and thin and quite honestly, she doesn't want it any other way. She doesn't want her life interrupted in ANY WAY. Being interrupted makes her see red and she doesn't like it when she sees red.

As she sits outside at her picnic table, Buttons sniffs the air and growls a low growl. Gwyneth shushes him with her dirty finger as they both watch a squirrel scurrying across the muddy ground. Retrieving her harpoon that is lying next to her on the bench of the table; she quickly snatches it and shoots it so fast that Buttons doesn't realize what happened. He blinks his eyes as Gwyneth picks up the dead squirrel. He then licks his chops as he watches Gwyneth toss the poor dead animal on top of the picnic table.

Pulling out her knife from her back pocket, Gwyneth slices the squirrel wide open. Buttons growls once again. Gwyneth turns to look at him. They stare at each other's eyes for a moment until Buttons backs down; whimpering and lowering his head.

He knows he will get some; he just has to be patient.

William repeats this sentence in his head, *"I should've brought ear plugs. I should've brought ear plugs."* He definitely should've brought ear plugs or at least left Roman at home. He can't take much more of his gibberish and bullshit ideas about making a movie in these woods. He feels like he's about to rip what's left of his hair right out of its roots.

They stroll past a "NO HUNTING" sign as Roman stops to take a breath. He pulls down his orange mask and exhales; making a blowing noise that sounds like a swirling tornado.

William pulls out his binoculars once again and scans the area. He spots the shack from a distance. Roman starts whining like a tired toddler as his mask becomes loose. He tries tightening it and replaces it back over his mouth.

"I said we are going west. Let's go," William demands.

Roman plays with his mask some more as he looks ahead; squinting his eyes as if he's trying to focus on something far away.

"But dad, I see something up ahead. Come on, let's check it out! It could be something creepy going on!" Roman is ecstatic. He isn't sure why, but he feels this adrenaline rush wash over his entire body. He feels as though he's hit the jackpot.

"Be quiet and get down," William orders.

"Dad you're acting weird," Roman replies, searching through his backpack. "Where's my binocu—" William slaps the backpack out of Roman's grasp.

"I told you we're going west. I shouldn't have brought you here. You never listen to anyone. Not me, not your mother and definitely not your sister."

Hearing the crunching noises of leaves and twigs, both William and Roman quickly turn as if they just saw a ghost. William spots a deer.

"It looks like a house up ahead. I want to see if anyone is there," Roman says, ignoring the deer and his father.

While keeping an eye on the deer through the scope of his rifle, William angrily protests, "No, we need to just leave. It could be dangerous. Besides, who lives in the woods?"

Roman thinks for a moment; staring into the abyss.

William continues to watch the deer through the scope. Silence cuts through the air like a knife inside of a tub of butter. The wind blows the leaves off the trees and the sky becomes darker as rain clouds pass by.

Roman is still staring into nothing as he thinks about bringing his camera to these woods.

The deer suddenly takes off. And so does William.

"Follow me! Let's go!" William yells over his shoulder at Roman.

Roman ignores his father once again and peeks through the scope of his rifle, pointing north. "Someone who wants to hide," Roman says to himself.

The kid has become incredibly defiant over the years. In the past month, William has admitted to his therapist that he often wishes that Roman had finished high school as of now so he could kick him out. He's wondered time and time again why he doesn't listen. Roman has acted out his whole entire senior year and no one can figure out why. He's never admitted to anyone why his behavior has become so shitty. His sister constantly nags him but he doesn't talk to her about his anger and defiant issues. It's a mystery that no one can solve.

Roman creeps closer toward the shack as he licks his lips. He's nervous and scared. His heart is pounding out of his chest and he feels like he's about to be sick. His hands are shaking as he places his finger on the trigger. He doesn't see anything for a moment. It's like time is at a standstill. He's creeping so quietly and slowly that he can't even hear his own footsteps.

He stops walking to dig out his knife from his fanny pack with his right hand. Still holding the rifle with his left hand, he continues to peek through the scope. He doesn't want to take his eyes off of what he is seeing ahead of him. He's curious but dumb at the same time.

Suddenly, Gwyneth appears. Roman watches her shove a squirrel through the sharp edge of a fireplace poker. She walks over to the burning campfire and cooks the squirrel as if it's a marshmallow for a S'mores snack. She spins the poker in circles; careful to cook each side of the dead animal. Roman can't believe what he's watching.

He hunkers down but slowly takes a few steps toward the shack.

He steps on a branch.

No one said that he's smart. Only book smart. His brain works like a handful of rocks. If only he would've listened to his father. If only he wasn't so hot-headed and tempered like a grizzly bear. If only he wouldn't have stepped on that damn branch.

Buttons perks up from lying on the ground. He growls that low growl. Gwyneth quickly looks up from her campfire and searches the area. In a flash, she drops the fireplace poker and runs toward the shack.

"Shit!" Roman whispers.

He continues to hunker down while watching Buttons through the scope. Gwyneth stands in the doorway of the shack. She clicks her tongue.

Buttons growls but whimpers as he searches the woods. Gwyneth clicks her tongue once again and then bangs her fist on the shack's front door. Roman watches Buttons run away and head toward the shack; finally listening to his master.

That dog kind of reminds him of himself; curious and defiant. That attitude gets you in deep trouble, especially if your name is Roman St. Rose. And, especially if you're a dog named Buttons who is owned by a psychotic killer named Gwyneth.

Roman looks around the woods. His father is gone and he feels like he might die at any second. His boots are frozen to the muddy ground. He's so scared to move that he doesn't know what to do. He knows that this mad person will come after him once the dog is safely inside. He knows he should start running away but he wants to see what this person is going to do next.

He doesn't know if this person is a man or woman or what kind of weapons they have in the shack. His mind is overthinking the possibilities and he doesn't notice Gwyneth walking out of the shack with her wire. She spreads it from one tree to the next; tying knots at the end of each one. She makes a circle; keeping her area intact.

Buttons watches from the doorway and barks. He sniffs the air as his saliva drips into the muddy ground. He's drooling, he's hungry for that squirrel and he just wants to take a nap. He wants to chase whoever is out there. His head turns to the right, then to the left, then straight ahead again; right into the direction where Roman is hunkering behind a tree.

Gwyneth snaps her fingers at Buttons and he lowers his head. Gwyneth places her finger up to her lips and shakes her head no at the dog like he understands what her gestures mean.

Suddenly, Roman is grabbed from behind. He jumps and quickly turns to face his father. William places his finger up to his lips and whispers, "Shhhhh." He then lifts his rifle and spots Gwyneth through the scope. Gwyneth's eyeballs search the woods as she points her harpoon.

Roman holds his chest. "Damn it dad! You scared the shit out of me!"

"I know I can smell your fart." William lowers the rifle. "Stop being a wuss. Let's go NOW. I specifically told you to follow me. You're going to get yourself killed out here. That damn deer ran off. It's getting late. We need to head back."

Roman watches Gwyneth once again through the scope. He waves his hand at his father as if he's telling him to go away. William suddenly grabs Roman's arm.

"NOW!" William growls; trying not to be extremely loud.

"Geez! Alright! Let's go Debbie Downer!" Roman whispers.

William shakes his head and thinks to himself once again, *"I should've come alone. I should've come alone. I should've come alone."* He lets go of Roman's arm.

Roman takes one last peek through his scope and then heads west. William watches his son walk away. His heart pounds with nervousness. If only this kid of his would listen. If only he would've come out here alone. If only Roman was more mature. He could talk to him like an adult instead of some punk kid who thinks he knows everything in life.

William takes two steps and then stops. He slowly turns; peeking through his scope. He takes one last glimpse of her.

He smiles.

Chapter Eight
6 years prior

Gwyneth absolutely loves that adrenaline rush she receives after she kills one of her victims. Her heart races with excitement. Her mind's electricity quickly zaps from one side of her brain to the other. Each zap loves to scream as it tries to make a mad dash out of her skull. Sometimes she can't even think about her next move because the bright lights leave spots onto her eyeballs. She seems blinded by the impact of each zap as it strikes like a lightning flash.

The sound of the electricity nearly deafens her ears. This ringing sound pulsate her ear drums; making her temples pound so hard that it feels like the face of a hammer is crushing her skull. One day her skull is going to burst open and the zapping of the electricity will finally be set free.

Like her. Set free. Free as a bird with her wings spread.

That's how she feels right now. Free of that disgusting and hateful Fisherman. Free of hearing his whining and crying. Free from hearing his begging and pleading to be released. It was an awful thing to hear. She would've rather have been clawed by a bear.

Speaking of bears, she just remembered the leftover bear meat that's in her refrigerator. She could feed the puppy some of that! She's been worried about how to feed him and properly take care of him. She doesn't want to end up like her mother and not understand how to take care of an animal. She never wants to hurt him or put him in any type of danger. That would crush her heart to pieces; kind of like that hammer is trying to do to her temple. The feeling is overwhelming and it's making her feel sick to her stomach.

Her migraine makes her head want to explode into thousands of microscopic pieces of brain matter. That's the only after affect that she hates the most about ending someone's life. Her excitement ends up torturing her brain; causing a headache the size of California. She could never understand it. Of course, she doesn't understand a lot of things but that actually blows her mind. One day, it will literally blow her mind and that's what she will get for killing people.

Tit for tat Bitch.

Gwyneth chuckles at her own joke as she trudges through the muddy woods. Buttons is frightened as his head peeks out of her Eskimo hood. He remembers the area quite well as his body immediately starts shaking. He sees the path that leads toward the pond and begins to whimper. He's scared out of his mind. He isn't sure if she's going to drop him off and leave him in that same exact spot they met. He likes her. He doesn't want to leave her.

Gwyneth has her ten inch needle hidden inside of her glove once again. She won't have any problems with stabbing anyone who tries to stop her. Her brain should be marked lethal. She will protect this innocent dog at all costs. No one will take him away from her now.

She isn't sure if the Fisherman has family or anyone who will come out to look for him. She has to be careful and not be seen. She knows how to tip-toe and stroll in quietly like a Ninja.

She knows she's tired though as she walks while slumped with her harpoon over her right shoulder and a Unicorn backpack fitting snug over her sore back.

Her back is always sore from the beatings and whippings she received as a young child from her awful mother. But now, it's extremely sore from pulling and lifting the fat man through the woods and onto the picnic table. Her neck is feeling the burn from carrying his fat ass.

Gwyneth approaches the same spot where the Fisherman was fishing. The dragonflies are flying above the smelly water. They soar through the sky like beautiful angels with bright halos. The blues and purple colors sparkle from the brightness of the sun. It periodically peeks out of the dark and rainy clouds. It looks like it's trying to scream, "Help me! Help me!"

She feels the same way, sun. The same exact same way.

Gwyneth spots the Fisherman's tackle box next to his dented cooler. His butt even broke the top of the cooler! She can't even imagine what kind of life he lived; just a pig slurping through his trough. Like a couch potato; eating everything in sight.

Buttons peeks out of the hood once again and whimpers when he sees the pond. Gwyneth searches the area with her tired eyes. This place is actually a beautiful spot to sit and fish. Maybe even read a nice book.

Or, maybe it's a nice enough spot to kill your wife.

Gwyneth looks toward the open meadow behind the pond. Bushes have grown alongside a fence that stops people from trespassing. The fence looks old and rusted.

She then glances at the trees swaying from the wind at the right of her. The dark clouds have stayed put and refuse to leave. The sun is completely gone now. She suddenly feels this overwhelming sadness and she doesn't understand why. The sun just wants to have fun too. Just like her. She wants to go home to her shack and laugh and play with her new found friend.

But she came here for the rest of the Fisherman's belongings. Well, maybe not that nasty cooler, but the tackle box will do.

She spots the dead fish that the Fisherman caught earlier. And maybe she'll take that too.

Looking around the area one last time for other human contact, Gwyneth picks up the piece of fish and shoves it into her backpack; along with the tackle box. Gripping Buttons from inside of the hood, she lowers him to the ground. He sniffs the air toward the trees. The same trees Gwyneth just stared at mesmerized and dazed.

He then sniffs the ground where that dead fish once laid to rest. The wind blows once again and Buttons shakes his fur as if he's suddenly feeling cold.

Searching the area, Gwyneth spots a path of trampled grass and stones. As she takes a step to follow it, Buttons becomes reluctant. Gwyneth clicks her tongue, hoping that the dog will listen. He is extremely sketchy with this area and she's desperate to know why.

Buttons sniffs the ground; slowly following her toward the path.

Gwyneth smiles. Even though Buttons can't see this smile because of her makeshift T-shirt mask, she's happy. She's happy that he's being a very good dog. She's happy that he's warming up to her and he seems to like her.

Gwyneth slows her pace. Buttons hops in front of her while continuing to sniff the ground. The wind has picked up; causing the trees to erratically sway side to side. A storm is surely brewing and this makes her nervous. She is hoping to find some clues as to where the Fisherman came from before it starts pouring down rain again.

The rain has to ruin everything.

Just like her mother did.

She suddenly feels angry but she doesn't want to show it in fear that Buttons will run off. He will learn of her anger soon enough but now is not the time. She needs him to stay focused.

He's on a mission just like her. She doesn't know what his mission is exactly, but he seems to know what he wants to do. This thought actually excites her and she feels that adrenaline rush once again. She's just hoping that the migraine that's pounding her brain won't get worse.

She feels the first rain drop splash onto her eyelid. Her migraine has increased tremendously. That small drop of rain feels like a hammer to the face.

A slight drizzle comes across the sky; interrupting her thoughts. She spots Buttons up ahead of her. She needs to pay attention more instead of staring around the breezy sky and trees that look like they're ready to be pulled from the roots.

She suddenly feels disturbed in some way. Buttons is certainly not a burden, but she feels like she wouldn't be in this spot if she hadn't heard his cries for help. She feels like she would still be cooped up in her shack with no knowledge of this poor animal. She feels like she would still be alone and sad.

But she isn't now. She isn't sure why she feels this way.

These thoughts have interrupted her realization of her surroundings once again. She's caught up with Buttons; only noticing him because he stopped walking as he stares straight ahead with his big, beautiful, brown, sad puppy-dog eyes.

She sees it; approaching the small cabin with tiny steps of her feet as if it has arms to grab her and swoop her up into the air. She blinks in nervousness as she hears Buttons whimper.

The cabin is freshly painted in a light brown. The bushes have been neatly trimmed. Tulips and roses grow from a lovely garden. A porch swing slightly blows in the corner from the high winds. Pots of plants dangle from the roof of the porch screaming, "Help me!"

The wind might rip them off soon enough. Hey, Gwyneth might even take them as a souvenir if no one is home.

And that's what she's nervous about; someone being home.

She doesn't want to be seen. That's what she likes the most about living in the middle of the woods. No one is there to judge her or make fun of her for her lifestyle. It's peaceful and quiet.

She just wants to remind everyone; that's how she likes it.

Looking at the cabin closely, Gwyneth notices a lamp light shining through the front window. She quickly kneels down onto the wet ground. It's raining now and she curses herself in her mind for coming back out here. Now, she's stuck in this mess.

Buttons disregards her nervousness and follows the path leading to the steps of the front door. He hops onto the porch and sniffs the air. Gwyneth approaches with caution, lying low as she creeps toward the front door.

Her heart is pounding her chest like a drum just like the migraine is still pounding her brain. It won't seem to go away and this concerns her. This migraine has lasted longer than any others in the past. She isn't sure how concerned she should be or if she should just get over it.

Buttons scratches at the door.

He has more balls than she does. Well, he does have balls and it is sure making him seem brave. She doesn't understand why she's so nervous herself. She's killed people for Christ sake!

A curtain is slightly open; enabling Gwyneth to peek through the window. Buttons whimpers; scratch marks on the bottom of the freshly painted door from his bear-like claws. She clicks her tongue at him to get him to stop.

Of course he doesn't listen though and this causes Gwyneth to click her fingers in his face. He stares at her with his sad puppy-dog eyes. That look will always make her heart melt.

She pats him on the head and then places her fingerless-gloved hand onto the handle of the door. Her heart is pounding with excitement. Thoughts of what's inside for her zap across her brain just like the lightning.

Slowly turning the handle, Gwyneth opens the door. She's actually quite shocked that it's unlocked. Who leaves their front door unlocked?

Her childhood memories flood her brain. All she remembers is Ruby constantly locking the door and peeking through the windows to make sure no one was outside of the house. She was always scared of getting caught for her child abuse. She knew that the neighbors sometimes heard the children crying and screaming. It was only a matter of time before they were finally taken from her. Her anxious behavior always gave it away anyways.

Gwyneth cautiously enters the cabin. She can hear her heart beat right out of her chest. The anxiousness doesn't apply to Buttons. He trots right inside as if he owned the place.

The cabin is dirty. A multi-colored striped couch sits in the center of the living-room area. A small television stand with an equally small television leans against the wall. The place smells like dead fish and bad body odor.

A brown coffee table containing an empty coffee cup and a newspaper sits in front of the couch. Coffee stains dried up on the brown paint of the table. Bubbles have formed as if they're screaming for dear life. Gwyneth imagines herself popping the bubbles with her filthy fingernails. She chuckles with this childish thought.

She looks around the living-room trying to take everything in. Deer head plaques are hung on the wall above the television. The lamp shines brightly on a light blue end table next to the couch. A fruit bowl sits on the kitchen table. The apples are rotten. Maybe that's the rotten smell that she was breathing in through her mask.

Gwyneth quietly closes the door. Across the living-room, she spots a door halfway closed. Slowly approaching it, she peeks in.

No one is there.

She feels this huge sense of relief. She really doesn't feel like killing the owner of this cabin right now. All she wants is supplies to help her and her new found friend to live comfortably for a few weeks or at least a month. She needs things too and she feels no empathy for the poor shmuck that lives here.

BUT, if she HAS to kill someone now, she will. It might be a struggle since her pounding migraine still hasn't gone away, but she will do it for the sake of Buttons.

Pushing the door completely open, she enters the bedroom. There are more deer head plaques that hang above the four-poster bed. This makes her very angry. Those deer heads were perfectly fine to cut open and eat. That's what she likes to eat to survive. She knows what a waste of food is staring back at her with dead eyes.

Dead eyes. Like her. Like her mother.

Looking around, she spots a desk in the corner of the room. Tip-toeing toward it, she sees fishing wire, another small tackle box, nails and extra items for the harpoon.

Stealing the items, she places them inside of her Unicorn book-bag.

Buttons sniffs the bag, licks her dirty fingernails and then wags his tail like it's the first time meeting her again. She pats him on the head.

Gwyneth then takes the alarm clock off the nightstand. She desperately needs one of these in order to know the time. She can tell time a little bit but she wants to know what time it will be when it gets dark. She wants to know when it will be morning too.

Turning toward the dresser, she stops dead as if she spotted a ghost float in her face. Her crystal blue eyes stare straight ahead as if she's being hypnotized.

There sits two framed pictures on top of the dresser. One frame consists of the fisherman and a younger gentleman. Another picture holds the crooked smile of the fisherman while gripping Buttons by the back of his neck.

She quickly glances at Buttons. A realization hits her that she's standing right inside of the fisherman's cabin. Right inside of his bedroom. Right where his fat ass sleeps every night.

Well, DID sleep every night.

Exiting the bedroom, she enters the living-room area once again. She stops to listen to a clock ticking. Tick. Tick. Tick. In silence, it sounds like a drum beating ever so slowly. Normally it wouldn't bother her, but her migraine makes it impossible to drain the sound out of her brain.

She needs to lie down and take a break before her head explodes into tiny pieces.

As she enters the kitchen where the ticking of the clock comes from, she notices Button's dog bowls on the floor. She immediately takes them and shoves them into her bag. Then the poor girl takes it upon herself to raid the refrigerator. She's starving and she knows that her puppy is too. He's constantly panting and licking his chops.

She steals chicken, grapes, a piece of fish, a small bottle of juice, a package of hotdogs, a small bottle of Ketchup and three cans of beer. She isn't sure why she took the beer because she's never drank it before, but she shrugs her shoulders. She doesn't have a care in the world.

She searches the cupboards next. She has this sudden adrenaline rush. It's like she found a gold mine. She's so happy that she found this fat pig's house.

Tit for tat.

He deserves it. He shouldn't have abused Buttons.

Rummaging through the cupboards, she steals canned goods of oysters, tuna, peas, green beans, potatoes and corned beef hash; whatever that is. She's never eaten corned beef hash let alone heard of it. As she inspects the can, she shrugs her shoulders and tosses it inside of her bag.

Searching another cupboard, she steals a box of plastic utensils, paper towels and a package of paper plates. Noticing the dog food, she takes that as well.

She searches around the kitchen one last time. She notices a hand-written note on top of the kitchen counter. It's written by the fisherman to his son.

"Son, I went away for the weekend for a fishing trip. If I'm not back anytime soon, don't worry, I'm travelling and staying at different campgrounds. I'm taking the bus. Peace out son. Oh yeah, I left the door unlocked for you so don't worry about that either. No one ever comes around here. See you later."

Gwyneth glances around the living-room one last time as well. She notices a sleeping bag, a hiking bag filled with a tent and some clothes, and two fishing poles on the couch. Taking the items, she shoves the small bag of dog food and the sleeping bag inside of the hiking bag.

She steals a quilted blanket off the couch.

She feels so relaxed. She feels so alive! She hasn't had these kinds of things while living in that shack. This is all brand new to her. Maybe things will start looking up for her.

She enters the bathroom. Giggling like a school girl, she steals the fisherman's toothbrush, toothpaste, razor (which she looks at like it's from a different planet), and soap. She then takes a hand towel and toilet paper. She shoves all of the items into the hiking bag.

The sound of a car door slamming rips her out of her hypnotized thoughts. She was staring into space. She's mesmerized by everything she has found.

Well, stolen.

She frantically clicks her tongue at Buttons as he quietly growls. He then trots inside of the bathroom like he has no care in the world. Gwyneth softly closes the bathroom door.

The fisherman's son checks out the area as he makes his way toward the front door of the cabin. He stops at a hanging plant on the porch and inspects it. He carefully touches it with his manicured fingernails. He acts like bugs are crawling outside of the pot. He has this disgusted look on his face like he just took a huge shit in the toilet.

He wipes the little smudge of dirt that rubbed onto his finger onto his suit pants. He then peeks through the window toward the lamp light.

Gwyneth is completely frantic and scared inside of the tiny bathroom. She also feels sick to her stomach from the shit smell that's wafting through her mask and into her mouth.

Looking for an escape route, she notices the window next to the shower and opens it quietly. She then picks up Buttons and places him back inside of her hood.

Peeking out of the window, she sees that the drop to the ground isn't far. She could jump right out of it! This gives her an adrenaline rush so high that her anxiety shakes her whole entire body. She's not even appalled at the thought of jumping.

She throws the hiking bag and the fishing poles out of the window. They land on the ground with a thud. She waits for a second in order to hear the fisherman's son's movements once again.

She can hear the handle of the door.

Like a bolt of lightning that flashes in her brain, she climbs out of the window and jumps. She lands on her hands and knees. She feels like a ninja on a mission to kill thy enemies.

The fisherman's son enters the living-room area and suspiciously looks around. He too listens to the ticking of the kitchen clock. He hears the rain pound on top of the roof.

"Dad! Are you home? I told you I was coming today. I guess that's why your front door is unlocked?" the son asks as he strolls through the cabin.

He looks around and waits. He has a dopey look on his face like he just smoked a batch of marijuana. His black, slicked hair is now standing up like it was dowsed in hair spray. He loosens his tie as he scrunches his nose from the bad odor of the cabin.

"Dad? Hello!" he shouts to an empty living-room.

Gwyneth grabs her belongings off the wet ground and makes a run for it. She looks back over her shoulder as if the son was chasing her.

The fisherman's son tosses his keys onto the counter next to the note. He picks up the note and reads it. He shakes his head and smiles.

Chapter Nine

Today is not the day to feel like this. Gwyneth was already feeling anxious and sad about the continuous torture from her Bitch of a mother. But this? This has to happen now? It hit her in the chest like a ton of bricks. The poor kids didn't even get a chance to have some kind of a warning.

They could've taken off and ran away. They could've left that beast high and dry. That would've been more fulfilling and satisfying. That would've been brave and smart. At least they would've been together. That's all the children ever talked about. Their secret pact was to never allow someone to separate them; even in the worst circumstances.

But now, that circumstance has come full force, knocking them on their asses.

Or knees.

Gwyneth's twelve-year-old body is kneeling on her knees; crying uncontrollably. Someone has called Child Protective Services. The Caseworker, Lindsay Omega, is trying to take the hands of Gwyneth's brother and sister. Her beautiful dark skin glistens from the sunlight piercing through the window of the kitchen. Her mesmerizing light-brown eyes sadly watch the tears of Gwyneth's eyeballs drop to the kitchen floor like rain drops.

Her mind races as she watches the boy slip out of her grip. In some kind of crazy fashion, he runs around the living-room in circles as he screams at the top of his lungs.

She understands this hyper activity and knows that the boy is doing this for attention. Maybe he's even trying to get Ruby to yell at them in front of her. The crazy loon insists that she doesn't beat or yell at her innocent children. Many people would disagree with this insane notion.

People have seen and heard the behavior that comes from this disgusting woman. Little does Ruby know, someone who is extremely important in this town, witnessed the statement from one of these victims. She will never supply that information to this awful woman. It doesn't matter how much she begs or cries to know what has happened. She could rot in HELL without knowing the truth. She doesn't deserve the truth.

These children deserve a better life and they will have that as soon as Lindsay gets them out of there. She needs to get them out of here safe and sound.

The poor little girl is crying next to Gwyneth. Her small head rests on her sister's shoulder. Gwyneth clutches the girls' head in her hand. This is extremely sad to watch and Lindsay closes her eyes for a moment. This is the part that she absolutely hates about her job; taking the kids away from the home. It saddens her to the core of her belly.

These children need to be taken though. They need a stable environment. They need to be taken care of by responsible and loving parents.

They need to be reunited.

Ruby is frantically smoking a cigarette. She blows the smoke up into the ceiling as her hands shake with nervousness and anxiety. Her body is fidgeting like she's waiting for her crack dealer to arrive. Or maybe her marijuana dealer. It could be both.

She glares at Lindsay as if she just murdered her dog.

Lindsay ignores the ugly look upon this beast's face and tries to stop the boy from running around. It's like a firecracker blew inside of his butt. He's acting wild and screaming obscenities.

Ruby cackles like a witch.

Of course she did. That's her defense mechanism. It's what she does to be an asshole. It's what she does when she's nervous. It's what she does to bring attention to herself.

She puffs her cigarette a second time and blows the smoke toward Lindsay. Lindsay waves it away with her arm and coughs as the smoke slides right into her throat.

Lindsay becomes angry. She could literally wrap her hands around this woman and squeeze the life out of her. She wants to squeeze as hard as she can and watch Ruby's eyes pop out of her head. She wants to dig her freshly painted red nails into her neck and make her bleed.

Lindsay tries to suddenly shake these thoughts out of her mind.

She tries to remember what her boss always tells her, "Don't make it personal."

Personal my ass, she thinks. It is personal. Child abuse is no joke.

The little girl suddenly peeks at Ruby for a response to Lindsay's coughing.

"I'm sorry kiddos, but it's time to go. Say your goodbye's darlings," Lindsay interrupts the silence from Ruby. She can't take it anymore. She can't stand being in the same room with this beast much longer.

Ruby inhales her cigarette. Of course she wants to speak at this moment.

"I don't understand who would've called you. You need to tell me woman!"

"Like I told you two weeks ago, that is confidential information. I cannot tell you anything of that nature. Now, please help me control your son," Lindsay says as calmly as she can.

She doesn't want to get reported for having a bad attitude. It's happened before and she will be damned if she lets this pig of a beast ruin her job.

It's taking everything in her power to not punch Ruby right in her smirk of a crooked smile.

"This is bullshit! People need to mind their own business! I'll call your boss if you don't tell me," Ruby threatens. Her voice is like a whiny little child who doesn't get their way.

Lindsay looks away and rolls her eyes. "You seem to be more concerned over who called us. More than the fact that I am here to take your children away." Lindsay shakes her head.

"I will get them back!" Ruby shouts.

"I highly doubt that. You have TWO child abuse cases open. We have enough evidence to support these allegations. If you don't mind Ruby, I have to take these children now."

The boy continues to run in circles while screaming. This makes Ruby chuckle. She honestly doesn't give a damn that her son is making a mockery of himself. He looks like a fool.

Lindsay stops him by the door.

"Oh and…" Lindsay continues, "Gwyneth's caseworker will be here later this afternoon to pick her up. Please make sure she's ready as well."

Lindsay manages to grab the boys' hand. He desperately tries to get out of her grip.

She softly whispers in his ear, "We will stop and get some treats. Does that sound good?" Lindsay is desperate herself to get the HELL out of this house.

The boy nods and reaches for his sister. The girl smiles at Gwyneth with tears in her eyes. Lindsay then grabs the girls' hand. Gwyneth's sister struggles; fighting to get out of her grip.

"You're hurting her!" Ruby shouts.

"Not any worse than you," Lindsay fires back.

"No! No want to leave Gwyneth," the little girl pleads.

Gwyneth suddenly jumps up from her knees. Lindsay becomes slightly anxious.

Gwyneth gestures the "stop" sign with her hand toward Lindsay.

"I have to take them sweet girl," Lindsay replies.

Gwyneth frantically holds up her hand and then points toward her bedroom.

If only people would listen and pay attention to her. This is what frustrates Gwyneth so much more than being made fun of by her mother. People don't care to understand. People don't take the time to educate themselves on people like Gwyneth.

However, Gwyneth doesn't understand that Lindsay sure does understand and acknowledge how Gwyneth's mind works. Lindsay has been working with children like Gwyneth for fifteen years. She's seen and heard it all. She knows and can imagine how these kids are feeling.

She's been there. And it wasn't fun.

"She wants sompin'," Gwyneth's sister pipes in.

Gwyneth hurriedly leaves the living-room and then enters her bedroom. She runs to her dresser. She's drenched in sweat and her black hair is sticking to her forehead.

She thrusts open the top drawer and picks up two handmade necklaces. They're made with red yarn and a golden button. She holds the necklaces softly in her hands like she's picking up a newborn puppy. She kisses them and then places them on her heart.

Gwyneth returns to Lindsay at the front door. She points to the necklaces and then points to her brother and sister. The twins are in tears. Their bodies are shaking. They have no idea of what will become of their future. They have no idea what's going to happen to their sister.

Lindsay nods, "Of course sweetie." She smiles. Gigantic white teeth sparkle in the doomed entryway. She softly touches Gwyneth's cheek. It's sticky from her tears.

The twins' take the necklaces from Gwyneth and places them around their necks. The twins are completely emotional and begin crying while wrapping their arms around their sister. Lindsay's eyes fill with tears but she turns her head so they can't witness her emotions.

She's usually tougher than this. This case has really hit her hard. Maybe it's too close to home. This situation is similar to her own past and she's caring too much.

She's taking it personal.

In order to get out of here, she has to push these kiddos a little bit more. As they continue to hold Gwyneth, Lindsay picks this as the perfect opportunity to put on their coats and hats.

They let go of Gwyneth to help her. They then take Lindsay's hands and head outside to the porch. Lindsay breathes a sigh of relief. Thank GOD they're out of there. The house smells of cigarette smoke and feces. The walls are stained yellow from the blowing of the smoke. The place should actually be condemned and once all three children are out, Lindsay plans on reporting the building to the township.

Ruby is nothing but an unfit mother.

As they approach Lindsay's car, the little girl gestures toward Gwyneth and gives her a heart sign. Her brother smiles with tears pouring down his cheeks. He also gives Gwyneth a heart sign.

In the doorway, Gwyneth blows them a kiss.

As the twins climb into the car, they reach their hands out of the window. Gwyneth reaches out to them. She knows she can't touch their hands or fingers but she closes her eyes for a brief moment and imagines herself getting into the car with them.

Ruby stands in the doorway next to her, crossing her arms in anger.

Lindsay rolls down the window and pleads, "Remember Ruby, the caseworker will be here around three o'clock for Gwyneth! Make sure she's ready!" She drives off.

While the poor child hysterically cries in the doorway, Ruby pushes her back inside of the house. If Gwyneth was only strong enough she would've knocked the Bitch on her ass.

She might be strong enough, who knows? Gwyneth has never had the "balls" to physically hit her mother. She has no idea if she can take her down or not.

As she contemplates this scenario in her mind, Ruby becomes even more frantic than what she was. She looks like a drug addict itching for more poison to slip into her body.

Oh wait, she is a drug addict.

Ruby is shaking. Her body is cold and clammy. She feels like she's going to vomit.

Gwyneth feels like she's about to be thrown into the black hole. She has this feeling of sadness in the pit of her stomach. She might not ever see her siblings again. This thought makes her want to vomit right into her mother's pale face. It would be amusing to see the vomit spew right into her mouth and down her throat.

That will teach her. That will teach her to keep her mouth shut.

The beast snatches a cigarette out of the pack. Her hands are shaking wildly as she lights it up and inhales a long drag. She then blows the smoke into Gwyneth's face once again.

Ruby is yelling, "This is all your fault you little wench! I bet you told on me that day we went to the park! The Sheriff was there. That's it! You must have told him something when he was giving out candy! I saw him talking to you."

Gwyneth would never admit if that were true or not.

The yearning to know this information burns inside of the bottom of Ruby's abdomen. A fire has ignited deep inside of her stomach. The anger pulsates on the sides of her temples. She's scared out of her mind and she's thinking of what to do next.

As she takes in another puff of her cigarette, Gwyneth frantically shakes her head no.

"I've had enough of your lies girl!" Ruby pauses as she contemplates what to say next. "And ain't anybody comin' to take you away from me. No one can take care of you like I can!"

Ruby grabs Gwyneth by her hair and drags her to the girls' bedroom. She is about sick and tired of being dragged by her hair. Pretty soon, she's going to be bald if this Bitch doesn't stop.

Once inside, Ruby snatches Gwyneth's Unicorn book-bag and shoves clothes and a hairbrush into the bag. She then tosses loose paper, markers and a pencil inside.

Gwyneth watches her intently with a confused expression upon her face. She's actually excited about this caseworker coming to get her. She wants to be away from her mother but she wants to be with her siblings at the same time. Why couldn't Lindsay just take her too?

She doesn't understand why and she never will.

"This is crazy girl! No one is taking you from me. You're going to hide until the cows come home!" Ruby shouts.

Until the cows come home? We don't have any cows. The only cow in this house is you.

Gwyneth can't believe what she's hearing. Sometimes she doesn't understand what her mother is saying and sometimes deep down she thinks she knows what her mother means. She's always meant to feel and think stupid so she doesn't really know what her mother means.

And sometimes, she doesn't care what her mother means. She doesn't care to understand.

Ruby grabs Gwyneth by her arm and drags her into the kitchen. She hears a slight pop, not completely sure if the beast pulled her arm out of the socket. She feels a small burning pain underneath her armpit. She stops herself from whimpering so she doesn't get smacked in the face or head. Whimpering and crying is not allowed. Even though she does it often, she doesn't feel like getting hit right now. She doesn't want to be called a "baby."

Ruby tosses two bottles of water and a bag of small donuts into the bag. She suddenly starts to chuckle nervously. There's something seriously wrong with this woman.

Ruby continues, "We're going to play hide n seek. Wouldn't you like that? That's your favorite game isn't it?"

Gwyneth is then dragged into the living-room. She struggles to get out of the beast's grip. Gwyneth is becoming frantic because her mother is acting out of control.

Ruby shoves a ten inch sewing needle, a container of small silver needles, thread, scissors and a bag of buttons inside of the book-bag. She then tosses three of Gwyneth's dolls inside of the bag. She's like a wild woman on crack. She's crazy and psychotic.

"I know these three are your favorite," Ruby says, pointing to the dolls. She notices Gwyneth's confusion on her face. "I have to get you out of here! We need to go, quickly!"

Gwyneth is now crying as she rubs her eyes with her fists. Ruby ignores her and then shoves the girls' coat, gloves and hat on top of her head. She puts on her boots and ties the laces tight.

Gwyneth cringes. The laces are so tight she might lose blood flow. That would definitely make her mother feel bad for her actions. Wouldn't it?

Gwyneth would hope so but deep down she knows that's not the truth.

"I'll have to give you some extra stuff in case something happens," Ruby continues.

Gwyneth is extremely confused as she continues to watch Ruby shove an extra pair of gloves and a small blanket inside of the now stuffed book-bag.

"I'm sorry Gwyneth. This is for your own good!"

Her own good? She doesn't even know where she's going. How could this be for her own good? She has no clue what her mother is up to. One thing she does know, whatever her mother is thinking of doing, is probably illegal.

Well, Gwyneth doesn't know what the word, "illegal" means, but she does know that it's something that she shouldn't be doing.

Lastly, Ruby then grabs an extra coat and a pillow out of the closet as she yells, "Let's go!"

Gwyneth is having a hard time trying to remember the last time she was in her mother's car. They walk to the park. They walk to the store. That's how the community sees their filth. That's how residents see Ruby's behavior.

She doesn't sugar coat anything in front of anyone. She yells. She hits. She calls the children nasty names. Sometimes she even leaves them on the sidewalk alone while she secretly sneaks behind a building to buy her drugs off of her drug dealer.

Ruby doesn't even wait until they get home before she lights up her crack. The neighbors watch her sway from side to side as she walks like a drunken fool. That's what they think she is…. DRUNK. But she's not. She's high as a kite.

Either way, no one actually questions her. No one says a word.

They just stand outside on their porches and gawk like a crow perched on a cable wire. They whisper to each other as they say bad things about Ruby. Some of them even say bad things about the children. Gwyneth once heard an older lady call her "stupid" and "weak." Some man that Gwyneth has never seen before even called them "filthy rats."

They can't help it. It's not the children's fault that Ruby is a bad mother. It's not their fault that they're not allowed to take baths every single day. It's not their fault that they don't get enough to eat. It's not their fault that they live in a shit hole of a house.

And it's not their fault that this is the mother they were born from.

Gwyneth wishes every day that she and the twins could've been born from a loving and caring mother. A mother, who consoles them, feeds them, bathes them, buys them toys and protects them from whatever is bad in the world.

A mother who is there for them. Just a good… MOTHER.

But the kids will never see Ruby as a good mother. They will never know what it's like to be protected by Ruby the Beast. They will never see things her way.

Ruby pulls off to the side of the road next to the woods. It's a deserted area with a stretch of trees and a meadow. It's beautiful once the sun peeks out from behind the clouds.

The air is cold and Gwyneth watches her hot breath exit her mouth. Her breath smells like a sewage pipe. Her teeth feel sticky and slimy. She hates the way she looks and feels.

She feels disgusting. She feels gross. She can smell her own body odor. Ruby could've at least let her take a bath before they left to go anywhere. This is why she always feels defeated and worthless. She feels like scum. She looks like it too.

Ruby climbs out of the piece of tin she calls a car. It's a maroon-colored 1980 Ford Taurus. She bought it for two-hundred dollars off of another drug-infested mother who needed money for food to feed her four children. That's what she claimed anyways. No one actually saw her buy food. She was seen behind the grocery store buying her meth.

Gwyneth stares straight ahead as if she's mesmerized by the cloudy sky. She thinks she hears talking but she isn't sure what's going on. Suddenly, Ruby pounds on the window, swings the car door open and then grabs Gwyneth by her arm, dragging her out of the car. Ruby looks around the area; anxious that she's being watched by someone. She then quickly snatches the book-bag, coat and pillow off the passenger side floor.

Gwyneth is on her knees. She's crying uncontrollably. Ruby throws all of the belongings onto the ground next to Gwyneth.

"I need you to go hide deep into the woods. I will be back for you tomorrow night," Ruby tells the poor girl. Gwyneth is confused.

She glances into the woods then back at her hateful mother. What the hell does that mean? She knows nothing about these woods. Woods have bears and deer and other animals who like to eat and kill humans. She doesn't want to die. She doesn't want to be eaten alive. That's not how she pictured her future to turn out. That's not how she wants to live.

Looking up at her mother with tears in her eyes, she frantically shakes her head no.

Ruby is sad. "I used to come here when I was younger. Used to do bad things in these woods. No one comes around here though. Not anymore. It's deserted. It gets extremely cold in this valley. That's why no one comes here. This road ends about a half mile east. There's a farm at the end of the road. Don't go there! EVER! They're bad people up in that farm. They'll kill you!" Ruby's eyes light up like she just watched a match torch the woods to the ground.

Gwyneth is frantic and in shock. She continues to shake her head no. Ruby swiftly and quite suddenly, grabs her daughter's shoulders and shakes her.

"Wake up girl! Listen to me for once! Ain't no caseworker comin' to take my baby away from me! There's nowhere else for you to go. I have no one Gwyneth. There's nowhere else for you to hide," Ruby shouts.

The beast is teary-eyed. Gwyneth mouths the word, "No." Ruby shakes her once again and then grabs her by the chin. She doesn't feel any pain. It's like her whole entire body is numb. She doesn't know who or where to turn to. She doesn't know what to think anymore.

Ruby continues, "You have to. Do whatever is necessary to survive. Go hide and I'll be back for you tomorrow night. I'll tell the caseworker you ran away from home. I'll come back to get you and we'll run away together."

It seems as though Gwyneth doesn't hear a word she is saying. Her eyes are in a trance. She points to Ruby's car and quickly picks up her items off the ground.

Ruby is exhausted and tired of trying to explain anything to this girl. It's like she has no brain cells. She can't function with this child anymore. She needs a break.

Grabbing Gwyneth, she drags her inside of the woods. The child kicks her feet and tries to wiggle out of Ruby's grasp. The beast is actually quite strong. This surprises Gwyneth since her mother only weighs about ninety pounds. Gwyneth feels like one of her rag dolls. Her hair catching onto branches as it's being pulled from the scalp.

She yelps in pain. Is this how Death feels like? Is she going into the black hole? Will she spin in circles and vomit from sickness? Will she ever be able to punish her mother for what she's about to do? Will her mother even feel any remorse for her actions?

Questions that will never be answered.

Once they are further into the woods, Ruby stops. She glances toward the direction of her car. She sees the smoke coming from the exhaust pipe. Her fingers are frozen and her cheeks are bright red. She's itching for a hit of her crack and she needs to get the hell out of here.

She makes Gwyneth try to stand up. The girl feels like a pile of bricks. She's refusing to stand until Ruby slaps her across the face. Sniffling, she has tears of her own flowing down her cheeks as she pats Gwyneth on the top of her head.

Gwyneth is hysterical as she holds her stinging cheek with her filthy hand.

"I'm sorry pretty girl. I do love you. I'll be back here tomorrow."

She heads toward her car but suddenly spins around yelling, "Don't follow me!"

Gwyneth reaches out her hand toward her mother. She looks defeated, worthless and sad. She feels like the energy is draining from her entire body. She can't seem to focus on anything that is coming out of Ruby's mouth. It's like the black hole is circling inside of her brain.

Ruby suddenly sprints toward her car. Gwyneth watches her. The emotional pain is unbearable. Yes, this woman was a disease to her, but how could she just leave her like this?

Abandoned and broken.

Her heart feels like it's been snapped in half. It's pounding with every breath she tries to take. Her anxiety has sky-rocketed. It's like a rocket has shot up into the clouds.

She's watching it explode into a thousand pieces; the burning embers landing onto her skin.

Gwyneth suddenly snaps out of her dark state of emotions and runs with her items toward the sound of the car door slamming shut. The Unicorn book-bag bounces on the girl's shoulders like it's taken a ride on a horse. It pounds on her back like a hammer. It's heavy and it's weighing her down; making her run slower than necessary.

Ruby speeds off; tires screeching in the silence. Gwyneth stops running, trying to catch her breath. She sadly watches Ruby drive away.

Her breathing is hard and fast. Her throat is dry. She needs water, anything. Her throat feels like it's on fire. It feels like she's being stabbed a hundred times in the neck.

Ruby looks back at the woods through her rearview mirror. She spots Gwyneth falling to her knees and crying up into the dark sky. The beast is crying; slamming her hands onto the steering wheel.

"Damn you Gwyneth! Damn you!" Ruby yells to herself.

What kind of mother have I become?

A bad one. A hateful one. An awful one. A heartless one.

Gwyneth is scared as she searches the woods in silence. She can hear the trees swaying in the wind. She feels the cold as it blows onto her wet face. Her tears pour down her cheeks. Her body is shaking badly. Her eyes dart like she's watching a lightning bolt flash across the sky.

Now what is she supposed to do?

Chapter Ten

If the woods could talk, they could warn Gwyneth about the dangers that lie ahead. The trees could whisk her away and guide her through the fog. The roots could trip her feet and stop her from moving along deeper into the forest. The wind could blow her away; all the way back to her mother's shit hole of a house. It's possible.

Only if the woods could talk.

At this moment, there are no pretty dragonflies flying above a corpse-smelling pond. That's for later. Right now, all she has is silence and the freezing cold whipping through her knotty hair.

She wonders where her siblings are. She wonders if they're in a nice, beautiful home with loving and caring parents. She wonders if they're sitting with Lindsay somewhere eating ice-cream. She wonders if they're thinking about her.

Slowly gripping her items, she drags them further into the woods. She doesn't know which direction to take and she isn't sure if there are any animals currently on a human hunt. This thought tugs at her heart. She doesn't want to die this way. She always thought that she would die at the hands of her Bitch of a mother.

She doesn't know which one is worse.

She's scared; jumping at every sound of nature.

If Gwyneth could talk, she would scream obscenities up at the sky. She would've called the beast a Bitch and she would've told her how bad of a mother she truly was. She would've told her siblings how much she loved them. She would've told them not to be sad.

As she drags her extra coat through the dirt, she stops to take a breath, sitting on a tree stump. Remembering the bottle of water, she opens her book-bag, takes one out and gulps it; water dribbles down her chin and onto her lap. As she tries to stop crying, she takes another deep breath. She feels like she's hyperventilating. She has no idea that that's the word to describe her harsh breathing but she knows that something is wrong.

She can't breathe. She can't think. She's hungry and thirsty. She's hot from crying and getting all worked up. Her skin is sweating but she's cold at the same time. It's confusing her.

If only the woods could direct her in the right direction. She wishes for a Guardian angel to tell her what to do. Right at this moment, she needs all the help she can get.

Maybe her siblings are luckier. Maybe they are snug in a warm bed. Maybe they're drinking hot chocolate and sitting by a fire. Maybe her sister has their new mother playing with her hair and combing it. She loved it when Gwyneth brushed her hair and put it in pigtails.

Gwyneth is calm now. She grabs her belongings; putting her book-bag over her shoulder once again. She holds her coat and pillow snug in her arms like a baby.

She walks deeper into the woods. She can no longer see the road. She can no longer see the pretty meadow. She has no idea how far she's walked but she's tired. She's tired of walking. Her feet hurt and her legs feel like Jell-O. Her toes are numb. Sweat pours down her face even though it's cold. Her face is as red as an apple. She just needs to take a break for a while.

She suddenly stops; listening to voices laughing.

What the hell? There are people in the woods? The beast said no one comes around here! They could be the bad people from the farm. Or they could be innocent people, just like her.

Dropping to her knees, she peeks behind a tree. In the distance, she can see two eighteen-year-old boys. Her heart skips a beat. She's never talked to a boy before, besides her 5 year-old brother but he doesn't count. She never went to school. She's never had any friends.

It looks like the boys are building a shack. Gwyneth watches them quizzically.

Peyton is short and thin with scrawny arms and spiked brown hair. It looks like he stuck his finger in a socket and electrocuted his head. He's wearing a light-blue and white wind-breaker jacket with matching blue pants. His black hiking boots are covered in dry mud and grass.

The only thing Gwyneth likes about his appearance is his bright blue eyes. They remind her of her own eyes. It's the only part of her body that she likes.

His eyes sparkle like diamonds. They're quite mesmerizing and she doesn't like the fact that she can't stop watching him. It's like his eyes are carrying a sign that reads: "Look at me I'm bright and beautiful!" She's never seen such pretty eyes on a boy.

She's looked at plenty of boys at the park, but, none of them had eyes like the crystal blue waters of the ocean. None of them had the power to manipulate her way of thinking.

She takes her eyes off of Peyton and watches the other boy slam his hammer on a nail. George smiles a cheesy grin as his light-green eyes shine from the sun trying to peek out from behind the clouds. His black hair is slicked back like it was doused in hair gel. He's wearing a black jean jacket with a white T-shirt. His blue jeans are covered in dry mud and his green hiking boots look soaking wet from rain. He's tall with some meat on those bones.

They look dirty. She likes them dirty.

As she quietly watches them, she creeps closer to get a better view.

Even though Peyton Ora has those dreamy eyeballs, she can't help think bad thoughts about George Crest. She thinks he's adorable. But she knows that he won't talk to her. She knows they will be scared of her. They all are. That's why she doesn't have any friends. People think she's a freak because she can't speak. Even though her speaking ability is out the window, she does have a brain… well somewhat. Her brain isn't all there either.

THAT'S why they're scared of her.

Both boys are hitting nails with a hammer as they pound on the wood. The noise vibrates inside of Gwyneth's eardrums. She isn't particularly fond of loud noises but she doesn't mind it this time. That's because she doesn't mind watching these boys hard at work.

Peyton is of course goofing off and laughing hysterically. He must think that everything is funny for some reason. This puzzles Gwyneth because she doesn't hear George tell a joke.

She creeps closer; trying to hear what they're saying.

She must look like a weirdo, a stalker and a thief in the night. Someone or something looking to pounce on its' prey. Hey, maybe she will get a chance to actually pounce on one of them. This thought makes her giggle inside. She can't believe that she's thinking these dirty thoughts. That's never happened before and she isn't quite sure how to handle it.

She looks like a twelve-year-old in heat; a cat that wants to hump. Noises that go bump in the night. She has this weird feeling going on throughout her body and she doesn't know how to respond. She's never felt this way before. She feels tingles in areas she's never experienced.

She watches Peyton look around the area. "Dude, no adult needs to know about our shack. That would ruin everything. But, we'll definitely have parties though," Peyton laughs.

"Parties galore… ha-ha! Man I can't wait!" George exclaims.

"It was so cool for Ethan to come by and hook everything up. You know, his dad is in construction so he knows what to do. I guess we gotta pay him back for the work he did. Somehow…" Peyton says as his mind trails off.

George stops to think for a moment. "Pay him back with the parties we're gonna have!"

That seems like a sensible idea. It's definitely something they can do. They don't have cash or rich family members to help pay for their debts. They don't have valuables to sell.

Peyton nods. "He might accept that as payment. Who knows? Either way, I ain't giving him money. He volunteered to help. We didn't ask."

"Well…" George begins to say.

There's a sound of a branch snapping. George stops and looks at Peyton. Peyton turns towards Gwyneth's direction. He looks out at the trees swaying in the wind. George squints his eyes; hoping to spot something in the distance.

"Dude, did you hear that?" Peyton asks.

"Yeah I heard it. You look paranoid. Chill dude. It's just a branch," George laughs.

Peyton calls out to the woods with his hands formed into an "O" around his mouth, "If someone is there, you better leave or you'll be sorry!"

George continues to laugh. "What are you gonna do? Pound a nail in their eyeball?"

The boys laugh together. Gwyneth licks her lips and creeps closer; stepping on another branch. She closes her eyes and curses at herself in her mind.

Dumb ass. Stupid Bitch. You couldn't be quiet huh?

Peyton is now frantic. "Who's there?! Come on out ASSHOLE!"

"Maybe it's a deer," George whispers.

Gwyneth ever so slowly approaches them from behind a tree. Peyton is in shock and he's speechless for a moment. Gwyneth holds up a hand in surrender and kindly waves.

"What is this? This is bullshit! Now someone else knows about our shack!" Peyton spits as he yells. That's all he seems to be worried about. He seems to focus on the shack more than the fact that a mute with psychological problems has now stepped foot on their turf.

George stares at Gwyneth; watching her every move while whispering to Peyton, "Get a grip." He nods at Gwyneth. "Come closer so we can see you better!"

Peyton angrily turns towards George. "What the hell are you doing George? We don't even know her."

"She looks lost."

Gwyneth slowly approaches the boys. She can feel her heart pound inside of her chest. She isn't sure if she's scared of what they might do to her or if she's scared of what she might do to them. She doesn't want them to be bad people. She likes looking at them. She likes George's smile. It can light up a room.

Hell, it lit up her heart. She feels this weird flutter in her belly. She feels the blood flowing through her veins and pumping rainbow-colored hearts into her skin.

She suddenly searches the area as if another person is going to pop out of nowhere and hit her in the back of the head. That's just how she thinks. It's all in her mind.

George interrupts her thoughts. "What's your name?"

Gwyneth points to her mouth and then shakes her head no.

George continues, "So you can't talk?"

Gwyneth sets all of her items onto the ground and then opens up her book-bag.

Peyton yells at her, "Don't do anything stupid! I have a hammer and I will hit you with it!"

Gwyneth pauses. She's trying to understand what Peyton is asking of her. At first, she glares at him like he's a beast from another dimension. As she grabs her bag, she realizes that he thinks that SHE is a bad person. This kind of makes her angry. She's not a bad person. She's never hurt anyone. As much as she's wanted to kill her mother, she never did.

Gwyneth looks at George and makes an "opening zipper" motion with the Unicorn bookbag.

George is annoyed with Peyton. "Calm down," he tells him.

Gwyneth shakes her head once again and points to her bookbag while eyeing Peyton. She suddenly feels this hatred for this boy and isn't completely sure why. He's protecting his property. He's protecting his sacred area. She does understand that much.

George is eagerly watching her. He nods as if giving her permission to go into her bookbag. George realizes this is ridiculous and immediately feels guilty.

Peyton watches her while whispering, "This better be good."

George slaps Peyton on the arm. Sometimes he has this urge to punch Peyton in the mouth when they run into negative situations. Although, meeting Gwyneth might be a positive situation, he still feels like Peyton is stepping over the boundaries and he needs to zip his lip.

"You're always a grouch. Always getting us into trouble. Shut up for once," George pleads.

Gwyneth retrieves a piece of paper and a pencil. Peyton is suspicious once again.

She writes her name, "Gwyneth," on the paper and then hands it over to George.

George is curious as he takes the note and reads her name a few times. "That's a pretty name. So, how did you end up here Gwyneth? Where are your parents?"

He hands her the piece of paper. She then writes, "Mama drop me. Be back tomorrow night for me." Her hands are shaking. She's scared about what Peyton might do or say.

Peyton snatches the paper from her hand and quickly reads her sloppy writing. "So she's picking you up tomorrow?"

Gwyneth nods. She quickly blinks multiple times as she waits for the blow of his loud and obnoxious yelling. She had enough of listening to her mother yell. She thought she was "yelling free" before she stepped foot onto their territory. Deep down, she was excited to not have to hear the cackling of her mother's croak voice. She was excited to get a break for a day.

Peyton starts acting wild. "What kind of mother just drops off her kid in the woods? What the hell is this bullshit?!" He crushes the paper into his fist and throws it at George. George picks it up quickly and smooth's out the crinkles.

He ignores Peyton, turning towards Gwyneth. "So Gwyneth, where are you going to stay until then?" He already has a plan in his mind but he wants to see what she'll say.

Gwyneth shrugs her shoulders.

"Well you're not staying here!" Peyton yells.

George angrily turns to Peyton. He isn't exactly sure why he's so mad at his best friend. Maybe it's his bad attitude towards this innocent girl who was basically left for dead. She must have had a bad time growing up and George feels as though Peyton has no compassion or empathy for her whatsoever. Peyton can be better than that and George knows this.

Peyton continues yelling, "What? Don't look at me like that! We have no idea who she is or if she's even telling the truth! Her mom dumped her here?! Give me a break!"

"Give her a chance dude! We don't know anything. Maybe she was dumped. Maybe she wasn't." George hands the crinkled piece of paper to Gwyneth. "Either way, we have to help her." George is adamant in helping this lost soul. That's what she looks like; a lost and lonely child who has nowhere to run to. It's obvious that she has no one to care for her.

George has two younger sisters. One of them is a twin with his brother. He can't even imagine any of his siblings going through something like this. He can't even imagine his parents dumping any of them in the woods.

"We don't HAVE to do anything! This is stupid!" Peyton whines.

George ignores him once again and speaks to Gwyneth with a gentle tone, "You can help us finish building the shack. We have to leave in a few hours to get more stuff from my house. Then we'll be back. But you have to leave when we do. Okay?"

Gwyneth nods. She has no intention of leaving once they're gone. She's going to sit her butt right on the floor and wait until they come back. She doesn't want to be exposed inside of these woods. She needs to take cover and seek shelter. She's scared of the crazy animals that she might stumble upon. There's no way she's listening to their bullshit anymore.

"My name is George. And this is Peyton."

Peyton angrily shakes his head and crosses his arms. Gwyneth feels a giggle deep inside.

His temper tantrum reminds Gwyneth of her twin siblings. They would cross their arms and huff while crying when they didn't get their way. It was quite amusing at times. Gwyneth would get this urge to bust out laughing but she would stop herself so she wouldn't upset them more.

George continues, "Do you know how to use a hammer?"

Gwyneth shakes her head "no" like she has a head full of screws. She glances at the ground about ten feet away; noticing boxes filled with clothes and a couple of coats. Another box is opened. It's filled with candy bars, chips, beer and a map. Next to the box sits a small, antique desk. The brown paint is chipped; it looks like an animal dug their claws into it and scratched it like they were the Wolverine.

A small card table with two chairs and a sign that reads: "NO HUNTING," sits on the ground next to the desk. Gwyneth nods her head towards the items.

"Oh that stuff? We got that furniture from a curb! The neighbors were throwing it away. I decided to take them for our shack," George answers in excitement.

Gwyneth nods; smiling at George as if it's the first time she's laid her eyes on him. She's mesmerized again and doesn't seem to notice George trying to hand her an extra hammer.

"Let me show you how to do this," George tells her. His sparkling, white teeth gleam in the sunlight. The sun is poking through the clouds. She has hopes for a sunny night.

And, maybe a fun night.

She's never had fun with boys before. She's always wanted to "hang out" as she's heard people say at the park. She liked going to the park because she listened to people's conversations in order to learn new and exciting things about life.

Peyton is angry and cracks open a beer. He watches in silence as George teaches Gwyneth how to hammer the nails into the wood. It's such a simple task and Peyton rolls his eyes as he watches how dumb Gwyneth looks. He's still suspicious of her and deep down he thinks that she is here to hurt them. She probably wants their shack.

He glances at Gwyneth's belongings on the ground. The book-bag is wide open. He sees a sewing needle and a pair of scissors.

Gwyneth excitedly hits the nail with the hammer repeatedly. George nods at her and smiles again. Peyton knows George too well and he believes right now that his best friend is flirting with this dirty girl. She's literally filthy. She's got dirt underneath her fingernails. Her teeth need brushed and her clothes smell like cigarette smoke and urine.

Peyton watches in disgust as George says, "You got this! Pretty simple huh?"

Gwyneth nods at George but then glares at Peyton as if he's trash on the side of the road.

"So why don't you talk? Is there something wrong with your voice? Do you not like how you sound?" Peyton asks as he watches Gwyneth intently.

Gwyneth looks confused and continues to glare at Peyton.

George cuts in, "If there was something wrong, you don't make fun of her."

"I'm not making fun of her. I asked a simple question," Peyton replies as he rolls his eyes.

Gwyneth points to her private area. Peyton is in immediate shock as if she just sliced his throat. His eyes are wide and he has this evil grin that makes the skin at the corner of his eyes crinkle with excitement. His blue eyes sparkle with mischievous thoughts.

What a pervert. That's not what she even wants.

While she does the pee dance, George asks, "You have to pee?"

Ah yeah, it's obvious. She wants to say this but she can't. She sees the fire in Peyton's eyes as the wheels turn in his brain. It looks like he's mesmerized himself but then he suddenly blinks and gives her a dirty look. He glares at her like she's scum on the Earth.

Gwyneth nods, trying not to be a smart ass about it. George points towards a different direction for her to have some privacy.

"Pee over there. But you have to use a good leaf to wipe with. Don't use a poison ivy leaf."

Gwyneth is confused. It's written all over her face. She doesn't understand some of the things that these boys are saying. They don't make sense to her and she's trying not to look like an idiot. But it's too late. Peyton already senses her discomfort and shakes his head.

George continues, "I'll show you. Come on."

She follows him through a path of trampled grass as he approaches a poison ivy leaf. He points to it as he encourages her to bend down to take a closer look.

"This is poison ivy. Don't ever touch this. You can pee over here," he says pointing to a section of trees. Gwyneth nods then smiles.

She quickly realizes how bad her teeth must look. Immediately, she stops smiling as the sadness displays across her face. She wishes that she could be normal. She wishes that she didn't grow up in such a disgusting environment. She wishes that she had a loving mother.

All of these wishes that will never happen.

George senses that something is wrong but he hesitates to ask. He walks away, leaving her to her business.

He isn't sure what to say or what to ask. She suddenly looks sad and distraught and he doesn't want to upset her even more. Her attitude and persona changed quite quickly and he firmly believes that she might have something seriously wrong in her brain.

Maybe Peyton is right. She needs to get going on her merry little way.

George returns to the shack. As he watches Peyton guzzle his beer, he shakes his head and chuckles. Peyton drinks way too much. He doesn't even care that he's not the legal age yet. George keeps warning him that one day he's going to get caught. Peyton always laughs and shrugs his shoulders like it's no big deal.

George pounds the last nail into the door of the shack. He tests it out by opening it and closing it. He shrugs his shoulders as if the crookedness is no big deal.

"It works," he says as he opens and closes it a second time. "A little loose but we can fix it later."

"That's what you get for letting Miss Weirdo help," Peyton replies.

"Dude, knock it off," George is irritated. He believed for a split second that Peyton might be right, but this putting her down and calling her names has to stop.

Peyton is outraged. "No, you knock it off with all this nonsense! We're gonna get caught now. Her mother is going to come back tomorrow to look for her. She's gonna find this shack. Our whole idea will be out the window because of some little twerp."

George is silent. Sometimes he lets Peyton rant like a child until he feels better.

Peyton continues, "So what would we do now Mister Smarty-Pants? If she goes home, she might tell someone."

George shakes his head in disagreement, "Nah, I don't agree. She doesn't even talk!"

Peyton takes another swig of his beer.

"Besides," George continues, "I think she will keep it to herself if she wants to continue to come here with us."

Peyton is shocked as he spits out some of his beer. The liquid pours out of his nose and onto the ground. He coughs and chokes as if someone just punched him in the face.

"What?" he asks still coughing. "Are you insane? She is not coming here."

"Why not?"

"Why not? Dude! She's a Goddamn weirdo!"

Gwyneth finishes her business and heads back towards the shack. She hears the boys talking about her so she stops to listen in on what they're saying.

She had a sinking feeling that they would say bad things about her. Most people do. They never want to give her a chance to show what kind of person she can be. She's not her mother and she's always wanted to prove that to people.

But that's hard when people look at her like she's a diseased freak. It's hard when people make fun of her for not being able to speak, for being dirty, for not understanding a lot of things and for not being smart.

Peyton swigs the last of his beer and crushes the empty can in his hand.

"Look Peyton," George says angrily, "I don't know what her deal is, but she can come here if she wants."

Peyton suddenly throws the crushed can at George's head. It lands on the ground.

George picks it up angrily and throws it towards Peyton's head. He quickly moves out of the way. For a second, George thinks that Peyton is about to laugh. He has that shit-eating-grin on his face. But he doesn't laugh. He becomes angrier.

"No, she can't. We're gonna have to kill her!" Peyton yells.

"Kill her?! You're crazy! She's probably no more than eleven or twelve! Just let her be," George pleads. He can't believe his ears. He can't believe that his best friend of fifteen years just threatened to kill an innocent child.

Peyton suddenly pushes George. "I guess I'm gonna have to take her out myself!" Peyton yells. George is extremely shocked. He's always known Peyton to be an asshole but he's never heard of him killing anyone. He's never heard of him threatening to physically harm someone.

Gwyneth approaches them from hiding behind the trees just as George pushes Peyton back. George stops and smiles at her once he sees her coming towards them.

Ignoring them, Gwyneth heads towards her Unicorn book-bag. Peyton watches her suspiciously as he picks up his hammer and a nail.

Gwyneth's mother's voice is in her head, "Do whatever is necessary to survive."

Chapter Eleven

How can anyone survive in this type of habitat? Well, besides the squirrels, the bears, the deer, chipmunks, skunks and any other wild animal that humans stumble upon in the woods. How can anyone, "do what's necessary?" What is NECESSARY?

Is it killing people? Killing those wild animals? Chopping down trees? Starving to death until you run into the chance of killing a wild animal and eating it? Not bathing for days, maybe even weeks so the little bit of water that you have can be saved to drink?

How do you necessarily survive in the woods; especially when you're all alone?

And especially when you have mental issues?

What are you supposed to do when you overhear someone talk about killing you? What are you supposed to do if someone was being nice to you but they associated with that exact person who threatened the kill?

These exact questions don't even float through Gwyneth's mind. She's not even thinking of any questions as a matter of fact. Her mother's words taunt her brain. The woman isn't even around and she's making her go crazy. It's like deep, growling voices are whispering in her ears.

She can't stop the sound. For a moment, she covers her ears with her hands. She's panicking. She's frantic. She feels this sudden anger burst from her heart. She feels this rage that she's never felt before; not even towards her mother. She doesn't know where it's coming from and she doesn't understand it. For a quick moment, she doesn't like it.

Ruby has threatened her life countless times. It's not something that she's never heard.

The beast of a woman treated her like dog shit for the past twelve years. This solid feeling of hatred is different. Gwyneth doesn't know how this feeling came about inside of her body and she can't describe it in her own mind. She can't even speak of it. That's the worst part.

She can't tell these boys to screw themselves. She can't yell at them and call them an asshole. She can't tell them anything without having to write it on that lousy piece of paper.

She can scream though. She's half tempted to scream at the top of her lungs but her mother has her afraid of the farm people. She doesn't want them to hunt her down like a wild animal and kill her on the spot. She doesn't want to die like that.

And she doesn't want to die at the hands of these punk kids.

Gwyneth calmly digs into her bookbag and pulls out her ten inch sewing needle. Her heart is pounding out of her chest and the anger feeling is hooking onto her brain… fast. The hook reminds her of a fishing hook clawing into an innocent fish. He's just swimming in the water; minding his own business, just like she was.

She was strolling through the woods ever so quietly while minding her own business. That's when they took her; hook, line and sinker.

She shows the boys her sewing items like they're prized possessions.

Peyton laughs. "Oh yeah, you can make us pretty doilies for the shack."

Gwyneth doesn't even know what a "doily" is. This confusion shows on her face and makes Peyton laugh harder. He tosses his hammer to the ground.

"I need a break. This is getting to be too much," Peyton whines.

Once again, he sounds like a child not getting his way; a little baby.

Gwyneth stole his favorite toy away from him, now go cry like a little Bitch.

He lies down on the ground as if he's exhausted from working all day. He blows out a long breath from his mouth as he looks up at the cloudy sky. The sun is hiding again.

Maybe the sun is hiding from Gwyneth.

George tosses his hammer and sits down next to Peyton. Peyton continues to laugh like a hyena. The sound vibrates throughout Gwyneth's body and mind. It sounds like nails scratching on a chalkboard. The hairs on the back of her neck stand up. Goosebumps form on her pale skin.

And she's angry.

"We should bring some nasty girls here so we can do nasty things," Peyton suggests.

Gwyneth joins them. She drops to her knees next to Peyton. She inspects the needle like it's the first time she's ever touched it. The sharpness gives her tingles inside of her belly. Some type of excitement jolts her insides like a firecracker exploding. Her heart is racing like it is running a marathon. The pounding feels like it's going to rip her chest to shreds at any second.

Peyton chuckles, "Are you going to be nasty to me? Maybe we could just use you."

George ignores Peyton's ignorance. He turns to Gwyneth, "Are you going to make something for the shack with all that thread and yarn?"

Gwyneth nods and smiles at George; acknowledging his kindness. Peyton laughs and shakes his head as he watches storm clouds passing by.

Gwyneth suddenly frowns and looks at George with puppy-dog eyes. Then she glances back at Peyton as he relaxes on the ground. She doesn't understand why he's being so mean to her. He doesn't even know her. She thought people were kinder than this; better than her mother.

"You better not tell anyone about this shack... especially your mother. If you do, I will hurt you. No, as a matter of fact, I'll kill you," Peyton threatens.

George interferes, "Will you stop it Peyton? Just stop.... threatening her won't help."

Gwyneth continues to inspect the needle because she doesn't know what else to do. She can't have a normal conversation with people so she just sits and listens when people talk to each other. She does it at the park. She tends to eavesdrop on conversations. That's how she learns about new things like what people like to eat, where they like to shop, the latest gossip and news and what people like to do for fun.

She watches other mothers as they take walks while pushing baby strollers. She watches older kids bully young kids and take their money from their pockets. She watches drug deals. She watches dead beat dads as they stare and fantasize about those mothers who are taking walks while pushing those baby strollers. Their eyes are perched on these women while their bad ass children run around screaming as they push other little kids to the ground.

Peyton laughs hysterically; interrupting Gwyneth's thoughts. The bubble cloud of dead beats was just popped; making her eyes blink repeatedly.

A sudden force rips through Gwyneth's brain and she lifts the needle up into the air like a psychopath. The tip of the needle then suddenly comes down; slicing through the inside of Peyton's right eye like a knife spreading butter.

Peyton screams at the top of his lungs. George is frozen in shock. His eyes are wide and it seems like his brain isn't registering what he's witnessing. This only lasts for a few seconds before George snaps out of some reality demon portal he was stuck inside of.

He screams.

Birds fly out of the trees. Worms crawl back into the dirt. Bugs scurry off into their hiding spots. The wind picks up as the storm approaches. Thunder and lightning is now in the sky but the rain hasn't surfaced as of yet. A cool breeze hits Gwyneth's face.

The smell of in-coming rain seeps through Gwyneth's nose and for a split second, she closes her eyes to take in the fresh smell. She and her sister would hear the thunder and watch the clouds from the kitchen window. Running outside to the yard, they would inhale that smell of in-coming rain. They would then stand in the middle of the yard while waiting for it to pour into their mouths to get something to drink.

Ruby would angrily swing the front door open and yell at them to come back inside. They would giggle like school-girls and run inside to get their asses beat.

Gwyneth suddenly opens her eyes and watches George lose his balance onto the ground. She lifts the needle a second time and stabs Peyton's left eye while watching George at the same time. Peyton is screaming and crying; trying to reach his bloody face with his shaking hands.

George is fast on his feet and suddenly tackles Gwyneth with a bear hug. She falls to the ground; dropping the needle. They struggle in a fight; George tries to grab Gwyneth's wrists. He sits on top of her; crushing her airways.

Peyton is in agony as he continues to scream in horror.

George continues to hold Gwyneth down as she becomes enraged.

She feels like her arms are growing bigger and her body is turning green like The Hulk.

She kicks her feet as she struggles; panting and out of breath. She feels like she's losing.

Quickly, she lifts her head and spits right into George's face. He removes his hands from her wrists to wipe the spit with his sleeve. He stands up; not realizing her action was a diversion. He's disgusted by her and her behavior; the look is displayed across his face.

"You're disgusting! All I wanted to do was help you!" he yells. He then turns to Peyton, "I'm going to get some help!"

George turns to run but Gwyneth quickly swings her leg; tripping him. He falls; cracking his face onto the ground. Blood immediately starts oozing from his nose and mouth. He wants to cry, but he doesn't want to sound like a little Bitch. He can't even believe that he's worried about that right now. This girl has a string on his back like a puppet and it's making him angrier. He wants to kill her. Peyton was right and now he feels horrible for not believing in his best friend.

Gwyneth is frantic once again. Her whole entire body is shaking. She can't think straight. Those lightning bolts are zapping once again. It strikes the right side of her brain and then quickly strikes the left. She feels dazed for a moment and isn't sure what to do. She has to act fast or these boys are going to kill her.

She blindly searches for her sewing needle. She's staggering like a drunken idiot leaving a bar. Her vision is blurred from the lightning flashes. She's sweating profusely and her face feels like it's on fire. She's angry but scared at the same time.

She spots the sewing needle and dives for it. George is lying on his back while holding his bloody face in his hands. He's screaming and crying now. The pain is unbearable and he suddenly feels weak. His body is frozen in time and he's trying to make sense of all this.

Gwyneth stands over him. She's like a cloud blocking the sun; a demonic shadow-figure.

George is shaking; terrified of this twelve-year-old. While lifting his bloody fingers in the air above his face, he muffles, "Gwyneth! It wasn't me being mean. I was nice to you!"

Gwyneth kneels; a branch stabs her knee but she ignores the pain. With sadness in her eyes, she stares at George as he cries. The guilt is taking over her heart but she still feels that hardening anger. She knows that she must kill them both now. George could easily run home and tell the police. They would come looking for her and she doesn't want that. Her mother would be so angry with her if she showed up tomorrow and she was gone.

With much pain and regret, Gwyneth quickly stabs him in the right eye. She tries to cover up his screaming mouth with her hand but he's frantic; shaking his head as the needle penetrates into his iris. Bloody tears slip down the side of his face.

She instantly pulls the needle out and tries to stab him in the left eye but she misses because he lifts his arms to block her. *Not only is he cute*, she thinks, *he's quite smart too.*

But she's smarter….

Holding him down with as much strength as she possibly can, she stabs his left cheek. He screams in agony while still struggling to get her off of him.

He's weak and he gives up for a split second. Gwyneth is weak in the knees. It's not because she's been kneeling and fighting in a struggle for the past few minutes, it's because she really cared about George and was beginning to like him. But she realizes at this very moment that she can't catch any feelings for anyone from now on. It makes her weak and she needs as much strength as she can possibly endure.

None of this makes sense to her sensitive brain. It's like living in a nightmare.

One minute she's with her mother and siblings at their house and then the next minute she's in the middle of the woods killing two complete strangers. She probably would've ended up killing them anyways. Peyton was such a pain in the ass that he would've driven her crazy.

Just like her mother.

So she should say… he would've driven her even CRAZIER and thinking of Peyton makes her feel this way. She can't explain why or what is making her brain tick like a time bomb when it comes to this boy. Well… it ticks like a time bomb when she becomes angry over anything.

As she watches George's left eye light up like a firecracker and his right eye ooze with blood, she plunges the sewing needle into his left eye.

He screams a blood curdling scream.

The home of William and Joni St. Rose has always been up for discussion throughout the community town folks. The couple tends to boast about their riches; buying a yacht, multiple expensive vehicles, a state-of-the-art camera system, a pool and a bowling alley built into their basement. He might be the Sheriff in town, but he doesn't make THAT much money.

Joni's money-making abilities have always been a secret. No one around town knows that before her marriage to William, she and her ex-husband robbed a jewelry store. They sold the jewelry; making millions. They were never caught.

William doesn't even know and Joni likes to keep it that way. She's a mysterious person and many people don't like her. Although, she does have a talent that mesmerizes the town; her painting skills are out of this world.

She paints. She auctions off her paintings and makes money that way. That's what William thinks and believes every time anyways. Sometimes it's hard for her to sell these paintings so she then claims to have sold a couple of them in order to present a wad of cash to William. However, that wad of cash had actually sat in a secret vault that was built inside of the garage.

William is oblivious to this situation obviously. He's out working for more hours than he is at home. He has no idea what she does. He has no idea how sneaky his wife actually is.

Sneaky indeed. Sneaky enough to kill her ex-husband because he threatened to go to the cops about their jewelry heist. It was a spur of the moment desperate kill because she knows deep down that he didn't mean those threats. He was mad. They just got into an argument about splitting the money. He, of course, wanted to pay their driver more money than what was discussed. He wanted to give some away to charity. She wasn't having ANY of that.

So she killed him and dumped his body into some secluded woods, out by the farm. Of course, William was assigned to the case. This was before his "Sheriff days."

He immediately became "aw" struck by Joni's beauty and vibrant personality. He was her shoulder to cry on. The one she confided in about the loss of her husband.

He was a fool and didn't do his research.

Joni lives this luxurious and fabulous life. Sometimes she doesn't want to deal with their bratty kids, but for the most part, her life has gotten way better than what it used to be.

If only those kids wouldn't act all "high and mighty."

Speaking of those seventeen-year-old twins, they're hanging out in Roman's bedroom while trying to finish their homework. Things have been tense between them lately.

Roman is on his bed, chewing on his hot grilled cheese sandwich; smacking his lips like a cow. Marybeth glares at him as she sits at Roman's computer desk. She's trying to write a paragraph about what she plans to do after college.

She has no clue either. Sometimes she yearns to have a husband and a growing family, but then other times, she wants to be single and live a party life. There's no in between for her. She currently does not have a boyfriend because she finds most boys immature and stupid like her brother. She's too mature for her age. She prefers older men but that would cause problems between her and her father. He, on the other hand, would not be okay with her dating someone over the age of eighteen. This thought always crosses her mind; actually pissing her off.

Marybeth squints her bright blue eyes and scrunches her nose as if Roman just farted.

Maybe he did and she just didn't hear it. It was one of those "silent but deadly" farts. He laughs like a hyena and snorts his nose like a pig; choking on his sandwich.

"Good, that's what you get. Do you seriously have to eat like that? What the hell is wrong with you?" Marybeth asks. She wants to laugh but she holds it in like lava inside of a volcano ready to explode. He's such an idiot.

Roman laugh harder; pieces of his sandwich spits out of his mouth. He tosses the sandwich onto his plate. His mind is somewhere else. He looks around the room like he's just discovered the smell of his fart for the first time.

Excitedly, he stands up from his bed and paces the floor.

"I cannot wait to show you that area dad and I hunted at," Roman tells Marybeth.

He suddenly returns to his sandwich and shoves the rest of it into his mouth.

He looks like he's going out of his mind. As a matter of fact, he looks like he's going through withdrawals. He's extremely excited and can't stop thinking about his big plans. He is very hyper and that's what makes him look creepy and weird. His friends tell him that pretty much every day of his life. He just has a ton of energy.

He continues to pace the floor.

"I thought that area was restricted? Dad was the one who restricted it! That's really weird of him!" Marybeth exclaims. The wheels are spinning in her brain as she takes a bite of her grilled cheese sandwich. She moans like it's the best thing she's ever eaten.

"Yeah, I was a little confused as to why he took me there. That was the first time. We were always told that was a bad area to go to," Roman replies.

"Well I don't want to go there," Marybeth whines. "Besides, it's cold and snowy. We'll get sick!" She hopes that Roman will finally take that as a "no" for her answer. He's been bugging her about going into these woods.

Of course he pleads, "Oh but please Marybeth? You said you would! You can't take that back!" He's becoming anxious. He's terrified to go alone.

"Oh yes I can! And I am!"

Chewing the last bite of her sandwich, Marybeth rubs her temples. She closes her eyes and sighs. She doesn't understand why her brother insists on putting her through so much bullshit in her life. He always makes her do things that she doesn't want to do. He always wants to take her to creepy places that she doesn't want to go to.

Two years ago, he made her go to a haunted house where his friends worked.

Of course, Roman had his friends prank her the whole time. They would only jump out in front of her. They physically chased her down with the chainsaw at the end of the maze. They pretended like they were stabbing her with a butcher knife.

She's been traumatized since then and refuses to go anywhere like that with him ever again.

Roman is suddenly frantic and jumps off of his bed.

"I want to show you that woman!" he pleads.

"You are so weird Roman. Are you sure that you saw a woman? I think you're eyes are playing tricks on you. It was probably a deer."

"Everyone must think there's a hoard of deer there!" He pauses and takes a breath. "See for yourself then since you know everything!"

Roman notices that one of the bulbs is out on his string of Christmas lights. They're stapled to the wall next to his bed. Some of them are blinking like they're possessed.

"Once one goes out, they all go out!" Marybeth laughs.

Roman glares at her. Sometimes he just wants to pull her big, blonde, curls right out of her scalp. He wants to punch her in the face and make her nose bleed.

He knows that's just awful to visualize, but sometimes it makes him feel better after she's made fun of him. He hates when she makes fun of him.

Marybeth rolls her eyes, "Okay, okay. You win. I don't like the idea. It sounds scary and dangerous. We shouldn't go there like dad says. But, I'll go to see for myself."

Roman excitedly claps his hands. "Alright! You won't regret it… I promise!"

Chapter Twelve

The night before was rough and the morning came faster than Marybeth could've imagined. Roman kept her up with his shenanigans about the woman in the woods. He has this mentality of a lost child. Sometimes he acts like he's five-years-old again; acting like a fool. Not to mention, he's extremely embarrassing in public. He's loud-mouthed and doesn't know when to stop behaving like an imbecile. It's gotten out of hand lately and Marybeth isn't sure what to do about him. It is completely exhausting.

One thing she does know, she has to dig into some information about this mystery woman and who she could possibly be. The only place that she could possibly find this type of information is her father's office.

Her father's office; it is off limits to her and Roman. Her mother doesn't even come into his office unless he requests her presence. Joni likes to leave him be while she plants her garden, cooks their meals, watches TV and does her crossword puzzles. She likes to hang out by the pool as she wears her skimpy bathing suit while the pool boy cleans it; trying not to stare at her boobs.

Joni winks; making the poor boy blush. His excitement shows below the belt and she giggles like a school-girl while sipping her vodka and lemon juice.

Marybeth thinks that she's a pig. Joni doesn't realize that her daughter watches her from the kitchen window as she pulls the strap of the bathing suit down past her armpit. The pool boy takes a glimpse of her breast. Then, she laughs like a hyena.

That kind of laugh for some reason makes Marybeth's blood boil.

It makes her anxious and it makes her heart race. Just like it is now as she quietly opens the door of her father's sweet-smelling, clean office. It smells like honey and blueberries.

Marybeth spots the blueberry candle on the large, cherry-wood desk that sits in the center of the room. A black leather chair sits behind the desk; waiting for its owner to plop his butt right on it as he drinks his morning cup of coffee.

A beautiful grand piano sits in a corner. Marybeth can remember her father playing it one Christmas evening when they were six-years-old. They sat on his lap as he played "Jingle Bells." He hasn't played much since. Joni has complained that it "sits there and collects dust." She demands that he gets rid of it if he isn't going to play it.

He ignores her of course but it still sits there; collecting dust.

It's been a long time since Marybeth stepped foot into this office. Her father has been secretive with his investigations lately and this discovery actually annoys Marybeth to her core.

Her father used to come to her with questions and advice. This was of course illegal, but William is the Sheriff. No one knows that he asked a teenager for advice with the law.

That would be considered absurd and unprofessional. Oh, what would the community think?! Townsfolk already believe that William St. Rose is a joke of a Sheriff. He's the talk of the town. People respect him of course, but they think he is a naïve man for marrying Joni.

His wife is not very-well liked and they constantly tell William to divorce her. His buddies think that she has something, "up her sleeve." But, they can't pin-point specifically what it is.

It frustrates his buddies to have no proof. No proof of infidelities. No proof of any lies.

They don't have the time or the energy to watch her like a child. They are not babysitters. They just wish that their friend would, "wake up and smell the roses."

Marybeth wanders around the office like she has all the time in the world. She stares at the library of shelves containing hundreds of books, magazines and newspapers that cover the walls of the whole entire room.

Two, red-plush, cushioned chairs are turned facing the desk. They look comfortable and sleek. No one sits on them so they look brand new. They aren't sunken in from the weight of people's butt imprints.

Marybeth places her sweaty hand on the nearest chair; it's soft and squishy. Her whole body is perspiring. She's scared shitless to be in this room. She's scared to get caught, that's what her problem is. She's been a dare-devil lately alongside her brother. He's become a bad influence.

She glances up at the family pictures hanging on the wall; designed like an analog clock. Roman's mischievous grin on his face while he and Marybeth are gathered arm-in-arm around a camp fire at their father's log cabin up north.

That picture was taken two years ago… the last time they took a family trip.

Marybeth sighs. William has worked skin deep into his investigations for the past two years that they haven't been able to spend any quality time together. She was hoping to take at least one more family trip before her and Roman leave for college.

Maybe her mother can convince her father.

Marybeth chuckles. Hell would freeze over before that Bitch would do anything to get the family together. She's only worried about herself and the things that she wants to do in life.

"Dad, are you in here?" Marybeth whispers as she knows damn well that he is one hundred percent not in the office. *But, he could be hiding in the closet,* Marybeth thinks.

She finds her thought to be extremely silly and she bursts with laughter.

Maybe she's going crazy. Roman seems to be lately. She must be next.

She hears the sudden sound of her mother walking through the kitchen and downstairs to the gym area of the basement. She's probably wearing a skimpy gym outfit and holding a tall glass of vodka and lemon juice in her newly manicured fingers.

Marybeth quietly closes the office door.

Snooping around, the runs her fingers on top of neatly stacked documents sitting on the corner of William's desk. Next to the stack of documents, a current newspaper clipping is folded neatly with the headline in bold letters: "ABUSIVE MISSING WOMAN FOR TWO WEEKS."

She didn't realize that her father was investigating this case. It has been all over the news and this "mysterious" woman has been the talk around the community.

The pastor at the church claims to have known her. He hasn't yet explained in depth on HOW he knows her but he did mention that he thinks she came into the church a few times to pray for her sins.

Thinking about past cases, Marybeth approaches a shelf filled with newspaper clippings. She runs her fingers through each and every one of them; glancing at each headline.

Noticing a much older newspaper, she gently pulls it out of its spot.

Her heart races as she grips it into her hand. The newspaper is incredibly fragile. It looks as though it was opened hundreds of times. It is tattered and ripped in a few areas.

If her father caught her in here snooping around, he might get angry enough to beat her ass. Although, she doesn't really know why she thinks this because William is not and was never an abusive father. It was always her mother who did that type of discipline to her and Roman when they were younger. Of course now, she would never try to put her hands on them because they are old enough to retaliate. Roman does believe that Joni is afraid of him.

And she is.

Three years ago, Joni and Roman got into an argument about him eating all of her healthy snacks. She was on a health kick and was dieting and exercising. Roman did admit to eating all of her snacks just to piss her off because he doesn't like their own mother.

Joni slapped him clear across the face. The only witness to this slap was Marybeth. William was out on a case and to this day, he has no idea of the exchange between his wife and son.

Roman's face had turned bright red. He later admitted to Marybeth that he was so embarrassed because he felt like a five-year-old all over again.

In an instant, Roman gripped Joni by her jaw and slammed her up against the wall of the kitchen. It must have spooked her a lot because her nipples hardened and she cried out in pain.

"I'm only going to say this to you once," Roman whispered in Joni's ear. "If you ever hit me like that again, I will kill you."

Joni was in shock but she still smiled, "Promise?" she laughed.

'I'll do more than promise."

Marybeth was flabbergasted. She had never seen or heard of Roman doing or saying anything like that… EVER.

It was the last time that their mother hit him.

As Marybeth reverts her attention back to the newspaper clipping, she reads the bolded headline: "MISSING GIRL? WHO KNOWS

THE TRUTH?"

Confused, she returns to the desk and picks up the other newspaper. She briefly remembers this "missing girl" story but can't quite point her finger on the details. This case might be one that slipped through the cracks. Marybeth doesn't like unsolved cases. It breaks her heart knowing that people are out in the world missing or possibly killed without justice.

Sitting cross-legged on the newly, shampooed, carpeted floor, Marybeth spreads the newspaper clippings out like a fan. She lets them rest onto the floor as she pulls her cell phone out of the pocket of her jeans. She quickly snaps a picture of both headlines of both newspapers.

As she's reading the articles and comparing notes in her intelligent mind, a hand suddenly grips her shoulder.

Startled, she holds her pounding chest. She glances up at William.

He doesn't seem angry, just irritated that she's in his office without permission.

"Uh… hi," Marybeth says with a smile to minimize his irritation. "Do you happen to know these women from these particular articles?"

"What in the hell are you doing? And why are you in my office?" William bellows.

Strutting toward the desk, he tosses his keys. They make a loud "clunk" sound as they land angrily onto the cherry-wood. Gulping his coffee, he stares at Marybeth while waiting for her answer. His bright, blue eyes, burn through her own eyeballs like hot lava. It reminds her of staring into the pits of Hell; a blazing inferno.

Marybeth swallows hard. The silence in the room makes her throat sound like a shark swallowing a mouthful of ocean water.

Marybeth clears her throat, "I uh... I came here to talk to you but I didn't realize you left. So, I went through your collection of newspapers… which is kind of weird I might add. But, I came across these two very interesting stories."

As she points to the articles, William heavily frowns. He holds his coffee cup to his lips; eyeing her suspiciously. He doesn't seem like himself this morning and this actually concerns his daughter. She thinks that he does look mad, now that she stares into his blazing fury.

"Well… I didn't know them personally but I heard rumors."

Marybeth is skeptical of his answer. "What kind of rumors?" she asks.

Sighing, William places his coffee cup onto the desk and sits onto his leather chair. He knows that this girl will not give up. He knows she is seeking answers to something he isn't ready to talk about just yet. He wants to come up with all of the facts first.

Marybeth stands up from the floor. Tossing the newspapers onto the desk, she plops her behind onto one of the plush, red chairs.

She notices that her father hasn't shaven. The stubbles actually make him look younger. His iconic, slicked-back hair-do is now disheveled. It looks like he just rolled right out of bed and never changed into pajamas last night.

William sighs again. "I heard that the woman was recently brutally murdered. Some people claim to have witnessed the murder in broad daylight, right in the middle of a parking lot! But I investigated those claims… they are simply untrue."

Marybeth is surprised and shocked at this revelation.

"Do you believe that they have any connections? I mean, these two women in these clippings?" Marybeth dares to ask. She instantly regrets the question because the look upon his face says it all. There's something that this man knows and he doesn't want to tell her.

"I have no idea," he answers, "one of the many mysteries of these towns around here."

She genuinely believes that answer coming out of his mouth. He looks exhausted and defeated. She hasn't seen him much lately because of the twelve hour shifts he's been working every day for the past two weeks straight. He definitely needs a break.

And she wants to help. She NEEDS to help.

Turning a page of the most recent newspaper, she continues, "A mystery indeed." She pauses, thinking. "Hey dad, I do have another question though."

"What is this? Twenty questions? You're just like your mother." William asks, irritated.

He suddenly opens the drawer to his desk and pulls out a Cuban cigar. Popping it into his mouth, he holds it with his wet lips.

Marybeth turns another page, careful to keep her eyes on the newspaper. William does not like to be questioned for any of his actions. It's his business and no one else's.

"So… why did you take Roman to the restricted area? You told us to not ever go there. We were just a bit confused is all."

William nonchalantly lights the cigar and inhales. He then slowly blows the smoke up into the air. His eyes are tired. His exhaustion is weighing him down like a bag full of bricks. His body is sore and weak. He hasn't gotten much sleep in weeks.

"Well," William begins, looking at his library of shelves, "I was in hopes that would excite Roman a little more… being in a restricted area and all. I would prefer if he would hunt with me and get excited like I do. It just made things worse."

"How so?" Marybeth presses on the subject.

Her father inhales once again. He plays with the ashes in the ashtray.

"Your brother seems to think that he can do what he wants. You guys are still seventeen and live under my roof. I have been a Sheriff for many, many years. I have seen it all. I try to help children as much as I can… considering I did not have a great childhood myself. But, I seem to not be able to help Roman, and that bothers me tremendously."

Marybeth quietly turns another page. She's not even reading any words that are printed. She's staring into the abyss as if the newspaper is blank. She's trying to process some of this information. "So you took him out there to change him?"

William chuckles. "Sure, if you think of it that way." He pauses. "Hey, look at me."

Marybeth slowly glances up from the newspaper. William slowly inhales his cigar. The smoke is filling the room, making Marybeth want to gag. It's not her favorite hobby that her father does. In fact, she hates it. She's told him to quit several times. But, she thinks she can tell the man what to do as well, just like his demanding wife.

William continues, "You kids don't have to be afraid of me. I know I can be rough sometimes, but I'm just trying to make you guys tough for the real world out there. Roman wants to make movies, which is fine, but he's cocky and arrogant. That's going to hurt him someday."

Marybeth giggles and nods her head in agreement.

"We just don't want to disappoint you," she says.

William puts out the cigar in the ashtray, crushing the embers like they're runaway ants.

"You will never disappoint me. Not like I have been by others in the past."

Grabbing the newspapers from Marybeth, he scrolls through the articles. She stares at her father's stubbles on his chin. *He doesn't look too bad with hair on his face,* she thinks.

"I really wish I knew where this woman was. I questioned the neighbors. No one talked to her. She kept to herself. She moved to this other town by herself years ago."

"Other town?" Marybeth asks.

"Yes, the neighbors said she lived here in our town. They said she had some sort of 'mystery' about her."

William takes a sip of his cold coffee and scrunches his nose in disgust. Standing up, he looks out of the bay window behind his desk. Gazing at the backyard with the beautiful snow lying on the ground, he watches a squirrel skitter across the electrical wires. He then stares at the neighbor's Christmas lights that shine brightly this early morning.

"You hungry?" he asks.

"Hell – I mean heck yeah! Mom went down to the gym a little bit ago. She didn't make any breakfast."

"Let's go my sweet girl. You choose the place."

Chapter Thirteen

Ruby, being the Bitch that she is, would've said, "Those boys deserved it."

They deserved it alright, especially Peyton. Peyton was a very bad boy. He was mouthy and arrogant. Gwyneth doesn't like mouthy and arrogant people. Her mother is mouthy and arrogant. Maybe that's another reason why she doesn't like her mother.

But, you cried like a little Bitch just an hour ago, Gwyneth reminds herself. *She left you high and dry and you cried over her.*

No, she thinks to herself, *I cried because I don't want to be alone.*

Her brain laughs as if she's going crazy. Her mind has gone mad and now she talks to herself in her brain. It confuses her, making her look around the woods as if someone is directly talking to her.

Well, you can't talk anyways, her brain reminds her.

Holding a marker in her fist, she quickly covers her ears and shuts her eyes for a moment. She can't let her brain beat herself up. She can't put herself down. Her mother did a great job of doing that herself. She doesn't need help from her stupid cerebrum.

She needs to figure out what to do next.

Hunched over the picnic table like The Hunchback, she glances at her drawing on a piece of paper. She blinks as she stares hypnotized at her pencil with a broken eraser and her ripped box of markers. She seems to be in a trance, staring at her drawing of dolls with buttons for eyeballs in their eye sockets.

Her mind is truly screwed up.

Thanks to her mother.

She always wondered why she ended up having Ruby for a mother. Why couldn't her mother be rich, or beautiful, or loving? Why couldn't she grow up with a caring mother alongside a caring father? Why couldn't she grow up in a happy home? Why does that only happen to certain people? *Everyone should live happy.*

Well, that's what Gwyneth thinks. That's what another small child thought on the news channel one morning as Gwyneth and her beast of a mother were eating Ruby's famous runny eggs and burnt toast. The toaster was even sick of her mother's shit.

The small child was crying because she got lost inside of a store while her mother was outside selling drugs. The incident was plastered all over the news because the mother tried selling the drugs to a cop. As soon as she pocketed the money, the cop pulled his gun out and pointed it straight at that child's mother's forehead.

The woman panicked and grabbed the cop's gun; accidently pressing his finger that was placed on the trigger.

Her brain matter had plastered all over the passenger seat and window of her beat up, "soccer mom," van.

Gwyneth watched with her own tears in her eyes as the child looked at the news camera with tired eyes and asked, "Why did I have to be born with this kind of mother?"

Gwyneth played with the runny egg with her fork as she glanced at Ruby. The Beast was smoking a cigarette while shoving a burnt piece of toast in her mouth.

The poor girl had definitely lost her appetite. She wasn't sure if it was from her mother's disgusting eggs, the crying tears of the child on the news, or if was because of the fact that this woman's head had been blown to pieces.

Or maybe it was because of Ruby's nasty eating habits. She ate like a pig snorting through the trough. The burnt toast was stuck between her yellow teeth.

Crying, Gwyneth tossed her fork and stared at her food on her plate.

Ruby sharply turned her head, "Look at me," she demanded.

Of course, Gwyneth ignored her.

"I said look at me you filth!" Ruby yelled.

Gwyneth blinks back tears as she stares at Peyton and George's dead bodies lying on the ground next to her. She was really looking forward to being their friend.

Ruby's voice is loud, "LOOK AT ME!" screaming inside of Gwyneth's brain.

Still locked in her trance, she draws a stick figure of herself next to the dolls with her black marker. She then draws a bubble above her stick figure head. Inside of the bubble, she draws two eyeballs and writes the word, "Me."

After finishing her drawing, she glances at the boys. Then, she quickly looks back at the piece of paper, and then back at the boys as if she's contemplating on drawing the dead bodies of the boys. She would have to add some red to emphasize their blood.

She loves to draw. It's the only thing she does best. Even her brother and sister told her so. They said, "You are the best drawer in the whole universe Gwyneth!"

She smiles as she remembers them laughing as soon as the words came out of their mouths. They weren't being mean. Their sister tickled their feet; making their brother fart loudly.

Gwyneth uncontrollably giggles as she grabs the red marker and colors big red dots on her drawing around the dead bodies of her new friends.

Her drawing is now complete. She picks it up and glances at the shack. *Should I hang it up inside or outside?* She asks herself.

Shrugging her shoulders, she stands up from the picnic table and moves all of her drawing materials to the bench. Sighing, she looks down at her tired and broken body. She hates being this skinny. She's always wanted to eat healthy and become fit enough to take on the world.

Staring at Peyton, she nods.

I must find strength, she thinks to herself. *I can do this. I don't care what that beast said.*

Grabbing Peyton's arms, she struggles a bit as she tries to lift his heavy body on top of the picnic table. To her, his body feels like five hundred pounds worth of bricks.

She's perspiring once again as she feels the muscles on the back of her neck start to pull. His blood wipes onto her coat as she whimpers; struggling to lift him up over the bench.

Lifting everything from the torso and up, she manages to get that part of his body onto the bench. But then she quickly grabs his legs as she realizes that the top part of his body had started to slide off of the bench. This is such a struggle for her and she feels like giving up.

She feels like a fool for trying to do this. Whatever THIS is. She's out of her mind.

After finally lifting Peyton's legs on top of the bench, his left arm dangles off of the bench; his pointer and middle finger glide gently over the mud on the ground.

The smell of his blood seeps inside of her nose; as does the smell of her breath. She scrunches her nose as she looks once again at Peyton's blood on the sleeve of her coat. She touches it with her pointer finger; licking blood and dirt off of that same finger as if it's a lollipop. She tastes bitterness, saltiness and some kind of taste that she can't even describe.

She spits; feeling disgusting and thinking how gross she must look.

Sighing again as if she has a breathing problem, she takes a deep breath and lifts Peyton's upper half of his body once again; struggling to lift it on top of the picnic table. He slides off but Gwyneth quickly grabs him by his shirt and gently places him back onto the bench.

She doesn't want his body to slide off the bench. That would make her completely angry. She might even try to scream at the top of her lungs. Her frustration has taken over her body like poison. She feels numb and stupid. She feels as if what she's trying to do is pointless. All she wants to do is to get him on top of this damn picnic table.

She has to perform surgery. The excitement engulfs her heart like fire.

She suddenly smiles as if a magical spirit whispered in her ear.

Trying once again, she steps onto the picnic table herself and then with all of her might, she pulls on Peyton's top half of his body. She then rests her legs and butt on top of his belly as she struggles to lift his legs onto the picnic table.

After realizing she finally did it, she stands up on top of the picnic table and stretches out her arms as if she's "Rocky Balboa" on the steps of the Philadelphia Museum of Art.

She's so happy that her face hurts from smiling so hard. She hasn't even realized that the temperature has dropped even more and she will soon be a freezing cold mess.

She can worry about that later, even though she should worry about it now since the frigid cold slices through her airway and into her lungs. She can see her breath; blowing through the air like the smoke of a cigarette. She forms her mouth into an "O" and purposely blows out air.

I'm smoking, she excitedly thinks to herself. *Smoking into the depths of Hell.*

She suddenly coughs. She feels her throat tighten.

You have work to do. Worry about that later.

She jumps down from the picnic table and makes her way toward her Unicorn book bag.

Her heart is racing like it's running a marathon. The beating feels like it's trying to break through her chest wall. Her breathing is hard and fast. Her body feels like it was just given a boost of electrical energy. The messages in her brain are lightning fast.

As she rummages through her book bag, she pulls out her black thread, a pair of scissors and her ten inch sewing needle. She glances back at Peyton lying on the picnic table. She then glances at George as he still lies on the ground; deader than a doorknob.

She suddenly feels bad for George. He was trying to be her friend until Peyton had to ruin it. She whimpers for this loss of her dear friend lying on the ground as she slowly walks toward Peyton as if he's about to sit up from the picnic table and say, "Haha."

Gripping the needle in her fist as if she's about to chisel through a block of ice, she leans forward over Peyton and looks at him with hesitation in her eyes.

He deserves it, her mother's voice chants inside of her brain. *He deserves it because of how he made you feel. He made you feel stupid. He made you feel worthless…*

DO IT!

Gwyneth searches the area as if she has an audience watching her every move. Her heart is pounding and feels like it's about to rip through her skin.

The trees sway in the soft breeze. The cold air freezes her tears on her cheeks. She breathes in this cold air and closes her exhausted blue eyes as if she could fall asleep right here in this moment. She takes in her quiet surroundings. These woods are beautiful and angelic. She's never seen something quite like it. Being cooped up in a broken house has made her realize how beautiful the Earth truly is. She's missed out on so much.

Opening her eyes, she looks down at Peyton's bloody eyes and face. He was a beautiful boy too but his attitude got him killed.

As she licks her chapped lips, she uses her ten inch sewing needle that's gripped inside of her right fist in order to dig Peyton's right eye out of the socket. Then, using her fingers of her left hand, she pulls the eye out as she makes a popping sound with her lips.

Sometimes she likes to amuse herself in order to feel happy.

She giggles as she cuts a piece of thread with the scissors.

She feels as if she's floating on a cloud. She feels happy and content. She feels like she just accomplished something huge in her life. She feels like she got the job done.

She finally killed someone who made her feel like shit.

She suddenly sighs. *Too bad it wasn't Ruby Glacier.*

As she slowly tries to slide the thread through the loop of the sewing needle, her hands start to shake with nervousness. The sweat continues to pour down the sides of her face and down her back; making her feel cold and clammy. The cold breeze makes her body shiver.

She's unable to slide the thread through the loop.

Feeling frustrated, she suddenly falls into a fit of rage. It feels like someone pushed her into a fiery pit inside of Hell. The inside of her body feels like it's on fire. The rage has taken control and she can't seem to stop it. She clicks her tongue in anger.

She slams the sewing needle on top of the picnic table and cries like a baby; placing her bloody fingers on her face and eyes. She cries inside of her hands; making sure she covers her face as if people are standing in crowds watching her every move.

The wind picks up and blows the hood of her coat off her head. She quickly puts it back on and shakes from the cold. She glances at the shack. She knows it's time to go inside.

DO IT!

Her mother's voice is like the plague. Sick and demented. Torturous and demanding. She's not even here and she's driving Gwyneth over the edge.

She takes a deep breath and slowly lets it creep out like a blown candle. She has to get a grip on herself. She can't believe that she's letting her mother torture her in these woods. She needs to become strong enough to fight her mother's voice inside her head. She needs to become strong enough to fight anything that tries to hurt her in any way.

And she did…and the beginnings of friendships have become lifelong.

She giggles.

Picking up her scissors, she cuts a piece of Peyton's white shirt. She stares at it like it's a newly discovered piece of cloth. She then places the piece over her mouth and ties it at the back of her head like a mask.

Taking another deep breath, she picks up the needle and thread once again.

Slower than the first time, she eagerly slides the thread through the loop of the needle. As she tries to tie a knot, she immediately becomes frustrated again. She's struggling and she doesn't understand why. She doesn't understand why this is so hard for her to do. *Just tie the damn knot and go on your merrily little way!*

She clicks her tongue again.

Clicking her tongue had become a bad habit ever since she turned three-years-old. It was a coping mechanism whenever her mother infuriated her or if she became frustrated about anything that she tried to do. Ruby used to smack her across the face whenever she did it. Ruby used to say that the noise annoyed her and it sounded like nails scratching on a chalkboard.

Gwyneth never knew what the noise sounded like when a nail was scratched on a chalkboard so she never understood why her mother hated it so bad.

Sometimes she couldn't help it.

And she can't help it now. She's angry, annoyed and frustrated and all she wants to do is finish Peyton's surgery so she can go inside the shack to collect some kind of warmth.

As a matter of fact, Gwyneth was always angry, annoyed and frustrated growing up with that beast of a woman. The clicking of her tongue had stopped for a-while but it came back in the last year or so. Gwyneth remembers the day she did it again after so much time had passed.

Ruby looked at her like a deer caught in the headlights.

Honestly, she looked stupid with a dumb look on her face. She looked at Gwyneth as if it was the first time she ever heard the poor girl do it.

Gwyneth knew what would happen the moment the noise shattered Ruby's brain.

The slap across her mouth sent her to the floor. She bit her lip so hard that the blood immediately drizzled toward her chin. She quickly licked the blood with her tongue and then wiped her mouth with the stained sleeve of her sweatshirt.

Gwyneth hurriedly shakes this memory out of her mind. She

doesn't want to re-count what happened after she wiped blood on a newly cleaned sweatshirt.

Looking at the thread like she's actually performing surgery, Gwyneth finally ties the knot.

Excitedly, she runs back to her book bag with her scissors and then digs for one of her dolls. Grabbing the first one she finds, she cuts the buttons off of the doll's eyes.

She's moving fast. She has this sudden adrenaline rush. She's so excited that she wishes she could sing a song. She wishes she could sing loud for all the animals in the woods to hear her. She wishes that a crowd of people were watching her right now so she could shake their hands and hear them say what a great job she has done.

But then she suddenly feels sad and lonely. She doesn't want to be alone.

With sad eyes, she stares at Peyton and George. *I shouldn't have killed them,* she suddenly thinks. *Why did I do this? They're young like me. And they're so cute. Am I a killer now?*

Returning to Peyton, she hesitates once again. After a minute of staring at him like she's looking at a ghost, she slowly sews a button into Peyton's right eye socket.

She quietly giggles and pauses for a moment. Then she giggles again but louder. As she continues to sew, she laughs harder. This overwhelming joy takes over her body.

Looking up at the sky, she hysterically laughs; sounding like a hyena.

Chapter Fourteen

A light snowfall has blanketed the ground; revealing the boot prints of Roman St. Rose. Behind him, the dust from the snow twirls into the air like a tornado after each step. The crunch of snapping ice-covered twigs and fallen leaves resonate like the banging of a drum inside of these quiet woods. He looks up at the swaying of the trees. They appear to be "shushing" the boy as he trudges his way deeper into the unknown.

Alone.

The armpit of his green, suede, jean jacket carries a clipboard, a notebook and his sister's pink feather pen. He was in too much of a hurry to care about the details of the materials that he brought along. Maybe the woman in the woods will be impressed with his sense of style.

He knows that what he's about to do is wrong but he doesn't care. He's a seventeen-year-old "punk kid" who does what he wants. He doesn't care what anyone thinks; including his entire family. He definitely doesn't care what his mother thinks.

She's a whore in a hand basket. He can't stand looking at her or even talking to her. She makes his skin crawl with bugs. She makes him want to stab his ears with a knife every time she yells at him like he's a child. Sometimes, he gets this sudden urge to stab HER in the ears with a knife. He would feel incredibly satisfied if that were to actually happen.

Roman shakes his head. He doesn't want the thoughts of his mother to ruin this interview. He stayed up all night in order to prepare himself for the questions he's about to ask of this mysterious woman in the woods.

Only, she doesn't know that he's coming for an interview. He figured he would surprise her with a dazzle of his charm in order to get the answers that he's seeking.

Of course, he's not really sure WHAT answers he's seeking. He doesn't expect this woman to immediately admit to a total stranger of why she lives secluded in a dark forest.

He chuckles.

"If only I could live alone in a dark forest," Roman says out loud to the trees.

They sway as if they understand.

If only trees could talk. They could tell stories for days. They could tell the world what the daily habits are of a twenty-four-year-old serial killer.

Roman searches the area as the snow becomes thicker; landing on top of his cherry-smelling blonde hair. He curses at himself for not wearing a hat.

He feels like he's been walking for hours; consistently checking behind his shoulders to see if anyone is following him.

He chuckles again. No one would be following him. No one knows where he went. As a matter of fact, no one knows that he's gone from the house.

His mother went out bowling with her friends, his father is at work in the office and his sister went shopping at the mall with her friends. He refused to sit alone at home like some kind of loser. However, he didn't expect to come out here alone. He expected Marybeth to come with him for this very important interview of a lifetime. He needed a helping hand, another listener and someone smart to help guide him through this process.

He's never interviewed anyone before. He doesn't have the social skills necessary.

Roman suddenly stops. "What the HELL am I doing here?" he asks himself. "I have no clue what I'm doing and she probably won't talk to me."

The sky is darkening and it will be nighttime soon. Roman realizes this but he shrugs it off as if it doesn't bother him. It should bother him because he doesn't fully understand the consequences that may occur during this asinine adventure.

The thick snow is sticking to his clipboard. He quickly tucks it deeper into his armpit; worried that it will get wet. The feather pen peeks out from the clip that's attached to the top of the clipboard as if it's asking for someone to help.

"I'm already here dumb ass! Move it along!" he yells up into the sky.

The darkened clouds look below as if they understand what he just yelled. There seems to be eyes all over him as if every environmental creature and plant grew eyeballs overnight.

These specific woods are quiet. Animals and trees know better than to make loud noises. Well… SOME animals. Some of them have no clue about what awaits them as soon as they enter her territory. Some of them don't even care.

Just like Roman; a careless animal with incredible stupidity.

He slows his pace as he spots the shack in the distance. His eyes are blurry from the wet snow that purposely lands onto both of his pupils. If the snow could talk, it would tell him to turn back. It would tell him to leave and never step foot into these woods again.

He suddenly stops; listening to the jingling sound of aluminum cans.

"Shit," he whispers as he quickly hides behind a tree.

He pulls out a small set of brass binoculars out of his jacket pocket.

He's shaking and he's not sure if it's from the freezing cold weather or if it's from finally reaching his destination. He quickly curses at himself for not wearing gloves.

Peeking through his binoculars like a creeper, he watches the shack while searching the area. He sees no sight of Gwyneth or her dog.

He tries to hold his breath so he can hear any kind of noise. He peeks over his shoulder once again and then quickly looks through the binoculars.

No Gwyneth and no Buttons.

Grabbing his clipboard from underneath his armpit, he unclips the pink feather pen. He writes on the first page of his notebook: "Not home. Entering the shack alone today."

He then quickly clips the pen back into its safe spot and then places the clipboard back underneath his armpit. He takes a deep breath. He has no idea what he's getting himself into. He thinks that this area is filled with rainbows and butterflies.

Trudging toward the shack once again, he suddenly trips over a trip wire. He's sent flying onto the snowy ground; dropping his binoculars and clipboard.

As he lies on the ground, he stares up into the snowy sky. "Shit," he repeats himself.

He wonders why he came all the way out here by himself. He questions his actions. He questions his intelligence. His brain is asking questions lightning fast and he doesn't have the answers to any of them. He doesn't know if he should continue on or just get the hell out of there. He cries inside as if this interview is a missing piece of his heart.

There's an emptiness feeling in the pit of his stomach. He doesn't want to leave without at least trying to talk to her. He has so many questions that he needs to ask her.

He just NEEDS to.

Slowly, he stands up and grabs his dropped items. He notices that his notebook is now wet and whines, "Aw man!" as he quickly wipes the snow with his freezing cold hand.

Squinting his blurry eyes, he tries to focus on the shack. The sun is almost completely set and he will soon see absolutely nothing. He then curses at himself for not bringing a flashlight.

What an asshole.

Taking two steps forward, he hears Gwyneth's click of her tongue.

That sound is like a thousand knives stabbing Roman's brain. His heart skips a beat. He quickly rubs the wet snow out of his blurry eyes with his cold finger-tips. Butterflies flutter inside of his stomach. He feels the vomit as it creeps through his throat and into his mouth.

Shaking his head no, he hurriedly swallows the vomit as he tries not to make any sudden moves. He's scared, freezing, lonely and completely unprepared for this interview.

Gwyneth walks around the east side of the shack with Buttons trotting behind her. Roman quickly hunkers behind a tree; the vomit tastes making him gag.

This whole situation has made him sick to his stomach. He can't believe that he put himself into this horrible nightmare. He has no idea what he was thinking.

No, I do know, he thinks to himself. *I thought she would welcome me with open arms but I quickly realize that she definitely will not do that!*

Buttons stops and sniffs the air as they approach the door to the shack.

He growls.

"Of course, you asshole dog," Roman whispers.

Gwyneth quickly stops and searches the area. She suddenly becomes angry and stomps her dirty black boots toward the tree line. She peeks through the trees; moving her head like a pigeon. She then places her gloved hand over her eyes; shielding them as if the sun was blocking her view. She can't see a damn thing with the sun almost completely set.

Roman bends at the knees as he leans against a tree. "Shit," he says once again.

Closing his eyes, he takes a deep breath and holds it in.

Gwyneth stares into the trees like a hawk waiting for its prey. Roman clutches his belongings to his side as if it's the last time he will touch them. His eyes are still tightly shut as he mouths a silent prayer. A silent prayer? He never prays.

Gwyneth storms toward the shack. Roman quickly opens his eyes wide enough to clearly see another planet in the sky. He wishes he was on that planet right about now as he peeks around the tree and watches Gwyneth enter the shack with Buttons growling behind her.

"Let's just get this over with," Roman says to a tree covered in thick ice. Too bad the trees couldn't save him from this mess. Too bad the trees couldn't lift him up into the air from the blow he might endure from this crazy woman.

Roman steps out from behind the tree; clutching his clipboard between his fingers, he lifts his arms up into the air in surrender.

Buttons turns; growling and barking at this "punk kid."

Roman locks eyes with Gwyneth as she stands in the doorway of the dirty shack. "Ma'am, I'm not here to hurt you," he pleads.

Buttons continues to bark like a rabid dog.

Gwyneth charges toward Roman with her fireplace poker.

"Please!" Roman begs, "Ma'am, I just want to ask you something!"

He pauses for a brief moment as he watches her come closer. Her rage and irritability says it all. She looks like a mad woman. She looks like she hasn't slept in days. She looks filthy. Above all, she looks exhausted.

Roman makes a run for it.

Gwyneth clicks her tongue. Buttons makes a run for it; chasing after Roman.

If this situation right now taught Roman anything, it would be to never step foot into the woods alone knowing full well that a crazy woman lived there. He learned his lesson. He should've listened to his sister. Marybeth told him to never go inside of this restricted area by himself. She begged him not to dwell on this woman's past or even her future.

She begged him not to go alone…. EVER!

Roman sprints through the woods with Buttons on his heels. The dog is barking as he nips at Roman's ankles. The boy is crying; running as fast as he can.

Instantly, Buttons jumps into the air like a flying Frisbee as his slobber dangles from his fangs; landing on top of Roman's back.

Roman falls to the ground.

This is not the time to give up, he thinks to himself. *Get up!*

He quickly grabs the clipboard off the ground and hits Buttons in the head. Buttons stops to whimper for a second but then immediately jumps on top of Roman; trying to bite his face.

Roman uses the clipboard as a shield as he struggles to get the dog off of him.

"Get off of me you mutt!" Roman yells.

Buttons suddenly perks his ears and turns his head toward the direction of the shack. Roman holds in his breath; unsure if he should let it out. His heart is racing. His head feels like it's ready to explode from the migraine that is forming in is brain.

Is this it? He asks himself. *Is this my time to die?*

Buttons barks in Roman's face one last time and then takes off toward the shack.

Roman lies on the ground; staring up at the dark sky.

Gwyneth would consider Buttons to be one of the best dogs in the whole entire world. He has always been extremely loyal and very well-behaved. However, the one thing that Buttons doesn't like… is his master's temper. It does scare him a bit. No, it scares him a lot. Sometimes, it scares him to the point to where he pees right where he's standing.

She can be vicious sometimes, just like this fat man with the white beard and mustache.

If only the woods could talk. They could tell Gwyneth exactly what happened to Buttons and maybe she wouldn't have such a bad temper toward people who enter her territory.

Buttons was once alone and vulnerable. If only the woods could tell her that she and her dog end up being just alike. The woods could tell her to calm down.

No, no one would have the nerve to tell her to calm down. She's angry for reasons that strangers would never understand, or care about.

No one would understand this fat man with the white beard and mustache either.

It's getting dark out as the red truck pulls up to the side of the road.

Buttons doesn't understand that this fat man is fifty-five-years-old; old enough to understand that what he's about to do is neglect and abuse.

He climbs out of the driver's side of his brand new, red Chevy truck. He opens the back door and grips the puppy into his fist. Without thinking for even a second, he then suddenly tosses the puppy into the woods like a sack of potatoes. He tosses him like he's a rag doll waiting for death to come sweep him away.

The puppy whimpers. The white-bearded man kicks his dirty, gray, hunting boots toward the poor thing; sending dirt flying into the air and into the puppy's eyes.

The white-bearded man yells, "Go on! GET! You bad ass dog! If my wife finds out, she's gonna kill me for doing this! You had to be the bad one out of the pack!"

The man kicks his boot once again. The black Labrador puppy scurries away further into the woods as his little heart pounds with fear.

Who would do such a thing? Why are some humans so cruel toward animals?

Buttons doesn't understand what is happening as he watches the white-bearded man climb back into his truck. He speeds off; not even looking back.

Sniffing the ground, the puppy whimpers as he quickly glances toward the empty road. He sniffs the air and slowly turns; making his way through the quiet woods.

He sniffs the ground as he walks; stopping to chew on a dead leaf.

His stomach growls with hunger. His mouth is dry and feels like he's dying of thirst. The white-bearded man could've at least fed him before he dumped him off like a lifeless corpse. He could've given him just a little bit of water to get by.

Sniffing the air once again, the puppy picks up his pace; trotting through the woods like he has no care in the world. He looks like a happy child skipping through a park.

He consistently sniffs the air and the ground as he looks around the wooded area. He climbs over tree stumps and crushes fallen leaves with his little puppy paws. He sniffs a wrapper of some sort by a tree and licks it with his small tongue.

He walks deep into the woods for what seems like hours. His breathing is hard and fast. The drool from his tongue drips onto the cold ground. He licks his chops; hoping to spot a critter.

The sky is completely dark but he continues to sniff the air.

Straight ahead, he suddenly approaches a cabin where a hanging plant blows in the wind from the roof of the porch. The sound of crackling fire is coming from the backyard of the cabin.

This must be it! The puppy's heart races with excitement. He sniffs the air and follows the smoke to the back of the cabin.

Who knew he would get this lucky? Maybe for once, he can finally be happy.

Trotting around the corner of the cabin, the black Labrador approaches a campfire with two men sitting in camping chairs smoking a cigar.

Hearing a noise, the fisherman turns in his chair.

"What the hell? Look at this son," the fisherman says.

His son turns in his chair and spots the puppy. "Awe look at this cute little thing! I wonder where he came from," he answers as he takes a hit of the cigar.

The son stands up and slowly searches the area. He's not completely sure if there are any humans trying to sneak upon their turf. they can't ever be too careful.

There have been times where complete strangers stumbled upon his father's place of residence and tried to rob him. A lost, hiking couple even tried to kill his father for his food and guns. No one has even come close to completing their task.

The fisherman is too smart and keen for his own good. Yes, he may be old, but he is extremely wise and intelligent. He knows how to handle vicious humans.

The fisherman's son approaches the dog and lets him sniff his cigar-smelling fingers.

"He's cute," the son continues. "Are you gonna keep him?"

The fisherman doesn't answer as he lifts his sloppy behind off the chair. The heavy stomping of his weight on the ground slightly scares the puppy, but then he immediately feels warm and fuzzy as the fisherman pets him on the head and then gently rubs his ears.

"I don't know if I want a dirty animal in my home," the fisherman answers.

"Seriously dad?" the son questions, "You need a companion. I don't always get a chance to visit. You're here all alone, all the time."

"I like it that way," the fisherman responds.

Turning from the puppy licking his chicken-greased fingers, the fisherman steps away and approaches his shed. The door makes a loud "creaking" sound and the puppy jumps. The fisherman's son soothes him as his father grabs his harpoon and a flashlight out of the shed.

"Come on puppy, let's catch us some dinner."

As the fisherman and the black Labrador make their way toward the woods, the son shouts, "I guess you're keeping him?!"

Chapter Fifteen

Turning eighteen is an exciting time for most teenagers. It's time for them to become an adult and take care of themselves. However, some teenagers end up taking care of themselves at a younger age. This happens simply because their parents are unfit, the child runs away or because one of them is suddenly abandoned inside of creepy woods.

She's not excited. In fact, she's still angry. She's angry at her mother for making her celebrate her eighteenth birthday in a forest of greens and browns. She's angry at her siblings for never having the balls to come look for her. She's angry at every single person who steps foot inside of her woods.

HER woods. Her territory.

It's been six years of being alone. But, thankfully she's not anymore. This thought does at least make her feel somewhat grateful. It makes her even smile behind her T-shirt mask every once in a while. Finding a companion can truly change a person for the better.

But it hasn't for her lately for some reason. She can't shake this angry feeling.

She's even angry at squirrels for trying to scatter away from her. She's angry at birds that fly over her head as they taunt her. The sharp tip of the harpoon usually flies through the air, but then misses those damn birds by an inch. Gwyneth swears she can hear laughter from their beaks. Of course, she's become delusional in some sense. She knows they're not laughing at her but sometimes she hears her mother's scratchy voice inside of her head, "Those damn birds are laughing at you because you're stupid."

Sometimes, Gwyneth even believes that statement. Inside of her head, she even catches herself thanking her mother for the honesty. Usually, she can shake the negativity from her mind, but lately, she's been thinking about the people who claimed to have "loved" her.

She's been thinking about her siblings a lot lately. Sometimes, she even wishes that her siblings were stuck in the woods with her. They could live happily ever after in her shack.

But, she knows that will never happen. And that's why she's incredibly angry.

Angry at the world as she trudges through the woods with Peyton's old, "NO HUNTING," sign gripped inside of her gloved hand. Her harpoon rests quietly on her back.

She can see the road in the distance. Her heart skips a beat as she spots two hunters pulled over on the side of the road in a red truck. From what she can tell, they're dressed in bright orange vests. She understands these kinds of people. They hunt for animals, just like her. She understands from learning the bad habits of that fat fisherman.

Fifty-five-year-old, John Roland, and his buddy, fifty-three-year-old, Ray Smith, climb out of the truck. John is a big man as well; making Gwyneth's heart skip a beat. He reminds her too much of that sloppy fisherman; dumb-looking and mean.

"I have to piss like a race horse!" John shouts.

Gwyneth quickly hunkers behind a tree; stepping on a branch and a pile of dead leaves. She holds in her breath from fear.

Not of fear for almost coming into contact with other human beings. But, in fear for being so close to the road in six years. She doesn't come this far out of her territory. This is new to her and she had a sinking feeling before she left, that she shouldn't wander this far from the shack.

John finishes urinating and searches the woods as he zips the zipper to his green hunting pants. His green boots are caked in dried mud.

"Hey Ray!" he shouts to his friend, "I think I just heard something. Might be a deer. Or possibly a dog…"

"Why the heck would it be a dog?" Ray asks as he inhales the rest of his cigarette. He flicks the butt of the cigarette onto the dirt and puts it out with his boot.

John whispers to himself, "You never know what can happen in these woods."

John hurriedly jogs toward the truck and opens the back door. He pulls out his hunting rifle.

Gwyneth hasn't learned much in the past six years, but she has learned that people who carry hunting rifles are people who look for animals to kill. They mostly kill deer, but she isn't surprised if this fat man would slip up and shoot a dog or a cat.

Ray is shocked to find John so adamant about following a sound. "We don't have time for that right now. My wife is going to kill me. We're already late dropping off the dog cage to her sister's house. Supper is surely ready."

"Do you do everything your wife says? I'm going to hunt," John responds.

"No, but you should. You're always in trouble with your wife."

John chuckles.

The big red farm sits on the opposite side of the road; engulfed in a huge corn field. Black shutters display over the windows. A newly built deck wraps around the whole entire house. A homemade wreath containing sunflowers and roses is placed neatly and centered in the middle of the front door. A giant red porch swing sways in the cold breeze.

The owner of the farm is perched inside of his corn field like a hawk. He's standing on an upside-down bucket that was filled with corn. The corn now lay strewn over the ground; looking up at their owner as if they're asking why they were dumped out of the bucket.

He spots Ray from the field as he looks suspiciously through the scope of his rifle; pointing it at Ray's head. He suddenly eases his anger as he recognizes his friend.

"Hey!" the owner shouts, "Ray Smith! Is that you?"

Ray turns away from John as the stubborn man enters the woods. Ray spots the owner of the farm waving with his rifle. He excitedly waves back.

"Yes it is! How's it going Morgan Wildfire?"

Gwyneth watches John enter the woods like a snake as he grips his rifle in both hands. She continues to hide behind the tree as her sweat slides down from her forehead to her mask.

She can't get caught now. Her life here isn't over yet. She has so much to learn and so much to do here with her friend. She can't let anyone take her dog. She thinks that people come into her woods to steal her shack and her dog. She thinks people want to kill her and steal every item that she has fought to find. She simply cannot have anyone hurt her lifelong friend.

Gwyneth ever-so-slowly begins to pull out her ten inch sewing needle from inside her glove.

"Hey John!" she can hear Ray shout from the field. "Come say hello to Morgan. His wife made some brownies and coffee. We sure could use some right now! It's been a long day hunting… what do you say?"

John whispers to himself once again, "Ahhh bullshit. Fine."

He exits the woods as he looks over his shoulder. A light breeze makes him shiver.

He stares at the woods suspiciously for a moment before he places his rifle back into the truck. Taking one last sweep of the area with his tired eyes, he turns and crosses the street; giving Morgan a handshake and Ray a pat on the back.

Gwyneth exhales a sigh of relief and then quickly places the, "NO HUNTING," sign into the wet mud. She pulls out her hammer from her coat pocket and quickly and quietly pounds the sign into the ground. She feels her heart beat like a drum with every pound. The sound vibrates in her ears and her head feels like it's about to explode.

She doesn't understand why she's in a hurry. She doesn't understand why she's suddenly afraid of seeing these men. She's witnessed people enter her territory before in the past and she's never been scared of them… EVER.

She's strong and full of skills that she's never imagined she would ever be able to accomplish. She never thought that she would be able to take on life in general. She knows that she can take on these hunters. She knows that they will be dead in a heartbeat if they come back and try to kill her or Buttons. She knows that she can handle them.

It's too much pressure. That's what it is. She's been under a lot of stress. She's having a hard time concentrating on finding food and supplies. The thoughts of her family haunt her brain. Her dog is hungry and is in constant need of something to eat.

She skips eating for days on end just so that Buttons has something to fill his belly with. She's lost plenty of animals this past week because it's like her mother controls them too. Gwyneth can hear her mother's voice in her brain every single day telling animals to run. It seems as though these animals can hear her in some way, shape or form.

After placing the hammer back inside of her pocket, Gwyneth

searches the area. She no longer sees the men but she eyes the truck that sits parked alongside the trees.

She knows that she was called "stupid" for the first twelve years of her life by her mother, but now, she calls herself "stupid" in her brain for what she's about to do.

Sometimes she likes a challenge though. Sometimes she likes to be daring.

And sometimes she likes to do things that give her an adrenaline rush.

Gwyneth looks around the woods and listens to the quiet breeze. It slightly flips the fur hood of her coat; exposing her straggly black hair. She quickly places the hood back onto her head as she makes her way toward the red truck.

As she approaches it, she spots John, Ray and Morgan entering the farmhouse. Her heart is racing once again. It seems like that's all her heart has been doing lately. She's become a marshmallow. She's become too soft for her own good. She's becoming a scaredy-cat and she truly cannot wrap her brain around this discovery. She's confusing herself... about her own self.

She waits an extra minute as she stares at the farmhouse; expecting the men to come barreling out of the door as they run toward her with guns blazing.

She quickly climbs into the bed of the truck and immediately spots a dog cage and plastic bags. Her eyes light up like a Christmas tree.

Her happiness overwhelms her brain and melts her heart. The excitement is uncontrollable. Her smile pains her cheeks. She feels like she's hit the jackpot.

As she glances back at the farmhouse, she slowly lowers the tailgate of the truck. Slightly struggling, she tries to unload the dog cage. It's too heavy for her liking.

Well, this is why you like to stay in shape, she tells herself.

She knows all about that particular saying.

"Stay in shape," her mother used to tell her. "You don't want to grow up fat. Then you won't be able to do anything. You won't be able to move. Do you want to be fat Gwyneth? Huh? Is that something that you look forward to doing? I'm sure you will grow up fat. You like chips and cookies way too much. I'm sure you will gain some extra pounds."

She was such a horrible beast of a mother.

Gwyneth shakes those thoughts out of her mind as she pulls on the cage with all her might.

I need this, she thinks. *I need this for Buttons.*

She jumps down to the ground and then grips the sides of the cage with her fingers. As she lifts it upward, she pulls, dragging the cage through the bed of the truck. She notices a few scratches on the bed behind the cage and shrugs her shoulders.

The cage reaches to the tailgate and she pulls; making an "Ahhh" sound from deep inside her throat. She picks up the cage like, "The Hulk," and places it onto the ground.

Her breathing is hard and fast. She takes a moment to catch her breath as she watches for the men once again. She surely doesn't want caught now. She almost killed herself trying to get the damn thing out of the truck. She will put up a fight if she has to.

After letting her heart settle a bit, she takes the plastic bags and wraps the handles around her fist. Gripping the sides of the cage, she drags it into the woods.

No one said she was smart. But, she definitely feels smart. She feels accomplished. She feels excited for her dog. She feels happy. She feels like she's about to get away with it.

Now, she just has to worry about how long John and Ray will stay inside of the farmhouse.

She suddenly turns into that scaredy-cat once again. Her heart skips a beat as she imagines the men running toward her with their weapons. She does have her harpoon that she can use to defend herself, but, she still feels this sense of fear. There's two of them and one of her. And, what if the owner of the farm comes after her as well?

Well, he shouldn't. He should stay in his cozy home and tend to his wife.

After a few minutes, she approaches her "NO HUNTING" sign and takes a break. She peeks toward the farmhouse but she can't see much from the distance. She thinks she's far enough from the road to start rummaging through the plastic bags.

She pulls the items out of the bags one by one; her excitement exploding like shooting stars. She smiles at the packages of dog bones, a dog whistle, a small chalkboard with chalk and two baby dolls. She grips the dolls with shaking fingers and then hugs them tight against her chest.

Her eyes light up with happiness. She can't believe what she has found… well… STOLE.

Remembering where the items came from, she quickly glances toward the farmhouse once again. The truck still sits in its place on the side of the road.

Hurriedly, she places the items back into the plastic bags and wraps them around her fist once again. Gripping the sides of the cage, she continues dragging the dog cage toward the direction of her shack.

The cage is extremely heavy and she's running out of breath. She doesn't want to lose hope. She doesn't want to lose her strength. She must reach the shack in case those men come looking for her. She will feel safe there. She will be more prepared.

As eager as she is, she loses her strength and plops her butt onto the ground. Even though she feels defeated, she still feels a glimmer of hope in her heart. She will get this thing to her shack one way or another. She just has to take a break and get her breathing back to normal.

Normal. She's never had normalcy in her life. She's never felt normal. She's never looked normal and she sure hasn't smelled normal; especially in the past six years. At this point, she should know the ins and outs of these woods. She should know how to take care of herself.

Unlike her mother, who didn't know how to take care of her children. Gwyneth believes with all of her heart that she would've been able to take care of her siblings. Well, to a certain point. She knows that they would've had to take care of her with certain issues like reading, doing math and writing. She gets by with what she knows but it would've been nice to learn beyond what she has experienced in life so far.

She suddenly feels exhausted. All of the energy floats above her head like a spirit leaving their dead body. She closes her bright blue eyes but fights to keep them open.

They're blurry as she looks around the woods trying to spot her siblings. She's looking for her family as if they will pop out behind a tree. She's expecting her brother to shout, "Found you!" as if they're playing, "Hide and Seek."

She closes her eyes as a soft cloud floats inside of her head. She knows that she can't fall asleep but her body says otherwise. She is so tired.

She's tired of feeling exhausted. She's tired of thinking about her family. She has to get them out of her mind. But, she can't as she falls into a deep sleep; remembering that time of heartache and pain to the awful news that she and her siblings were told.

As a twelve-year-old, it would have been useful for Gwyneth to have that same type of strength and endurance as a grown twenty-four-year-old woman. Unfortunately, at twelve-years-old, she had no strength over her mother's temper.

She was a child. She was a lonely and vulnerable child who depended on her five-year-old twin brother and sister. She might as well have been five-years-old herself.

She acted like it. She looked like it. Her brain thought like a five-year-old. That was something that Gwyneth could never stomach.

However, she surprisingly understood that she was different from her siblings. They always tried their best to make her feel special and smarter than them. They tried to make her feel happy and loved. They wanted her to believe in herself.

One day, she finally did.

Gwyneth sits on a broken chair at her crooked desk inside her bedroom. Her twin siblings are sitting on her urine-smelling bed as they color a rainbow in their coloring book. They watch Gwyneth's tongue hang out as she concentrates on cutting two pieces of red yarn.

They giggle as her teeth chomp down on her tongue as if they are a pair of scissors.

On the desk, lie two gold buttons.

Gwyneth slips the end of a piece of yarn inside a gold button. She tries to tie a knot but she can't; making herself struggle with sudden anger. Frustrated, she sighs.

The twins stop giggling but they quickly look at her and then back to their coloring page.

Gwyneth ties the knot and smiles. She glances up at the twins and smiles at them. They notice her happiness and giggle once again. They turn back to their book and color a couple trees green and then the sun yellow.

Gwyneth continues her work and slides the tip of the second piece of yarn inside of the second gold button and then immediately ties a knot.

"Get your asses in here kids! NOW!" the children can hear Ruby shouting from the kitchen.

The twins panic in fear as Gwyneth stands and quickly grabs her homemade necklaces. She hurriedly places them inside of her dresser.

She takes the twins' hands. They look at each other for a moment. They seem to be scared for their lives. They're scared of what is to come and they have no idea what is coming.

They take deep breaths and exhale at the same time. Then together, they leave Gwyneth's bedroom feeling a fear like they've never felt before.

When they enter the kitchen, they sit down at the table. Ruby stands over them like a giant tarantula standing over their prey. She's ready to bite and chomp down on their tiny heads.

She looks angry and exhausted as she inhales her cigarette. She rudely blows the smoke into the children's faces. Gwyneth's brother waves his hand through the air as he coughs. His twin sister stares at Ruby with hatred in her light-blue eyes. She's teary-eyed and her face is red as an apple. She has this sudden urge to punch her mother in the face.

"We're havin' visitors today so you best be on your best behavior. I need you all to tell the woman that I don't yell or hit you," Ruby tells them as she glares straight at Gwyneth. "You got that?" she asks the poor girl.

The twins are confused but they nod in acknowledgement. Gwyneth glares back at Ruby. She fully understands that their mother is asking for them to lie.

Ruby continues, "Did you hear me girl? Or can't you hear either? Dumb mute. Don't be givin' anybody signs or signals either. Don't be writin' anything to them on your little papers."

Gwyneth nods as she looks at her siblings as they whimper. They whimper in fear. They whimper from pain that this beast of a woman has unleashed on all three of them.

They whimper as they watch Ruby stand eye-to-eye to Gwyneth. Ruby has no emotion and no sympathy. She stands with her back straight and her small boobs perk up as if they were just told, "ATTTEENNTION!"

"The lady will be here any minute," Ruby says as she stares into the eyes of a future serial killer.

Gwyneth's eyes pop open as if a light-bulb flickers inside of her brain. She glances around the woods and swallows hard. Her mouth is dry as her mask blocks her breathing. Her throat suddenly feels sore. She wonders if she was snoring.

She's wakened herself up plenty of times from hearing her own snoring. Just like right now in this moment. That light-bulb must've been her wake up call.

She panics as she remembers what she was doing. She quickly glances at the dog cage and the plastic bags filled with her goodies.

She searches the area and stops to listen for any human contact. All she hears is the swaying of the trees. After thirty seconds, she hurriedly grabs her items and heads toward the shack.

Chapter Sixteen

John Roland is indeed a big man. He was a big child as well; bullied for his weight in school. His mother used to hold him tight after getting ready for bed as he cried in her arms.

He looked different than most kids. He's always been taller with broad shoulders. However, as the years of bullying continued on, no one dared to try to fight him. His size is what helped him survive his school years. Everyone knew that he wasn't scared to throw a punch.

As a fifty-five-year-old, he still isn't scared.

He waves goodbye to Morgan and his wife and returns to his truck. As he approaches it with a confused expression upon his face, he notices that his tailgate is lowered, the tampered grass on the ground and the drag marks that are covered in mud.

"What the?" he asks himself as he glances back at Ray giving Morgan a handshake.

Turning back, he searches the woods with suspicious green eyes. He holds in his breath as if he's waiting for someone to pop out from behind a tree. He embraces himself for the impact.

But it doesn't come.

After thirty seconds of holding in his breath, he blows it out slowly and quietly. He then follows the drag marks to the edge of the woods.

Panicking, a thought crosses his mind. Realization has hit his brain as if someone suddenly punched him in the head.

He quickly turns back to the bed of the truck and notices that the dog cage and plastic bags are gone. He immediately feels the heat creep up to his cheeks and forehead.

The anger feels incredibly overwhelming as he sees flashes of light in front of him. It's like his eyeballs were struck with lightning. The anger engulfs his brain as his whole entire body shakes. He's ready to fight.

He's ready to kill.

As he retrieves his rifle from the backseat of the truck, he shouts, "Damn thieves! Punk ass kids!"

Angrily, he enters the woods unprepared and full of rage.

John was an angry teenager. The bullying and abuse from both students and teachers had taken over his life. It made him mentally unstable. He was unable to control his anger anytime someone said something mean and nasty to him. His teachers even made fun of his grades. They would call him, "stupid" and "weird."

John's mother was a single mother and his anger had taken its toll on her as well. She tried taking him to a therapist. He would talk for ten minutes and then walk right out of the office with no explanation as to why he was leaving.

She tried to put him on medication but he refused to take the pills. He would flush them down the toilet and laugh in his mother's face. She would cry about how expensive they were. He would shrug his shoulders and continue to laugh. On a daily basis, he would take his anger out on his mother until one day she had enough.

She kicked him out at the age of seventeen and he hasn't seen her since.

She's eighty-years-old living at a nursing home diagnosed with Alzheimer's disease. He doesn't know that though and he probably wouldn't care.

John stomps his dirty green boots through the woods like he's the "Jolly Green Giant." He points his rifle at every little sound; a squirrel scurrying up a tree and the leaves swaying in the breeze. He snaps branches with his big feet along the way; scaring himself.

He passes the "NO HUNTING" sign.

Laughing, he snorts like a pig. "No hunting? Ha! Come on out you little punks!"

He stops to look through the scope of his rifle as he searches the woods. Deep down, he actually hopes that he stumbles across a deer. Maybe even a bear.

His luck of finding deer on a scale between zero and ten has been a strong zero. He hasn't shot a good, solid buck in two years. Ray was lucky enough to shoot a white-tailed deer a week ago. At least Ray is a good friend and shared his Venison meat with John and his wife.

John chuckles. He wouldn't have shared his Venison with Ray even if he begged for it.

"That's why I'm going to hell," John says out loud.

He continues to walk but slows his pace. He's tired. He's been walking for what seems like hours. He knows it hasn't been that long but he's smart enough to know that he is deep inside of these woods. He's even smarter to realize that he shouldn't have traveled this far from the road.

He's terrible with directions. Remembering this characteristic of himself, he's suddenly scared of the thought of being lost. This is not an ideal place for being lost. He normally has his compass handy but he was so angry that he completely forgot about it.

"That's what you get dumb ass," he calls himself.

As he takes a few more steps with his big feet, he sees the shack in the distance.

"Gotcha punks!" he yells.

Taking one last step, John suddenly trips over a piece of wire attached between two trees. He falls forward but tries to save himself from the impact. He twists his body and lands on his back; staring up at the cloudy sky.

"What the hell is going on?" he asks.

The jingling cans abruptly interrupt Buttons' nap. He growls; glancing over at Gwyneth sitting at the picnic table. The dolls that she found inside of those plastic bags are held tight in between her gloved hands. She's touching an eyeball to the red-haired, freckled doll with her cold finger-tip as she listens to that disturbing sound vibrating her brain.

That sound is extremely disturbing to her brain. That means someone or something has come too close for comfort. Sometimes, when the sound pounds her brain like a hammer, she mouths a silent prayer as she wishes for those jingling cans to be a bear or a deer.

Sometimes, it's not an animal. And sometimes, she has to protect her territory.

She stops playing with her doll and slowly looks over at Buttons.

Clicking her tongue, she snatches the harpoon off the table and places it on her back.

John slowly sits upward from the cold ground as he feels a shooting pain crawl up his back. He cries out as he tries to get on his knees to inspect the wire he just tripped over.

"What are wires doing in the woods?" he asks dumbfounded.

That's how he feels… DUMB. Dumb for charging through the woods like a mad man. Dumb for thinking that at fifty-five-years-old, he can take on a person that he doesn't even know.

He's not even sure if there's a group of people. He has now put himself in a bad situation that he should've never done. He always acts like he's big and bad. He always thinks that he has all kinds of power to control people. He thinks that he's a bad ass.

Well, not right now as he cries like a little Bitch; holding his back in pain.

He isn't sure what to do but at this point, he doesn't want to give up. He glances back toward the direction of the road as he picks up his dropped rifle.

Turning back to the shack in the distance, he shrugs his shoulders and continues toward it; whistling as he walks. He's trying make himself feel as if this is no big deal.

But, his heart pumps faster and it feels like he's having a heart attack. He's never felt so scared in his life. He imagines a group of kids running out of the shack and attacking him.

As he continues to walk, he peeks through the scope of his rifle and spots the shack.

He suddenly stops; looking confused with a pale face. He looks like he might vomit. He's sweating profusely as he wipes his white beard with his freezing cold hand.

His fear has taken over his body. He feels sick to his stomach. He's shaking; unable to keep a grip on his rifle. He tries to focus on his surroundings but he can't seem to concentrate.

He suddenly hears the low growl of an angry dog behind him.

John whirls around; scared shitless and confused.

Buttons aggressively barks; exposing his baby sharp teeth.

Then, Gwyneth approaches John as she points the harpoon at his head. She watches Buttons. He seems angrier than she's ever seen him. She looks at John with a confused look upon her face as she watches the fat man smile at Buttons.

"I can't believe it! Puppy is still here! You're safe!"

Buttons continues to bark and growl as he creeps closer toward John; taking baby steps with his paws. Drool drips from his tongue as he licks his chops.

Gwyneth watches Buttons as he exposes his fangs like a rabid dog. He's obviously angry at the sight of this man and Gwyneth has no idea why. She's never witnessed her dog act like he's ready to bite the jugular of a stranger.

They've come across a few humans since she found him that day at the fisherman's pond, but, he's never acted so mean and aggressive. He looks like he's ready to kill.

John raises his hands in surrender. "Look lady," he says, "I don't want any trouble. I'll just be on my way now."

As he turns, Buttons suddenly pounces on the old man; knocking him to the ground. As Buttons chomps on his boot and ankle, John yelps in pain. Tackling him, he bites the man's arm.

Gwyneth clicks her tongue but Buttons ignores her. She then slips off her fingerless-glove and places the tips of her fingers inside of her mouth; whistling long and loud.

The dog stops; glaring at Gwyneth like she just stole a piece of steak from him.

He whimpers as she clicks her tongue once again; putting her glove back on.

Looking back at John and then glancing back at his master; Buttons then takes off toward the shack. His disappointment burns deep inside his belly.

Gwyneth takes John's rifle and motions with her head for him to follow her.

"Screw you Bitch!" he shouts.

But, he instantly regrets it as he watches her eyes fill with anger.

Gwyneth aggressively reaches her arm behind her back and grabs her harpoon. She places the sharp edge on John's cheek and then slowly slides the tip upward toward his eyeball. The tip slightly touches his right eye.

Holding in his breath, he leans forward on his elbows as he suddenly smacks the harpoon with his big bear claw. Gwyneth angrily hits him over the head. Lying on the ground, he cries out in pain and curses under his breath.

Gwyneth watches him as she points the harpoon at his head once again; pressing the tip on the injury she just caused. She clicks her tongue once again at John and motions with her head toward the shack.

While he lies in a fetal position and whimpers like a baby, Gwyneth angrily grips John's arm and pulls him toward her; trying to drag him. His heavy weight pulls a muscle in her neck.

Her anger explodes into thousands of shattering pieces of glass. All she sees is red and all she wants to do is kill him. Her brain flashes with lightning as if it's trying to send her messages from hell. There's no stopping her now. Her anger has taken over her body.

She wants to throw this man into that black hole. That serves him right for coming onto her territory. When will people ever learn?

Digging the harpoon's sharp edge into the fat man's side, he cries out in pain.

John slowly stands up as his knees buckle. Gwyneth grips onto his heavy orange coat and pulls him toward the direction of the shack. He limps in pain from Buttons' bite.

As they approach the run-down building, Gwyneth spots Buttons lying on the ground in front of the shack door. As the dog spots John, he growls.

Gwyneth gets this sinking feeling that this guy is definitely a bad guy and somehow, someway, he was involved with her dog. She had every intention of letting him go because she did steal his stuff. She feels as though it's her fault for him stepping into her territory.

She knows that he's the fat man from the farmhouse. And she knows that he has another friend who might get the courage to come search for him. That could create more chaos than she anticipated. She's not ready for more chaos. She's excited to play with her new toys and set up Buttons' new cage. This guy just had to ruin her plans.

Maybe I'll just let Buttons eat him, she thinks to herself.

After staring at John for ten seconds, she shakes her head and chuckles. *No way. He's mine.*

Gwyneth pushes him in front of a tree and he tries to catch his breath; leaning against it with his pained back. He winces as the sharp edges of the tree digs into the middle of his back.

Breathing hard, John says, "Well, I'm glad you found that mutt. He was always the rotten one. Seems to… fit well with you. You're a rotten apple that's fallen from the tree."

Swiftly, Gwyneth points the harpoon at John's head once again.

"Is that the best you got?" John asks, breathlessly laughing.

Buttons barks loudly and Gwyneth turns to glare at him.

"See," John continues, "He doesn't listen. Damn mutt. And by the way… hasn't anyone ever taught you to never turn your back on your enemy?"

Gwyneth is confused; turning to Buttons for help as if he completely understands what John just asked. Buttons is unaware of his master's glare as he slowly approaches John with teeth exposed. His drooling is out of control and drips onto the ground like spilled soup.

John is sweating and has become sick-looking. His face is pale as he tries to hold back his vomit. He definitely doesn't want to vomit. He's scared that the crazy woman will beat him again for doing it. He doesn't want beat. His head is pounding from her beating him the first time. It's pounding as if she's banging a drum on the top of his head.

Blood dribbles down the sides of his temples. It oozes that pretty color red that she loves so much. Red is the color of blood. Red is the color of hell.

Her two favorite things.

"I don't feel too well," John whines as he leans forward. "You should let me lie down to catch my breath." He suddenly vomits.

Stepping away from him, Gwyneth places her harpoon and John's rifle onto the picnic table. She trudges toward the shack as she clicks her tongue at Buttons. He runs inside almost tripping her. She glances back at John as she quietly closes the front door.

It doesn't close all the way of course because it's still broke, but she peeks through the crack of the door as she watches John stop vomiting. He looks around the woods as if he's looking for an escape plan. He wipes the leftover vomit from his lips with the sleeve of his coat.

Gwyneth thinks about what he said to her as she continues watching him.

Don't turn your back on your enemy.

She always turns her back on her enemy. But, her enemy is normally in a state of panic and cannot escape because they're tied up.

She thinks about this as Buttons nudges her gloved hand with his nose. She bends down to his level and rubs his ears. He whimpers and looks at her with those sad puppy-dog eyes.

She lowers her T-shirt mask and gives him a kiss on his head. Buttons licks her lips and then her nose. She giggles like a school-girl before replacing the mask over her mouth.

She approaches her desk and opens her container. She stares at the contents for a brief moment. Sewing has all she's ever known. Sewing is something that took many years to accomplish. She used to hate it because of her mother. But, it has grown on her like a wart. She never wants to get rid of that wart. And she will never stop sewing as long as she is alive.

The sound of the gooeyness of her victims' blood sends shivers down her spine. The texture of their eyeballs on the tips of her fingers makes her feel warm inside. Their empty sockets remind her of that black hole. She loves to stare at the emptiness as if the eyes will suck her inside like a vacuum and spin her in circles.

She's giving herself an adrenaline rush. Her heart pounds with excitement as it beats faster and faster as if it's running to catch a beautiful butterfly.

Turning her attention back to the container, she pulls out fishing wire.

Once finished, she steps outside to see John sitting on the ground and slumped over a tree stump. He hears the door slamming shut and quickly sits up; leaning his head against a tree.

"I think you really messed up my head. You didn't have to hit me so hard," he whines.

Gwyneth grabs the rifle off the picnic table and approaches John as if it's the first time meeting him. He could have some kind of trick up his sleeve and Gwyneth is always cautious.

She kneels down to his level and lowers the rifle.

"Hasn't anyone ever taught you to never lower your weapon?"

Gwyneth peeks down at the rifle gripped in her hands. Slowly, she looks back up at John.

Suddenly, John thrusts both of his big, bear claws around Gwyneth's throat; choking her.

She drops the rifle; kneeling on her knees, gasping for air and gripping his wrists with her fingers. She struggles; choking as she feels vomit creep up her throat. The smell of his vomit is making her sick. She imagines him throwing up over and over in her mind as he squeezes harder.

She digs the tips of her finger-nails through his skin of both his wrists.

He wails in pain as the skin breaks; exposing that beautiful red blood.

Buttons dramatically leaps out of the doorway of the shack and sprints toward Gwyneth and John. Without a thought in the world, he bites down onto John's arm. John lets go of Gwyneth's throat as he screams in terror. Buttons attacks him; biting his face, his head and the fat man's neck. He then bites his ears and nose.

Gwyneth quickly runs behind the tree that John leans against and wraps the fishing wire around the front of his neck; tying a knot behind the tree.

She clicks her tongue. Buttons suddenly stops biting at his victim and sits nicely on the ground. The black Labrador watches Gwyneth as she bends down to John's level.

He's gurgling. The wire has cut through his neck and blood is slowly oozing from its wound. His eyes stare straight ahead; unfocused and bloodshot.

Gwyneth taps her fingers on John's chest and then points to Buttons. She gives Buttons a thumbs-up. She then points to her ears and then points to Buttons.

My dog listens. Bitch.

John slowly dies. Gwyneth's eyes smile as she places the tip her finger on his head wound; licking the blood as she slips her finger inside of her mask. *Oh that beautiful color of red.*

Chapter Seventeen

Ray Smith is a tall and skinny man with a nice, clean, red beard. He loves to grow his beard super long for the winter time because his most favorite thing to do is to go hunting with his best buddy, John Roland. Ray is the complete opposite of his friend. Ray is nice to people and he treats everyone with respect. He loves his wife and kids. He loves to make them happy.

He always says, "Happy wife, happy life."

John Roland would always laugh at his buddy and say, "You're whipped man."

If being whipped means being alive with a stable home and a loving family, so be it. That's what Ray loves. That's what Ray wants. He doesn't want a miserable family like John has.

That's only because John is miserable himself. He makes his family miserable but he blames it all on them. He never wants to take any responsibility for his actions or words.

Ray usually shrugs off the complaints that roll off John's tongue. John does love his family, he just doesn't love himself. He never has.

Ray has told the man plenty of times that he should be a single man living in a bachelor's pad. John always laughs as if it's a joke. One time, he even acknowledged that statement by agreeing and saying, "I've made some regrets in my life."

Ray immediately regrets the fact that his buddy left ahead of him as he returns to John's truck. Morgan is at his heels; looking around the quiet area.

John is gone and this irritates Ray's soul.

Ray rarely becomes angry or irritated at people. When he does, it's always toward his friend.

"Great. Now where did this asshole go?" Ray asks with frustration.

Morgan looks smug but remains calm as he continues to search the area with his questionable eyes. His heart suddenly races as if it's running down the dirt road. He wishes that he could dig up that dirt road that ends at his farmhouse in order for people to stop coming down to this area. He's sick of seeing hunters and even strangers passing by as if they have something up their sleeve.

Of course, Morgan always looks at people as if they have something up their sleeve. Ninety-nine percent of the time… they do. There is absolutely no reason for people to drive down this dead end. There's no reason for anyone to take a hike or walk in this area. It's nothing but fields, trees and woods.

HIS fields. HIS trees. And HIS woods.

There are fields that lead to nothing. There are trees that sway in the breeze and mind their own business. And the woods have become a devil's playground.

Morgan feels no sympathy or empathy for John. He was warned not to go in the woods. Morgan is one-hundred percent sure that's where the man went.

"Probably spotted a deer again. Hey, you go on ahead. If he shows up, I'll take him home," Morgan suggests as he turns to look at his farmhouse.

Turning back, he watches Ray's eyes dart back and forth from one tree to another.

Ray eagerly nods. He has no interest in waiting anymore. "Well thank you farmer! I'll give you a call sometime! It was great seeing you and your wife again. Take care!"

Ray gives Morgan a handshake and then a pat on the shoulder.

As Morgan stares into the woods, he says, "No problem. It was great seeing you."

Hurriedly, Ray climbs into John's Chevy truck and speeds off.

Morgan swallows hard and smiles as he notices tampered mud and grass. He bends at the knees and places his fingers onto the drag marks on the ground.

Whispering, he says, "Fear. Her. Wrath."

After twelve years, Ruby Glacier stands at the edge of the woods as she glances around the area; tears in her tired eyes.

Tears. After all these years! She cries.

She cries up into the cold, snowy sky; lifting her head as she allows the flakes of snow drop into her pupils. She stares up into the

151

clouds as she remembers that her daughter would be twenty-four-years-old this year.

Twenty-four. A grown woman.

Ruby closes her eyes; the wet snow melting inside of her eyelids. She imagines gripping twelve-year-old Gwyneth by her shoulders and shaking her like a rag doll.

Those were the days when she was able to beat her children. Those were the days when she was able to scream and shout and boss them around. Those were the days when she didn't let them bathe every single day. Those were the days when she thought that she was the best mother in the whole world.

Those were the days when Ruby Glacier was delusional.

She's older now. She's seen a therapist. She's gotten mental help.

She's been put on medication. She's been living a life that she never imagined that she would have lived. She's been thinking about her oldest daughter for twelve years.

Ruby slowly enters the woods.

She's wearing a gray Eskimo coat with the fur on the hood and bright, blue, snow boots.

She glances behind her shoulder and then down at the snowy ground; staring at her boot prints as if she's never seen such a thing.

Her heart pounds loud and hard like a hammer. She feels butterflies in the pit of her stomach. A sudden headache forms at the base of her skull as the cold wind blows through the area. Her hood flies off her head but she immediately replaces it; holding on to it for dear life.

Searching the woods as tears slip down her cheeks, she whispers, "Do whatever is necessary to survive."

She takes a step forward but then stops and looks around. She has no idea why she came back. Deep down, she wants to find her daughter in here. But then again, she doesn't want to see her. If she does, then that means she has been living in these woods for twelve years.

And it would be all her fault.

Her fault for abandoning her precious, special, child. It's her fault for leaving her daughter unprepared and sick inside of a dark forest.

There's no way that she's living in these woods.

There's no way that Gwyneth has been by herself this whole entire time.

As Ruby reminisces about her children, she walks deeper into the woods; not even realizing how far she's walked. She didn't even realize that she continued walking in the first place.

She stops for a moment as she breathes in the cold air.

She feels this sudden fear. These woods smell of death and decay. There's some type of gloom that surrounds Ruby like an orb. She feels sadness and depression. She hasn't been depressed in years. Stepping into these woods has brought back feelings that she hasn't felt in a long time…. not since she's had her children in her home.

She feels this anger suddenly engulfing her mind. She's shaking as if the trees have taken her by the shoulders; inflicting pain with their sharp and pointy bark.

She knows that she should just turn around and leave right at this instant. She knows that she needs to climb back into her car and never come back.

She knows that her daughter is not here.

She's wasting her time and energy. She has more important things to do. She needs to go back home and get ready for her night shift at work.

But she can't. The trees are stopping her as they blow in the wind; whispering her name.

Ruby imagines branches pulling themselves out of the ground and then clinging onto her ankles; tripping her and making her land on her face.

The snow has picked up. The snowflakes land softly onto the palm of her hand. She stares at the crystal shape as it melts from her sweat.

She forgot her gloves in the car.

This realization makes her turn her body away… but the whispering in the wind makes her turn back; staring into the abyss.

Her eyes are like two black holes. She feels possessed somehow.

She can't shake this feeling of dread and fear. She can't seem to go back to her car. Her feet are frozen in their spot. It's like something is making her walk forward instead of back.

It's your own damn mind you idiot, she thinks to herself. *You're only scaring yourself.*

But she continues forward; walking deeper into the woods.

As she observes the area, she trips over a wire; falling to the ground and twisting her ankle. Lying in the snow while whimpering a prayer, Ruby holds her pained ankle with her cold hands.

You should've turned around, she thinks to herself. *You should've gotten back into your car!*

The shooting pain strikes her like a lightning bolt. Her heart tightens as she holds in her breath. She cradles her ankle like a baby as she pulls down her sock to take a look.

It is swollen and tender to the touch.

Ruby cries out in pain as she rocks back and forth on the snowy ground.

"What the hell am I going to do now?" she asks herself.

That sound would always make Gwyneth's blood boil when she was younger. It used to make her so angry that it enabled her from focusing on a calm or rational decision.

It used to make her insane. It used to make her see red.

But after all these years, she's taught herself to control that anger. She's taught herself to control her mind. She can be a cunning and stable killer. She's learned to suppress that anger. She's learned to calm herself even if the rage still boils from inside.

And it boils. It boils like hot water in a pot. She can't help the boiling. She's tried.

The rage boils likes the internal pits of hell.

But the boiling doesn't tip over the pot anymore. It doesn't make her see red anymore. It doesn't make her brain flash bright lights inside of her eyeballs.

However, it does give her that sudden electric shock of energy throughout her whole body. It sends shivers down her spine. It gives her that adrenaline rush that swoops inside her brain like a tidal wave. The water splashes against the walls of her cerebrum and slams against her skull.

It makes her eyes smile and her knees weak.

It helps her to make rational decisions.

Well, decisions that she believes are rational.

Her behavior is something that she has learned to control. She's calm and quiet as a devious predator. She's become smart and vigilant. She hasn't let her guard down in quite some time… and she doesn't plan to.

As she stands by the picnic table with Buttons, she listens to her tin cans jingling like a bell.

It's as if the world has suddenly moved in slow motion. She just finished fixing her broken harpoon. She slowly looks up from it. The excitement in her eyes could light up a firework.

Her blood is boiling but her brain tells her to calm down. It's like a light switch flicks on; on the back of a bright, neon sign that reads: "Calm your tits."

After slowly exhaling a breath, she places the harpoon on her back and clicks her tongue at Buttons.

While she continues to cradle her ankle, Ruby tries to sit up as she inspects the wire.

"What the hell?" she asks confused.

Without applying any pressure to her twisted ankle, she tries to stand up. She leans against a tree for support to catch her breath. She stood up too fast and now she sees swirls of lightning on the ground. She feels dizzy and light-headed.

She wants to scream in pain. She wants to scream at her foolish decision. She wants to scream at that wire. And she wants to scream at whoever put it there.

She wants to scream into that person's face. She wants to tell them how stupid they are. She wants to tell them how much they've hurt her. She wants to knock their teeth out of their mouth.

"So stupid," Ruby says. "I am so stupid!"

Gwyneth steps out from behind a tree as she points the harpoon at Ruby's head. Buttons is on her heels as he growls at their new victim.

Ruby is suddenly taken aback as she presses her cold hand to her chest. Her heart sounds like galloping horses through a meadow.

She squints her fearful eyes; eyeing Gwyneth up and down like she's trash on the side of the road. Ruby watches this crazy lunatic take another slow step toward her.

Ruby swallows hard. Her eyes are suddenly filled with sadness. "Gwyneth?"

There had to be something for these five-year-old twins to do. There had to be music and games and food. They were hungry. They were bored. But they were also tired.

They hadn't slept properly in all five years of their lives. Their mother made sure of it. She made sure that they never received a good night's rest. She always made sure that they only ate once a day so they wouldn't gain too much weight.

No, they were starving. They were exhausted. But, they were still somehow bored.

They wanted to color but there weren't any coloring books or any crayons. There weren't any extra pieces of loose paper to draw trees and houses.

They just said goodbye to Lindsay. She smiled and waved. She had promised that they were going to live a better life. She promised that their mother would never hurt them again.

They sit cross-legged on the living-room floor while playing Nintendo. They're wearing matching blue sweatshirts and the necklaces that their sister made for them.

They giggle as they watch "Mario" jump into the air as the sun swoops down and bumps him. *That damn sun,* the boy thinks. "Mario" dies; making the twins laugh out loud.

A very thin woman wearing a bright pink dress takes a step into the living-room from the kitchen. She smells like strawberry soap and the kitchen smells like cinnamon.

"Her name?" the little girl asks her brother.

He shrugs his shoulders. They immediately howl with laughter.

The woman looks sad as she sits onto the couch.

"I have to talk to you kids for a minute," the woman says.

She motions with her fingers for the kids to stop playing. They drop the game controllers onto the floor and look at each other as if they are about to get into trouble. Their little hearts pound with fear. They take each other's hand as if they're walking into a snake pit.

They slowly sit down on the couch and look at the woman with sad puppy-dog eyes.

"I have bad news kids. I just got off the phone with Lindsay."

A look of confusion is on their faces.

This isn't the time for sad news. They just started to feel comfortable. They just started to feel happy and loved. They were getting used to this new life so quick. They're five-years-old; easily adjustable to a better life. It's something that they have been wishing for. This is something they have been preparing for. They like feeling happy.

"I have just been told that your mother and sister have been killed. Lindsay just gave me the news. She said if you need to see her for support, she would come over tomorrow evening," the woman tells them. Her face is red from the heat inside of the kitchen.

The strong cinnamon smell wafts inside the living-room like a spirit brushing past their shoulders. The little girl shivers as she cries into her brother's arms.

The woman is awkward and watches the children cry loudly. As she scoots closer to them, she fixes her dress as it lifts up the sides of her legs. As she crosses her ankles, she takes the children into her arms and consoles them.

She gives them a hug and a kiss on their foreheads.

"Sister," the little girl cries. Her brother kisses her forehead and hugs her tighter in his arms.

This was not the news that they expected. They expected to hear that this woman decided to adopt them. The little boy even thought that Lindsay was on her way back to adopt them herself.

They like Lindsay. They want to live with Lindsay. They want her to be their mother.

They are so confused. They have no idea where they are going to live. Lindsay told them that this woman would take care of them until her husband came home. Then the couple would decide what to do after a couple days of getting to know them.

She promised them a better life.

But they don't like this woman.

They don't like the way she dresses. They don't like her tone of voice.

And they don't like cinnamon.

The little boy chuckles as he thinks of this. His sister quizzically looks at him as if he's gone crazy. Crazy like their mother. Crazy like their sister.

Well, dead mother and sister.

"No like cinnamon," he says.

They laugh together with tears in their eyes.

The woman looks at them confused. She wipes the tears from her eyes. She feels helpless toward these children. She feels as though she must take good care of them. They have been through so much and now she has a chance to make things right.

"I can make you kids some other dessert," the woman suggests.

The kids think for a moment. "Pie," the boy says and giggles.

"Okay," the woman answers. "Pie it is!"

She gives them another hug. The boy kisses his necklace made out of red yarn and a gold button. He places his head onto his sister's arm as she too kisses her homemade necklace.

They cry together as the woman with the pink dress holds them tight into her arms. She watches the paused game of "Mario Brothers" and slowly smiles.

Chapter Eighteen

William St. Rose always, "played by the book," ever since he was elected as Sheriff of this small town. The community folk love him. They respect him. Even though some people have never respected his personal choices in life; they listen to what he has to say. They follow his rules even if they don't agree with them. The younger children look up to him. Some of the teenagers want to work with him.

Some of the women even want to sleep with him.

He chuckles every time he thinks of this notion. Joni would rip him a new asshole.

But, he's a faithful man. He's never cheated on his wife. Sure, women have put the moves on him, but he's instantly turned them down. He's a hard-working father and husband. He doesn't have time for games. And, he surely doesn't have time for another woman.

His work pulls him away from the one that he has. Of course, he does have his suspicions of his wife's infidelity. He knows that he's gone most of the time; leaving her to her own devices.

He's gotten angry with Marybeth when she mentioned the pool boy…

That girl is silly. Joni wouldn't ruin their marriage over some young pool boy.

But then again, some of the townsfolk have whispered secrets in his ear while he's out grocery shopping. His buddies have sat at the bar with him; nonchalantly telling him stories of witnessed accounts of Joni's cheating scandals.

No one likes her. That's it. No one has liked Joni since she stepped into this town many years ago. She was lonely and abandoned. She had been abused by her ex-husband.

William St. Rose has a heart of gold. That's why he took Joni into his home and took care of her. She was broke, sad and disheveled-looking.

She can be sweet, kind and loving. That's what people don't see. They don't see this wonderful side of her that he just can't get enough of. He loves her sweet kisses and soft hugs.

As William thinks of this, he smiles while placing his police vehicle in park. He glances left toward the woods. These woods look so peaceful and quiet.

A light dusting of snow has landed on top of the branches of the trees. They sway in the breeze as the wind picks up; blowing the snow into the air like a tornado.

William shivers. He has this urgent feeling of cuddling with his wife in front of the fire. He wants to hold her underneath their thick, wool blanket and kiss her softly on the lips.

He wants to tell her that everything will be okay.

She's been upset with him lately. She asked that he takes a vacation or take a few days off so they could spend some time together. He blew her request out of the water. He told her that she was insane for thinking that he would take time off at this time of the year.

Winter is the busiest time for some reason. The snow causes more crashes, heaters cause more fires in the area and kids become extremely bored. They like to misbehave and act naughty. The "Santa Claus" talk doesn't work for the older children. He likes to joke with them, which works, because they laugh at the thought of "Santa Claus" not placing presents under the tree.

Maybe he will take a vacation soon. He does need it. He needs a break from all this madness. He could ask his deputy to take over for a few weeks.

William turns his head; glancing to the right toward the field of the farmhouse.

The snow covers the old corn crops. The outside lights of the farmhouse shine brightly. The place looks like a museum. The huge bay windows are covered with beautiful red, silk curtains.

William looks up at the sky. He has no idea why he didn't wait to come out here until tomorrow. But, the urgency from John Roland's wife caught his attention and he just had to investigate the area.

It will be dark soon. Another night that he's out late and not cuddled up with his wife. It's another night of not saying goodnight to his children before they trudge up the steps toward their rooms;

getting ready to sleep snuggly in their beds.

William stares straight ahead toward the dead end road as he imagines Roman and Marybeth tucked under their nice warm blankets. He imagines himself kissing their foreheads and reminding them of how much he does love them.

He sighs but the thought of his children soon vanish as he notices another pair of tire tracks in the grass that leads to a connecting field. He then follows the gravel driveway with his suspicious eyes; stopping at the farmhouse once again.

A small table sits on the porch next to the front door. A large red candle sits on the table. The wind blows the flame like a spirit floating in the air. The porch light shines bright as if it's waiting for a guest to arrive. As if the owner of the house is waiting for William's arrival.

William shakes his head and chuckles. His overreactions sometimes put him in a bad spot. Being the Sheriff makes him think that everyone is suspicious, even if a person means well.

A bright light and a candle doesn't mean that the owners are expecting him. It just means that they like to decorate their porch and make it look inviting.

It just means that they are warm and welcoming.

Maybe he should take some pointers. Maybe he should ask them for some advice on how to look warm and inviting.

William chuckles again.

He exits the vehicle and adjusts his holster. He then adjusts the waistband to his pants. He's lost a little weight because he hasn't been eating much. Not being home has given him slight depression and he isn't sure how to take care of this problem.

The cold air immediately smacks his cheeks like the hand of his father. The sting reminds him of the ugly look that his old man used to give him when he was drunk off his ass.

He hated his old man. His father drank a thirty-six case of beer every day and would take his frustrations out on William and William's older sister, Annie.

He would beat them to a pulp. William would show up to school with bruises on his eyes and forehead. Annie would cry to her teacher as she showed her the bruises on her back.

That was the last time that his father ever laid another hand on them. That was when William's mother finally found the courage to leave his father and press abuse charges on him.

He died in prison. Another inmate found out why William's father was sitting in a jail cell.

The dispatcher's voice on the vehicle's radio breaks his thoughts. The silence of this area is suddenly overwhelming. He's used to the town's main road with its loud Christmas music and kids running up and down the street as they laugh and play in the snow.

He's used to conversations and people saying hello. He's used to car horns and the engines revving up to a green light. He's used to the hustle and bustle of a busy small town.

As William imagines the townspeople walking up and down the sidewalk waving to him like he's the President of the United States, the owner of the farmhouse stands on his porch; lifting the binoculars to his suspicious eyes.

Morgan spots William pacing in front of the woods.

He chuckles, "Well, that was fast."

William's thoughts of the townspeople suddenly disappear as he steps toward the edge of the woods. His hands are on his hips as his eyes squint from the snow landing on his eyelids.

They dart from tree to tree. He feels unsure as this sudden feeling of creepiness climbs inside of his mind. He's unsure if he is actually seeing moving shadows or if it's his own imagination. These woods might be quiet and peaceful, but they give William the Heebie-jeebies. He doesn't like this feeling and it makes him nervous as hell.

Morgan emerges from the field with his shot gun holster wrapped around his shoulder and chest. The shot gun rests on his back as if it's hiding from the big bad wolf.

"Well hello there Sheriff!" Morgan exclaims, startling William.

William quickly spins around like a whirlpool.

"Good evening farmer. How's your day been so far?" William asks.

Morgan shrugs. "Same as always I guess… What brings you here in this cold evening?"

William's mind is spinning like a washing machine. He searches the area once again as he contemplates on how to answer Morgan's question. He glances up and down the dead end road as his eyes squint again toward the woods.

His eyes are tired and playing tricks on him. They're blurry from the wet snow.

"Well…" William responds after a long pause, "looking for a missing person. John Roland. You know him?"

Morgan nonchalantly nods his head as he ponders a response. He notices the flame to his red candle blows out from the strong gust of wind. It's as if the wind is telling him to be quiet.

Morgan watches William shiver in the cold. He wants to laugh but he holds it back. What does the Sheriff expect when he isn't even wearing a winter coat? The man likes to show off his smaller physique. He likes to show off his muscles as if Morgan is afraid of him.

He would shoot a bullet into the Sheriff's brain without any hesitation.

Morgan doesn't care about muscles and huge biceps. He cares about people showing up on his property uninvited. He cares about people thinking that they can maneuver their way through his woods without permission.

And he certainly doesn't give a shit that William is the Sheriff.

"Sure do," Morgan answers as he places his gloved hands on the strap to his holster. "Lives about a little ways going west. Near the grocery store."

"That's him. You see him lately?"

Morgan nods. "As a matter of fact, I have."

William waits for more of a response. He quickly realizes that the farmer isn't spewing more information. He crosses his arms like a tough guy.

He's actually freezing but he doesn't want Morgan to sense how ridiculous he looks without a winter coat. He would like Morgan to believe that he is a tough guy.

NO, he IS a tough guy.

And he isn't scared as the farmer stands in front of him with a weapon hiding behind his back. The farmer feels nice and toasty as he wears his bulky blue suede coat with a hood.

"And?" William asks, pushing for more information.

Morgan mocks William and crosses his arms over his chest. The strap slightly tightens as the shot gun lifts a half an inch over his back.

"AND… he was here earlier with Ray Smith. They stopped here after hunting. Dragged their tires onto my property from that field over there…" Morgan points past his driveway and toward another set of woods a mile from the farmhouse. "Drove right through my fields. I guess John had to suddenly take a piss and couldn't wait. They stopped next to my driveway and at the edge of these woods." Morgan points again to the woods that William stands next to.

Morgan continues, "I spotted them and invited them into my farmhouse for some coffee."

William nods as the information swims throughout his brain like fish in a fish tank.

"Sounds about right," William agrees. "Ray said that John had wandered off after spotting a deer in the woods. BUT, he did mention that you volunteered to take John home." William pauses; waits for a reaction from Morgan. There is none.

Morgan continues to cross his arms, looking bored and tired.

"Did you do that?" William continues.

Morgan smiles innocently; revealing brand new dentures. He uncrosses his arms and places his hands on his hips.

"No actually… I drove him to the gas station down the street from his home. He said he wanted to buy some lottery tickets. He said he wanted to win and get the hell out of this town."

Morgan's response spins the neurons in William's brain like the wheel of a bike.

"So, let me get this straight. Ray left John after he spotted a deer in the woods. John took off and came back to find Ray gone? Did John return to your farmhouse?"

"Of course," Morgan smiles. "Pounded on my screen door like he was the police."

William raises an eyebrow and chuckles. He thinks… no he KNOWS that this man is playing with his mind. He seems to have the upper hand in this conversation. William needs to turn it around before he makes himself look like a fool.

William smirks.

Morgan seems suddenly nervous. "I apologize Sheriff. Sometimes, I lose my manners when my property is invaded upon."

"So, you think that's what this is? An invasion of your privacy?" William asks curiously.

"Of course," Morgan replies. He feels a sense of anger. His cheeks flush. "These two men came through that field in John's truck," Morgan continues as he points toward the field once again. "Which is where those tire tracks come from. That field is also MY property. They're actually lucky that I didn't push the issue further. There is to be no hunting on these grounds because it's all MY property. AND," Morgan crosses his arms once again, "those woods are my property as well. John entered those woods to hunt, which I might add, is illegal. So instead of taking negative action, I invited them to have some coffee to discuss the property layout of my rights." Morgan's frustration is revealed but he remains calm as he uncrosses his arms again.

William nods and places his hands on his hips again. He looks at the tire tracks that have destroyed the dirt road. He stares at the mud that now lies on top of gravel in the driveway.

"Okay, seems fair," William agrees. "So he returned to your farmhouse and then you gave him a ride to the gas station?"

Frustrated, Morgan answers, "That's what I said, sir."

Morgan emphasizes that word SIR. William can take a hint. The farmer just wants to be left alone with his property and his wife. He just wants people to stay away.

William understands this. He wishes for it too. But unfortunately, he can't have his wish. He is the Sheriff of this town and he must give the townspeople fair justice… even if they are being assholes. Sometimes, he wishes that people would stay away from him. But they can't and they won't.

He can't stay away either. It's in his nature.

William suddenly nods as the information processes through his brain. "Okay Morgan. I get your point. Thank you for your cooperation." William pauses for a moment and peeks into the woods once again. "One last thing, would you mind if I search the woods?"

Morgan smiles, replying, "Be my guest."

"Thank you." William answers as he shakes Morgan's hand with freezing fingers. "Have a good night."

The sun is setting and a cold gust of wind blows through the area once again.

Morgan half turns toward his farmhouse but stops. "I wouldn't take too much time Sheriff. It will be dark very soon."

William doesn't answer as he contemplates this realization.

"Oh and…" Morgan looks back at William, "next time, wear a coat."

He takes off toward his house as he waves, smiling.

William slowly nods. He feels this sudden anger. Morgan made him feel like a fool. He made him feel stupid and incompetent. He made him feel like he didn't know what he was doing.

At this point, he's been in the police force for twenty years and has never let anyone make him feel like Morgan made him feel.

But he understands the man's frustration. William would be livid too if he had to deal with strangers constantly appearing onto his property and destroying it.

William turns back toward the woods and then looks up at the sky. The snowy clouds are covering the sun. The bitter cold makes him shiver.

He hopes he doesn't freeze to death.

William's lips are turning purple as he creeps through the woods with his gun drawn. He scared himself half to death after stepping on fallen branches.

He glances over his shoulder as if someone is chasing him with an axe.

His cheeks are red and numb from the cold. He can't feel his hands and feet. He can't understand how he forgot his damn coat. What a fool.

His infamous black jean jacket with white fur is lounging on his office chair back at the police station. He was in a hurry when John Roland's wife called. She was frantic; saying that she thought her husband could have gotten hurt in the woods. She said maybe he shot himself by accident. She said that he's never late for dinner. John likes to eat. Food is his passion.

William ran so fast out of the door without realizing how cold it really was outside.

By the time he was halfway to the farmhouse, he realized that he had no coat.

This sense of urgency has made him realize that he really does need a vacation. Running out of the station in the winter time without a coat means that he's exhausted and needs a break.

The woods are becoming darker and his visibility is becoming less clear. The sudden gusts of wind seem to be telling him to turn back.

He should turn back and head home. He should cuddle up with his wife. He should tell her how much he truly loves her. He should apologize for never being home enough. He should hug his kids and tell them that everything will be alright.

But he can't.

He has the duty as Sheriff to find this missing man. This is his job… HIS passion.

William pulls out the flashlight from his back pocket. Switching it on, he suddenly stops. He spots the "NO HUNTING" sign three feet away.

His heart pounds as he exhales his breath.

It's only a sign William, get a hold of yourself, he thinks to himself.

He continues on as his teeth chatter. This will definitely make him sick. He will have to take time off for sickness instead of having a nice vacation.

Flashing the light toward the ground, he notices footprints in the snow.

He stops, searching the area with the light. He's shaking and he's not sure if it's from the cold or from the sense of fear that has suddenly swallowed his entire being.

He finds his courage and continues to follow the footprints.

He gets his courage from his mother. William smiles as he thinks of her hard-work.

She was always a strong woman; she just hid it from her husband. She was terrified to show that she wasn't some weak-minded "slut" that William's father made her out to be.

Her courageous fight against the old man was what really opened William's eyes. He always knew that his mother had it in her. He always knew that she was strong and intelligent.

She was intelligent enough to put her abusive husband in prison. She was intelligent enough to save her children from the old man's wrath.

William stops walking again as he spots something shiny toward the ground.

Bending at his knees, he flashes his flashlight. With a quizzical look, he notices fishing wire tied between two trees just a foot in front of his boot.

"Very interesting…" he says, trailing off into a vision of satanic group members running toward him with crucifixes and a rope to hang from his neck.

Carefully stepping over the wire, he continues to flash the light toward the ground; hoping to find other traps as clues.

Clues to what?
He does not know.
But he wants to find out.

Chapter Nineteen

Gwyneth absolutely loves the snow. She likes collecting it in a bucket for water for her favorite animal. She likes to stick her tongue out every now and then to taste the sweetness.

She loves the smell of it and the feel of it. She loves to roll snowballs into her palms and throw them at Buttons. Excitedly, he wags his tail and barks up into the air. He runs to her; jumping on top of her chest and knocking her down into the snow. She laughs like a hyena as he licks her forehead. She hates laughing like a hyena but sometimes she can't help it.

They like to roll around and tackle each other like school kids.

Gwyneth loves to build a Snowman.

Last year, Buttons leaped up into the air and plowed right through her Snowman. Covered in snow, he then leaped on top of Gwyneth; the snow covered her whole face as she landed hard on the ground. As soon as she bumped her head from his wildness, Buttons whimpered.

But Gwyneth laughed as she wrapped her arms around her best friend and gave him kisses through her mask. Buttons licked the snow off her coat as a way to say, "I'm sorry."

Winter time is her most memorable time with Buttons. They have so much fun together. She laughs most of the time and becomes extremely happy spending time with her beloved dog.

But then other times when they are interrupted from their snow time, she becomes annoyed and frustrated. She becomes an animal herself.

She becomes a rabid dog. When this happens, Buttons usually stays away. He doesn't like her crazy mood. She scares him half the time because he isn't sure what she will do.

Snow time this year has had to wait.

And Buttons is becoming impatient.

Just as Gwyneth has become impatient as she sits at the picnic table; cleaning off the blood from her fishing wire. The blood is sticky and covering her fingertips.

Buttons lies on the snowy ground next to her as he watches her; anticipating for their fun time. Every time she slightly moves, he suddenly sits up as if she's about to roll a snowball in her palms. He then realizes that she has no desire to make a snowball; making him plop back down onto the ground and sigh with sadness.

Buttons has been sighing a lot lately. He wants to have fun. He wants to run around in the snow and catch a Frisbee. Gwyneth hasn't had any time to play.

Buttons opens his eyes as his master throws the bloody fishing wire onto the ground. Sniffing, he thinks it is food. But he immediately recognizes the wire and lies back down.

The poor dog is restless. He wants to run wild and crazy. He wants to play in the snow with his favorite human. He wants her to build a Snowman so he can run through it.

That has been their tradition for the past six years.

Buttons sighs once again but immediately perks his ears. He growls a low growl toward the woods. He suddenly sits up; perched and ready to run.

Gwyneth feels that anger deep inside her belly. The electricity in her brain zaps her skull. All she sees is bright lights as she follows Buttons' gaze toward the woods.

She sees a light in the distance.

Her eyesight is blurry as she glances over at John Roland's dead body leaning against a tree.

That poor schmuck. He should have just left her woods alone. He should've just gotten into his fancy truck and drove home to his wife.

Fat bastard. Why can't people just LEAVE HER ALONE?

William continues through the woods as he feels the crystals forming onto his skin. His ears are partially clogged as the wind blows its cold air right through them. His throat hurts with every swallow of the cold wind. His lips are chapped and bleeding.

He feels like he's stuck in a nightmare.

He's realized that he is definitely a fool. A fool who thinks he can conquer the world. A fool who thinks that he can save everyone. A fool who thinks that he can accomplish any mission that falls into his lap. A fool for believing that he can handle this bitter cold without winter clothes.

He wonders what Joni would think of him right now. He wonders what his children would think. Hell, he wonders what his deputy and fellow officers would think of him.

He knows exactly what they would all think…. That he's an IDIOT!

"Stupid son of a bitch," William calls himself as he shivers.

He can no longer feel his body as he shines the flashlight onto another wire trap.

Slowly stepping over it, he says, "I wonder what we have here."

One thing is for sure, Gwyneth will ALWAYS protect her best friend. Even if they don't have their "fun time" in the snow, Gwyneth will forever make sure that her dog is not harmed by any stranger who steps foot into her territory.

She's beyond infuriated. She's exhausted. All she wants to do is spend quality play time with her beloved dog and it seems as though SOMEBODY keeps stopping her.

Maybe they aren't meant to have play time this year. So far, they have been lucky to have a small amount of visitors lately. But, between having to hunt for supplies and food, Gwyneth hasn't thought much about play time until yesterday.

This makes her feel suddenly sad for Buttons. The poor boy just wants to play. However, he doesn't understand the consequences of his playing. When they play in the snow, Buttons becomes extremely loud and this places them in danger. People in earshot can possibly hear them laughing, barking and throwing snowballs.

That's why she keeps him quiet. That's why she makes him go inside of the shack.

Gwyneth hurriedly clicks her tongue at Buttons. He immediately lowers his head and follows her directions. He tries to give her those sad puppy-dog eyes.

As he enters the shack, Gwyneth quietly begins to shut the door. She stops; noticing his sadness. She pets the top of his head with her bloody fingers. He licks them as he tries to nibble on them like he was given a fresh dog bone.

She rubs his ears and clicks her tongue once again. He suddenly stops licking her fingers and sits onto the cold wooden floor of the shack.

Patting his head, she then quietly closes the door. Peeking through the crack, Gwyneth can see a tear in the corner of Buttons' right eye as he too peeks through the crack. She closes her eyes. *We will play good boy, don't you worry,* she thinks.

All of these mixed emotions are overwhelming her heart as it pounds like a drum.

She's mad but sad at the same time. She's mad that people keep bothering them. She's sad because she knows that her dog is ready to finally play in the snow.

But, she has to take care of business first.

Returning to the picnic table, she retrieves her harpoon. Her hands are shaking and her heart continues to pound through her chest. She feels this sudden adrenaline rush as she makes her way behind the tree next to John Roland.

Her boot accidently kicks his frozen arm and she instantly panics.

She's always so keen and quiet like a Ninja. She loves to creep up onto her prey and then bite them like a snake. She loves it when they least expect it.

She's nervous now. Making any slight sound will give this intruder an idea of where she's hiding. She usually doesn't slip up like this.

Damn you John, she thinks in her nervous mind. *Damn you to the black hole!*

Ahhh… yes. That black hole.

She likes to envision dead bodies swirling inside of that black hole. She likes to remind herself that's where all of her victims go. That's where they rot.

And she loves it.

The thought just makes her giddy inside. Her thoughts make her feel ecstatic. Her brain helps to make her feel happy whenever she feels nervous.

She quickly peeks downward and notices that she's standing on John's hand. But then, she hurriedly looks back up as she hears the crunching sound of a twig snapping.

William walks past a set of trees and then approaches Gwyneth's campfire area.

He slowly and carefully lifts his flashlight to expose the outside of the dilapidated-looking shack. The flashlight is shaking as it shines onto the picnic table, the small fire-pit with a dying fire and then Buttons' dog cage. The flashlight moves to the water well and then to more trees.

William then points the flashlight back at the shack as he notices a small light shining through the front window. He sees some sort of shadow figure inside.

He's instantly terrified. He's freezing his ass off and he has no idea what to do now. His teeth are chattering and his whole entire body is shaking. He knows now that it's not only from the bitter cold; but from fear.

Fear of the unknown. Fear of what's inside of that shack. Fear of who has been living in these conditions. He's in fear for being killed out in these woods and no one will ever know.

He didn't get a chance to say goodbye to wife and kids. He didn't get a chance to kiss them on their foreheads and tell them that he loves them. He hasn't gotten a real chance of watching his kids grow up. They're twelve now. They're fierce and strong like warriors.

Something he needs to be.

He needs to be fierce right now. He needs to be strong.

But he's lost feeling throughout his body. He's weak. He can't fight fairly. He doesn't have the strength. He's barely holding on to the flashlight.

He suddenly hears a dog growling.

Frantically, he swiftly moves his body from right to left as he uncontrollably shines the flashlight throughout the area. The light twirls like a baton.

The dog barks.

He can't see a thing. It is pitch black outside now and his pupils are tired. The snow is falling harder; flakes are softly landing onto his eyelashes.

He could literally fall asleep where he stands. Well, if he were to do just that, he would for sure die. He would become a block of ice. He knows that he wouldn't make it out of these woods alive and this makes his heart burst into flames.

With a scratchy voice, William calls out, "Is anyone out here? Expose yourself now."

Lifting his gun, he frantically searches the area once again. He's not sure where to look. He's not sure where to step. He thinks about the trap wire and immediately stops himself.

He shines the flashlight onto the snowy ground but he doesn't see any wire.

He inhales a deep breath and then slowly exhales. He then takes small steps toward the shack. He has no idea why he is even doing this. He wants to turn around and go back to his car. He wants to erase this witnessed area from his mind.

He doesn't want to know who lives here. He doesn't want to know why.

But he can't seem to turn back. He seems frozen in his boots.

Everything is numb. Everything hurts. And he feels like he's going to die.

"I'm not here to hurt you," William continues.

He suddenly feels tightness on his heart. *Maybe I'm having a heart attack,* he thinks to himself. *Maybe it will explode and shatter my soul. Maybe this is where I am going to die.*

As he hears the sound of the wind twirling like a tornado, he quickly turns around. His flashlight falls upon John Roland's dead body.

Every thought of his own death soon fades away from his brain as he rushes toward John.

William feels for a pulse.

Realizing that the man is surely dead, he quickly stands up straight. He has this imagery of someone standing behind him... waiting to crush his skull.

The image is gruesome. The image is wicked. It reminds him of a horror movie.

He envisions his brain scattered all over the beautiful crystal snow. He imagines some kind of sharp object being impaled through the side of his temple.

He quickly looks to the right. Then, he sadly looks to the left.

He is sad. He's sad for John Roland. Sad for the man's wife and kids. And sad for his own family once they find out that he was brutally murdered by some psychopath out in the woods.

He has to do SOMETHING. He can't just stand around here shivering and shaking.

Remembering his mother's courage, he turns back toward the shack.

"Come out come out wherever you are," he teases. "I just want to talk. Set things straight, that's all." His teeth chatter as he tries to speak intelligently. He's never been so cold in his life.

Buttons continues to bark. He peeks through the window and

spots William. William's flashlight quickly shines into the dog's eyes. Buttons then whimpers as he hurriedly jumps down from the card table. The poor dog has no idea what's going on. He's stuck inside and can't get out in order to help his master. SHE NEEDS HELP!

William sighs a breath of relief. *At least I know now that the dog is INSIDE,* he thinks.

"Beautiful dog you got there," William tries again. "What's his name?"

There's still no answer from anyone. He's starting to think that the owner of the shack isn't even home. The person left their dog inside from the blistering cold.

Well, at least they're smart, William laughs in his brain.

As he approaches the door to the shack, he flashes the light onto the dog cage once again.

He suddenly hears some kind of noise but he isn't sure what it is. It sounds like a crunching noise of someone stepping onto the snowy ground.

Quickly turning, he looks at the picnic table and spots John's rifle. Then, he looks at the fir-pit once again. The fire is completely out. He wishes that it was a full-blown blazing fire. Maybe he could then feel some kind of heat. Maybe his body could thaw out like frozen meat.

"Looks like you've made yourself a home here. Do you mind if we have a little chat?" William pauses, waiting for a response, "Please?" he asks.

As William stands just a few feet away from the shack's front door, the sharp edge of the harpoon flies past his head; piercing the wooden wall of the shack.

William jumps as if his feet are on fire. His eyes are wide and he instantly feels helpless.

The flashlight shines brightly on Gwyneth as if she's a star from the sky. William quickly realizes that she's gripping onto her harpoon and is pointing it straight at him.

William suddenly thinks that this scenario is a cruel trick. He thinks that this psychopath is playing a game. But, he decides to play along. He loves to play games. Especially with someone who thinks that they are big and bad.

Well, he can be big and bad too.

William is sarcastic as he says, "Well there you are. I didn't think anyone would show up."

Gwyneth steps sideways with her untied shoe-laced boots. William points his gun at her head. *Two can play at this game,* he thinks as he suddenly feels an adrenaline rush.

"Now listen," William continues, "I don't want any trouble. Just lower your weapon."

But, Gwyneth continues to point the harpoon at William's forehead.

Stupid, she thinks to herself. *He really has no idea what he's getting himself into.*

"Okay, have it your way then," William says, popping Gwyneth's thought bubble. "I'll go first if you wish," William threatens.

The Sheriff walks over to the picnic table. Gwyneth eyes him suspiciously as she follows him. The harpoon is snug between her gloved hands. She's actually been holding onto it so tight that her hands feel cramped and sore.

This sudden thought seems to distract her mind from what's important. She needs to get this man out of her territory or she just needs to kill him.

NO! YOU NEED TO KILL HIM!

William slowly places his gun onto the picnic table as he raises his hands in surrender. The cold wind bursts through the area and it feels like it has blown his fingers right off his hands.

Why do I continuously put myself in these types of situations? He asks himself this as he contemplates on just running and hoping for the best. *Boy, do I need a vacation.*

"See that?" William asks Gwyneth. "No harm." He continues to raise his arms into the air.

Of course he gets no response. The man has no clue that she doesn't talk. He also has no idea what this girl is capable of.

"So what happened to John over there?" he asks as he nods his head toward John's lifeless body. "Did he piss you off?"

William braces for an impact, but none comes. He looks at her quizzically. He isn't even sure if the girl understands what he's saying. He could be wasting precious oxygen.

The Sheriff sits down on the bench to the picnic table. Gwyneth continues to point the harpoon at his head. She wants to just shoot him right here and right now.

But she doesn't. She realizes that this man in front of her knows who John is.

I knew it! She thinks. *I knew someone would come out here for that fat ass!*

She slowly takes two steps toward William. She doesn't want to get too close. That could be bad for her. He could grab onto her harpoon and shoot her. She cannot let that happen.

He might even kill her poor Buttons. She DEFINTELY can't let THAT happen.

Her anger gets the best of her and she takes another step.

"Did he invade your privacy too?" William taunts.

He knows that he's slipping on a thin line. Whoever this person is, they're ready to kill at all costs. They're ready to protect their home. They're ready to protect their best friend who is frantically panting inside of the shack. The poor dog is whimpering and scratching at the door.

If he were rabid, he could bust right through it with no problem.

Gwyneth takes another step but William continues to keep his arms and hands raised high up into the air. The cold wind blows and he can smell the sweaty scent of his armpits and deodorant.

Why the HELL didn't I wear a coat???

William looks at Gwyneth with sadness in his eyes. He suddenly feels bad for her.

"I'm not here to hurt you. I'm here to get some information. Do you understand anything that I am saying?" he asks. He wants to beg on his knees for a response.

Buttons is now out of control. His anger and sadness has grown stronger and he can no longer hold back. He whimpers louder as he scratches at the door; pulling on it with his claws.

He barks over and over again. The loud noise is starting to beat inside of Gwyneth's brain like a hammer pounding on nails. Her heart is beating faster and faster.

The electricity in her brain shoots across from right to left; piercing the walls of her cerebrum. It might explode into thousands of pieces. It's all in a matter of time before she explodes herself. She can't handle it anymore.

Buttons moves to the window sill and scratches at it. Gwyneth's brain is filled with smoke and she wants it to burst. She NEEDS it to burst. The tension is rising and her mind is confused.

Gwyneth suddenly runs to the window and smacks her hand on the glass. She stares at Buttons for a brief moment. The dog stops scratching and growls at his master.

"What's your dog's name?" William asks behind her.

Gwyneth angrily turns and stomps her boots toward William. She tries to pace herself but her anger has taken over her whole entire body. It's as if she cannot control it anymore.

William braces for the impact. *Now it's coming,* he thinks to himself.

The tip of the harpoon is placed directly onto his forehead. *This is it. I'm dead.*

"You don't have to point that at me anymore. I said that I'm here for some information."

Just a foot away from William, she then places the tip of the harpoon on top of William's head. She imagines his brains blowing up into bits and pieces. She imagines blood spewing like a waterfall. She then imagines dipping her fingers into the oozing blood and drinking as if it were a glass of sweet tasting wine.

William's hands are still raised.

But, he quickly realizing that they're becoming sore and tired. However, he thinks that if he lowers his hands, that he's giving up. He's letting her win. He would be letting his guard down and he can't let that happen. Giving up is not an option. He needs to fight this battle on his own terms. He needs to win fair and square. He needs to talk some sense into this mad man.

"We don't have to do this. We can just talk. Or, I'll just talk and you listen."

The wind blows extremely hard. The snow twirls into the air like a spinning wheel.

William unexpectedly lowers his head to block the cold air from blasting his face. He accidently bites his lower lip. He immediately tastes blood. His lips are so chapped and dry that his sudden movement makes the top lip rip apart the skin.

He cries out in exhaustion. He just wants to go home. He just wants to sleep in his nice warm bed with his beautiful wife. He just wants to cozy up in front of a fire. He just wants to take a sweltering shower and let the water flow all over his freezing body.

He's starving. His stomach growls despite the pain that circulates his veins. It's excruciating pain that he can no longer handle anymore.

The wind blows again.

William looks up this time and sees Gwyneth's hood blow right off her head.

He catches a glimpse of her face.

Gwyneth irresponsibly lowers the harpoon in order to place the hood back on top of her head. Sometimes the cold air messes with her brain. Sometimes she doesn't think straight.

William leans forward. "Oh my dear GOD… GWYNETH?"

Chapter Twenty

Gwyneth hasn't heard that voice in twelve years.

TWELVE YEARS!

It's been twelve years of quiet bliss from that scratchy, hyena laugh. It's been twelve years of not smelling the bad odor of her mother's stank breath. It's been twelve years of not being punched, kicked, hit or tortured. It's been twelve years since she's been called "deaf, dumb and blind." It's been twelve years since she's looked into her mother's eyes.

And it's been twelve years since her mother told her that she would be back for her. She told her to do whatever was necessary in order to survive. She told her that they would run away together and live a better life. She told her not to cry. She told her not to worry.

SHE TOLD HER SHE WOULD BE BACK FOR HER!

Twenty-four-year-old Gwyneth understands this situation. She is far from STUPID. She understands that her mother had absolutely no intention of returning to those woods for her daughter. She understands what kind of mother she grew up with for only twelve years.

TWELVE YEARS!

Twelve years of torture. Twelve years of cigarette butts burning into her skin. Twelve years of her eardrums bursting from the loud screaming from her mother's croaky voice. Twelve years of living inside of an unhealthy house filled with mold and dust. Twelve years of being poked and prodded until the anger spewed hateful words.

Twelve years that she spent inside of a home. Twelve years to use regular running water.

Well, SOMETIMES.

Twelve years of eating actual food instead of eating animals in the wild.

Well, SOMETIMES.

And twelve years of not seeing that dumb look upon her mother's ugly face.

She's still ugly with her witch-looking nose. Still ugly with the wrinkles underneath her eyes. Still ugly with her crooked yellow teeth and food crumbs all over her lips.

Except… Gwyneth doesn't notice any of those things. Her mother's nose is smaller. Her teeth are white and shines bright like a diamond. Her lips are fuller and covered in red lipstick. Her long black hair is brushed straight past her shoulders without any knots clumped at the back of her head. Her cheeks are rosy. And her smile looks sincere.

Gwyneth lowers the harpoon. Staring at her mother suspiciously, she watches her face wrinkle in pain. The beast rubs her twisted ankle and whimpers like a child.

As Gwyneth watches her, Ruby almost falls over but she graciously holds herself up by grabbing onto a thick branch hanging from a tree.

Gracious? When has this woman ever been gracious?

She belongs in hell. No wait… she belongs in the black hole. She deserves to spin inside like clothes inside of a dryer. She deserves to bust her head against the walls of the black hole. She deserves to be swallowed inside of the tornado of the black hole. She deserves to DIE inside of the black hole. That would serve her right.

Because… she deserves it.

She deserves to die.

Gwyneth angrily lifts the harpoon once again and points it at Ruby's head. She quickly takes a step closer toward her mother. She's ready to pierce the harpoon into her mother's eyeball.

As a matter of fact, her ten inch sewing needle is lying nice and snug inside of her glove. She's ready to stab her death. It doesn't even matter where she stabs her, as long as the Bitch dies. Just as long as she stops breathing. As long as Gwyneth doesn't have to look at her face, this time, EVER AGAIN!

Gwyneth gazes at Ruby. She suspiciously looks at her mother's body from her head and then down to her feet. The beast has gained some weight. She's dressed well and looks healthy.

Tears fill Gwyneth's sad blue eyes.

Ruby welcomes her daughter with open arms. "It's me baby, your mama. I can't believe you're still here after twelve years! I can't believe my eyes! I thought you were dead!"

Ruby truly and sincerely thought that her oldest daughter was dead. She truly cried over this notion for many years. She would lie awake at night in her bed and cry herself to sleep. She thought about her daughter every day of her existence.

How could this happen? Ruby asks herself as she stares at Gwyneth's teary eyes. *How the hell could a stupid little girl like her survive out this wilderness?*

Ruby's last words replay in Gwyneth's mind once again, "Do whatever is necessary to survive." "Do whatever is necessary to survive."

Well, she has. And she's been perfectly fine without this beast. She's been perfectly fine on her own. She doesn't need another human coming into her life and telling her what to do. Especially… THIS human beast. She doesn't need nor wants her mother back into her life.

Gwyneth blinks. Her tears fall to her cheeks.

She hasn't cried in twelve years. She hasn't seen this ugly human being for twelve years. This woman has not made her cry in twelve years.

And she doesn't understand why she's crying now. She doesn't understand why or how this woman can instantly make her feel emotional.

And the woman clearly doesn't understand how bad her daughter wants to kill her.

"I've come back for you!" Ruby exclaims.

Gwyneth slightly shakes her head. She can't believe what she is hearing right now. She knows that she is slow and doesn't understand a lot of things, but she sure as HELL can't understand why her mother would say such stupid words after all this time.

Ruby's voice is in Gwyneth's head once again, "I'll come back for you tomorrow. Go hide."

The echo suppresses her brain. The echoed voice is driving her crazy. She's done everything that she possibly could during these past twelve years to get rid of that echo of her mother's voice. She worked so hard to forget about her mother. She worked so hard to forget about her life before the shack. She's done everything to make a stable life for her and Buttons.

And now this Bitch comes back.

Gwyneth violently shakes her head no.

Ruby steadily and easily holds out her hand. "Baby, it's me. You don't have to be afraid."

Limping, Ruby takes a small step toward Gwyneth. "I'm a little hurt with my ankle. Could you help me dear?" she dares to ask.

HELP? DEAR?

Who the HELL does she think I am?

Gwyneth hasn't realized that her harpoon dangles from her fingertips. She forgets for a split second where she is and who is talking to her. Her mind has veered off into a winter wonderland. She's envisioning herself and her siblings jumping into piles of snow.

She sees her little brother running in circles as her little sister throws a snowball. She sees herself building a Snowman in their backyard. She sees her brother running into the Snowman and falling face first into the snow. She sees them all laughing and playing.

Her tears spill onto the top of her T-shirt mask.

She suddenly snaps out of her memory. She watches Ruby look at her with that dumb look on her face. That dumb look that she was forced to stare at for the first twelve years of her life.

There she is! There's the REAL Ruby Glacier! The girl knew she would see it soon!

Gwyneth lifts the harpoon higher and points it directly into Ruby's face.

"Now stop it child. It's your mother. Snap out of it. You don't want to anger me do you?"

Gwyneth has tremendous speed. She's taught herself to think and act fast in dangerous situations. She's taught herself to never listen to her victims as they taunt, cry or threaten her well-being. She has taught herself to hate the world.

And that's what she's doing.

Quickly and fiercely, Gwyneth shoots the harpoon. The sharp edge slams into Ruby's twisted ankle. The woman screams in agony and falls to the snowy ground.

Crying, she spats at her daughter, "What have you done?"

Something I should've done a long time ago.

Gwyneth grabs her mother by her hair and twists; pulling a few strands out of her scalp. Ruby screams; blowing out her daughter's eardrums.

Buttons barks. He whines from the awful sound coming from her mother's mouth. Gwyneth clicks her tongue at Buttons and nods her head. He runs ahead toward the direction of the shack.

Ruby's cries sound like a dying animal on the side of the road. Her tears have caused boogers to slip out of her nose. The boogers are sliding into her open mouth.

She stares up into the cloudy sky and screams her head off.

Gwyneth starts walking toward the direction of the shack; dragging her mother by her hair. Ruby tries to kick at her with her good foot. She misses and slams her foot against the ground.

"Let me go you little Bitch!"

Gwyneth does contemplate this. If she were to let go of her mother, she would leave for good. BUT... she could also possibly tell someone that she is indeed living in these woods. That would mean that other human beings would step into her territory and that is something that she does not want to deal with. She always makes sure that her dog is safe... and letting Ruby go is not safe. It's quite dangerous actually and Gwyneth recognizes that issue.

Instead, Gwyneth picks up her pace.

Being seventeen is quite exciting for Marybeth St. Rose and her brother, Roman. Being seventeen usually means that turning eighteen is only one year away. Being seventeen means college applications and your high school career is soon to end. Being seventeen means that you can SOON move out of your parents' house.

Lately, Marybeth doesn't think that life is all rainbows and butterflies. She's been thinking a lot about college and moving out of her parents' house. She's been thinking a lot about living in a dorm. She's been thinking a lot about not being around her brother as much anymore either.

This all saddens her. This makes her so sad that she actually ripped two college applications right in half and then threw the pieces into the fireplace.

She doesn't want to move. She doesn't want to leave her father. She doesn't want to leave her brother. Hell, she doesn't even want to leave her mother.

Lately, she's felt emotional. She doesn't want to grow up into an adult. She wants to stay young for the rest of her life.

But, she knows that that is not possible. She knows she has to step up and be a woman. She knows that she has to take care of business.

All of that just makes her sad. Her life as a teenager will be over before she knows it. And she knows that this doesn't bother her brother one bit. She knows that Roman is tickled pink for leaving their parents' house and moving onto college. She knows how excited he truly is about making films as well. And she's happy for him. She's happy that he found a passion.

Sometimes, Marybeth believes that Roman should be a detective instead of playing around with silly films. She thinks that he would make a great detective.

He's intelligent and pushy. He would for sure get the information needed to solve a case.

Maybe that would make their father happy about his future. *A detective is a cop right?* Marybeth wants to talk with Roman about this idea of hers. She wants to let him know that he should look into a more realistic career path.

As they walk home from school, the snow blows into their eyes, into their face and onto their heads. They're almost to their house and Roman has done nothing but complain.

Marybeth wants to stop him from continuously blabbing about homework, his dopey friends and his love for movie-making. She hasn't gotten a word in for fifteen minutes.

He's been complaining about his "rotten teachers," their "asshole" principal and their dirty "whore" of a mother. He said that he can't wait to move. He said he would never visit her again.

Marybeth tries to change the subject. "Have you applied to any colleges yet? I find it to be so exciting to graduate at seventeen!" Marybeth says, interrupting.

Roman is out of breath. He coughs as the cold breeze blows into his lungs. "As a matter of fact, I applied to a filming school. I know dad won't be happy about it. I want to do what I want to do. Not what he wants."

Marybeth chuckles. *What a baby.* "You have the right to do what you want. It's your life. Don't let anyone tell you otherwise. I know dad is rough, but it's tough love."

Maybe that idea of detective work will have to wait until later, Marybeth thinks to herself.

"It's been rough having a Sheriff as a father."

"We've just had a rough life in general. I mean, we barely

remember when we were little. Like we have amnesia or something. We had speech problems growing up. The speech therapist was nice to us though."

Roman laughs. "Yeah, she was. It just seems like dad hides things from us. You get that feeling too? Like he knows secrets or something."

Marybeth ponders her brother's statement for a moment.

He is RIGHT. Their father is very secretive. Marybeth has been playing detective for many years herself. She knows that their father has something up his sleeve. Many people like him do.

Marybeth shrugs her shoulders. "I feel like that about mom. Like they're both hiding something from us."

They cross the street. Roman trips over the curb and loses his balance. Marybeth laughs at him as he falls to the snowy ground. He laughs along with her and then decides to make a snow angel. While spreading his arms and legs, he stares up at the snowy sky.

Marybeth joins him; spreading her arms and legs to make her own snow angel.

They laugh in unison. It's been such a long time since they've played in the snow. It's been such a long time since they've done anything together as a matter of fact.

They are always too busy to spend any time together. Their father is extremely busy and their mother could care less to spend any time with them. Marybeth always tries to make plans with the woman but she always has some kind of excuse as to not to.

Marybeth sticks her tongue out to let the snowflakes land on its warmth. They immediately melt in her mouth and this makes her laugh loudly.

They probably look like two insane people making snow angels on the side of the road.

An elderly couple drives past the teens in their new Lincoln as the wife stares out of the window. Her eyebrows are scrunched in the middle of her face. She looks concerned.

The woman then tugs on her husband's coat sleeve and he suddenly stops the car. Marybeth looks up at the vehicle and waves the couple away. The husband steps on the gas.

"People are so nosy," Marybeth laughs.

Roman chuckles. "You got that right."

Marybeth is the first one to stand up. She then pats the snow off her coat and boots.

Noticing that the old woman is completely turned around in the passenger seat and staring at Marybeth, she waves at the Lincoln as it continues slowly down the street. The old woman flicks Marybeth off with her middle finger. The girl howls with laughter.

"Bitty old Bitch," Marybeth says.

Roman howls with laughter.

His sister watches him as he continues to make his snow angel without even thinking about getting up. He doesn't want to get up. He doesn't want to go home and see his Bitch of a mother.

He watches Marybeth as she holds out her hand to help him up. He hesitates for a moment. Noticing his sister's annoyance, he then nods; grabbing her gloved hand.

"So listen," Roman continues, "Tonight I want to take that walk in the woods again." He watches Marybeth roll her eyes. "Look, I know my first encounter wasn't successful…"

"Successful?!" Marybeth interrupts. "You know, I am really not happy about this. You said that you were scared for your life!"

"I was! But it will be different this time. I will have you with me and I will be better prepared. Please Marybeth… I need your help," Roman begs.

Marybeth sighs. She feels angry but she also does want to help.

"Fine! I'll go with you so you don't get into any trouble," Marybeth answers with a sour puss look upon her face. She doesn't truly know why she just agreed to his rendezvous.

They reach the driveway to their house. They walk past their father's car.

"Okay great! Because I have a master plan!" Roman exclaims.

When Gwyneth was eighteen, only six years after her mother dumped her into the woods, she was extremely hopeful and dedicated to finding her family.

She used to have these dreams where she would run into the arms of her five-year-old siblings. She imagined herself as an eighteen-year-old, but for some reason that she doesn't understand, her brother and sister would be little kids.

She assumed it was because it was the last time she ever saw them. The last time she saw them was when they were inside of Lindsay's car; crying and waving goodbye.

GOODBYE. For the last time.

The image of their crying little faces used to haunt her for years. She used to cry herself to sleep on her dirty cot of a bed and make herself sick from being so upset.

She wants to find her family. It's been six years.

She even wants to find her mother.

That's why she's sloshing through the mud in her too-small-sized black boots. Her toes hurt from the pressure. Her heels are digging at the back wall of both boots.

She's taught herself to ignore the pain. She's taught herself to toughen up and not act like a baby. She knows that she needs new boots… and SOON!

She isn't even sure how far she will make it in these boots. She has this sinking feeling that she will be walking for a very long time.

She feels exhausted as she carries Buttons in the hood of her coat.

Sometimes he accidently pulls on the hood with his claws, causing her to choke.

The poor thing isn't doing it on purpose. He doesn't have much room to begin with. But, she doesn't have a leash for him yet and she doesn't want him to run away.

It doesn't help either that the Unicorn bookbag on her back is constantly tugging at her shoulders. She just wants to cry. She just wants to turn around and forget about it.

Gwyneth opens her map like a fan. The creases inside of the map remind her of mountains.

She wishes that she was living in the mountains instead of a set of woods for illegal hunters. She just wants to be left alone with her dog.

Left alone.

What am I doing?

Gwyneth reaches the spot where her mother dumped her. She stops.

The memories come flooding inside of her brain as if she was abandoned just yesterday. Her mother's voice is inside of her head, "I'll be back for you tomorrow. Go hide."

Gwyneth blinks and shakes her head. Tears fill her eyeballs once again.

She's tried so hard to not cry over this woman again. Seeing this spot after six years has brought back unpleasant memories. Memories that she would like to erase from her mind.

Why do I let her do this?

All Gwyneth wants is to see her siblings one last time. All she wants is to see if they are okay. She wants to know where they are. She wants to know if they are living a good life like Lindsay promised them.

Lindsay also promised that Gwyneth was going to live a good life.

Glancing down at the map, she then looks at the dirt road ahead of her. Her tears drop onto her cheeks and then flow onto her filthy T-shirt mask.

I'll be back for you tomorrow. Go hide.

Gwyneth closes her eyes. Another painful reminder of her childhood swirls her brain.

She's back at that awful shit-stained house. She and the twins are outside in the backyard. It's freezing cold and none of them are wearing coats, hats or gloves.

They're shivering and crying as the wind blows into their faces. Gwyneth's straggly black hair blows behind her head. The wind pierces inside of her sensitive eardrums like a sharp icicle. It feels like a stabbing pain as her eardrums pulsate like a beating heart ready to explode.

Ruby stands in front of them with a belt in her gloved hands. She's wearing a long, light-brown, coat and a dark-brown hat that points up into the air like a sharp knife.

She looks ridiculous with that dumb look on her face.

So ugly, Gwyneth thinks to herself.

She then wonders why she has such an ugly-looking mother. Gwyneth has been told by the townspeople many times of how beautiful she truly is. Well, they would say, "You would be beautiful if you were all cleaned up and had your hair brushed."

Gwyneth never knew if she should've taken that as a compliment or not.

Ruby is yelling, interrupting Gwyneth's thoughts, "Okay so, who was the one who threw my yarn into a tub of water?" She waits five seconds for a response. "WHO?" She screams.

Gwyneth is frantic. She glances over at the twins as they cry hysterically.

"I'm gonna ask one more time or you're all getting beat."

No one answers.

Ruby takes a step toward the twins.

Gwyneth's heart is pounding, her head is pulsating and it feels like she's about to vomit. But… that's how she feels almost every day of her life.

Sick.

Sick and *tired*.

Gwyneth quickly raises her hand. She starts crying hysterically. She knows now that she will be punished. She knows that she is about to get her ass beat to a bloody pulp. There's no way that she will allow the twins to take the fall for something that SHE did.

Of course she threw that Bitch's yarn into the water. She deserved it. That woman deserves every bad thing coming to her.

She deserves to die.

Gwyneth steps forward and waves her hand as Ruby lifts the belt high into the air to beat her five-year-old sister.

Ruby glares at her with evil eyes. "I knew it would be you!"

The sting from the belt hurts the poor girl to her core.

Gwyneth's eyes snap open. She can't help the tears flowing down her cheeks.

Glancing back down at the map, her eyes wander to the words, "MOTHER," "SISTER," and "BROTHER," written across the top of the page.

She slowly looks up as if the devil just took over her body. She's angry.

Shaking her head no, she crumbles the map into a ball and then heads off toward the shack.

Chapter Twenty-One

Of course this makes Gwyneth puzzled yet again. What are the chances that another human being actually KNOWS who Gwyneth is? How can this be? She doesn't remember this man from a hole in the ground. He's an alien to her. A stranger.

Speaking of the ground, it feels as though Gwyneth is sinking right through it. Her small, black, boots are being sucked inside as if there's quick sand trying to swallow her.

Her mind races with questions. That lightning bolt strikes the sides of her brain. It zaps quickly as it bounces up and down. The zaps are giving her an instant migraine.

Her head is pulsating and it feels as if it's about to explode.

Sometimes, she wishes that it would just explode already. The pain is unbearable and she can't think straight. Sometimes, it makes her brain wonder if what she's seeing is actually real.

She doesn't know this man so how the hell could he know her name? How could he even recognize her with this T-shirt mask on?

And, WHO THE HELL IS HE?

Gwyneth stares at William as if he just transformed from a different dimension. Did this man just climb through some kind of portal that she doesn't know about?

Is he even real? Is she hallucinating again?

She often hallucinates. She sees her mother running through the woods like a Banshee. She sees her siblings sitting at the picnic table while coloring trees and flowers.

Sometimes, she sees her mother chopping down trees for firewood.

She chuckles as she thinks about that scenario. Ruby would have NEVER chopped down trees. That means she would be doing some kind of work around the shack. If she was living in Gwyneth's territory, she would make her children do all the work… just like she did at her shit-hole house.

Lazy Bitch.

Gwyneth laughs.

William slowly lowers his arms. They're definitely sore and tired. AND this girl is completely out of her mind. She laughs at the most oddest times.

William looks around the area and then behind his shoulders. He looks past Gwyneth as if there's someone standing behind her.

What the HELL is she laughing at?

"I cannot believe what I am seeing. I have been looking for you for years! And here you are! You're living here!" William exclaims. He's flabbergasted. He cannot even fathom anyone living in these kinds of conditions. Who would do such a thing?

WHERE THE HELL IS RUBY?

He wants to know and he wants to know NOW where that Bitch is hiding.

He frantically looks around the area once again; waiting to spot Ruby running toward him with an axe. Or… maybe a knife. Or… maybe one of her ten inch sewing needles.

Gwyneth quickly snaps out of her thoughts and raises the harpoon to his face.

"I should've been there for you," William continues, "You wouldn't be in this mess! Living in filth. Living out in the cold during the winter. I'm so sorry Gwyneth."

William looks defeated as he lowers his head. He feels like a failure. He feels like he didn't do enough to find her. He feels like Ruby did this to punish him.

"I should've done more when I called CPS," William admits.

Gwyneth stares at the man for a good solid two minutes. It feels like a lifetime. It feels like she's been looking at this man for days as he shines the flashlight toward his face.

She doesn't recognize him at all. It's been six years since she lived in that small town with her family. He could be anyone that she passed in the grocery store. She could've passed him at the park.

The park….

Gwyneth is sad and her mind instantly shuts down. She's ready to sleep. She struggles to keep her eyes open. She could place her head on this man's shoulder and just cry herself to sleep.

He doesn't seem like he will harm her. He's talking to her like she's a normal human being. He isn't making fun of her or calling her names. He isn't telling her that she "could" be beautiful.

"It's time for you to come home now," William encourages.

Ruby's voice is inside of Gwyneth's head, "I'll be back for you tomorrow. Go hide."

Gwyneth shakes her head no.

She then lowers the harpoon toward the ground and frantically shakes her head no once again. She is NOT going anywhere! She is not leaving this shack and she sure as HELL isn't leaving her Buttons. This man is an INTRUDER!

"I'm begging you," William pleads, "Please come with me. You can live a normal life…" He contemplates his next words, "…I'm not your mother."

Gwyneth's eyes widen.

She places her hand on top of her head to make sure that the coats' hood doesn't fly off again. The wind is too strong for her liking and she's ready to go back inside to warm up.

She can't comprehend the words coming out of his mouth. She can't understand how he knows her mother. She doesn't know this man and at this point, she doesn't want to. She wants him out of here! She wants him out of her woods!

Gwyneth raises the harpoon once again and signals with the weapon for William to leave.

But the Sheriff shakes his head no. "No. I am not leaving you."

She signals a second time but William doesn't respond.

This man has no idea who I REALLY am.

I will kill him.

Angry, Gwyneth pulls out her ten inch sewing needle from the hidden compartment inside of her glove. She's had enough of this man's games. He thinks this is a joke.

And she doesn't understand why she won't just stab him right now. Stab him in both eyes and then go get her thread and scissors.

She suddenly shoves the tip of the needle onto William's right eyelid; careful not to stab him yet. She wants him to beg for his life. She wants to hear him scream in agony.

That's what she loves. And he will not take what she loves away from her.

William begins to cry.

How dare this man make her feel bad for what she wants to do? She wants to kill him but he's making it so hard for her. *WHY THE*

Gwyneth removes the needle from his eyelid and then signals for him to leave once again. She points the needle past the clearing and into the trees.

As he stares at the picnic table, he cries harder. His teeth are chattering; making a loud sound alongside his cries. The sounds are vibrating inside of Gwyneth's brain. She can't stand this noise and her head is about to explode again.

She envisions her brain splatter and blood landing on top of the Sheriff's head.

She giggles. She can't help it. The thought just tickles her fancy.

Slamming her fist onto the picnic table, William is startled and looks up into her eyes. She points the needle once again through the clearing and into the trees. She stabs the air as if the needle is a magic wand.

William suddenly stands up from the table and grabs his gun.

Quickly, Gwyneth lifts the harpoon off the ground and points it at his head.

William is angry. "I'm not going to shoot you! Fine… if this is what you want, then I'll leave you be!"

Buttons barks. He peeks through the window, watching William like a hawk. The Sheriff watches Buttons and imagines him busting through the glass and running toward him. He imagines the dog jumping on top of him and biting his neck.

He seems to be hallucinating himself and he needs to get to a doctor. However, he feels as though he might die here for some reason. This girl would just let him suffer in pain. BUT, she does want him out of here and all he wants to do is give her what she wants.

William flashes his flashlight back to John's body.

"You must dispose of his body," William demands. "I'll make you a deal Gwyneth. I'll leave you here alone on one condition."

Gwyneth lowers her harpoon and eyes the Sheriff suspiciously.

"Stop killing," William continues. "Stop this nonsense. If I find out that ANYONE else has been killed here, then I will come after you and hall you off to jail. You understand me?"

Gwyneth doesn't respond.

Is he nuts? Not kill anyone? What planet did he come from?

This request has given her instant anxiety. There's no way that she could live like that. What if more people enter her territory? What if they are dangerous? What if they come here just to kill her and Buttons? He expects her to not defend herself and her best friend?

There's absolutely no way that she would agree to that.

Buttons is hysterical. He's barking non-stop, whining and crying. He's scratching at the door again as he tries to get out. Pretty soon he's going to break the front door. That will cause a lot of problems for him. His master will be extremely mad.

He doesn't care though. He just wants out.

William waits for a response. But, he knows that he will not get one.

"You can let your dog out now. I'm sure he keeps you safe."

Gwyneth watches William shiver from the cold. He walks away from her, leaving her standing alone. But, she continues to point the harpoon at the back of his head.

She contemplates ending his life right now. He's leaving. He might go and tell his fellow officers that she's living here. They might decide to investigate the situation.

That would put HER in another situation where she would have to kill someone. AND he doesn't want her to do that. He doesn't want her to be a murderer.

Gwyneth chuckles.

She decides to reel in the rope to the harpoon. The sharp edge shines in the moonlight.

She glances up at the moon, wishing that she lived there instead. She could live up there and watch everyone suffer and die down here on Earth.

Now THAT would make her happy.

William stops. Looking at John one last time, he stands over his lifeless body. Pointing his finger, he makes a cross across his chest.

While in prayer position, the sharp's edge of the harpoon flies above his head; striking the tree. William whirls around. His heart is in his chest. He feels like he can't breathe.

She's taken him by surprise. He might have a heart attack right at this moment.

Gwyneth signals him with the harpoon to get out.

"Don't make me regret my decision," William threatens, trying to catch his breath. "If I do, I'm sure I'll be back once again. You can count on that."

William leaves. Gwyneth watches the light of the flashlight disappear through the woods. Buttons is going crazy inside of the shack. The poor thing just needs to go to the bathroom now.

Gwyneth thinks about what William told her to do. No, what he DEMANDED her to do. She thinks about everything that he said to her. She thinks about running through the woods and finding William frozen to death on the ground.

Gwyneth giggles up into the cold air.

William is just an earshot away. He hears her giggling and suddenly stops.

And smiles.

Gwyneth has had enough of her mother's bullshit. She's had enough of her cries. She's had enough of her threats. She's had enough of her screaming and yelling obscenities.

Her behavior only proves that the Bitch hasn't changed one bit.

She might be nice to everyone else, but she's surely not nice to her daughter. She never has been so why would it stop? She's never been a good mother. She's never taken responsibility for her actions. And, she's never APOLOGIZED.

Gwyneth doesn't expect an apology. She knows that it will never come out of her mouth. This Bitch will die a Bitch. She will die a heartless human being. And Gwyneth is okay with that. But, she's pretty sure that Ruby won't be okay with that.

She won't be okay with dying here. She won't be okay with being buried in the woods where no one will be able to visit her grave. Gwyneth will make sure that her body is dug deep into the dirt. She will make sure that the beast suffers.

She's always deserved it.

Gwyneth approaches her shack with Ruby's black hair tangled in her gloved hand. She has the perfect spot for the Bitch to rot.

While she opens the dog cage, Ruby struggles and tries to kick at her daughter. Her boots slam onto the cold, hard, ground. She cries out in pain as her twisted ankle slams sideways.

Gwyneth punches Ruby right in the face. This sends shivers down the girl's spine.

Ruby stops wailing her arms and places her hands on her nose to stop the bleeding. Gwyneth pushes her inside of the dog cage. Ruby kicks at the door with her good foot as Gwyneth tries to slam it shut.

Ruby kicks her daughter's hand; making the cage stab at the inside of her palm.

Gwyneth then reaches behind her back and grabs the harpoon. Ruby slightly sticks her head out of the cage just as Gwyneth swings her weapon. Ruby hurriedly moves out of the way; missing the harpoon by an inch.

Gwyneth slams the door shut and locks it with the wire that's tied to it.

The girl is out of breath. This Bitch is giving her a run for her money so to speak. She's exhausted from dragging her ass for five miles into the woods. Gwyneth is lucky that her mother is still skinny. She wouldn't have had the strength or the energy to drag her if she was fat.

Ruby begs, "Please Gwyneth! I'm not a dog! Let me go!"

Gwyneth ignores her as she heads toward the shack.

This beast really doesn't know her daughter anymore. She's stronger. She's intelligent. She's wise. She's skillful. And she knows and understands how to torture her victims.

Gwyneth imagines plunging her ten inch needle into her mother's temple.

But, that's too easy. The beast must suffer. Her death must be nice and slow.

And she knows just what to do.

Gwyneth rummages through the refrigerator. She's glad that she's wearing a mask considering that the refrigerator has a nasty rotting smell to it. The smell is trying to rip her mask apart. She scrunches her nose and shakes her head at herself.

She's been quite lazy lately with keeping the place clean.

She picks up a dead bird and watches the blood drip onto the bottom of the refrigerator. She makes a mental note to clean it up later.

Buttons plays with his empty bowls. He's kind of giving his master a hint. He is dying of thirst and needs some water for extra strength. He's been extremely thirsty and hungry lately and Gwyneth can't keep up with him. She's trying her hardest to get him some food.

Using his paws, the poor thing turns the bowls onto their sides. Gwyneth takes this hint and fills one bowl up with a milk carton that's filled with dirty water. She's only been able to collect rain water because her water well has been having issues. It's old and she doesn't understand what she needs to do to fix it.

She's contemplated on leaving her woods to go hunt for a repair man and kidnap him. She has this elaborate plan that once he finishes the job, she would then kill him. No witnesses and no other people have to be involved.

Of course, she's been too scared to actually leave her woods. She's been too scared to knock on the door to the farmer's house.

That would surely scare her half to death. He's a scary man.

Gwyneth slabs the dead bird onto a chicken-juiced paper plate and grabs the fireplace poker. She watches her poor dog slop up the water.

She feels like crying. She feels like a failure to her dog. She loves him so much and she feels as though she isn't doing enough for him. He's like her child that she needs to take care of.

The poor thing needs food. Hell, SHE needs food. She's starving but she always makes sure that her dog eats first. She will eat later. That's why she's cooking up this bird for him.

As she exits the shack, she completely ignores her mother's cries.

What a baby.

Approaching the fire-pit, Gwyneth places the dead bird through the sharp tip of the fireplace poker. She sets the bird over the crackling fire.

Her toes are cold and she places her feet closer to the fire. The warmth licks at her boots like she used to lick the top of her ice-cream cone.

MMMM... ice-cream. It's been so long.

Thinking of the tasty treat makes her mouth water.

"Can I at least have some water?" Ruby whines.

Still a baby.

Gwyneth reluctantly heads back to the shack. Besides, she doesn't want her mother to die of thirst. She wants to kill her. It's the only way. If she has to feed her and give her water like her dog, she might as well fill her up before she reaches her impending doom.

While Gwyneth is inside, Ruby tries to untie the wire. It's extremely tight and she can't even get it to move an inch. She pulls with all her might. Her face turns beat red like the blood that bleeds from her nose.

She's too weak and she knows this. She just wants the hell out of here. She wants to go home to her nice warm house. She wants to kiss her husband on the mouth and make sweet love to him. She wants to forget all about this THING that she gave birth to.

She wishes that she never had Gwyneth in the first place. That's what she gets for being a whore. That's what she gets for falling in love with a man who didn't love her back.

That's what she gets for believing a liar. That's what she gets for putting her heart on her sleeve. That's what she gets for messing around with a married Sheriff.

And that thought has haunted her for twenty-four-years.

Ruby bangs on the cage. Hopefully there are hunters around. They could hear her cries for help. Maybe they could come and rescue her. She needs rescued from this crazy ass Bitch.

"HEEELLLPPP!" Ruby screams at the top of her lungs. "Can anyone hear me?"

Gwyneth storms out of the shack with Buttons' dog bowl filled with water. She angrily steps in front of Ruby as the beast grips onto the sides of the cage.

She throws the water into Ruby's face.

Gwyneth actually cringes after she does it. She knows that was wasted water but it was definitely worth it. The look on her mother's face is priceless. It's filled with such hate.

Gwyneth wants to laugh at that dumb look on her mother's pitiful face. But, she holds her laughter back. This isn't a laughing matter and she's taught herself to control her giggling.

Ruby spits at Gwyneth. The spit lands onto the snowy ground. "I should've killed you that day instead of dropping you off!"

Gwyneth throws the dog bowl but it clangs against the dog cage.

Ruby continues, "Don't worry dear daughter. I hate you too!" she smiles, showing bloody teeth. The blood from her nose has slipped into her mouth.

Ruby grabs the bars of the dog cage and violently shakes it.

"Somebody please help!" she screams.

Gwyneth can't help it this time. Quietly, SHE LAUGHS.

Chapter Twenty-Two

Marybeth blinks as heavy snowflakes land on her eyelashes. She doesn't know how Roman talked her into this silly adventure. She doesn't know why she even agreed to it. She doesn't want to do this. She doesn't want to be here.

The snow is coming down harder and making her visibility useless. The air is teeth-chattering. At least two inches of snow has stuck to the ground; just waiting for their boots to crush it like a bug. This is not fun for her and she wants to go home.

Most importantly, these woods are incredibly scary. Marybeth feels this sudden fear inside of her body. At first, she thought she was shaking from the cold, but then, she quickly realized that her shakiness is from the terrifying trees and the tornado sound of the wind.

Not to mention, these woods give her an eerie feeling of death and decay.

Marybeth is trying to be hopeful for her brother, but as soon as they stepped foot inside, she immediately felt as if her soul was taken over by a demon. This negative energy revolves around them like a spiritual orb. She's imagining evil ghosts flying past their heads.

This isn't her idea of a fun time. This is not what she expected either.

She didn't expect to feel so numb and exhausted. It feels as if someone or something is tugging at her boots and pulling her along. It feels as though she can't breathe.

As she glances down at the ground to make sure that they're not stepping on hidden trap wires, her Santa hat falls off her head. Her blonde curls blow in the breeze.

She's suddenly angry and emotional.

She quickly snatches the hat off the ground and places it back on top of her head. Snow is clinging onto her black, pea coat with gold buttons and she notices this inconvenience as a nuisance. She angrily wipes the snow off her coat with her gloved hand.

She's crying and her sniffles break Roman's concentration. He tries to look at her face but she turns away. She doesn't want to upset him.

Roman opens his mouth to ask her if she's okay but he decides against it. He knows what her problem is. He knows that she is not enjoying this little trip. She tried to get out of it multiple times and he wouldn't let her. He kept making her feel guilty by saying, "You promised!"

As he trudges through the snow, he thinks about her feelings. He immediately feels awful about everything and he wants to apologize. He just can't seem to say the words.

He's not an apologetic person. He's an asshole quite honestly and he's always acknowledged that he's received this rotten attitude from their mother.

Joni is an awful human being and she's making her son the same exact way.

Roman shakes his head; causing his Elf hat to dangle back and forth on the top of his head. He's carrying a string of Christmas lights and a plastic bag containing a fresh piece of steak.

Marybeth glances over at the bouncing lights as they drag on the snowy ground. Roman nonchalantly glances over at her; watching her as she shakes her head in annoyance.

"I told you that I want to decorate her shack with Christmas lights," Roman replies.

Marybeth is angry. "You don't even know who 'HER' is!"

"You are such a Grinch!"

"Call me what you want but I disapprove of this. We are bothering this poor woman!"

"Poor woman!" Roman exclaims. "You don't even know who she is either. What a joke. Besides, I have been watching this woman ever since me and dad went hunting a few weeks ago. We stumbled upon her shack then. This, I already mentioned to you."

"Roman, apparently she wants to be left alone. She lives in a shack in the woods!"

This boy just doesn't get it. He doesn't understand who he could possibly be messing with. He told her the stories. He told her what happened the last time he showed up uninvited. He told her how scared he felt. He told her that he thought he was going to die!

What an idiot, Marybeth thinks to herself. *I have an idiot for a brother.*

Roman pauses for a moment. Holding his breath, he searches the area.

Angrily, he glares at his sister. "Will you keep your voice down?! She has a dog that we need to look out for!" Roman quickly looks away.

This piece of information was not shared with her. *Of course he didn't tell me this! What kind of an asshole doesn't share this important information!*

Marybeth is sarcastic. "That's just wonderful. I would love to be eaten alive."

Roman suddenly slows his pace.

"We need to approach this situation slowly and carefully," he demands.

Marybeth thinks for a moment. She thinks about the two missing women from those newspapers that she saw in her father's office. She thinks about the gap in their disappearances.

Her detective skills kick in and she suddenly feels this excitement at the pit of her stomach.

"I wonder if all of this is connected," she says.

Roman is confused. "What are you talking about?" he asks angrily.

"A couple articles I read about. Disappearances of women and such. No one knows anything. Or… no one wants to speak up."

"Interesting…" Roman trails off.

"I think it's possible that the mysterious woman in the woods… is one of the missing women. It could happen. Maybe she killed someone and ran from law enforcement."

Roman ponders this scenario. He thinks that Marybeth is wrong but he doesn't have the guts to tell her this. She would instantly become upset and accuse him of calling her stupid. She's the most sensitive girl he's ever known and he doesn't want to hurt her feelings right now.

"Listen; to tell you the truth," Roman says, "I have been doing some research about those stories. I truly believe that the young girl is the one who lives in that shack."

Roman pauses and waits for a response. Marybeth seems engaged inside of her own mind and he isn't quite sure if she's even listening to him.

But, he continues on anyways, "I also think she killed her mother too. I read that the little girl was killed after she disappeared. However, I don't believe that. I do believe that the mother abandoned her and then left town. They were both pronounced dead."

Marybeth shakes her head no. "That's crazy," she says.

Roman knew that she would disagree. She always does. She thinks that she knows everything. She thinks that she can solve cases better and faster than he can.

And he must prove her wrong. He must show her that he's smart enough to figure out murder cases as well as she does. He has to show her that he's just as reliable.

Roman suddenly slows his pace once again. He thinks that he heard something.

He isn't quite sure what he heard, but he definitely heard something moving around in these creepy woods. It could just be his imagination. He's been imagining a man running around with a chainsaw. He pictures this psychopath chopping up their bodies and throwing them into the pits of Hell. He watches this killer in his mind as he eats their body parts.

Roman shakes the idea out of his brain. He immediately hallucinates; thinking that he heard his brain jingling with Christmas bells.

What is it about these woods? Are they making us go crazy?

Marybeth searches the woods. She suddenly stops; listening to the trees swaying in the wind. She watches a squirrel climb up a tree.

As Roman watches the squirrel as well, he lets out the breath that he was holding. He rolls his eyes. They are worrying way too much about being killed. If the woman doesn't want to talk, then they will gladly leave. He doesn't want any confrontations. He doesn't want his sister to be in any kind of danger. And he sure doesn't want them to die.

Marybeth's teeth chatter. She's freezing and her cheeks are rosy.

"I have a very bad feeling about this. I feel sick to my stomach. I'm seriously shaking," Marybeth whines as she tightens the scarf around her neck.

Roman ignores her and begins walking again. "No bodies were

ever found. If this woman is that little girl, I want to talk to her. Ask her if she would allow me to interview her for a documentary. It's for my film project."

Marybeth shakes her head. She's surprised that her neck doesn't hurt from shaking her head so much at him. Her brother is truly an idiot.

"You're crazier," she says. "I can't believe we are here for a stupid film project."

Roman turns toward her to defend his passion, but, he stops as soon as he hears the growling dog standing in front of them.

Buttons slowly approaches them with his teeth sharp and his mouth wide.

Roman takes baby steps toward Marybeth. He then steps in front of her as he says to Buttons, "Hey now puppy, calm down. Remember me? I got something for you."

Marybeth is terrified as she watches Buttons creep closer. His teeth are like fangs and he's ready to bite. His silky black fur is covered in snow. He looks healthy and clean.

"I guess this is her dog?" Marybeth whispers.

Buttons growls louder this time. He takes another small step toward Roman.

"I'm not sure about his name," Roman whispers back as he slowly slips his gloved hand inside of the plastic bag. He pulls out the rare piece of steak and shakes it at Buttons as a tease.

Roman is arrogant now; a smirk upon his face. "I came prepared for this."

Buttons licks his chops and watches Roman suspiciously as he takes another step. Roman shakes the steak again and laughs; taunting the dog because he, "has no brain," like his father makes it a point to tell everyone.

As Buttons takes another step, just two inches away from Roman, he suddenly turns his head back toward the direction of the shack. He then quickly looks back at Roman with drool dangling from the outside of his mouth.

He whimpers just as Roman tosses the steak onto the snowy ground.

Buttons takes off toward the shack.

Marybeth shakes her head again; hearing the sound of jingling bells. Well, she THINKS she heard the sound of jingling bells.

Maybe she's going crazy too.

"You shouldn't have taunted him like that... ASSHOLE," Marybeth says.

Gwyneth looks worried as she stands next to the fire-pit with large burning tree stumps. She's created a bonfire and at this point, she doesn't care if the smoke is spotted. She is freezing and she needs to warm up. The past couple days have been way too cold and she can't take it anymore. This is sometimes the only problem she has in the winter time. She doesn't like to be freezing cold. She likes to feel the warmth of a cozy fire.

As she lowers the dog whistle from her mouth, she spots Buttons running toward her.

Gwyneth clicks her tongue. Buttons barks and then looks back past the clearing and toward the trees. He licks his chops again. He clearly wants to chomp down on that beautiful piece of steak. The poor dog imagines himself eating the juiciness as it slips down his throat.

Gwyneth points past the clearing and toward the direction of where Buttons came from. Buttons whimpers; lowering his head. Gwyneth watches him intently.

He then looks back once again, licking his chops for that piece of steak.

Roman picks up the piece of steak and places it back inside of the plastic bag. He chuckles as if Marybeth just told a joke.

But his sister rolls her eyes.

"I really don't think we should do this. It's not too late to turn back," Marybeth pleads.

It really isn't too late to go back. The crazy woman in the woods did not see them there, only her mangy mutt. The woman doesn't even know that they're almost to her shack. They could turn around and run back to the car. They could drive away and act like nothing ever happened.

But of course, Roman would not allow that to happen. He would not allow them to leave without trying to get any viable information from the mouth of this psychopath.

And that's what she is... a psychopath. Who decides to live in the woods? How can a person survive that type of environment?

Marybeth knows that she hasn't gotten a chance to see the shack yet, but she's almost one-hundred percent sure that it's not the best standing building in the block.

And she's pretty sure that this woman will not talk to them. She's pretty sure that the crazy lady in the woods will try to kill them. She's tried to tell Roman this time and time again but the kid is just so determined to prove her wrong. He tries to prove her wrong any chance that he gets.

He thinks that every situation can be rainbows and butterflies.

He needs a major wake up call.

Roman is suddenly angry with her. "Leave then, Marybeth! Her shack is my mission. I'm not going anywhere but there. I need this documentary to happen." He pauses, "Could you imagine?" He looks up at the sky as if he's asking the clouds for an answer.

Snowflakes drop onto his face and he laughs. He laughs loudly up into the sky as if the snowflakes told him a joke. He thinks that everything is a joke. Marybeth reminds him almost every day that not every situation is something to laugh about.

"Imagine what?" Marybeth asks annoyed.

She's ready to leave but she doesn't want to leave him alone. He will likely die. He begged for her help because he thinks that she has the power to fight any battle that comes her way.

She might be strong but she's not THAT strong.

If the woman in the woods wants to kill them, she will. She doesn't seem the type to play any games. Anyone who lives in the woods and chooses to be alone definitely does not want to be bothered. That is a fact that smart human beings can comprehend.

BUT, her brother isn't smart most of the time.

"That I would be the one to solve the pieces of the puzzle. That I would be the one to sacrifice my life in order to find out the truth about these missing women!" He pauses as he waits for Marybeth's response. She looks at him as if he's a fool. "I would be a hero! A legend!"

Marybeth is extremely irritated. He doesn't seem to be taking this situation seriously as usual. As usual, he looks like a dumb ass.

"You're nothing but a jackass! Get over yourself!" Marybeth yells.

"Ye have no faith. Whatever. Let's keep going, we're almost there."

Almost there? She doesn't want to be almost there! She wants to turn around and go home. She has this sinking feeling in the pit of her stomach. She's overwhelmed with feelings of fear and helplessness. She thinks that she will be helpless once they reach their destination.

She came here to help. She came here to fight her brother's battle.

But she doesn't think that she can.

"The only thing that you're going to do is get us killed," Marybeth accuses.

Roman waves his hand as if what she just said was the most ridiculous thing he's ever heard. He seriously needs to wake up out of this nightmare. He needs to leave… and fast.

Roman spots the campfire smoke.

Gwyneth has listened to her mother's screams and cries for far too long now. She doesn't know exactly how long but she has this sense that it's been hours.

She hasn't seen a clock or a watch in quite some time. As a matter of fact, she doesn't even know how to tell time. She used to because her siblings taught her. The one that she found at the fisherman's cabin six years ago broke on the way back to her shack.

As she thinks of this notion, she becomes angry with herself. She's angry for not educating herself in the last twelve years. She could've hunted for educational books.

Who is she kidding? Educational books are not easy to find. Hunters don't carry math books or writing books. They carry rifles to shoot deer or bears for food.

BUT no one has a shot a bear in her woods.

Gwyneth is angry as she cuts the wire off the dog cage door with her scissors. Ruby watches as she waits patiently to escape her daughter's wrath.

Ruby looks sick and exhausted. Her mouth is still covered in blood. Her lips are dry and cracked. She's cold and shivers as the wind blows through the trees.

She tries to ignore the cold but she's been left out here for too long. She feels as though she will have hyperthermia if she doesn't get out of here.

She imagines herself running toward her car and jumping inside of it.

That's what she should have done in the first place.

If she knew that her crazy Bitch of a daughter was hunting her like an invaded animal, she would have never driven out here.

She should've stayed in her cozy home and got ready for work. But instead, she thought about her abandoned baby and wanted to go back in time to finally end these hurtful memories.

She wanted to end everything once and for all. She wanted to see the area one last time because she had absolutely no intention of ever coming back after this visit.

What a crock of shit.

Gwyneth opens the cage and drags her mother out of it.

Ruby pleads, "Gwyneth, please! What is wrong with you?"

What's wrong with me? She thinks to herself as she glares at her mother with disdain.

What kind of question is that? Is this woman stupid?

Well, Gwyneth already knows the answer to that question. Of course she is. She dumped her daughter in the woods like she was a disease. And she never came back.

Ruby's voice is in Gwyneth's head once again, "I'll be back for you tomorrow. Go hide."

Gripping onto Ruby's hair, she pulls at it, making her mother look up at her.

Ruby stares at her with tears in her eyes as she pleads with her sadness. Gwyneth stares back, unpleasant memories flooding her brain like an overflowing swimming pool.

In one swift move, Gwyneth's ten inch sewing needle is inside of her fingertips.

And she slices her mother's throat.

As it gushes out that beautiful red blood, Ruby reaches for Gwyneth in desperation.

Chapter Twenty-Three

Gwyneth's mind is twirling in large circles like a Hula-Hoop. She's making herself dizzy as she thinks about her body spinning like a wheel.

Her eyes dart from Buttons to the trees at the edge of the clearing. Buttons is clearly trying to warn her. She wishes that the damn dog could speak. She wishes that SHE could speak.

She wishes that she could yell and scream at every single intruder who steps onto her territory. She wishes that she could tell them how she feels.

She wishes that she could've told her mother how she felt.

But, it's too late for that. It wasn't meant to be.

She wasn't meant to live a good life with the woman who gave birth to her. She wasn't meant to live with a father who didn't want anything to do with her growing up.

No one came to save her. No one came back for her.

And that is something that she's gotten over… until she came across the beast in her woods.

Why would she ever come back here?

Gwyneth is suddenly frantic but she tries to keep herself calm. She's been handling her fear for years and it's not time to let her guard down.

Running to the picnic table, she snatches her fishing wire. She then runs to the edge of the trees with her bright, blue, boots fitting nice and snug on her feet.

Hurriedly, she places this additional wire around the surrounding trees in front of the picnic table. Her hands are shaking and her mind is racing.

Who in the hell is coming now?

Why can't people just leave her alone?

She's probably asked that question every day of living in these woods. She was under the impression that these woods were private property but no one ever listens. No one reads her, "NO HUNTING," sign. No one pays attention as they walk through either; constantly tripping over her wire because they're nothing but careless creatures.

And she doesn't care if they get hurt. She doesn't care if they bleed to death.

As she makes her way toward the shack, she clicks her tongue at Buttons. He follows her and they go inside; quietly closing the door. She does not want her precious best friend getting hurt. He might be only six-years-old, but he needs to makes sure that he takes care of himself.

Quite honestly, Gwyneth is getting sick and tired of living this kind of life. She loves the woods, but she wants to live somewhere warm and inviting. She wants to eat her favorite foods again. She wants to use running water out of a faucet.

Every day she hopes. But every day she's still stuck in her shack.

Roman and Marybeth spot the shack from a shorter distance. The campfire is blazing hot.

Marybeth's mind is going berserk. She's having a hard time thinking straight. Her body temperature has dropped and she feels weak in the knees. She feels like vomiting.

Roman suddenly stops her with his hand; just short of a trip wire.

She slowly closes her eyes and then opens them as if her eyelids had plans to glue them shut. Her mind is irrational and she can't focus on what they are doing anymore.

She doesn't feel well and her stomach is growling.

Roman whispers, "We have to be super careful. I once witnessed her attaching wire around the trees." He's still holding her back with his arm.

Marybeth whispers back, "Seriously? We need to…"

Roman suddenly places his finger to his lips to shush her; cutting her off. He points downward toward the wire that she didn't even care to notice.

This psychopath is very skillful and knowledgeable. She seems cunning and determined to catch her prey. This is not a good sign for them and Marybeth has had enough.

She's had enough of this nonsense of Roman's interview. She's had enough of him not listening to her. She's had enough of him talking about his wants and needs.

What about hers? She WANTS to get the hell out of here. She NEEDS a hot shower, some food and a good night's rest. She's sick and tired of her brother's selfishness.

Roman tugs on her sleeve. She looks at him with death in her eyes. She's so angry with him. If she had the strength, she would punch him square in the face. She would laugh too because he deserves it. She would then kick him where the sun doesn't shine.

As she imagines doing this, he tugs on her a second time. She rolls her eyes as he points again. She doesn't care about any wire. *I just want out of here!*

They bend down together and inspect the wire. Without thinking, Roman repeatedly flicks it with his fingers as it shakes like salt and pepper shakers.

Marybeth slaps his hand. "Will you stop it dummy?! I swear you have no brains!" she yells.

He's not going to have any brains when I'm done with him.

She pushes his hand away from the wire. For a split second, it looked like he was about to flick it again. She has this sudden urge to flick his eyeballs. She wants to punch him in the head.

They both slowly stand up. Cautiously, they step over the wire.

Marybeth waits for something to happen. She refuses to move in her spot. It's as if her boots are frozen to the ground. She's shaking uncontrollably. She can't handle being out here any longer. She doesn't want to see the shack up close and personal.

That is HER personal space… whoever she is. That is her home that they are about to invade. This is her territory and they are there to destroy it.

Marybeth believes with all her heart that Roman has something planned that he hasn't mentioned. He seems to be too excited for this. He's not thinking rational. He's being secretive and she doesn't like it. He's being a snake in the grass.

The sound of her jingling cans outside vibrate inside of Gwyneth's whole body. Her anxiety is through the roof of the shack and she's becoming angry and irritated.

These people won't stop. They won't stop bothering her. They won't let her live a peaceful life. They won't let her enjoy the finer things in life like playing in the snow with her dog.

That's all Buttons wants to do. But she can't promise him that right now.

Gwyneth peeks through the cracked front door.

Ruby mouths a small prayer for herself. She knows that her life is about to end. She knows that her daughter has finally gotten what she wanted: her mother buried six feet under.

The beast is lying inside of the dog cage again with a bandage taped around her neck. The ten inch sewing needle didn't complete the job.

Gwyneth's chalkboard and a tiny piece of blue chalk lie next to Ruby's pitiful body.

Gwyneth is sitting on the bench of the picnic table as she places a piece of chicken through her fireplace poker. Her campfire blazes bright as she then places the chicken over the hot flames. The smell of the food makes her stomach growl. She hasn't eaten all day because she's been too busy handling the beast.

Ruby gently taps the cage with the chalkboard.

She wants to beat this Bitch with it. She wants to hit her over the head and then run out of the cage. But she isn't sure how far she will get with a broken ankle. Gwyneth made sure to break it with her harpoon. She made sure that she wasn't able to escape at all.

This girl is smart. She's strong and capable of taking care of herself.

Ruby realizes this and starts to cry. Her dumb, mute, daughter finally toughened up. Maybe leaving her out in the wilderness was something that she HAD to do.

Gwyneth leaves her fire and approaches the dog cage. She eyes her mother suspiciously.

Ruby taps the cage once again with the chalkboard.

All she needs is this Bitch to open the door. Open it so she can escape.

Gwyneth takes the chalkboard from Ruby through the bars of the cage. The words on the chalkboard are just a jumbled mess to her and she doesn't know what it says.

She turns the chalkboard so Ruby can see her own words written. Gwyneth points to them.

Ruby points to her bandaged neck.

She can't talk, just like her daughter.

Gwyneth is irritated. She stares at the words one last time and tries to read them. She understands the words, "Go now," but it's the next two words she doesn't understand.

Ruby points to her mouth and then waves her hand in circles.

The next two words are, "Won't tell," but Gwyneth still doesn't understand, frustrating her even more. She's mad at herself for not understanding four simple words. She can count four words. She knows that much. It might not be a lot, but at least it's something.

She feels the heat rise on her face as she glares at Ruby.

Suddenly, she throws the chalkboard at the cage, startling her mother half to death. She then storms off toward the shack once again.

She enters the shack and slams the door. She doesn't want to deal with her mother anymore. Maybe she should just let her go and live. After all this time, all she's ever wanted was to kill her mother. And now that she has the perfect opportunity, she wants to back out.

She doesn't understand why. She doesn't understand her own mind. She wants to see this woman suffer like she did. She wants to see the blood from her body shoot out like a squirt gun.

These second thoughts are making her angry.

She just wants her mother out of her life again. She wants her to disappear and never come back. She thinks that she should let her live.

As she contemplates on releasing her mother, she packs her filthy Unicorn bookbag with a bottle of water, a piece of chicken from her disgusting refrigerator and a blanket.

She's making herself angry with her own thoughts.

As she exits the shack, she glances over at her pitiful mother as she tries to keep warm inside of her fancy coat. Gwyneth wants to kick her own ass for not taking the coat in the first place.

Her mother's white tank-top and gray sweatpants are destroyed anyways. Blood is caked on them and they're dirty from her being dragged around inside of the cage.

Gwyneth should've taken those too. She should've just let the Bitch sit there bare naked and freeze to death. That would've killed her quick.

Gwyneth suddenly rushes toward the cage and opens the door. She drags Ruby out by her hair. She's surprised that she still has any hair from as much as Gwyneth has pulled out of the scalp. She might look bald by the time she's done with her.

She rips the bandage off her mother's neck. The old Bitch cries out in pain as more blood oozes from her wound. Ruby places her hands over her neck; trying to stop the bleeding.

Gwyneth then snatches the harpoon off the picnic table and tosses it over her shoulders. It lands on her back with a thud. Then, she does the same with her book-bag.

She looks over at her chicken cooking inside of the fire and sighs. Eating will have to wait until later. She removes the fireplace poker out of the fire and then places it on top of the picnic table. She licks her lips as she glances at the chicken. The smell is extremely appetizing.

Clicking her tongue at Buttons and nodding her head for him to run inside the shack, she grabs Ruby by her armpits and begins dragging her through the woods.

Memories of her childhood flood her brain. She's tired of thinking about the past. She's ready to move on and forget about it. She wants to forget about her Bitch of a mother.

Dragging her mother for five miles is exhausting and she's ready to go to sleep. She is extremely tired and feels as though she's becoming weaker. She needs to sleep for a couple days in order to get her strength back. She has never felt so exhausted in her entire life.

Even as a little girl.

She would sneak in a nap or two while Ruby was crocheting ugly blankets for the twins. Gwyneth would hide inside of her closet while her siblings colored on her bed. They were her "look outs." They made sure to wake her up when Ruby finished a project.

Gwyneth did this for her siblings as well. The twins would hold each for warmth inside of Gwyneth's closet. The house was always cold because Ruby didn't believe in heat.

One time, the twins almost got caught. They crept out of the closet just as Ruby stepped inside of Gwyneth's bedroom to question her about where the twins were.

Ruby had her suspicions of something going on, but she never figured out what they were up to. She used to threaten to beat them with belts if they didn't tell her what was going on.

That was the story of their lives.

Gwyneth reaches the exact same spot where her mother dumped her twelve years ago.

As she approaches the edge of the woods, Gwyneth stares at the exact same spot where her mother parked her car on that awful day.

Ruby's brand new vehicle is sitting in the same spot. The engine is still running.

Gwyneth contemplates on leaving with her mother. She could just climb right inside the passenger seat and take off without a look back.

Of course, she would have to go back to her shack to retrieve Buttons and personal items.

But knowing her luck, she would come back to an empty road. Ruby would not wait for her and Gwyneth knows this to be true.

She left her one time before, she would do it again.

This thought actually makes Gwyneth sad for a moment. She doesn't understand why she's even sad in the first place. She knows that her mother doesn't love her. She hasn't been sad in many years because she's pushed all of these memories at the back of her mind.

She's been strong and independent. She's been calm and wise when it comes to interacting with other humans. She's taught herself to act rational. She's taught herself to not care.

But, now she cares. She cares that her mother doesn't love her.

This thought haunted her brain for so long and she actually made herself forget. She made herself forget about her mother. She made herself forget about her siblings.

She made herself forget about her life before the wilderness.

Her wilderness. Her woods. Her territory.

They are something that is part of her now. She can't leave. She can't leave her precious shack with space for only her and Buttons.

She can't leave her fire-pit. She can't leave her trees. She can't leave her useless water well.

She plans to get it fixed soon.

She has lots of plans. These plans only include her and Buttons.

Her plans don't include this Bitch.

Ruby nods her head as if she just understood Gwyneth's thoughts.

She mouths the words, "Thank you," as she continues to nod her head.

Thank me for what? Gwyneth asks in her mind. *For letting you go? Well, I shouldn't. I should kill you right now.*

Ruby then signals for Gwyneth to help her stand up. The girl complies as she stares at Ruby's broken ankle. The bone is protruding through her skin and blood oozes down the sides of her socks and boots.

Gwyneth lifts her up. Ruby leans on a tree for support. The beast is sweating profusely and she looks absolutely sick. Her neck wound looks infected.

Ruby nods once again and mouths the words, "Thank you."

Gwyneth suddenly doesn't like to be thanked; especially by her mother. She doesn't like doing good deeds for anyone. No one has ever done any good deeds for her. No one has truly helped her in the time of need. No one has ever THANKED HER before.

This thought is taking time to process. This whole situation is taking time to process.

She still can't believe that she's chosen to let her mother go.

She doesn't want to let her go. She wants to watch her suffer in pain. She wants to watch her die a horrible death and she wants to be the one to do it.

Ruby signals with her finger for Gwyneth to come closer. Gwyneth hesitates at first. She has absolutely no trust in this beast. She never will.

But Gwyneth slightly leans forward. She can smell the cigarette smoke from her mother's breath. Some things just never change. She knew that this Bitch wouldn't stop smoking.

She had always imagined her mother accidently swallowing a cigarette and choking to death. She imagined the smoke burning her throat and setting her on fire.

Now THAT would have been a sight to see.

Ruby is whispering as Gwyneth moves her ear closer to her mother's mouth. "If… I… didn't… leave… you… how… would… you… be?"

Gwyneth stares at her mother's crusty lips. She stares at her bloody neck.

She then stares into the eyes of this monster.

A monster that she's wanted dead her whole life. A monster that never deserved to give birth to the children she had. A monster that deserved to die a long time ago.

Ruby continues, "Lindsay… told… me… you… were… dead."

That SHE was dead? How could Lindsay do such a thing?

Gwyneth is quite shocked. Her mind is racing as she wonders if her mother is lying once again. She's wondering if someone told her mother to come here. She's wondering if there's some sort of plot against her. She's wondering if other people will show up to kill her.

Gwyneth starts to cry.

Again, she doesn't know why she's letting this woman release her tears that she's held back for many years. These tears have not slid down her cheeks for a very long time and she never planned to let them. She feels weak when she cries. She feels like a baby.

And she's not a baby.

Not anymore.

Suddenly, Ruby reaches behind Gwyneth and grabs her harpoon off her back.

Gwyneth has been waiting for this moment. She's been waiting for her mother to so something stupid that would help change her decision.

She's been waiting to finally kill her.

In an instant, Gwyneth lifts her ten inch needle out of her glove. Stabbing Ruby in her right eye, she twists her weapon like a screw driver. She then stabs deep into Ruby's neck wound and then slices it a second time.

The sweet sound of juicy blood sends shivers down Gwyneth's spine.

This is her happy place. This is what she was born to do and this is where she will stay for the rest of her life. No one will take that away from her.

And this beast will never hurt her again.

Ruby falls to the ground as she cries in agony. Her gurgling screams worry Gwyneth considering how close they are to the road. She doesn't like to be close to the road. She feels exposed. She doesn't like to feel exposed. It makes her worry too much.

And she thinks that she will get caught.

By who? By many…

She quickly glances at the field across from the dirt road. She looks up and down the street to make sure that no one is nearby.

Ruby reaches out toward Gwyneth; blood on her hands and fingers. Gwyneth watches her as the blood continues to ooze from her neck wound.

Unable to hold herself up any longer, Ruby lies down on her side as a lonely tear slides onto her temple and into her ear.

Gwyneth kneels on both knees and leans into her mother's face;

watching her as she exhales her last breath. Her mother's eyes are open and staring at Gwyneth for help.

Her eyes look like two black holes.

Ahhh…. the black hole.

She's finally where she belongs.

Opening the Unicorn bookbag, Gwyneth pulls out the blanket.

She stares at her mother as if she's going to jump up and say, "I'm not dead Bitch!" She envisions her getting up and strangling Gwyneth's neck with her bare hands. She envisions her stabbing Gwyneth's eyes with her ten inch sewing needle.

Shaking the thoughts from her mind, she reaches for Ruby's gray Eskimo coat with the fur on the hood. She rips it off of her; leaving her lie there in just her white tank top.

Gwyneth puts on the coat. She then pulls Ruby's blue boots right off her feet.

This gives her the bright idea to finally take off her small black boots. She places the old ones inside of the bookbag and then slips on the blue boots.

Gwyneth feels accomplished. She feels happy and safe once again. She feels like this weight has been lifted off her shoulders.

She's finally killed the beast.

Her siblings would be proud. They would hug her and kiss her on the cheek while telling her how proud they are of her.

Gwyneth smiles behind her T-shirt mask as she wraps the blanket around Ruby's dead body.

She hasn't truly smiled for a long time.

Grabbing her mother by her broken ankle, Gwyneth starts her journey toward the shack, dragging the dead body of Ruby Glacier.

Chapter Twenty-Four

Gwyneth's mouth drools like a dog as she craves for some hot apple pie.

She's been thinking about this dessert quite a lot since her mother stepped foot into her woods. She used to love to plop a big spoonful of whipped cream on top of her pie because her mother actually let her do it; which was a huge surprise. She never let her do anything.

She thinks of this delightful dessert as she continues to peek through the cracked door of the warm shack. Burning logs blaze inside of the fireplace to warm up her beloved dog.

Buttons peeks through the crack of the door as he listens to boot-crunching noises coming from outside. He growls a low growl as he stares up at Gwyneth with sadness in his eyes.

It's as if he can smell that juicy piece of steak from inside of the shack.

The poor dog imagines his teeth sinking into it and ripping it apart. He imagines the steak sliding down his throat and into his hungry belly. He imagines being stuffed and full.

Buttons whimpers.

Roman and Marybeth slowly make their way toward the picnic table.

Marybeth is intrigued but shocked to find that someone is living in such conditions. The shack looks as though it might fall over any minute. The door is crooked and hangs off of its' hinges. If there are any, she can't tell. The place looks like a Hell-hole.

She spots a crayon-colored family portrait of a woman and a dog on the front of the shack door. The woman's hood covers her entire head and the dog is perched on his back legs.

Two, small, blue dots indicate the woman's eyeballs underneath the hood.

Marybeth's eyes wander to the picnic table; a frightened

expression upon her face.

Roman looks around the area; hoping for this, "woman of the hour," to step outside and greet them. He hopes that she welcomes them with open arms this time around.

He hopes and prays that she agrees to an interview.

But, the sudden, quiet, environment makes him nervous. It's as if the wilderness is telling him and his sister to get the hell out of her territory. The trees seem to warn intruders as soon as they arrive but these people never listen. Roman and Marybeth did not listen.

The sudden, quiet, air finally helps Roman to realize that he's been acting a fool. His mind is telling him to turn around and leave. His heart races with fear. He is suddenly terrified.

He's reached his destination safe and sound but now he's wishing that he would've listened to his sister. He's finally realized how stupid he sounds by telling his sister that this woman will talk to them. He knows deep down that she will not respond. She didn't the first time and he has no idea why she would this second time. He's done nothing but act arrogant.

He's been foolish and careless. He's been blind for not seeing the truth and foolish for dragging his poor sister through dangerous territory. He realizes that he's put her life in danger and that is something that he's never wanted to do. It's something that he's never planned to do.

Maybe his father is right… he's a selfish asshole who only thinks about himself.

As he thinks about his behavior, he suddenly stops Marybeth once again with his arm; pointing toward the extra wire around the trees that Gwyneth just placed.

Cautiously, they duck their heads as to not catch their hats on the sharpness of the wire.

Roman suddenly thinks that they even LOOK foolish for wearing Christmas hats. They look foolish for carrying Christmas lights; in hopes to help the woman decorate.

He has no idea what he was thinking. He has no common sense.

Marybeth is right; this woman wants to be left alone. She could be a killer and he's now placed both of their lives inside of the killers' hands. She will crush them in her fist like an ant.

He's placed them inside of a spider's web. She's ready to pounce on her prey any second.

As they approach the picnic table, Marybeth places a gloved hand over her mouth.

She whispers, "What the hell?"

Roman's eyes widen. "Is that what I think it is?! A dead body?!"

They approach Ruby Glacier's lifeless body. They simultaneously bend down to observe her eyeballs. Roman scrunches his face in disgust. He covers his nose with his hand.

"I recognize her from the newspaper clippings! That's Ruby! The woman who vanished a few weeks ago!" Marybeth exclaims. She suddenly feels accomplished like she solved a puzzle.

She is the real hero here. She will be the legend.

She knew she would figure it out. She knew all along that SHE would make a better detective than her brother. She will follow their father's footsteps.

Roman doesn't listen to his sister as she brags about her puzzle-solving skills. "Is that a button in place of her eyeball?" he asks as he reaches out to touch the bloody button.

Marybeth quickly grabs his hand as they both immediately realize that they are staring at a DEAD WOMAN. She's deader than a doorknob and they have no idea what to do next.

Straightening upright with horrified looks upon their faces, they stare at each other.

The harpoon's sharp edge quickly impales through Roman's right eye.

Instantly killing him.

Roman's body, the piece of steak and the Christmas lights fall to the ground at Marybeth's feet. As she steps back, staring into her brother's empty eyes, she screams in horror.

With tears in her eyes, she looks up as the door to the shack hangs wide open.

Childhood memories flood Marybeth's brain. She's running through a backyard with Roman as they chase each other with tree branches. They laugh hysterically as Roman trips over his own feet and land face first into the snow. He looks up at his sister with snow in his teeth.

As Marybeth blinks tears, she remembers her father hugging her tightly and kissing her on the forehead as he promises to take great care of her and Roman. That's what he promised.

She's lived a great life. She was well taken care of and loved by many. Her mother was a pain in the butt, but she realizes now that her mother did truly love her.

She wishes in this moment, that she could hug her parents and tell them that she loves them. She wishes that they were sitting on the beach at an expensive resort as they sip lemonade or some kind of flavorful juice. She wishes that they would've taken one last vacation before college. She also wishes that her brother wouldn't have brought them here in this nightmare.

Gwyneth stands in the doorway, pointing the harpoon straight at Marybeth.

The girl blinks, unsure of what to do. It's as if her boots are frozen to the ground once again. It's as if the snow is pulling her through the wet mud. She can't move. She can't think clearly.

All she can do is stare into the face of a heartless killer as everything moves in slow motion.

Marybeth takes off; running as fast as she can as the snow creeps inside of her socks.

Gwyneth clicks her tongue at Buttons.

Oh that sweet sound of his master's clicking. Sometimes, he loves to hear it. And this time, he knows that he's in for a treat. She smells sweet and tasty. The poor dog imagines devouring her neck and biting through her veins. He imagines tearing her apart and ravishing her heart.

Buttons takes off toward Marybeth.

Gwyneth watches and listens intently as Marybeth cries out for help.

As the poor girl runs, she frantically looks behind her shoulders.

Her life flashes before her eyes. It's as if a strike of lightning zaps her brain. She sees herself playing in the snow with Roman. They are making snow angels in the front yard of their father's house. The neighbor drives past and waves. Her mother is building a Snowman.

She can't believe that her mother is outside playing with them. But she quickly remembers that Joni used to play with them when they were little. She seemed to love them more at that time in their lives. The hate didn't begin until they turned into teenagers.

Marybeth's thoughts are distracting. She slips on the wet snow and falls to the ground.

Buttons flies through the air like a Frisbee and pounces on the poor girls' head. Growling, he bites at her ear and then down to her shoulder. He then tries to nip at her neck.

She desperately tries to fight off this rabid-looking dog. There's slobber everywhere and he's biting her as if he hasn't eaten in days. He does look hungry and this makes her feel bad.

But, the pain is excruciating and her energy level is decreasing by the second. She feels out of breath and unable to control this dog's anger. She can't believe that she actually feels bad!

Marybeth knows now that she's going to die today. This fact is right in front of her face.

She knew that this would happen. She told Roman that he was putting them in danger.

She warned him of the repercussions of his actions. She isn't sure if he finally realized this notion before he died. She isn't sure what his thoughts were or how he was feeling.

Marybeth screams, "Someone help me! Please!!" But she knows that no one will hear her.

Buttons rips apart her coat sleeve of her arm as her cries fill the quiet woods.

No one can hear her. No one can see what is happening. No one will show up to save her.

She knows this. She knows that her death is inevitable and she's preparing for it.

She smells the sweet scent of her blood. Her energy is completely gone and she smiles up into the sky. If she's going to die, she's going to die in peace. She's going to die happy.

As she takes her last breath, Buttons bites a chunk of skin, blood, veins and fat out of the side of her neck. The blood squirts like a squirt gun. Gwyneth loves to watch that happen.

Lying on the snowy ground, she bleeds to death.

Gwyneth approaches the dead body; patting Buttons on the top of his head as he eats.

She stares at the young girl, wishing that she had her good looks. Her blonde curls and beautiful blue eyes are astonishing. Gwyneth can't wait to dig her fingers into those bright, dead eyes. She can't wait to make this girl look even prettier. She would love to do a make-over.

She grabs the girls' ankles as Buttons continues to feed; dragging her through the woods like a rag doll. Gwyneth is overly excited about this sewing project.

She's never had anything so beautiful.

Gwyneth's heart is filled with pure love. She's never seen such beautiful people in her life.

She can't believe that these two stumbled upon her shack. She hasn't felt this excited since she was a little girl. She feels a different kind of adrenaline rush. It feels soft and cozy.

Her excitement always consisted of killing animals for food. Her excitement is continuously toward the love of her precious Buttons. And, she doesn't understand why she feels this way.

She's never been excited about intruders stepping into her woods. She's never been excited to have "friends" over to her house. It's as if she's a child again.

She wonders if she should offer them a cup of water. Maybe she should offer them a piece of chicken bone left inside of the fire-pit or one of her dead birds from the refrigerator.

Gwyneth giggles as she drags Roman's dead body closer to the picnic table and next to Marybeth. All of this pent up adrenaline is giving her the energy that she needs.

She moves like a rocket shooting off toward space. Lifting Roman, she slightly struggles but is able to toss him next to Ruby on top of the picnic table.

Picking up her needle and thread, she closely inspects the second knot that she prepared before she was rudely interrupted. Well, they're not rude anymore.

Just dead.

Plucking the second button off the table like a feather, she begins to sew it into the socket of her mother's left eye. She doesn't want to complete this work sloppy, but she can't wait to finish her mother so she can move on to bigger and better things. Her mother was a washed up, disgusting, pig who deserved to die. She doesn't deserve a fancy burial either.

These new creatures that she happened to snag like a fish out of water; deserve great care and relaxation. They do deserve the best even though they intruded onto her property.

Buttons continues to chomp his teeth into Marybeth's inside guts.

Without looking up from sewing, Gwyneth clicks her tongue. Buttons' head pops up as if he was just digging into the ground. There's blood on his snout. He licks his chops.

Gwyneth finishes her sewing. Buttons watches her intently as she stands up from the bench and drags Marybeth closer to the picnic table. Buttons growls.

Gwyneth stops for a moment; her eyes glaring at her beloved dog.

They seem to be having a misunderstanding. He must think that his eating is endless. He must think that he can spend the rest of the night feeding on this poor, innocent girl.

Innocent girl? Gwyneth questions in her mind.

She isn't innocent at all. She stepped inside of an illegal territory; her and this boy.

What makes them so special? She kills everyone who crosses the line.

And now, Buttons is crossing the line. He has the nerve to growl at her like she's incapable of punishing him. She's quite shocked actually. He's never growled at her like this before.

Gwyneth spots the bag of steak on the ground. Maybe that will fill him up for the night.

She has this sudden urge to tease him with it. She's never felt like being mean toward Buttons… EVER. But, his growling has really upset her and she isn't sure why he's turned on her like this. She isn't sure why he's behaving like a lunatic.

Well, he didn't TURN on her. He was just simply eating his meal. He was interrupted, that's all. He was interrupted by her clicking sound. Maybe he doesn't like that sound.

Gwyneth pulls the piece of steak out of the bag.

Buttons whimpers.

She hesitates for a moment.

She knows that she can't tease her Buttons like that. He's very precious to her. He's extremely loyal and will do anything for her. He just happened to be incredibly hungry and that is quite understandable. She loves this dog with all of her heart.

She watches as Buttons whimpers a second time. He lowers his head as if he understands that growling at her was a mistake. He didn't mean to do it. He's just hungry.

Gwyneth tosses the steak onto the ground.

Buttons devours it like he devoured that piece of fish when they first met just six years ago.

Her poor pup is only six-years-old. He's still wild and free. He still wants to run and play in the snow. He wants to jump through a

Snowman.

Gwyneth thinks about this as she watches him eat that piece of rare steak. She imagines them running through the snow as Buttons playfully tackles her.

It's time for them play in the snow; after she finishes the job. She will build a Snowman and chase her dog like she's five-years-old again.

She wishes she would've had Buttons as a small child. He could've helped save her from all of those beatings from her mother. He could've been there for her emotionally.

But, that would make him older and she doesn't want him to get older yet. He has many years ahead of him and she doesn't want to think about losing him.

The thought makes her quite sad.

She can't even imagine living her life without Buttons. She was lonely and frightened all of the time. She felt insecure and stupid as if she didn't know how to survive on her own.

That isn't her anymore.

And she knows this. She might not know a whole lot, but she knows that she's incredibly strong. She knows that she can survive whatever comes her way.

She isn't afraid of anyone or anything. She's stood up to a bear once and killed it before it had a chance to attack her.

She's very smart. She knows just enough to get her by. She doesn't have to know how to divide or subtract. She doesn't divide or subtract anything as a matter of fact.

And she doesn't have to get to know people either. She wants to be left alone with her dog. She wants to live in her shack and sleep on a dirty cot.

She wishes that she could tell people this. She wishes that they would understand her choices in life. *Everyone has a choice to live the way they want to live.* Well, that's what Gwyneth thinks and believes. Her mother used to tell her that everyone has a choice.

Ruby also used to tell her that if she chooses to be a bum for the rest of her life, then that was HER choice. Ruby Glacier used to give out advice as if she knew what she was talking about. She felt so smart and determined to give adequate advice to her children.

She used to tell the twins that one day they were going to make a choice that would make them look stupid. She said that this choice would most likely be the worst choice of their lives.

Gwyneth ponders this as she leaves Buttons to his eating.

She enters the shack and approaches the desk. Lifting the container, she grabs extra thread.

It's time to get busy.

Chapter Twenty-Five

William St. Rose pulls his police cruiser into his driveway. Placing it into park, he rests his head onto the steering wheel. The Sheriff has had such a long day and he is hoping and praying that his beloved wife doesn't complain about their kids.

Every day for the past two weeks, he's come home to her ranting and raving about their bad attitudes and Roman's, "pig sty of a room."

William usually sits and listens to her bitch and moan. He normally nods his head and agrees to whatever is coming out of her mouth. But quite frankly, he has this sudden urge to scream in her face. Sometimes, he wants to tell her that they throw an "attitude" because she's a Bitch.

But, he doesn't. He doesn't have what his buddies' call, "the balls," to call her a Bitch. They tell him that she's a cheater and that he needs to get rid of her. They constantly remind him that she is only with him for the money.

But he argues… what money? He doesn't have money like they think he does. But of course, his buddies don't know about all of HER money. And they never will.

William unzips his Sheriff jacket and grabs the hidden pack of cigarettes from inside of the jacket pocket. He glances at the front door and quickly replaces the pack inside of the pocket.

What a chicken shit. He's too scared to tell his wife that he's smoking cigarettes again.

She absolutely hates them. It took every bone in his body to fight for his Cuban cigars. He told her that he WAS NOT giving those up. He agreed to give up cigarettes.

That was three years ago. He needs them more now than ever before.

His children are leaving him alone with this crazy lunatic. They're going off to college and he whole heartedly blames it on his wife.

She's tough as nails. She doesn't care about anyone's feelings.

She never used to be like that. She enjoyed spending time with the children when they were younger. She used to play card games and Hide n' Seek.

They used to hug her when they came home from Kindergarten. They used to plant huge kisses on her cheek and tell her that they loved her. They adored their mother.

William isn't quite sure what happened.

Maybe she got sick and tired of their shit. When they turned thirteen, they used to play nasty tricks on her and laugh about it for days. They used to say that it was a joke and for her to, "stop getting her panties in a bunch." She didn't even understand that statement so they made fun of her for not understanding. It was quite embarrassing for her.

Something must have happened between the three of them and no one will tell him. He's asked numerous times what the hell happened and none of them will fess up.

Joni just blames it on them being, "little asshole teenaged kids."

William craves a cigarette as he thinks about the fight that he and Joni had the night before. He closes his eyes and silently prays that she has gotten over this fight.

Sometimes, she will fight with William about the fight that they had the day before and it will last for days on end. She is relentless and annoying. Maybe that's why his kids are frustrated with her. No, maybe that's why they HATE her.

The words that come out of her mouth are so hurtful that the kids choose to ignore it.

They choose to not let her bother them anymore and William needs to take their advice.

They've told him time and time again to ignore her nasty words. They know that she only says these nasty things to piss them off. She even admits it to their faces.

William closes his eyes, "God, help me."

As he enters the foyer, he waits for Joni to approach him. When she doesn't arrive, he slams the front door. He isn't even sure why he slams it. Maybe, it was to get a rouse out of her. Sometimes, he wants to start some bullshit just to see what she would say or do.

He takes his jacket off and carefully hangs it up on the coat rack. He doesn't want his cigarette pack exposed for her to see. That would start another huge fight that he isn't prepared for… a fight that he really doesn't have the energy to deal with.

He smells the delicious aroma of food cooking in the kitchen. He smells the candle scent of strawberries and cream wafting from the living-room.

His spirits are high. She's cooking AND she lit romantic candles.

Maybe she finally realized that she was acting like a huge Bitch last night.

One could only wish.

William enters the kitchen. He watches Joni place food onto a plate as he places his holster onto the kitchen table. He likes to have it near him in case something serious ever happens.

He isn't sure what could happen, but he isn't too sure of his wife's behavior lately.

As he takes a seat, he slowly lifts his wine glass and sniffs the drink. He then takes a sip of the red wine; sloshing inside of his mouth like mouthwash.

"What a long day," William starts the conversation, "What's for dinner?"

William isn't sure if she is still upset about the words that came out of HIS mouth last night. He said some awful things that he regrets. He doesn't like fighting and he doesn't like saying mean things to the people he loves.

William waits for a response as he glances at his gun lying nicely on the table in front of him. Of course, he would never shoot his wife, but, if she became a knife-wielding lunatic, well, he would shoot her on the spot.

Joni turns from the stove. She's dressed in a cute, red, apron with a yellow sunflower printed on the front. Her dress is white and long; touching the tips of her toes. She's shoeless; exposing red-painted toenails. She's only wearing black eyeliner on her face and her hair is pulled up into a pony-tail. Her smile is bright. Her teeth glow in the kitchen light.

William doesn't remember seeing her look so plain. She normally wears enough make-up to cover up the face of three people. She's always dressed in tight clothing and she wouldn't dare put her hair up into a pony-tail. She loves to make fun of women who do just that.

He LOVES this new look. He loves the smile on her face.

Joni gives William a kiss on his cheek.

And lately, she hasn't approached him with such love.

William immediately eyes her suspiciously. He desperately tries to hide the fact that he thinks that she's plotting his death. Butter him up and then slice his throat.

She places his dinner plate in front of him; next to his gun.

He's waiting for her to tell him to take it off the table. She doesn't like guns. She doesn't like it when he flaunts his weapon all over the house as if he's God's gift to criminals.

Yes, a gift from God. He's placed onto this Earth to help criminals get back on their feet.

But, she doesn't say a word about his gun. She doesn't say a word about their fight last night. She doesn't even say a word about the smell of his cigarette breath.

"Fresh chicken strips and veggies," Joni replies.

William shakes his head. "Just because you're on this ridiculous diet, doesn't mean that I have to succumb to it," he whines as he scrunches his nose like a two-year-old.

Joni dismisses his statement with a wave of her hand. "Oh, you can get over it dear. You can afford to lose a few extra pounds." She smiles with bright, white, freshly-brushed teeth.

William is sarcastic, "What a great support system I have."

Joni giggles and then sits across the table from her husband. She devours her vegetables.

William continues to eye her suspiciously. He doesn't want to put his guard down completely. He has to admit though, he likes this new Joni. He likes the positive attitude and the upbeat of her tone. This is how she used to be. This is how she used to talk to him and the kids.

Of course, this new attitude also makes her look suspicious.

It is quite sudden AND after a big fight.

William continues, "Hungry huh? I'm sure with all that exercising you do."

He pushes his plate to the side and then gulps the rest of his wine.

He gets up from his seat and glances at Joni. She doesn't respond. She's not even looking at him as she shoves a piece of chicken into her mouth.

He becomes incredibly surprised that she's not yelling at him to sit down and eat his dinner.

He walks to the counter and pours more wine into his glass.

"So, where are the kids?" he asks before shoving the glass into his mouth.

Joni is shoving another piece of chicken into her mouth. "What do you mean?" she asks as she swallows her food. She then swigs a huge gulp of her own red wine.

"I called both of their cell phones. Neither one is picking up."

Joni places her empty wine glass onto the table. "They're upstairs. Doing what teenagers do," she answers as she shrugs her shoulders.

"And what exactly do teenagers do?" William asks as he takes another swig of his wine.

He's going to be drunk by the end of this conversation if he doesn't slow it down. He's starving and has no intention on eating this food that she's placed in front of him. He's ready to head to the burger joint alone and enjoy the juiciness of a rare burger.

Joni eats a bite of her vegetables. "You're overreacting… again."

"Am I really? 'Again' huh?" William asks defensively.

The man has the sudden urge to punch her in the face. He knows that he won't though. She would call the cops on him and he would be arrested. He doesn't need his fellow police officers calling him an abusive husband. He would never live it down.

Of course, with the way they act, they might even ask what she did to deserve it.

"Yes. Dear. AGAIN," Joni says, "You overreact to every little thing they want to do in life. You want them to do what YOU want them to do." Joni takes a pause to finish eating her vegetables. "It's not fair," she claims.

William is angry and almost chokes on his gulp of wine.

"Fair! You want to talk about fair?!" William dramatically pauses for his next words.

He knows that he really should calm down with the drinking, but he can't help it. This stupid Bitch expects him to eat diet food instead of a real meal.

"You know what's not fair?" he asks as he gulps the rest of his wine, "Living in the woods like some kind of animal! Living alone with a mutt!"

"What the HELL are you talking about?!" Joni yells.

"WHERE THE HELL ARE THE KIDS???!!!"

Joni slams her fork onto her plate. "I told you! UPSTAIRS!!"

William leaves the kitchen in complete anger. He's lost his marbles. He isn't even sure why he's yelling at her. She's done everything she could to make tonight good for them and he had to screw it up. He had to make her look suspicious even when she was being nice.

William stomps up the steps; followed by Joni.

He can feel the hairs on the back of his neck stand up. He's sweating profusely. He loosens the collar of his white shirt as he steps into the hallway.

He knew he should slow down the drinking. He feels drunk already and light-headed.

He has this urge to elbow Joni in her face. He wants to watch her fall down the stairs and break her neck. No, he wants to push her.

Hell, he can't even make up his mind on what he wants to do.

He feels her breath on the back of his neck. He just wants to turn around and slap her right across the face and he doesn't know why. He's never had these types of thoughts before.

He's never wanted to beat her so badly. She's been getting under his skin for the past two weeks and he's ready to bludgeon her to death.

But, he immediately regrets these horrible thoughts. His heart pounds with sadness. He loves his wife and he would never intentionally hurt her. He's never laid a hand on her.

And he doesn't understand what has come over him. He's starting to wonder if a demon crawled inside of his soul. He's wondering if he's been possessed.

William barges into Roman's bedroom.

The smell hits him instantly.

The smell of sweat and gym socks, the smell of burnt bacon, the faint smell of lavender and the smell of Marybeth's perfume.

William is taken aback by the mess. Joni is right. His room is seriously a pig sty. He can't even believe that Marybeth steps foot into this room. She is a very tidy and clean person.

Dirty clothes lie on the floor next to the clothes hamper, newspapers and books are scattered all over his unkempt bed. His sheets dangle on the side of the bed; exposing a yellow-stained mattress. Plates of uneaten food are stacked on top of his dresser.

Dust is caked on every single piece of furniture. A spilled drink has stained the carpet in front of the door.

William shakes his head as he looks around the empty room. No sign of Roman or Marybeth. William closes his eyes for a brief moment. He doesn't understand why his children would just leave the house without saying a word to their mother.

His heart starts to pound like a beating drum. He notices the children's cell phones neatly lying on Roman's nightstand. Why wouldn't they take those with them?

William quickly checks the closet as if the kids are five-years-old again.

Joni stands in the doorway with her arms crossed. An angry expression upon her face as she watches her husband frantically search the room as if they're pretending to hide.

William turns toward Roman's bed. He quickly notices the boy's filming documents scattered on top of his pillow. He picks up the notebook that's clipped to a clipboard. On the top of the page, Roman's handwriting reads: *"We're going back tonight."*

Joni pushes past William; snatching the clipboard out of her husband's hand. She reads the message on the notebook. She is suddenly confused and feels hopeless.

"They were here!" she yells, "Where the HELL did they go? And what the HELL does this mean?" She tosses the clipboard onto the bed.

"I know exactly what it means!" William shouts into her face. The shower of his spit stings her eyes. She suddenly cries; wiping William's saliva from her eyeballs.

William stares at her with tears in his eyes. She looks so upset and frightened. Since he stepped foot into his home this evening, he's done nothing but treat her like garbage.

He suddenly realizes this terrible act of bad behavior as he watches her pull a tissue out of her apron. She blows her nose. She's crying for her children and all he can do is stare at her.

He quickly pulls her into his arms and squeezes her tight. She cries into his chest. He caresses her head while whispering, "Sshhhh."

"I'm so sorry!" Joni wails, "They must've left when I went down to the basement to exercise! It's all my fault!"

William's tears spill down his cheeks.

He isn't even sure why Joni is crying.

Maybe she feels bad for treating them badly. Maybe she feels guilty for not paying any attention to them. Maybe she feels horrible for not being close to them for the past four years.

Or maybe she's guilty of hurting them.

William is suddenly suspicious of his wife once again. He's become suspicious of her behavior since he stepped foot inside of the house. Lately, she's been nothing but suspicious.

She's acting differently. This isn't Joni St. Rose. Maybe her body has been possessed by demons. Maybe she killed their children. Maybe she's hiding the bodies.

Marybeth has never left this house without her cell phone.

Maybe they did it on purpose because they didn't want to be bothered. Maybe they didn't want to be caught. Or maybe they truly forgot their phones because they were filled with excitement; excitement of becoming detectives themselves.

William thinks that he knows exactly where they went. Roman has become obsessed with some of these, "missing persons," cases. He's become obsessed with solving murders.

As William thinks about this scenario, he slightly grins. Maybe his son will follow in his father's footsteps after all. Maybe he's wanted to become a detective and he didn't want to tell William quite yet. Maybe he will move on to the police academy.

This nonsense of filming movies will finally end. His son will finally get a real job and have a family of his own. He will finally become a real man.

William lets go of Joni as she continues to cry. She seems emotional and caring right now.

This woman truly loves her children.

He isn't sure why he's doubted her in the first place. He's doubted her since the beginning of their relationship; which is terrible to ever admit. He would never tell her this. She would never forgive him. She might even divorce him and he doesn't have the energy to fight with her about houses and cars. And he doesn't want to fight about his children. They will always be his.

But of course he has doubts about Joni, he's a Sheriff!

But, sometimes being the Sheriff destroys relationships. It can destroy marriages.

It has for him.

He can't lose his children. That is not an option. That is not in the cards for his life.

William hugs his wife one more time as he stares at the clipboard on the bed.

"We're going back tonight."

He kisses Joni's cheek.

Without another word, William rushes out of the door.

Chapter Twenty-Six

Gwyneth feels that butterfly feeling in the pit of her stomach. She feels her heart race with excitement. That familiar adrenaline rush swallows her veins like hot lava.

She can feel the temperature rise throughout her entire body. She can see the cold air sizzle from the heat of her skin. Her face feels like it's on fire. For the first time, she wants to take her T-shirt mask right off her mouth. The steam from her hot breath busts through the mask like a torpedo. She watches the smoke as it flows through the air. It reminds her of cigarette smoke.

It's that nasty habit of Ruby Glacier.

It's a habit that Gwyneth refuses to succumb to.

Of course, Gwyneth has never stumbled upon a pack of cigarettes in twelve years. She hasn't gotten the chance to actually smoke one as an adult.

She did try one when she was eleven-years-old. Her siblings promised to never speak a word to their mother. They kept their promise because Gwyneth was never beat for it.

The beast had finally found time to take a shower. She was incredibly smelly and the dingy house smelled like shit stains and dirty vagina.

Gwyneth spots the pack of cigarettes on the kitchen table next to her mother's half-eaten chicken legs. The chicken wasn't fully cooked all the way through. Gwyneth was surprised that her mother wasn't vomiting. She should've gotten sick.

On second thought, Gwyneth was happy that her mother wasn't vomiting. That would've made her breath smell ten times more awful than what it already did.

Gwyneth wants to vomit just thinking about her mother vomiting. The thought is too much for her and she tries to tuck that memory in the back of her mind.

Her siblings watch their sister in fear. Not for fear of Gwyneth becoming addicted to the nasty cancer stick, but for fear of their sister getting caught.

Gwyneth swiftly picks up the pack and stares at the cigarettes as if they are snakes in the grass. She waits for them to chomp on her fingers. She waits for their teeth to crush the bones of her hand. She waits for her fingers to put them back down on the table.

But they don't. She won't allow them to.

She looks up at her siblings with mischievous eyes.

Her sister is in tears. Her brother repeatedly turns his head toward the bathroom as if Ruby will walk through the doorway at any second. Their hearts are pounding through their chests.

Gwyneth can hear her veins pulsate with every beat. The butterflies in her stomach are making her feel queasy. Her mind is racing with tons of questions.

Do they taste good? Will I smoke like my mother? Will I like them?

She wants to answer, "No," to every single question. However, she isn't too sure. If her mother loves them, maybe she will too. Maybe she will become addicted. Then, she would have to tell her mother so they could share her extra packs that she keeps hidden in her drawer.

On second thought, if she does become addicted, she will just steal them. Her mother would not allow her to share cigarettes. Ruby already complains about the prices of them.

Gwyneth slips a cigarette out of the pack. She then pulls the lighter out of the pack as well; looking at it with confused eyes as if it's a freak of nature.

She's watched her mother a thousand times place her finger on the flint wheel and button. She feels confident that she can quickly light this bad boy up and puff a smoke.

Gwyneth places her finger on the flint wheel, but it doesn't do anything. She slides it again, but she doesn't think that she's doing it hard enough.

The shower turns off. Her brother looks back at Gwyneth with a frightened expression upon his face. He waves his hands at her; motioning for her to hurry up.

Gwyneth quickly slides her fingers once again against the flint wheel. Nothing happens.

She doesn't understand what she is doing wrong.

Her brother hurriedly moves his twin sister inside of the doorway to be the "look out." He then rushes toward Gwyneth and snatches the lighter out of her fingertips.

He places his thumb on the flint wheel and quickly shows Gwyneth that she has to press the button at the same time. He hurriedly glances at his twin sister.

She waves her hand for him to hurry up as she peeks down the hallway. The bathroom door is wide open and Ruby is getting dressed.

The flame suddenly appears and Gwyneth stares at the brightness as if it's a star in the sky. She's immediately mesmerized as the flame moves side to side from the blow of her breath.

Her brother taps her on the shoulder.

Gwyneth looks at his terrified eyes. She glances back at her sister as she peeks through the hallway once again. Her sister whispers, "Hurry up!"

Gwyneth quickly places the tobacco rod to her lips. Her brother frantically shakes his head no and then snatches the cigarette. He turns it around and shoves the filter part between her lips.

Gwyneth glances back at her sister as she frantically whispers, "She's coming!"

Gwyneth places the tip of the cigarette into the flame. She inhales like she's watched her mother do thousands of times.

As Gwyneth hysterically coughs, her brother replaces the lighter inside of the pack of cigarettes and then places the pack onto the kitchen table.

Their sister watches Ruby drop something inside of the doorway to the bathroom. She watches her bend down to pick it up.

Gwyneth inhales a second time; choking as she coughs.

Gwyneth's brother waves his hand through the smoke to hide the smell. Gwyneth is coughing as she spits inside of the kitchen sink.

She doesn't like the taste. It is surely disgusting to her. She feels like she popped a couple of mints into her mouth and then chewed on them excessively. Her mouth feels tingly.

Her brother hurriedly snatches the cigarette out of Gwyneth's fingers and then turns on the water. He lets the water run all over the cigarette to put the fire out.

Their sister bolts from the doorway and sits on the floor next to her coloring book.

Gwyneth and her brother look at each other with desperate eyes.

Her brother quickly drops the cigarette down the drain of the sink and then grabs Gwyneth by her arm. He drags her to the floor next to their sister.

Ruby pops her head into the doorway of the living-room. She eyes her children suspiciously.

That infamous dumb look is upon her face.

"What are you doing?" Ruby asks as she sniffs the air.

"Coloring," Gwyneth's brother answers. He lifts the coloring book into the air.

"What's that smell?" Ruby asks.

The children sniff the air with their noses. Gwyneth even looks around dumbfounded as she snorts her nose like a pig. Her siblings want to bust out laughing but they hold back. Her brother's eyes are wide as he's ready to burst into laughter.

"What smell?" Gwyneth's sister asks sweetly.

"Cigarettes," Ruby replies as she glares at Gwyneth.

"It always smells like that in here," their brother answers.

Ruby watches them with rage in her eyes.

The children hold in their breaths. They prepare themselves for screaming and yelling.

Ruby suddenly turns away; ignoring them. She stomps down the hallway and slams the door to her bedroom. The house rattles like a snake.

The living-room air fills with children's laughter.

Gwyneth exits the shack with her extra thread. The memory of her siblings laughing in the living-room that day makes her giggle. It was the best day of their lives.

She returns to the picnic table.

She suddenly realizes that she forgot extra buttons. This angers her but she quickly tries to calm herself down. She's having a good day. There's absolutely no reason to get mad over something so silly. And she knows that her anger is silly.

Glancing down at the front of her mother's gray Eskimo coat, she shrugs her shoulders.

She can handle wearing an open coat for years to come. At least it's nice and new. It should last her for quite a-while. She isn't planning on buying one anytime soon.

Gwyneth giggles again as she cuts the bottom two buttons off her coat with her scissors. She leaves only two buttons left.

She's ready to get to work.

Approaching Roman as he lies on top of the picnic table, Gwyneth shoves her fingers into his right eye socket. She pulls the eye out of his skull.

Buttons licks his chops.

So does Gwyneth.

She is starving and this eyeball looks scrumptious. His blood smells delicious.

She rubs her fingers against the sliminess of the eyeball. The texture makes her weak in the knees. She wants to devour it but the look on her dog's face saddens her.

He's starving too. He needs to eat more than she does.

Gwyneth then shoves her fingers into Roman's left eye and pulls it out of the socket.

Her stomach growls but she ignores the pain.

She tosses both eyes to Buttons. He devours them as if he hasn't eaten in years.

Well, days. Still, it's been a long time. She needs to cut the bodies for meat and pack them inside of her refrigerator. She CANNOT wait to do that to her mother.

She's been, "biting at the bit," to cut her mother into pieces for many years.

She can't contain her excitement. Her blood pumps through her veins as if someone is punching them with their fist. She feels as though her veins might burst through her skin.

Gwyneth bends at the knees and leans toward Marybeth. She smells her sweet-smelling perfume. It reminds Gwyneth of peeled oranges.

She smells her hair; a faint scent of strawberries.

Gwyneth is craving a bowl of fruit. Her mother would buy her and her siblings some fruit for a special treat if they behaved well. She would always buy oranges, strawberries, grapes and apples. She would cut them into tiny pieces and place them onto paper plates.

Gwyneth can taste the sweetness of an orange. Those were her favorite. Her sister would eat the strawberries and her brother would devour the apples.

Gwyneth smiles as she thinks about her brother shoving a piece of apple into his mouth.

She giggles; placing her gloved hand onto Marybeth's black, pea coat. She places the tips of her fingers on top of the gold buttons.

She wants this coat as well. This one is beautiful.

Grabbing the scissors once again, she cuts two buttons off of Marybeth's coat. Her excitement continues as she stares at the gold color of the buttons.

It reminds her of the flame from her mother's lighter.

She stares into space as she remembers her brother's frightful expression. He knew how to light a cigarette. It was very impressive. She didn't know that he paid attention to details that well. He was only five-years-old. He was truly smart.

Straightening, Gwyneth eyes her mother as if she's about to climb off the picnic table. She glares at the beast as she feels the heat rise into her face.

Angrily, Gwyneth stomps the snow with her bright, blue, boot like a bull.

She reaches the other side of the table where her mother lies. She places one hand on Ruby's arm and her other hand on Ruby's stomach. She pulls her mother's body off the table and slides her onto the bench. Ruby's head hits the bench with a loud thump.

Walking back over to the other side where Roman lies, Gwyneth pushes his body over to the spot where Ruby was laying. Their blood combines together on top of the table.

Gwyneth giggles. Her happiness fills the air. She has never felt this happy as an adult.

She has an idea and this is the best idea she's ever had!

Struggling, she lifts Marybeth's lifeless body onto the bench. She takes a moment to catch her breath. She loves to get exercise, but lately, it's been a lot and it's definitely tiring her out.

She has plans to sleep for a couple days once she cuts their bodies for food.

Then, she will have play time with Buttons.

Holding in her breath, Gwyneth lifts Marybeth's body onto the picnic table next to Roman.

She's sweating profusely and she needs a drink of water. She knows that will have to wait. Time is ticking. She doesn't have much daylight time left and she needs to get more work done.

Licking her lips behind her mask, she begins the process of

sewing her mother's coat buttons into Roman's eyes sockets.

The sound that it makes reminds her of a rubber duck being squeezed inside of a bath tub filled with water.

Buttons finishes eating Roman's eyeballs. While watching Gwyneth, he heads into the shack. His mouth is dry and he's dying of thirst.

He sniffs the air of the shack as he licks his chops. His mouth is drooling for water.

He whimpers as he licks the empty water bowl.

He hasn't had fresh water since yesterday morning. The saliva is getting out of control; dropping onto the floor like a waterfall. The wetness absorbs inside of the wooden floor of the filthy shack. She needs to clean the place up.

Buttons suddenly jumps onto the counter and into the sink. He licks the water tap for water but there isn't any dripping out. The water tap inside of the shack hasn't worked for years either.

Whimpering, he jumps down.

As he paces the floor, he watches Gwyneth through the doorway of the shack.

Gwyneth sighs as she listens to Buttons' whimpering. She knows that he wants water. She knows that he needs it, now. He's probably extremely thirsty.

She knows this, but she can't seem to stop sewing. She wants to finish before the sky turns completely dark. She needs to take much care into this boy and girl.

They were destined to be together.

She cuts the thread; finishing her sewing on Roman's eyeballs.

Oh, he looks adorable! Just like my man doll I had when I was nine!

Gwyneth then slides more thread through the loop as she listens to Buttons' cries. She can't stop now. She will be done very soon. It won't take her long. She promises Buttons inside of her brain that she will hurry up and get him water.

Of course, he can't hear her but it was worth a try.

Gwyneth begins to sew Marybeth's buttons inside of her eye sockets.

She suddenly feels as if she has to be in a hurry. It's actually making her angry.

She doesn't like to be rushed. She likes to take her time and get things done the correct way. She doesn't like to half-ass a job. She wants her sewing skills to look perfect.

Now look at my sewing Ruby! My sewing is better than yours, Bitch!

She trembles as the sky turns darker. Her poor dog wants water. She can hear him scratching at the wooden floor. She can hear the clinking sound of Buttons' paws against the water bowl.

As she carefully places the tip of the needle inside of the eye socket, she hears Buttons barking like a wild animal. It sounds as if he's throwing his water bowl against the wall.

Gwyneth shakes her head. *Wait a couple minutes you damn dog!*

She feels the pressure. She feels trapped. She feels frustrated and annoyed.

She wants to scream at the top of her lungs, but she can't. She wants to scream and tell Buttons to wait a minute, but she can't. She wants to beat him for disrupting her, but she can't do that either. She's never beaten her dog and she doesn't want to start now.

As her heart pounds, she licks her lips; carefully sewing the next button into Marybeth's left eye socket. She should be a professional seamstress.

However, she doesn't even know that word. Gwyneth calls it, "sewing person."

Buttons continues to bark. He gallops through the shack like a horse; playing with his water bowl as if it's about to attack him.

He bumps into the card table, almost knocking it over. He then bumps into his master's sleeping cot. If this is what he has to do to get a little attention, then that's what he has to do.

Gwyneth feels overwhelmed. Her damn dog is making a ruckus inside of the shack but she doesn't want to stop to discipline him.

She's almost finished.

She slides the tip of the needle inside of the socket one last time.

Finishing, she stares at Marybeth and Roman; their beautiful buttons for eyes. She admires their new look. This is the best job that she's ever done.

As she hears the clatter of a water bowl, she smiles at her piece of artwork.

Morgan Wildfire's family has owned the farmhouse for two-hundred years. Morgan inherited the farmhouse from his father, Samuel

Wildfire, at the age of twenty-five.

Unfortunately, Morgan's father was diagnosed with cancer at the age of sixty. Six months later, he passed away only two days before Morgan's twenty-fifth birthday.

It was the worst birthday of his life.

Morgan's mother, Abigail Wildfire, tried to commit suicide after she finished baking Morgan's birthday cake. He found her lying in the bathtub after slitting her wrists.

After treatment at the hospital, Morgan sent Abigail to a mental institution.

Three months later, a fellow patient stabbed his mother with a fork on the side of her temple; killing her instantly. That patient was then shot by security guards for trying to stab the warden of the institution.

Morgan made a vow to his family that he would take great care of his land and the farmhouse. He promised to make sure that no one would destroy any part of the property.

Samuel Wildfire wasn't well-liked. During his ownership of the land, people accused him of being a crooked business man. People called him a liar and a thief.

Samuel stole the farmhouse from his brother, Edgar Wildfire, and he had lost all respect from his family and friends. He had even lost respect from his wife, Abigail.

The news of his possession of the farmhouse was plastered on the front page of their newspaper. He was called a traitor and a slime-ball.

People would show up at the farmhouse and try to shoot Samuel from across the woods.

It was also a hectic time for Morgan. He made no friends because the school-children called him a thief as well. They claimed that he would end up just like his father, a low-down, dirty, crook. They bullied him; throwing food in his face during lunchtime. They called him stupid and ugly. One day, they managed to break his glasses by throwing a huge snowball at his head.

Morgan cried a lot. His father told him to "toughen up." Samuel was a strong man and didn't take any crap from anyone. He begged his son to become strong like him. He begged him not to worry about what the children were calling him. Samuel even told him that if he had to get into a fight in order to protect himself, then his son had his full permission.

Morgan took advantage of that statement.

In tenth grade, another boy walked up to Morgan one day and slapped him on the side of the head. Morgan turned around to face his bully. Everyone stood in the hallway and watched intently. No one thought that Morgan had the balls to do anything about it.

He punched that boy square in the nose; breaking it. When the boy fell to the ground, Morgan repeatedly kicked him on the side of his stomach. He then stomped onto his chest.

The boy rolled over in pain; crying for his friend to help. Then, Morgan stomped on the boy's back with his boot; breaking his ribs and his back at the same time.

Morgan was sent to a juvenile facility for the remainder of his school career.

When he returned two years later to the farmhouse, it was as if nothing changed. His father was still hated and his mother hated her life.

Morgan was devoted to his parents. His vow to take care of the farmhouse has been a sacred vow that he will never forget.

That's why he's standing on his patio watching a thirteen-year-old girl through his binoculars. He watches her creep out of the field.

Her dirty, brown, hair hangs to her shoulders. The front of her light-purple shirt is caked with mud. She's wearing black shorts and muddy socks. There are no shoes on her feet.

She looks lost and lonely. She looks frightened as she shakes with fear.

Morgan watches her step onto the end of his gravel driveway.

She rubs her arms for warmth. She then blows hot breath into her palms.

Morgan glances up at the sky. A rain storm is coming. The clouds are dark and dreary.

The girl enters the woods.

Morgan shakes his head. When will people learn to stay away from his territory? His property is not for everyone to step into. This property is HIS. He earned this property and he will forever protect it. He will make sure that people suffer the consequences.

Placing his binoculars on the patio table, Morgan grabs his loaded shot gun.

Sighing, he turns to his wife who is standing at the screen door.

He smirks.

Chapter Twenty-Seven

The thirteen-year-old girl is terrified of the wilderness. She wonders why she even stepped foot into these woods. She's cold and confused. She's hungry and thirsty.

She suddenly remembers why. She remembers that her rotten, younger, brother told her to travel inside of these woods. He told her that she would find enough animals for food. Their family is starving and they volunteered for *her* to make the trip.

She doesn't even have a weapon. How in the world is she going to kill an animal?

They're extremely poor. They live inside of their older brother's van. Their parents were killed two weeks ago by a hunter in the next county.

They have nowhere else to go. They have nowhere to turn to. They have no other family members to help them through this tragedy.

So, they sent their sister to do the dirty work. She was told to search for animals as if she was in a scavenger hunt. They told her she wasn't allowed back inside of the van until she brought back food and supplies. They even wanted her to find water.

The younger brother heard wild stories about the farmhouse. They told her to stay away from the house. They told her she was allowed to enter the woods to find food.

The older brother was told by a friend that these woods were great for hunting deer and bears. He was told that many people had the chance to kill cubs.

The girl feels foolish. She feels trapped.

She can't believe that they made her do this.

Seeing the farmhouse up close and personal made her shit her pants.

Now, her shorts are soiled. The smell is making her stomach queasy. Vomit creeps up through her throat. She swallows it like water.

As she creeps through the woods, her poor feet steps on tree branches and leaves. The moisture soaks her socks. She softly cusses under her breath.

It would be nice to have a decent pair of shoes. Her white ones broke in half just two days ago while running through a field. She tripped; causing the hole at the bottom of her shoe to become bigger. She cried; knowing that her brothers would make fun of her.

That night, they managed to make a fire for warmth. Her older brother grabbed her shoe and stuck a burning tree branch through the hole. The shoe caught on fire; burning his thumb.

"Dumbass," the girl says, thinking of her older brother.

Sometimes she wishes that she was an only child. Sometimes she wishes that she had a sister to play with. She hates her brothers. They treat her like garbage because she isn't smart enough. She doesn't have the brains that they have. She wasn't destined to be an intelligent child.

This makes her sad. It makes her vulnerable.

And it makes her weak.

She is extremely weak. That's why she doesn't understand why her brothers sent *her* out into this forsaken place. These woods are scary. She has no intention on being in here for long.

She plans on staying away for a little bit of time to make it seem like she tried to find food.

She has no weapon to defend herself. She has no way of killing a deer or a bear cub.

She doesn't know what her brothers expect from her.

They must expect her to drag a dead animal through the woods, through the field and then another five miles down the gravel path behind the farmhouse.

They told her it was safe to walk through the gravel path. Her older brother told her that no one gets caught going that way.

She's a glutton for punishment.

She knows that they were lying to her. She knows that she's not very smart, but when it comes to those two assholes, she knows that they were messing with her head.

They don't care if she lives or dies. They already told her that if she doesn't return by the next morning, then they are leaving to go across the country. They said that they will not come looking for her.

They will just assume that an animal killed her instead of the other way around.

She knows that they planned on getting rid of her. They hate her. They always have.

Her older brother tried smothering her face with a pillow when she was a month old. Their father practically beat him to death. He couldn't sit down on his butt for two weeks.

This was just the perfect opportunity for them to leave her. They're probably on their way toward another state by now. They most likely left as soon she walked away from the van.

This saddens her as well. She left her favorite stuffed bunny in the backseat.

Her stomach growls loudly. She's so hungry she could eat a fly.

She suddenly stops and bends down toward the muddy ground. She can hear thunder in the distance. *Just great,* she thinks. *Now I'm going to be soaked too.*

She digs through the mud with her dirty fingers. She finds a worm.

This excites the poor girl. She smiles with yellow, crooked, foul-smelling teeth.

She pets the worm like a cat. "Hi there cute fella!"

Quickly, she shoves it into her mouth; chewing like a cow and smacking her lips.

Continuing through the woods, she glances up into the sky. The dark clouds are floating above her head. She laughs loudly. *Of course they're above my head! Everything hates me!*

She hates herself. She hates living this kind of life. She hates that her parents died.

As a matter of fact, she doesn't even know *how* her parents died. Her brothers came home one day and told her that they died and went to Heaven. They said it was a hunter in the woods.

Maybe they killed them, she thinks.

Shrugging her shoulders, she suddenly thinks of a bright idea.

Abruptly, she starts running.

Jumping over tree logs she looks like Superman flying through the air. She pulls on branches hanging from the trees as she runs like a wild Cheetah. She looks like a monkey climbing from tree to tree. She's fast and fierce.

Her feet sting from the sharp points of tree branches and rocks.

She imagines herself buying a new pair of shoes once she gets out of these woods.

No, she wants a pair of boots. She's never owned a pair of boots.

The girl suddenly stops as a raindrop lands onto her forehead. Giggling, she wipes it with her filthy fingers and then licks the raindrop from her hand.

Looking around the area, she picks up a tree log.

This is great exercise!

She bolts; running with the tree log under her smelly arm-pit.

She hasn't taken a shower in weeks. Her and her brothers stumbled upon an empty house. The owners weren't home. They left their backdoor unlocked.

Her older brother left them a treat in their toilet as well.

The girl giggles as she thinks of the huge turd that they all admired and laughed at. Her younger brother kept pointing to the toilet saying, "Oh, they're gonna love that!"

Her older brother took the longest shower. They made her go last. By the time it was her turn, the water was freezing cold. She didn't have the pleasure to enjoy her shower at all.

They are rotten to the core and they will get what they deserve someday.

Distracted by showers and turds, the girl suddenly trips over a root in the ground. It sends her flying through the air like Superman again.

Her face slams hard against the tree log; smacking her stomach onto the wet ground.

Crawling into a fetal position, she whimpers in pain.

Her busted mouth is bleeding. She touches the blood with her fingertips.

Her stomach feels like it was sliced in half. The pain is excruciating. She pictures a knife digging into her guts. She imagines her older brother cutting through her large intestine.

Slowly, she sits up. Raindrops fall onto her head.

She glances down toward her stomach and notices blood on her purple shirt.

"Oh no," she says, "I'm dying."

Ever so slowly, she tries to stand up.

She doesn't know what to do or where to go. She can't head back to the farmhouse. It's creepy-looking and scary. Besides, the owner will most likely kill her for being on his property.

Whimpering like a two-year-old child, she decides to continue through the woods. Hopefully she will come across a hunter. They can help her. Maybe they can take her home.

Maybe this was a great idea! Someone will find me and help me!

Gwyneth isn't one-hundred percent sure of when her birthday is, but she celebrates it before the snow falls. She knows that it happens right before the cold weather approaches.

Sometimes, she celebrates it twice: during the fall weather and whenever the first heavy snow hits the shack. She doesn't care. She can do what she wants.

If she wants two birthdays in one year, then she makes it happen. There's no one here to tell her that she isn't allowed. There's no one here to stop her.

This makes her completely happy. She's quite content turning eighteen without parental supervision. She's quite content with not having any parent figure bossing her around.

However, she does wish for a companion; an animal perhaps.

She becomes quite lonely during the fall season. She becomes even lonelier during the winter months. She doesn't have anything to cuddle with during the night.

She likes to have a small fire in the fireplace. It would be nice to have a cup of hot chocolate and a piece of hot apple pie.

As Gwyneth remembers the syrup dripping onto the apples, the closes the front door of the shack and makes her way toward the picnic table.

Hot apple pie would've been perfect for her eighteenth birthday.

She sighs as she sits down on the bench.

She sure misses eating her desserts. It was the only thing that the beast knew how to cook.

Gwyneth licks her lips as she sets her black and red marker onto the table. She opens her map like a fan and places it in front of her. She imagines hot apple pies jumping out of the trees on the map. This makes her giggle.

Using her dirty finger, she points at different sections of the map. She stops at an area covered in trees. Picking up the black marker, she circles the trees.

Gently, she continues to move her pointer finger throughout the map; stopping at another area with a row of houses. She draws a square around a house.

Connecting her finger to a small pond, she draws a triangle around the water.

Placing the black marker back onto the table, she then picks up the red one.

She imagines hot apple pies swimming in the pond. This makes her stomach growl louder and she bursts with laughter.

The sound of thunder interrupts her thoughts. She looks up at the sky as a raindrop plops onto the tip of her nose.

This rain sucks!

She reverts her attention back to the map. Dancing apple pies glow inside of all the houses.

On the top of the map, she writes the word, "SISTER."

Next to it, she writes the word, "BROTHER."

She knows how to specifically spell those words because her siblings taught her when she was ten-years-old. They made her trace the words fifty times. They didn't want her to ever forget how to write who she loved the most.

"Hello? Ma'am? Can you help me?"

Gwyneth is suddenly startled. Her body is frozen and her eyes are wide.

How can this be? Who the hell is in my woods?

Her black boots are frozen to the ground. She feels numb. The butterflies in her stomach are flapping their wings; making her want to vomit. She's shaking with fear.

Dropping the red marker onto the table, Gwyneth slowly turns around.

"Please help me," begs the thirteen-year-old girl, "I'm bleeding. I fell and I hurt badly."

Gwyneth suspiciously eyes her up and down. She stares at her mangled face; swollen and bleeding. She carefully glances at the girl's clothing. Her purple shirt is covered in blood and her socks are hanging half way off her feet.

She stares; unsure of what to do.

The young girl continues, "Hello? Did you hear me?" She points her bloody fingers at Gwyneth. Most of her nails are broken and dirt is caked underneath them. "See? There's blood. Do you have a Band-Aid?" she girl pushes for help.

Gwyneth continues to stare. Her mind is twirling in circles. She wonders if someone sent her this girl to taunt her. Maybe someone is playing a joke on her.

But who? She doesn't know anyone. No one knows where she's hiding. No one knows that she's been living here peacefully for the past six years. No one even knows her name.

The young girl stares at Gwyneth. "I'm talking to you girl."

Gwyneth slowly stands up from the bench.

Who the hell does this Bitch think she is?

She watches the girl for another moment. She suddenly feels sorry for her. She looks a mess. She looks like someone beat her to a pulp. She looks cold and hungry.

But, deep down Gwyneth truly doesn't care. This Bitch stepped onto Gwyneth's territory and now she must die. They all have to die. Those are HER rules.

Gwyneth holds up her finger; motioning for the girl to wait.

Turning, Gwyneth heads toward the shack; looking over her shoulder to make sure that this Bitch doesn't follow her. How dare she? Coming up behind Gwyneth like some sort of boss.

Gwyneth suddenly realizes that she could've been killed. She didn't hear a sound. The girl must have crept on her with quiet ease. She must take care of that problem immediately.

She never wants this to happen again. She wants to know as soon as possible as to when people approach her shack. This can NEVER happen again.

Once inside, Gwyneth panics.

She isn't sure why she's panicking. This is her home that she has to defend. She needs to be strong for herself. She needs to work through her fears.

Still panicking, she searches the shack for nothing. She opens cupboards and the refrigerator. She frantically opens her container on the desk.

Her brain suddenly lights up like a light-bulb.

She picks up her ten inch sewing needle. Eyeing it as if it's the first time she's ever seen it, she slowly slides it inside of her fingerless glove.

Her heart races with excitement. She's never been able to kill a young girl before. She can't believe that this dirty Bitch basically fell onto her lap.

With a smirk on her face, she snatches a paper towel off the card table.

She wonders how it will feel once the girl is dead. She wonders if she will feel sorry for her. She wonders if her heart just won't care at the moment.

She's craving for some fun. She's craving another killing.

She had a blast with Peyton and George. But, they were too easy. She wants to build a puzzle. She wants to figure out what will make this girl angry. She wants her to get mad and go after her. She wants this new friend to try to kill HER! She's ready for a fight!

While exiting the shack, Gwyneth sees that the girl has taken a few steps closer. She's bent over the picnic table; staring at the map. Her bloody finger follows the square and triangle.

Gwyneth is angry. She sees red. Her blood is pumping through her veins like a punch into a punching bag. That's what she wants to do… punch her and knock her ass out cold.

No, she wants to stab her eyeballs with her ten inch sewing needle.

Gwyneth is filled with rage as she stomps her boots toward the young girl. She doesn't even know her name. Quite frankly, she doesn't CARE what her name is.

She wants her dead.

The young girl sees Gwyneth in the corner of her eye. "I…I'm sorry. I didn't mean to make you mad."

Gwyneth shoves the paper towel into the girls' hand.

"Thank you," she answers as she wipes the blood from her mouth. She stares at Gwyneth with fear in her eyes. She has no idea what this freak is going to do to her.

She continues, "Do you live here or something? Like in the woods?" she asks.

The girl waits for a reply. When she realizes that she isn't getting one, she continues, "Can I live here with you?"

Gwyneth is completely shocked. She's NEVER had anyone ask her such a thing. She can't even fathom those words coming out of her mouth.

For a moment, Gwyneth isn't sure if the girl is joking. She looks around in search of people jumping out from behind trees. She imagines hunters approaching her with shot guns. She imagines a woman looking like her mother while holding a camera and saying,

"Caught you on camera!" She imagines an audience laughing at her.

Gwyneth finally shakes her head no and aggressively points her finger toward the clearing and into the woods. She then points her finger into the girls' face and then back toward the trees.

The girl continues to nag her, "I guess you can't talk huh?"

Gwyneth shakes her head no once again.

She points her finger into the young girls' face again and then back at the trees.

The girl ignores her. "Why can't you talk? What happened? Something with your throat?"

Gwyneth angrily shakes her head no and motions for her to leave again.

She's feeling frustrated and annoyed. Her anger has taken over her body and she is shaking with anxiety. She wants to puncture her throat to stop her from talking. She's had enough.

"Your voice box?" the girl asks.

Gwyneth glares at her; imagining herself stabbing the girls' swollen face.

"Your mouth?" the girl continues.

Gwyneth feels the hatred float inside of her soul. She feels her wrath.

In the blink of an eye, Gwyneth grips the young girls' throat and squeezes.

She chokes; coughing up her blood from her bleeding mouth.

Gwyneth suddenly lets go. While coughing and trying to catch her breath, the girl holds her neck with her cold fingers. She eyes Gwyneth suspiciously.

"Sorry I asked," she says, coughing hysterically.

Gwyneth grabs her by her hair and pulls her away from the picnic table. She's had enough of this Bitch. She needs to die now before she runs away and tells her family.

Gwyneth suddenly stops and thinks for a moment. She's completely torn. She wants to kill this girl but she also feels sorry for her. She looks disheveled and weak. If a bear caught sniff of her, she would be dead. She already smells like shit.

Speaking of shit, that's all Gwyneth has smelled since this girl stepped foot into her clearing. She can't believe that she's been walking around smelling like a sewer pipe.

The smell is travelling through her mask and into her mouth.

Gwyneth feels her stomach turn into knots. She feels queasy. The smell is starting to crawl inside of her mind.

Gwyneth pushes the girl and points past the clearing and into the trees once again.

"I'm not leaving you… I like it here," she looks around the trees. "I hate my brothers. They are mean to me. I… ran away. I hate my father too. I finally got away. I don't want to go back! Please don't make me!" the girl begs as she picks her nose.

Gwyneth stares into space for a moment. She imagines the girl spinning inside of that black hole. She imagines chopping her into itty-bitty pieces.

She watches the girl inspect her bloody booger. She pops it onto her tongue.

Gwyneth angrily pounds her forehead with her own fist.

The girl is excited. "Are you crazy?!! Because I am too!" she exclaims.

As she takes a step toward Gwyneth, Gwyneth takes a step backwards. The young girl giggles. Her giggle sounds just like Gwyneth's sister. The sound brings back memories that Gwyneth doesn't want to focus on right now. All she wants to focus on is killing this Bitch.

She gave her the option to leave and now she's refusing.

"I like to play games too!" the girl exclaims.

She takes another step. Gwyneth takes another step backwards.

Her heart is racing. She has no idea if this girl actually wants to play a game. She has no idea if she is being serious about living here.

Gwyneth thinks for a moment. She could use the help. She could teach her how to sew. She could teach her how to kill. She could help find food and supplies.

In an instant, the girl charges toward Gwyneth like a raging bull. She lowers her head. Gwyneth imagines fire blazing from her nostrils. She sees that her eyes are blood-shot.

The girl is screaming like a lunatic as she raises a tree branch into the air as if she's gripping onto a knife. Maybe a demon took over her soul. Maybe she took a crazy pill beforehand.

Gwyneth feels the heat spread throughout her body. Her sudden anger disperses like a detonating time bomb. She feels the flames lick at her chest. She feels the tug from her brain telling her to kill this crazy Bitch.

Gwyneth wastes no time. They tackle each other like vultures fighting for prey.

The girl tries to stab Gwyneth with the tree branch. It breaks; falling out of her hand.

Gwyneth quickly grabs her by her hair and pulls her down to the ground. The thunder in the sky slightly makes her jump but she doesn't let it stop her concentration.

The girl kicks Gwyneth square in the shin. The pain shoots up her leg like a rocket.

Gwyneth grabs the girls' foot and ankle; dragging her toward the fire-pit.

The young girl screams, "Get off of me! Let me go! I will kill you!"

Gwyneth suddenly feels the need to laugh. She would surely not kill her here and now. She must be crazy if she thinks that she can pull off her murder.

The girl manages to kick her foot out of Gwyneth's grasp.

Spotting a large-sized rock on the ground, the girl grabs it and quickly jumps into a fighting stance. She looks disheveled and scared. Her eyes are wide with fear.

"I'll hit you with this! I swear I will!"

Without another warning, the girl hurtles the rock. Gwyneth ducks; missing her head within a split second. She has to be fast. This crazy Bitch has a sudden energy boost.

Gwyneth pulls a muscle in her neck from ducking her head. She feels the burn brewing inside. The pain makes her want to cry. But, she won't do that in front of anyone.

The girl slips on wet leaves and loses her balance. Gwyneth charges at her like a speeding car with her head held high. She ignores the burn in her neck and runs toward the girl.

Gwyneth then lifts her forearms in mid-air and pushes with all her might; plowing into the young girl like a bulldozer.

The girl falls backwards toward the picnic table. She bashes her head onto the bench and then lands onto the ground. Gwyneth falls on top of her.

Blood oozes out of the poor girls' nostrils and mouth. She stares into Gwyneth's evil, bright, blue, eyes. She stares into the black hole; staring into the abyss.

The girls' eyes are tired and weak. Her body is shaking from the shock of the fall.

As Gwyneth stares into her eyes, she slowly slips the ten inch sewing needle out of her glove. She raises it high into the air.

Gwyneth's adrenaline is rising into the stormy clouds. It twirls into circles as it intertwines with the thunder and lightning. Her heart pounds with excitement. The lightning inside of her skull zaps the side of her brain; stinging her pulsating temples. It feels as though her brain is trying to puncture her skull; digging into the crevices.

Gwyneth's fist suddenly comes down with as much force as possible; shoving the needle into the girls' right eye. She twists the needle like a screwdriver.

Gwyneth is angry. She's angry for letting this Bitch get inside of her head. She's angry at herself for letting her guard down. She was seriously considering on letting her live in the shack.

With the needle gripped into her fist, she repeatedly stabs the girls' eye.

The last whimper escapes the girls' mouth.

Gwyneth stops; watching the girls' dead eyes stare up into the cloudy sky.

She wishes that she knew her name.

Blood has splattered all over Gwyneth's mask. She notices the mess as she glances down at her bloody, gloved hand. She's still gripping the blood-covered needle in her fist.

Abruptly, Gwyneth then realizes that she's lying on a dead body covered in shit.

Chapter Twenty-Eight

Gwyneth's breathing is fast and hard. Her lips are dry and she feels quite disgusting from all of the blood. She wants to jump into the water well and take a bath. As a matter of fact, she wouldn't mind drinking her bath water. Her throat hurts with each swallow of saliva.

Her bones feel brittle and her back is sore. Her left knee pulsates in pain from banging it off the ground. Her head pounds with a sudden migraine.

And her nose twitches from the smell of this shit-stained Bitch.

Slowly, Gwyneth crawls off the girl's lifeless body; her knees cracking with a "pop" sound.

She feels older than what she truly is. She feels like she's turning eighty instead of eighteen.

She then wonders how her body is going to feel once she turns thirty.

If she even makes it that far.

If people leave her alone she will live to be an old woman.

This thought saddens her exhausted brain. She doesn't want to be old. She doesn't want to have gray hair. She doesn't know what will actually happen *when* she becomes old.

Will she be able to hunt anymore? Will she be able to exercise and run through the woods? What will happen to her shack? Will it fall over? Will she have to build a new one?

And how would she do that? She doesn't have the materials to build a whole new house.

She contemplates this scenario. She must find materials before she turns old and gray. Hell, she might have to build a whole new shack NOW before it's too late.

Well, maybe she could wait a couple years just in case. It might be too soon to do it now.

She wants the new house to last until she's crippled with old age.

She wants it to fall down well after she's dead in the dirt.

Wait, how will she be buried? No one is here with her. She's going to die and her corpse will rot somewhere on the ground. She might even rot inside of the shack.

This thought is quite disturbing.

She looks down at the girl once again; wishing that she hadn't killed her. They could've become best friends. If one of them died, the other would be there to help bury them.

But then, who would bury the surviving friend?

There are too many emotions flowing inside of Gwyneth's heart and she doesn't like it. She doesn't like the fact that she's upsetting herself with thoughts of loneliness.

She truly is lonely. And this will haunt her for the rest of her life.

She doesn't want to be haunted by her own demons. Well, she doesn't want to be haunted at ALL but her own demons would make her afterlife a nightmare as well.

She imagines herself sitting at the picnic table with demons flying through the air above her head. They chomp down on her neck like a Vampire; killing her instantly.

Her blue eyes stare up into the sky just like this girl is doing now.

Gwyneth shakes these thoughts from her mind.

She's being completely unreasonable yet again. Sometimes, her imagination takes her by surprise; upsetting her mind and soul. Her soul doesn't like to be disrupted with silly lies.

Her soul likes to be left alone in the dark.

Just like her.

"Killing is wonderful isn't it?"

Gwyneth hears the man's voice from behind. Yet again, her back is turned and someone has crept upon it. This really needs to stop happening! She needs to come up with a decent plan in order to know exactly when someone is coming for her.

She's frantic as her heart feels a burning sensation. It might just burst into flames. It might rip out of her chest and bounce back into her forehead. She'll be set on fire.

This thought scares her half to death. She would never admit that to anyone but whoever is standing behind the golden door has put fear into her whole entire body.

Her eyes are wide and she has no idea what to do. She's scared to turn around.

Turn around and face who? Who is this man and why the hell is he in here?

As Gwyneth tries to catch her breath, she suddenly spins around with her needle high up into the air. She instantly thinks that this is a foolish and bold move, but what else is she supposed to do? How else should she react? Someone is once again in HER territory.

Morgan Wildfire points his shot gun directly at Gwyneth's head.

Dropping her arm as a way of surrendering, she starts to cry.

The tears fill her eyes and pour down her cheeks. She isn't quite sure why she's crying in the first place. She doesn't cry. It always makes her feel weak.

And she's not weak.

Her exhaustion has taken over her body and mind. This exhaustion has made her weak.

You let your guard down again Gwyneth! How can you be so stupid?

But, she's not stupid… just tired.

She's tired of dealing with intruders. She's tired of living alone. She confuses her own brain when she wishes for a companion, but then cries that she wants to be alone.

Her confusion is exhausting. Everything in her life is exhausting and right now she's prepared to give up. If this man wants to kill her, she will let him.

In a heartbeat.

Then what? What will happen to her shack? To her supplies?

Will he steal them? Will he bury them in the woods?

Her mind is overreacting once again. *Get a grip, Bitch!*

Morgan slowly takes a step toward her. His heart beats like a drum. He feels nervous and ashamed at the same time. Ashamed because he just watched this poor girl kill someone and he didn't do anything about it. He witnessed a murder and he let it happen.

She's the poor girl? Ha! The poor girl is the one dead.

But Morgan saw it. He saw the dead girl attack Gwyneth. He saw the whole thing happen and didn't stop her from killing the Bitch.

Morgan softly chuckles.

"I thought someone was here in my woods. Wasn't sure though. I'm glad I followed that girl you just killed. See for myself," Morgan says.

Gwyneth tightens her grip on the needle. If this man is looking for a fight, she's going to give him one. She will fight to the death for this property. This is HERS!

Morgan notices the tight grip of her hand. He doesn't miss a thing when it comes to standing face-to-face with strangers on his property. He's done this all before.

He's killed people who have refused to leave. He's shot at little kids running through the woods. He doesn't care. This is his land and he will do whatever is necessary to protect it.

He made this promise and he doesn't plan to break it anytime soon.

And this girl protected his land. She protects it from harmful people.

He can tell that she loves living here. She's made a life in that shack. She has a water well, food, a picnic table, a nice fire-pit and a weapon to help protect herself.

"There's no need for that," Morgan says as he glances at her clenched fist. "Honestly. These are MY woods girl. I say what goes on here. And if you act calm with me, I'll let you stay." Morgan pauses and waits for a response.

Gwyneth looks shocked but satisfied at the same time.

Morgan continues, "I see that you already made a home for yourself. I wish I would've thought of this to be honest. I'd love to live in the woods. But, I have a wife and a farmhouse to take care of….which is why I've killed people too."

Gwyneth is scared. She isn't quite sure what to think about this man. At least now she knows who he is. She's been petrified for the past six years to go near that farmhouse. Her mother warned her not to. Ruby told her that those people were bad. She told her that they would try to kill her if she was spotted in the woods.

Ruby also told her that if she was caught, she would be killed on sight.

This thought burns through Gwyneth's brain. She slightly lifts the needle; still gripping onto it like it's about to fall out of her hand.

Morgan lifts his shot gun and points it at Gwyneth's forehead.

He continues to speak as he peeks through the scope of the gun, "If you keep my woods safe, I'll leave you alone. People try to come into these woods and do bad things. Like drugs and sex," Morgan chuckles. "I guess murder is a bad thing too. But, I'll let it slide with you."

Gwyneth glares at him; still unsure of what to do.

She can't trust many people. Well, she can't trust anyone. Trust is something that she only had with her siblings. Trust is a sacred word to her heart. Trust hasn't been in her vocabulary since she was twelve-years-old.

Instead of facing her fears, she starts to panic. She wishes that she could talk to him. She wishes that she knew sign language to help signal some kind of words. She wishes that she had something to write with. She wishes that she could express these happy thoughts flowing through her mind like a waterfall.

She doesn't understand why the farmer is letting her live. Why does he want his land to be protected so badly? And why is he putting all of his trust into HER?

Gwyneth tries to calm down. This is the first time in her life that someone has faith and trust in her. This is the first time that someone has put something incredibly valuable into her hands.

Even her siblings didn't trust her this much.

And... her mother sure as HELL didn't trust her.

Morgan continues as he senses her uneasiness. "Listen girl," he says as he lowers his gun, "I don't want to hurt you. I want to keep you here. Okay? Take care of my woods."

He then turns to leave.

Just like that, he's willing to leave her alone and get on with her life.

She can't believe it. He's willing to let her live here all by herself. He's willing to put his property into her hands.

She suddenly wonders if she's dreaming. She slaps her own face to wake up. The sting hurts but she ignores the pain. She then pinches her cheek.

I'm wide awake!

How could this happen? How could she get so lucky after all these years?

The farmer turns back and smiles. "Hey listen, some advice. Set some traps so that you know when people are coming. Use some kind of wire or string. Tie them to the trees and then connect them to tin cans. The cans will jingle."

Gwyneth's eyes widen.

Why didn't she ever think of that? Oh wait, it's because she isn't as smart as she thinks she is. She believes that she's a genius compared to some people.

"It works like a charm," his smile is genuine and full of love.

Gwyneth catches the twinkle in his eye.

Morgan winks as he waves good-bye.

And just like that, she was left alone for the first time. A human being, who stepped into her territory, left her completely alone. He left her in awe. She didn't even have to try to talk to him. She didn't need to write any words. This is truly astonishing.

And she didn't get to thank him.

Gwyneth watches him leave. His shot gun placed over his shoulder like a bag of stones.

What the hell does she do now?

It is official; someone knows that she lives in the woods.

What if he tells a friend? What if he tells his wife?

Gwyneth shakes her head from these thoughts. He doesn't seem like the type to blabber his mouth. He wants her here. He wants her to take care of his land and his property. He wants HER HERE! She can't get enough of those words. She thinks it over and over again.

Boy, he must've been hit over the head as a child.

Who in their right mind would want a killer creeping through his woods?

Well, someone who has the same type of mind as Gwyneth. Someone who is cunning and strong. Someone who would risk everything for his valuables.

As her confusion turns into charm, Gwyneth waves back.

As Gwyneth smiles with a renewed feeling inside of her body, she approaches the kitchen sink. Turning on the water, she washes her bloody sewing needle.

The blood flows down the drain like a busted pipe.

She stares at it as she imagines the farmer's genuine smile.

He's letting her live here!

She can't over it. She can't get over his smile. He was so happy and excited.

As she smiles in delight, she washes her hands. The feeling of the cold water sends shivers down her spine. She can't imagine her life without her woods.

These are HER woods. She will protect them at all costs.

Taking off her T-shirt mask, she splashes the water onto her face and scrubs off the blood.

She feels this sense of ecstasy. She feels as if the farmer told her he loves her.

She's weak in the knees.

She can't believe that she's even feeling and thinking this way. The man has a wife.

Gwyneth imagines herself busting through the door of the farmhouse and slitting his wife's throat. She imagines the farmer pulling her into his arms.

She needs to slow down with her thoughts. Her area feels tingly inside.

Now, she's definitely crazy.

Returning to her colored container sitting on the desk, she neatly places her ten inch sewing needle back inside. She closes the lid as she imagines the farmer giving her a hug.

She picks up her fishing wire from the top of the desk and inspects it.

The farmer's words in her mind, *"Use wire or string."*

What a smart man.

But first, she has work to do.

She cuts two long pieces of the wire and smiles as she pictures the farmer giving her a kiss. She imagines his slicked-back, dark hair resting on her sweaty chest.

Her face flushes as red as an apple. She places her mask back over her mouth.

As she exits the shack, she smiles as she glances at the young girl's body lying on the ground. She really wants to know the poor girl's name.

She knew that she would want to know. She knew that it would bother her.

She likes to know people's names.

She's suddenly sad. She didn't get the name of the farmer.

Damn it you dummy!

She needs to do something in order to get the farmer out of her mind. She's never thought about another man like this before. She's never felt these butterfly feelings in the pit of her stomach. She's never wanted anyone so badly in her life.

Gwyneth peeks toward the trees where Morgan stood. She wishes that he would come back. She wants him to cuddle her inside of his muscled arms.

She needs to keep her mind busy.

Struggling, she tries to lift the girl's body on top of the picnic table. She's struggling because she's tired. This girl isn't more than ninety pounds.

She can handle ninety pounds.

Gwyneth places her body on the table; wrapping the wire around her wrists and then tying them into a knot underneath the table.

She suddenly giggles. The girl isn't going anywhere.

She sits back down on the bench in front of her map. Picking up the red marker once again, she writes the word, "MOTHER," alongside a question mark.

As thunder rolls, Gwyneth hears the sound of a dog crying in the distance.

As Gwyneth stares at her piece of artwork, she hysterically giggles.

As a twenty-four-year-old, she shouldn't be giggling like a school-girl. She should be calm and strict. She should stand here with her thumb up her ass.

Gwyneth laughs.

She hasn't seen anything so beautiful. This boy and girl are like puzzle pieces to her nightmare. They fit in like glue. They blew into her life like a cannon ball.

And she can't wait to display them inside of her shack.

She wants to place the boy in a sitting position on top of the card table. She wants to place the girl on the floor in front of the fireplace.

She thinks about hanging them up on the wall as pieces of art.

However, she doesn't have the necessary materials to do that.

She wanted to chop their bodies into pieces, but she decided against it. She wants to see their buttoned eyeballs for the rest of her life. She will only cut up her mother.

No one cares about her.

No one knows that she's even missing.

Those words sound like music to her ears. She hopes and prays that Ruby Glacier has no one at home waiting for her. She left her car on the side of the road.

Well, hopefully the farmer spots it and gets rid of it.

Maybe she should walk on over and tell him.

She walked over one time.

Two months after he showed up and told her that she could stay, she went to pay a visit. She missed him and wanted to see his beautiful face again. She wanted to see his smile.

Okay, so it was the ONLY time she's ever left the woods. It gave her too much anxiety. She felt exposed to the world. She felt like someone was going to take her away and return her to Ruby. She could never have that happen.

She left her woods and crossed the dirt road. She walked right up the gravel driveway and stared at the farmer as he stood on his porch with his binoculars.

She waved but he didn't wave back. He had a sour look upon his face. He was upset.

He probably wanted to kill her.

When Gwyneth came closer, she noticed that he was angry.

She stopped; gently placing her hair behind her ear.

The farmer waved her away. He told her to leave and to never come back to his farmhouse.

Gwyneth was confused. She thought he loved her.

Just as the farmer's wife opened the screen door, Gwyneth took off toward the woods. Looking back over her shoulder, she watched the farmer grab his wife into a hug and gently push her back inside of the house.

She lost the love of her life.

But now, she has a new love. She has two new people to add to her family. She just knows that she will be happy with Buttons and this boy and girl. She will dress them up and have tea parties. Well, not tea… just water.

She can make them chicken in the fire. She can bring them with her on errands.

Gwyneth feels ecstatic.

She feels like she hit the jackpot. She found her treasured gold.

She will take care of them for as long as she can.

Gwyneth smiles; noticing an item hanging from Marybeth's neck. She's confused but curious at the same time. She's like a curious cat. She always has to know what's going on.

Gwyneth didn't notice anything before. She was quite content finishing her work of art.

She lowers her head. With slow moving fingers, she strokes Marybeth's blonde curls; moving them out of the way. She's careful not to touch her cold skin.

Ever so slowly, she pulls down the collar of the pea coat.

She recognizes the necklace immediately and places her hand to her masked mouth.

Wildly, she shakes her head no. Her eyes are filled with tears.

She's suddenly hysterical, crying up into the air.

This has to be a joke. Someone is playing a prank. Where are the cameras?

Gwyneth frantically looks around the area as her tears stream down her cheeks. She sees no one. She hears no one. She knows that she's all alone.

Gently lifting the red yarn and golden button into her hand, she cries out. Her cries could wake up a sleeping bear. Her cries are of extreme sadness and loss.

How could she be so stupid? How could she be so blind?

Frantically, she touches Roman's neck. She feels his red yarn and golden button necklace. Forcefully, she pulls down the collar of his coat.

She gently touches his necklace with her gloved hand.

Crying out, Gwyneth pounds her fist into her own face.

She's killed her siblings.

Chapter Twenty-Nine

As they grow older, Roman and Marybeth become as curious as a cat.

Just like their sister.

Roman has a fascination with looking through Joni's closet. He likes to search through her clothes and shoes. He likes to plaster chocolate all over the closet walls and then laugh about the mess. He likes to break her valuables and pull apart her new tennis shoes.

He loves to go through Joni's shoe boxes while she is down in the basement exercising. He loves those shoe boxes. They hide notes written to old boyfriends. They hide old jewelry that Joni doesn't want to wear anymore. And, they also hide diaries filled with secrets.

Joni has a lot of secrets. Secrets that Roman has decided to keep to himself. He's never told Marybeth, he knows that she would never forgive their father.

William St. Rose has a huge secret; secrets that he keeps from his own children.

These old shoe boxes contain secrets hidden by William. One shoe box contains an old photograph of William, Marybeth and Roman as babies and another woman with crusty teeth.

Roman has tried so hard to figure out who the woman is without giving up his snooping capabilities. He has the skills of a Ninja. He moves quickly and efficiently as he reads old diary messages from Joni's pink flowered diary. One passage is dated the year that the twins turned five. This passage is certainly the biggest secret that Joni and William kept from their children; a secret that would tear Marybeth's soul right in half.

It would crush her heart into thousands of pieces; something Roman isn't prepared for.

This might sound dramatic, but Marybeth is dramatic. Sometimes, a little too dramatic.

Roman is thirteen-years-old. He feels like a child being told that

Santa Claus isn't real. He reads the sentences over and over until he's able to memorize them. He reads the passage word for word until his brain becomes exhausted. He reads until he can't cry anymore.

He can't believe his eyes. The words on the page seem foreign. They look like a scrambled mess of cursive letters. The words are written in blue ink.

Roman stares… HARD. His eyes become blurry and he can't think straight. He sees Marybeth smiling from ear to ear as they play in the backyard of a disheveled house.

Wait a minute… a disheveled house? Where is it? He's never remembered living in such a poor-looking house. It's dirty inside and smells like cigarette smoke and shit.

Joni St. Rose is not their real mother.

Tears fill his eyes as he reads Joni's passage:

"The twins finally came to our house tonight. William left to go shopping before they arrived. I can't wait for Roman and Marybeth to meet their father. I can't wait to be a mother to them. Even though I'm not their REAL mother, I will do everything in my power to make them feel comfortable. I will always make sure that they never find out about their REAL mother… Ruby Glacier. She is a dirty, disgusting rat. She will get what's coming to her."

Joni St. Rose is the dirty, disgusting, rat. Their father is scum of the Earth.

Roman places the diary back into the shoe box. He wipes his nose with the sleeve of his shirt. Joni will LOVE that; boogers on his sleeve. She will definitely yell at him for that one.

She will most likely call him, "a punk ass teenager."

They joke around a lot and laugh with each other. He doesn't want to laugh with her ever again. As a matter of fact, he never wants to see her face ever again.

He knows that's not possible. They live together. It's as if he and his sister live with a stranger. He has no idea who Joni truly is. And at this point, he doesn't care.

Maybe his father's friends are right; she's just some whore off the street that he fell in love with. Sometimes, she's heartless and cruel whenever their father isn't around. That's something that he never witnesses because he's gone at work all day long.

Roman is never going to treat her with respect ever again. She's not their mother, why should he listen to her? She's lied about who she is. She doesn't deserve respect.

Roman smiles as he thinks of this notion. She will get a kick out of his behavior now. She thinks that he was an asshole before; he's going to be a *major* asshole for the rest of his life.

And he can't ever tell Marybeth.

Becoming fifteen-year-old, "curious cats," can become quite alarming; especially if hidden secrets are snuggled up right under their noses; secrets that are snuggled like love-birds.

And it's right under the noses of Roman and Marybeth St. Rose.

Their curious behavior gets them into trouble. One day, it's going to get them killed.

As they sit cross-legged on the attic floor, they rummage through old boxes. Roman feels like a bad influence. He knows that his sister is only sitting here with him because he begged her to. He promised to do the dishes for a week if she follows his plan.

He doesn't really have a "plan," per se; he just wants company up in the attic.

Their attic is scary and cold. He needs her to hold his hand; just like he did when they were little. He was always a scaredy-cat with unfamiliar territory.

Actually, he wants her up there with him in case they get caught. He contemplated on blaming the whole idea on Marybeth. But, he can't do something like that to her. She will never trust him again. And he needs her trust. He needs her to follow his crazy "plans."

The attic floor is covered with old books and magazines. Tangled around their feet are old "Barbie" dolls and action figures. They are dirty and dressed half-naked. Their shirts are torn and Marybeth's "Ken" doll isn't even wearing pants.

Roman spent thirty minutes playing with his old Army boy action figure. Marybeth brushed the hair of her "Pink Jubilee Barbie" with a pink "Barbie" hairbrush.

Roman lifts his head; spotting a box hidden behind the Easter decorations. The box is labeled, "Twins stuff." Curious, he moves aside the box that Marybeth is rummaging through.

"Wait until we're done with this one," Marybeth demands.

Roman shakes his head and laughs, "This one peaks my attention. Let's check it out."

The box is heavy. He grunts as he drags it toward Marybeth. She rolls her eyes as he excitedly opens the box as if it's a Christmas present. His eyes light up like a star in the sky.

Marybeth eyes the box suspiciously. She wonders how long it's been sitting in that spot. It is quite obvious that the box has something to do with them.

Being Roman's twin has been draining. They look exactly alike. Sometimes they act alike.

One time, Marybeth was deathly ill and had to miss school. She was extremely upset because she had to take a big math test. She studied for three days straight.

Joni made her stay home. Marybeth made Roman dress up in a pink outfit of hers and wear a blonde wig. She made him study for a math test that wasn't even his. He was so angry and humiliated for how he looked. He was embarrassed to be dressed up like his twin sister.

Needless to say, Roman was never caught impersonating Marybeth. He took that math test with ease and scored ninety-eight out of one-hundred.

"What the?" Roman asks, trailing off as he scrunches his nose at the items in the box.

Curious, Marybeth slowly approaches the box as she watches the absolute look of disgust on her brother's face. What could possibly be the issue? Maybe he's a bit too dramatic.

Marybeth pulls out a dirty hairbrush. A mixture of black and blonde hair twists inside of the bristles. The handle is broken and covered in dried mud.

Roman pulls out a filthy red T-shirt and pink pants. He sniffs them.

Disgusted, he says, "These smell awful!"

"I wonder if I wore these," Marybeth replies. She too sniffs the clothing. Covering her nose with her hand, she shakes her head. "Oh my God those are terrible."

She really hopes that these pieces of clothing did not belong to her. She doesn't ever remember wearing this outfit in her life. She doesn't ever remember using this hairbrush.

Slowly, she sniffs the hairbrush.

It's not dried mud. It's dried poop.

Marybeth throws the brush back into the box and wipes her hands on her jeans. She whimpers as she thinks about touching old fecal matter. She hopes and prays that it wasn't her who smeared shit on a brush handle. Someone didn't wash their hands properly.

Moving on, Marybeth pulls out two pieces of paper. Both of them are colored with trees and grass. The sun shines brightly below a beautiful rainbow.

A dilapidated house is colored in pink. A Snowman sits next to the house. The Snowman's scarf is colored purple and his hat is colored in green.

Marybeth then finds the broken crayon pieces of pink, purple and green scattered on the bottom of the box. A yellow and red crayon show bite marks.

Roman picks up two homemade necklaces of red yarn and golden buttons.

He stares at them as if he's trying to magically remember them. He closes his eyes and thinks real hard. But, his mind is a blank. His mind is blackness. It's as if his brain crawled inside of the black hole. He can't remember a thing before the age of seven.

"I don't remember any of this stuff," Roman whines. "Do you?"

Shaking her head no, Marybeth says, "Not at all. I wonder why mom and dad kept this stuff from us." She reaches into the box once again.

Joni isn't our mother.

Roman wants to blurt those words into his sister's face. He wants her to know what a crook and scoundrel this woman who they call, "mom," is. He wants her to know that they're own father has lied to them for many years. He's a dirty scoundrel too.

But, he doesn't have the heart to do that. He can't. This secret will ruin her life. He knows for a fact that it will. She will go off to college in a few years and never talk to their parents again. And, Roman doesn't want that for their father. William has worked too hard with taking care of his children. He's worked too hard to keep his secret safe.

Marybeth pulls out a skein of black yarn. She's confused. Questions are popping into her mind like bubbles. Who used this yarn? What was it for? Did she sew? Did Roman sew?

She doesn't think that these questions will ever be answered at this point.

"I don't ever remember sewing anything," Marybeth says as she twirls the black yarn with her fingers. "Mom doesn't sew. Neither does dad."

Roman ignores her. He isn't sure why, but he's not worried about yarn at the moment.

Holding up the homemade necklaces into the air, he asks, "Did we make these?"

Marybeth looks confused. Shaking her head no, she stares at the golden buttons of the necklace. Her mind is blank. It must have fallen into the pit of the black hole as well.

She's frustrated. Trying to remember their past is like pulling teeth; painful.

She suddenly feels sad. They should know where all of this stuff came from. They should know who made these necklaces. There must have been someone else in their lives.

"Maybe," Marybeth answers after blinking tears, "It's crazy that there are two of them. Maybe something we made together to match. We are twins."

She does make a valid and obvious point. They made the necklaces. That would only make sense. *Of course it makes sense,* Marybeth thinks in her mind. *It's not rocket science.*

Roman places the necklaces onto the attic floor. Marybeth picks them back up and twirls the red yarn between her cold fingers. Her body is shaking. She isn't sure if it's from the cold attic or the goosebumps that have formed on her arms.

Roman pulls out more drawings from the box. There's a drawing with trees and a rainbow, another with rainy clouds with that same dilapidated house and a third with a pond holding fish.

Roman hands the drawings over to Marybeth.

"This might be something that we colored too. I think our childhood was so bad that we just blocked it out. Is that even possible?" Roman asks as he rummages through the box again.

Marybeth traces the outline of the drawings with the tip of her finger. "It sure is possible," she agrees. "This looks like three heads."

Confused, Roman takes the drawings out of her hands.

"Three black circles combined into three heads? I can see it. Stick figures I guess," Roman replies as he places the drawings onto the floor.

"Who's the third?" Marybeth asks.

Roman shakes his head and shrugs his shoulders. This doesn't seem important to him but it is for Marybeth. She wants to know who owns the third head. Did they have a triplet that they don't know about? Did the triplet die at birth? Who drew this drawing?

Marybeth has so many questions. Unfortunately, she knows that she won't get any answers from their father. William is extremely secretive. She knows this by his posture and the way he's answered questions in the past. He likes to change the subject when he feels pressured.

Marybeth knows that her parents are liars. She just doesn't know what they are lying about specifically. This issue has been a part of her own investigation for many years. She feels like that she's almost to the end zone with factual information. She will find out the answers to her parents' secrets. They both act suspicious most of the time.

And so does Roman. Marybeth thinks that he's hiding something from her.

They suddenly hear the sound of footsteps climbing the attic ladder.

Roman is frantic as he tosses all of the items back into the box. He looks at Marybeth for help but she stares at him wide-eyed. She hopes and prays that it's not Joni.

She will kill them. She specifically told the twins to stay away from this section of the attic. And Marybeth has always questioned… WHY? Why are they not allowed over here? What is she keeping from them? WHAT IS JONI HIDING?

William's head pops up from the opening of the attic door. He notices the books and magazines scattered all over the floor. He then notices the box with the big label, "Twins stuff."

He glares at Roman. He then looks at Marybeth with pity in his eyes.

"What's going on guys? What are you doing?" William asks as he climbs the rest of the steps to the ladder. The frown on his face is clear: he's PISSED.

Marybeth quietly chuckles. He reminds of her of a giant grasshopper invading the home of thousands of ants. He's a humongous predator that must be stopped.

Roman quickly glances at Marybeth as he waits for her to respond. She doesn't and this makes Roman nervous. She's going to leave it up to him to explain their shenanigans.

"Just looking through old stuff. Checking out this box here," Roman replies as he points to the, "Twins stuff," box. His finger is shaking. He doesn't understand why he feels so scared.

Maybe it's because they were banned from this section of the attic. They were warned to never go through this stuff. Joni threatened repercussions.

But he isn't scared of Joni.

He's scared of his father.

William quietly nods. He looks as though he might scream and yell but he holds back.

His face is as red as a "Stop sign." He looks as though he might blow his top.

Roman imagines smoke pouring out the sides of his father's head. It looks like his brain is about to explode with anger. The sweat on his forehead pours down the sides of his temples.

"Oh... well... that's just old stuff you guys used to collect," William answers.

"Dirty clothes?" Marybeth asks sarcastically.

Roman is shocked. His sister's "smart ass" answer was not something that he was prepared for. He can't help but chuckle. Of course, this makes William quite angry.

"Yes, smart ass. You collected dirty clothes," William responds as he grinds his teeth.

Marybeth glares at Roman. She knew that this would get them into trouble. She begged for them to not come up here without permission. She told him that they would get caught.

And he assured her that they wouldn't.

He said William was at work and Joni was out with her friends; the usual life that they live. They're left alone most of the time. He said, "What are the odds that dad comes home early?"

Well, the odds are staring at them in the face.

Roman pulls out the homemade necklaces from the box. He holds them up as if they're prized possessions. They dangle in the air as they intertwine like twins.

"What about these?" Roman asks as he glares back at William.

Two can play this game. Roman is sick and tired of William's lies. He's sick and tired of the secrets. He just wants his father to be honest with them.

Stubbornly, William shrugs. He takes the necklaces from Roman and inspects them as if they're trash. He touches them delicately with the tips of his fingers.

"I would assume that you two made these a long time ago. Now lets' go, dinner is ready."

William tosses the necklaces onto the floor. The golden buttons make a loud "thump" sound. This angers Marybeth to her core. This man is careless and has no sympathy whatsoever.

As William watches his children not budge a single inch, he sighs.

"It's time to clean this mess up. I brought dinner. Now move," he orders.

Marybeth doesn't understand why he's acting so strange. He seems worried. He seems to have anxiety over this box of items. And he doesn't want to answer their questions.

He leaves the attic.

Roman shrugs his shoulders as he watches his father's head disappear from the door. He stares ahead as he remembers Joni's diary again. He wants to tell Marybeth right now.

But, he won't; because he is a punk ass teenager.

Marybeth opens the box once again and inspects a pair of gray sweatpants. The smell of the pants is awful. They too smell like fecal matter. Marybeth scrunches her nose.

"These must be yours. And these pants smell like cigarette smoke and poop."

"No way that those are mine! I didn't shit my pants!" Roman is defensive.

Marybeth laughs hysterically.

She then pulls out a shit-stained pair of pink jeans.

"Ok then… THESE are yours!" she says howling with laughter.

Roman angrily shakes his head. "You're messed up in the brain."

Marybeth ponders a response. Of course she's messed up in the brain. Look at her parents and her brother for crying out loud. Her parents yell and scream at everything little thing.

Her brother thinks that they will never get into trouble for anything that they do. He thinks that they can walk around and do whatever they want. He seems to think that they can say whatever they want without any discipline.

Marybeth knows that they can't. She tries to talk some sense into Roman but it doesn't help. He thinks he knows everything. He thinks that he can get away with having bad behavior.

His behavior took a turn for the worst just two years ago. She doesn't know what happened and he won't explain anything to her. He likes to keep secrets as well.

This bothers Marybeth. They are supposed to be twins. They are supposed to care for each other and look out for each other. Marybeth seems to be the only smart one.

"Aren't we all?" Marybeth suddenly asks.

Roman ignores her once again. He doesn't want to get into any of this nonsense.

Reaching toward his sister, he hands over one of the homemade necklaces.

He looks at Marybeth and smiles for the first time in days. His smile is genuine and caring. This makes Marybeth's heart melt. The love between brother and sister is undeniable.

They both slip on a necklace at the same time.

"Now, we can wear matching homemade jewelry!" Roman exclaims.

"We are so lame," Marybeth laughs.

Chapter Thirty

Gwyneth feels this sudden rapid exhaustion filling inside of her brain. She's lost all sense of purpose. She's lost all sense of feeling. The lightning inside of her skull zaps the walls inside of her cerebrum. She's confused, she's angry and she's an emotional wreck.

She hasn't felt this type of pain since her siblings took off in Lindsay's car. She hasn't felt deeply saddened since that day when she felt lonely and frightened. She felt the biggest blow during that traumatizing time of her life. It changed her behavior for the worst.

But, no blow could ever compare to this. Under no circumstances did she ever imagine that she would purposely kill her beloved siblings. She loved them dearly and with all of her heart.

Gwyneth clenches both fists. She could literally kill herself over this. Her most important mission in life was to not only find her mother, but to find her beautiful brother and sister.

And here they are.

Dead.

She killed them in a fit of rage. She killed them without even finding out who they were first. But, that's what she's always done. Anyone who steps foot into her territory must suffer the consequences. They must be terminated at all costs.

Now, she's suffering the consequences of her own actions. Her eyes are wide with pain and sadness. Tears stream down her face and into her T-shirt mask.

What in the world has she done? Why did she kill them so fast? What kind of monster has she become? Her anger is out of control and it shows with the death of her own siblings.

Gwyneth's heart pounds with anxiety. It wants to explode into tiny pieces.

And she just might let it.

She wants to die. She wants to stab her own eyes with her ten inch sewing needle. She wants to shoot the sharp edge of the harpoon through her brain.

She screams up into the air, crying hysterically.

She never thought that a scream with that level of loudness could ever escape her throat. She never thought that she would ever feel this type of pain in her life.

And she's never wanted to die; even through the loss of her mother and being dumped into the woods. She's never known emotions to be this strong.

She feels weak in the knees. She feels heartbroken.

And she feels evil.

How could I do this to them?

Grabbing Roman and Marybeth simultaneously, she snuggles them into a bear hug. She rocks them back and forth like a baby as she cries out.

The pain is unbearable. Her heart is ripping through her chest. The guts from inside of her stomach feel tightened. She can't think straight and her eyes are a blurry mess.

Buttons whimpers, plopping his butt onto the floor of the shack inside of the doorway.

He watches her cry as his heart races. He doesn't know what to do. He's never seen her act like this before. He's never witnessed her crying hysterically.

The poor dog wants to play in the snow. He watches the snowflakes land on top of Gwyneth's hood to her coat. He watches her scream up into the air.

Speaking of the air, he suddenly sniffs it.

And growls.

Gwyneth kisses Roman's forehead with her masked mouth. She then kisses Marybeth's forehead. Her tears drop onto her sister's buttoned eyeballs.

Gwyneth feels this sense of anger. She's mad at herself. She's mad at the world for letting her do this. She's mad that no one ever tried to stop her from killing people. They let her live her cruel life because she forced them to. She killed people for bothering her. She forced people to leave her alone when all she wanted was her brother and sister.

And now she has them. But now they're dead. And it's because of HER.

Her heart pulsates with anger. The lightning zaps continue to slam against her brain like a car slamming into a telephone pole. They bounce from side to side like a basketball bouncing off the ground. It feels like a hammer pounding on a nail.

She can't take it anymore. She can't stand the pounding. She hates the lightning zaps. All she wants to do now is climb into that black hole.

Maybe SHE deserves to go inside of it and spin in circles. She deserves to be crushed with blackness. She doesn't deserve to live. She doesn't deserve to take care of her precious Buttons.

"What have you done?" a voice trails off behind her back.

That familiar man's voice pounds into her brain like a twisting screwdriver. The man waits for an answer. He pauses for a brief moment. But, Gwyneth doesn't want to turn around and face him. He told her not to so this. He did tell her not kill people anymore.

"GWYNETH! WHAT HAVE YOU DONE?!!!"

What has she done? Well, that's a stupid question. It's quite obvious what she's done. It's quite obvious that she feels remorse for her actions. It's the first time ever in her life that she's felt like this. It's the first time that she's seen her siblings in twelve years.

Wait a minute… it's not the first time.

Gwyneth suddenly remembers two weeks ago. She remembers her brother. Yes! Roman showed up here and tried to talk to her. He had a clipboard in his hand.

It all makes sense now. He was coming to talk to her.

This sudden realization has made her heart drop. She screams up into the air once again.

William points his gun at the back of Gwyneth's head as he slowly steps toward her.

"Answer me! Answer me girl, NOW!!"

Gwyneth places her head into Marybeth's coat. How could she be so stupid? How could she do this to them? How could she kill her precious baby siblings?

They were precious to her. She loved them so much. She loved their smiles and their giggles. She loved their beautiful drawings of trees, houses and flowers. She loved to make them laugh. She loved to hug them and hold them tight in her arms.

Looking up, she peeks at their dead eyes. She watches the blood ooze from the sewn buttons. She looks at their necklaces and remembers the day she dug them out of her dresser.

She softly touches their cheeks with her gloved hand. Her fingertips are frozen and numb. She can barely feel their flesh. Her heart is numb. And her brain hurts from the sudden migraine forming inside of her skull. It must be those damn lightning zaps!

As she feels the presence of William St. Rose behind her, she closes her eyes.

She waits for the bullet to blast her brain. She waits to die in this moment with her family. She patiently waits for him to pull the trigger.

She's become impatient as she increasingly waits.

But he seems to be crying behind her back. She can hear it. His cries are soft and quiet. She doesn't want to turn around and face him. She doesn't want to look into his saddened eyes. He seems to know who her brother and sister are. He seems to care for them as much as she does.

Gently, Gwyneth touches the buttons that are now their eyeballs.

Yes, what in the world has she DONE?

In a sudden fit of rage, Gwyneth tries pulling the buttons out of their eye sockets. The sound of the juiciness makes her sick. Her fingers are caked in blood.

She can't pull them off. She sewed them extremely tight. This boggles her mind.

This is the best job she's ever done.

She frantically searches the ground for their eyeballs. She looks like a maniac searching for nothing again. She's wild, pounding her fists onto the snowy ground.

She suddenly realizes that she tossed the eyeballs to her dog for a treat. She realizes that she had the urge to eat her family's eyes without a care in the world.

As she crouches on the ground like a pacing hungry tiger, she glares at Buttons in the doorway. She doesn't know why she's mad at him. It's not his fault. It's HER fault for acting stupid. It's HER fault for not giving them a chance to talk to her.

William takes another step toward Gwyneth; still pointing the gun at back of her head. He carefully watches Buttons from the doorway as he takes a second step toward his master.

Buttons growls at him; louder this time. He doesn't care to be quiet. He must save his master. She needs his help and he will be there for her!

Just like he's always done.

Buttons barks; exposing his sharp teeth as he crouches toward the ground. He carefully takes each step toward William and Gwyneth with ease; careful not to go too fast.

"Shut that mutt up or I'll shoot it!" William threatens.

Shoot her dog? There's no way that she will let THAT happen. Buttons is too precious to her; just as much as her siblings were. She cannot lose her dog too. She will kill William in a heartbeat if he pulls that trigger.

Gwyneth suddenly turns. She pounces off the ground and flies through the air; pushing William to the ground. Landing on top of him, she attacks him like a rabid dog. William's gun fires the bullet up into the air. The gun falls out of his hand and flies across the wet snow.

William suddenly grips Gwyneth's throat with both clenched fists and squeezes hard.

Buttons is there in an instant; sinking his teeth into William's arm.

William sees his children in the cloudy sky. Roman waves. Marybeth blows him a kiss. He smiles as a shimmering light illuminates the outline of their bodies.

Marybeth motions for William to come along. Roman points his finger toward the clouds. They laugh and jump up and down like small children playing at a playground.

Buttons suddenly chomps his bloody teeth into William's cheek. The Sheriff's grip loosens around Gwyneth's throat as he cries out in pain.

He watches Marybeth laugh and play patty-cake with her brother.

Gwyneth clicks her tongue at Buttons but he completely ignores her. Now is not the time to stop. He must kill this man and end this madness. He must save Gwyneth so they can have some play time. He wants to play in the snow and burst through a Snowman.

Buttons bites down hard into William's neck; pulling flesh from his bone.

Gwyneth clicks her fingers and then pushes Buttons away. The poor dog growls but steps back; looking at his piece of artwork. It's like a painting with splatters of reds and pinks.

Buttons winces as Gwyneth clicks her fingers a second time. He imagines his master hitting him and he suddenly snaps his jaw at her fingers like a shark; just missing the tips.

William whispers but Gwyneth can't hear what he's saying. Buttons continues to growl as if he's rabid. Gwyneth is feeling angry at her dog. She feels a sudden burning desire to hit Buttons for the first time. It's eating at her like bacteria.

She wants Buttons to go back inside of the shack and leave them alone. But, she knows that he's only trying to protect her. He's a very loyal and caring dog.

Do whatever is necessary to survive.

She doesn't hit Buttons. Instead, she slowly lowers her ear toward the Sheriff's mouth.

"All I wanted… was for my… children… to be together," William whispers.

Gwyneth is taken aback. His children? Who are his children? Roman and Marybeth? Gwyneth herself? WHAT IS HE TALKING ABOUT?!!! She wants answers! No, she NEEDS answers! She can't move on from this! She HAS to know!

God damn you Buttons!

Buttons sinks his teeth into William's head. Gwyneth clicks her fingers once again.

The dog refuses to leave. Gwyneth pushes him away. Buttons snaps at her gloved hand; nipping her pinky finger between his teeth.

Gwyneth yelps and waves her hand at Buttons. She points toward the shack.

William is out of breath and bleeding rapidly from his wounds. He blinks back tears as he stares into the beautiful blue eyes of his eldest daughter.

"I'm sorry I let you… down… pretty girl. I wanted… you… to come… home."

William smiles as he watches Marybeth and Roman open their arms wide for a bear hug. He hasn't hugged his children in years. This makes him sad but now he's able to finally spend the quality time needed with his favorite two people.

Roman and Marybeth watch William take his last breath.

His dead eyes stare up into the clouds.

Gwyneth is silent as she watches her father's tears stream down the sides of his temples. She blinks; sending her tears to drip onto William's forehead.

Suddenly, she screams up in the air. Her screams are loud and fierce. The squirrels scurry away, the tree leaves hide behind their own trunks and Buttons quietly steps into the shack.

As Gwyneth flails her arms as if she's swimming in a pool, the ten inch sewing needle slides out from inside of her fingerless glove. She suddenly grips it tight into her fist; slamming the tip inside of William's right eye.

Angrily, she stabs the eyeball repeatedly. Blood shoots up onto her face and into her eyeballs. Blood spews from his eye sockets and lands on the front of her mother's coat.

Oh Ruby. You sly devil you, falling in love with a Sheriff.

She should be angry with William. She should hate him like she hates Ruby Glacier. She should be happy that he's dead.

But, she's not.

She should be dead. Her mother is dead. Her siblings are dead. And now… her father.

I had a father!

Gwyneth stabs William's face; puncturing the needle through his skin and bones. She stabs his left eyeball; twisting and turning with the most anger she's ever felt in her life.

She's angry with herself. What in the world has she done?

Yes, father. I've killed my whole entire family. THAT'S what I've done!

Crying hysterically, Gwyneth lifts the needle high up into the air and swings it toward her own face. She braces for the impact. She braces for the pain that she's about to endure.

But, she stops her hand. The needle looks into her eyes with a mischievous grin.

She drops it to the snowy ground.

She climbs off of William; shaking and stumbling. Her legs feel like Jell-O and her whole entire body is numb from the pain; the pain of losing everyone who was in her life.

She wants to crawl into the black hole.

Buttons whimpers as he stands at the crooked front door. He watches his master stumble onto the bench of the picnic table. He wants to go to her but he's scared. He isn't sure what she will do. He's not sure if she will hit him like she felt the urge to do a little bit ago.

Gwyneth pulls her mask down off her nose and mouth.

As tears flow down her cheeks, she stares at Roman and Marybeth with such sadness.

She remembers their sweet smiles when she handed them those homemade necklaces of red yarn and golden buttons. They were full of happiness and love.

She imagines them kissing their necklaces as they wave to her inside of Lindsay's car. Marybeth is crying hysterically and Roman is blowing her kisses out of the window.

She then sees Roman tugging on his necklace and waving the golden button.

Gwyneth sees Lindsay wave and blow her a kiss.

That was the last time she ever saw them.

Leaning forward, Gwyneth hugs her siblings one last time. She removes Marybeth's blonde curls off her forehead. She then tucks a strand of Roman's blonde hair behind his ear.

In a sudden fit of rage, she stomps her mother's blue boots toward the shack; wiping her tears away. She wants to wipe all of her precious memories away from her mind.

She wants to end it ALL.

Buttons is petrified as he stands in the corner of the shack. He watches her grab the container with her sewing items off the desk.

She stomps back out of the shack.

Buttons then watches her dump all of the container's contents into the fire-pit. Picking up the harpoon off the bench, she slams it against a tree trunk; breaking it.

She then rips off Ruby's Eskimo coat and throws it to the ground. She stomps it into the snow; burying it like she needs to do with her siblings.

There's no way she's cutting them into pieces and eating them like she's a wild wolf. She will give them a proper burial. She will find flowers and re-plant them in front of their graves.

Gwyneth looks at her siblings as if they just whispered in her ear. The cold wind blasts her face and she shivers. *This will haunt me for the rest of my life.*

She returns to the entrance of the shack. Buttons peeks at her as he growls a low growl.

His master is wild and out of control. She's frantic as she rips all of her dirty coats off the hanging fishing wire. She then rips the whole entire wire off the wall.

She grabs the card table and slams it against the wall, twice.

She's angry. She wants to go back in time and change everything. She wants to go back and make her mother into a loving and caring woman. She wants to make her father stay with her mother so they can be a happy family together.

She wants to live her life all over again. She has better ideas. She wants to live a better life. Lindsay promised her a better life. She said that she would be taken care of. She said that she would live in a happy home with a parent.

Yes, her father. She was supposed to go live with her father!

But Ruby Glacier stripped that away from her. The Bitch didn't want her to live a happy life because she was miserable herself. She hated Gwyneth so she wanted her to suffer.

Gwyneth suddenly grabs a dog bowl and throws it; unable to control her temper.

The bowl accidently hits Buttons in the leg.

Buttons lowers his head; growling in anger at his master.

Stepping toward the stove, Gwyneth remembers the stories that her mother used to spew out of her disgusting mouth. She remembers Ruby talking about, "sleeping with a married man." Was the married man her father? *He has to be! I knew Ruby was a whore!*

The beast called herself a whore. She told Gwyneth inappropriate stories about what she and "The Sheriff," used to do in these woods. *The Sheriff! My father! You Bitch!*

And that's why you're DEAD!

It all makes sense to her brain. She wasn't smart then but she is now.

Gripping a pot off the stove, she hurls it across the room.

The pot hits Buttons' side of his stomach. Gwyneth is oblivious as she stands in the middle of the shack and screams her head off. She screams up at the roof as she clenches her fists.

Buttons exposes his sharp teeth.

The door to the shack is hanging wide open. The cold wind blows inside like a freight train.

Morgan Wildfire watches the shack as he hides behind a tree; peeking through the scope of his shot gun.

Buttons leaps onto Gwyneth, piercing his teeth into her face. Gwyneth is stunned and confused as she falls backwards onto the cold, hard, floor.

Her head bounces like a yo-yo off the floor of the shack; the lightning inside of her brain cracks like a whip and then disappears like smoke filling the air.

Gwyneth grips her head into her hands as Buttons continues to attack her. She tries pulling her arms away from his bites but he chomps down on her right arm as if it's a fresh dog bone.

Buttons bites at her face and neck. She's bleeding and crying hysterically.

She doesn't understand what is happening. She doesn't understand why Buttons is doing this to her. She doesn't understand why he's so angry with her.

Buttons bites her face once again. He bites her hands and her chest.

He bites the side of her neck.

Gwyneth is suddenly still.

The only loud sound is the blowing of the wind. The snow is coming down hard and fast.

A snow storm is coming. It's almost play time now.

Buttons stops and whimpers as he watches his master lie still on the wooden floor. The shack is freezing cold and the front door is banging against the wall as the wind roars through the trees like a herd of elephants.

Buttons is scared to death as he paces around Gwyneth's body.

He sniffs her and licks at her closed eyeballs. He doesn't understand why they're closed. He then licks the blood oozing from her wounds. The taste sends shivers through his belly.

He's dying of thirst. He needs water and food.

Pacing in front of the doorway, Buttons peeks out toward the woods and then back at Gwyneth again. He's confused and doesn't understand why she's not moving.

Morgan Wildfire spots Buttons through the scope of his shot gun; pointing the weapon directly at the dog. Buttons whimpers as he lies down next to Gwyneth; placing his head on her bitten chest. He then places his paws onto her stomach.

Morgan pulls the trigger….

About the Author

Angela Sanner is a full time writer while attending school for Writing and Directing film. She has written many works such as books, novels, poetry and film scripts of "Auditory," "Play Me A Song," and many others. She has directed three short films of her own which include: "A Dash of Charlie," "Her Seething Hollow," and "Leaving the Dead Rose." "Gwyneth Part 2" is currently in the works. She currently resides in Pennsylvania with her fiancé and two children.